"I deserved that promotion. I worked hard for it."

Still holding the glossy portrait of her parents, Louise crossed the imported-tile floor of her fourteenth-story grossly mortgaged condominium. "You need to mellow out and become one of the good guys," her boss had told her when she'd questioned why her promotion had gone to someone else. A bark of bitter laughter came from her throat at the inanity of his advice. Louise was a powerhouse in the courtroom. Aggressive, unyielding. Wasn't that what a lawyer was supposed to be?

If not, maybe she'd chosen the wrong profession. But she loved the law. She couldn't give it up now. So where could she go to learn to be a nice, people-person kind of lawyer?

Suddenly she had the answer. Bayberry Cove. The homey little burg on the edge of Currituck Sound near the Outer Banks where her best friend lived.

Louise walked toward the phone. "If Bayberry Cove can't turn you from a lioness into a pussycat," she told herself, "I don't know any place that can."

Dear Reader,

I have always admired and been a little bit envious of strong women. I am awed by females who enter politics or bravely insinuate themselves into occupations that traditionally have been considered a man's venue. Admittedly I'm from the generation that had to learn through experience that women could achieve whatever they wanted, be whomever they chose. Now I do believe it, wholeheartedly, and if I'd had a daughter instead of my dear son, I would have told her to strive for whatever her heart desired.

But since I didn't have that daughter, I created Louise, a woman you may have met in *The Husband She Never Knew*, and who now has her own story in this book. Strong, independent and bold, Louise stands for all that is good about being a woman in the twenty-first century. But more important, she also has a soft center, a pure heart that makes her compassionate, caring and vulnerable in the ways of love. I hope you enjoy Louise's journey to her heart's desire.

Cynthia Thomason

P.S. I love hearing from readers. You can write to me at P.O. Box 550068, Fort Lauderdale, Fl 33355 or e-mail me at Cynthoma@aol.com.

The Women of
Bayberry Cove
Cynthia Thomason

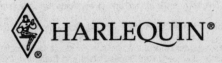

HARLEQUIN®

TORONTO • NEW YORK • LONDON
AMSTERDAM • PARIS • SYDNEY • HAMBURG
STOCKHOLM • ATHENS • TOKYO • MILAN • MADRID
PRAGUE • WARSAW • BUDAPEST • AUCKLAND

ISBN 0-373-71232-4

THE WOMEN OF BAYBERRY COVE

Copyright © 2004 by Cynthia Thomason.

This edition published by arrangement with Harlequin Books S.A.

® and TM are trademarks of the publisher. Trademarks indicated with ® are registered in the United States Patent and Trademark Office, the Canadian Trade Marks Office and in other countries.

www.eHarlequin.com

Printed in U.S.A.

This book is dedicated to the memory of
Amanda Sue Brackett. Dear sister, sweet angel,
your flame still burns brightly in my heart.

And a special thank-you to Florida attorney Adam Chotiner,
writer Zelda Benjamin's son-in-law, whose expertise
in the field of labor law kept me on the right track.
Any mistakes are entirely mine and not his.

Books by Cynthia Thomason

HARLEQUIN SUPERROMANCE

Don't miss any of our special offers. Write to us at the
following address for information on our newest releases.

Harlequin Reader Service
U.S.: 3010 Walden Ave., P.O. Box 1325, Buffalo, NY 14269
Canadian: P.O. Box 609, Fort Erie, Ont. L2A 5X3

CHAPTER ONE

LOUISE DUNCAN, who regularly apologized to friends and business associates for being late, was fifteen minutes early this morning. The Fort Lauderdale legal firm of Oppenheimer Straus and Baker didn't officially open until nine, but when Roger Oppenheimer had called her at home the previous evening and told her to be in his office at eight, Louise knew she'd be on time. She'd been waiting ten years for this call.

She exited the elevator on the top floor of the Moroccan-style building that had graced Las Olas Boulevard since the 1940s. Continuing down a wide hallway flanked with offices, Louise stopped outside Mr. Oppenheimer's door. She knocked lightly and responding to Roger's request, stepped inside.

He turned from the bank of windows and smiled at her. "Right on time, I see, Louise." He gestured for her to take a seat in a deep-tufted green leather chair, and he sat in a similar one on the other side of a mahogany coffee table. He lifted a chrome serving pitcher from a silver tray. "Coffee?"

Louise smiled back at him, growing even more confident in the cordial atmosphere. "I don't know. Did you make it yourself?"

Roger chuckled and poured a cup for himself and

one for Louise. "Yes, I did." He set his mug on a coaster and molded his thick fingers over the edges of the chair arms.

Louise peered at him over the rim of her mug. It wasn't her imagination. The good humor of the last moments was fading from his features. His eyes had narrowed, the lines around his mouth deepened. The time for small talk was over. That was fine with Louise. She was ready to hear the good news.

"Perhaps you know why I called you to the office so early, Louise," he said.

She set down her mug. "I think I have a pretty good idea."

"I wanted to speak to you in privacy, without the interruptions of normal business hours."

And so the others who have been considered for the promotion wouldn't be around when you tell me I'm the one who got it. Louise allowed herself a bit of mental gloating. "I think that was a good idea, Roger."

He moved his hands to his knees and leaned slightly forward. "As you know, since Harker Penwright left, the firm has been considering moving someone from inside the organization to his position of junior partner."

She nodded. Oh, yes, she knew. The promotion had been the subject of whispered comments at the water cooler and murmured predictions during happy hours. Two days ago, Louise had gotten wind of what she believed was the true inside scoop from her secretary, who'd heard from Oppenheimer's own assistant. The promotion was going to Louise.

"We all knew that a decision was forthcoming," she said.

Roger cleared his throat. "Right. And that decision was reached last night. It probably comes as no surprise to you that you, Ed Bennett and Arthur Blackstone were the principal candidates for the promotion."

Louise folded her hands in her lap and connected her gaze with Roger's in that direct way she was famous for in the courtroom. "I had assumed as much, yes." *Oh, this was going to be so sweet.*

Roger looked away from her penetrating stare and seemed to find something fascinating in the weave of the green-and-tan carpet. The first hint of unease prickled along Louise's spine.

After a moment, he looked up. "There's no easy way to say this, Louise. Especially since I am fond of you on a personal level. And of course I admire you on a professional one."

Louise turned cold to the tips of her fingers. She held her breath.

"We've decided to give the position to Ed," Roger stated with agonizing blandness.

Louise shook her head, replayed the stunning announcement in her mind several times to be sure she'd got it right. She leaned forward and stared at Roger's face, at the capillaries expanding and reddening in his plump cheeks. "You what?"

"I'm sorry, Louise, but in the end, all three of us agreed that this decision was best for the firm."

Uncharacteristically, words failed her. She blew out a long breath, blinked several times and finally uttered, "Roger, I have seniority over Ed by more than a year."

"I know, and we took that into consideration. Unfortunately, there were other factors that weighed more heavily in our decision."

"Other factors? May I ask what they were?"

"Louise, I don't want to go into this…"

"Roger, you owe me an explanation. You know you do."

He sighed heavily. "All right. Basically we feel that Ed projects a more appropriate image for the firm. He's wonderful with the clients. They like his give-and-take attitude with regard to decision making. He oozes confidence, Louise…."

"And I don't?" Good God, if there was one trait that clearly defined Louise Duncan, it was confidence, not pretended or fleeting, but real, no-nonsense confidence that Ed Bennett could only dream about.

Roger remained calm, his tone of voice even. "You do, of course, and for the most part your work in the courtroom is exemplary, but…" He rolled one shoulder, resettled his bulk in the chair. "Frankly, Louise, we've had complaints. You come across as somewhat intimidating, forceful."

"I'm an attorney, Roger. It's my job to be forceful."

"To an extent, yes. But you shouldn't necessarily act that way toward our own clients. Ed is dignified, solid, almost courtly. He's stable and reliable, the picture of old-company trust. In the field of corporate law, Louise, his demeanor is most impressive."

"You're saying I'm not stable?"

He had the nerve to smile. "I'm certainly not suggesting you need psychiatric help, but to a client who's contemplating putting the future of his empire in our hands, you come on a little strong." He threaded his fingers together, resting his hands in his lap. "Let me put it this way. Ed Bennett bonds with the clients. He's both compassionate and capable. And while there's no doubt that you're a top-notch litigator, Louise, you do have a tendency to bully everyone around you."

Louise couldn't believe what she was hearing. Ed Bennett was a complete toady in his perfectly tailored black suits, and shirts starched to such gleaming stiffness that he crackled when he swung his arms. And he was getting this promotion over *her*. Her pride was wounded beyond repair. Her dreams were shattering like old crystal. And so she heard herself utter words of self-betrayal and corporate capitulation. "I can change," she said. "I can listen to stories about backyard barbecues, and kids' educations, and family vacations to Aspen. That's what Ed does. I can do that, too. I can be nice."

"Of course you can, Louise, but not by nine o'clock this morning." He stood, effectively dismissing her. "I hate to cut this short, but Arthur Blackstone is due at eight-thirty, and I have to do this one more time. It's not something I enjoy, I assure you."

She stood up. "If you expect me to sympathize with you, Roger, you're going to be disappointed."

He chuckled a little. "I don't expect that at all. But please consider some advice. Take a break from the firm, a vacation. A couple of months. You've earned a mountain of personal days over the years. Sanders and Martin can take over your workload for a while.''

"You're suggesting I run off to some Caribbean island and sun myself for weeks?'' The thought was ludicrous.

Apparently oblivious to the absurdity of his idea, Roger said, ''Yes, that's a great plan. We want you on board, Louise. But take some time for yourself. Come back refreshed, renewed.''

And more in tune with Oppenheimer Straus and Baker, Stepford attorneys. "Fine,'' she said, opening the door to the hallway. "I'll see you in a few weeks, Roger.''

She passed Arthur Blackstone midway down the hall. He stopped her with a light touch to her elbow. "Did you just come from Oppenheimer's office?'' he asked.

"I did.'' A worried frown tugged at his lips. "Don't worry, Art,'' she said, empathizing with his soon-to-be-victim status. "It's not me.''

He exhaled. "Sorry, Louise, but if not you, then who…''

"Just one word of warning. If Roger offers you coffee, you might want to lace it with a shot of bourbon.''

AT NINE O'CLOCK that night Louise polished off a pint of Ben and Jerry's ice cream, licked the carton lid and tossed the empty container across the room into the wastebasket. Then she leaned forward on her sofa and reached for a cardboard box on her coffee table. Roger Oppenheimer had made it clear that her job wasn't in jeopardy, but she'd thought it advisable to clear her desktop of personal effects, since she might be gone for a couple of months.

She felt around in the box until her fingers grasped a chrome picture frame. Pulling it from the box, she stared at the portrait of her parents, both of them dressed in the white coats of their medical profession. Linda and Fritz Duncan had wanted their daughter to study medicine and join their successful OB/GYN practice. Louise had staunchly refused, and followed her heart into law. Her parents had supported her decision and had always remained proud of her accomplishments.

"You should see me now, folks," Louise said to the glossy image. "I deserved that promotion. I worked hard for it." Through a hiccuped sob, she added, "And now I think I might be just a little bit drunk." With her bare toe she rolled an empty wine bottle across the floor.

Still holding the photo, she stood up, crossed the imported-tile floor of her fourteenth-story condominium and went out on the balcony. A breeze from the ocean, less than a half mile away, washed over her. Revived, she looked across the rooftops of nearby buildings and settled her gaze on the silvery black sea, rippling to shore from the distant horizon. "Damn it. What the hell am I supposed to do for two months? Where am I supposed to go? I already live in a freaking paradise.

"Where do people go when they are told to mellow out and become one of the good guys?" A bark of bitter laughter came from her throat at the inanity of

Roger Oppenheimer's advice. Louise was a power-house in the courtroom. Aggressive, unyielding. Wasn't that what a lawyer was supposed to be?

If not, maybe she'd chosen the wrong profession. But she loved the law. She couldn't give it up now. So where did a person go to learn to be a nice, people-person kind of lawyer?

And suddenly she had the answer. She'd go to that little town in North Carolina where her best friend lived. What was the name? She struggled to remember it through a haze of muddled thinking. Bayberry Cove. That was it. A homey little burg on the edge of Currituck Sound near the Outer Banks. Vicki had moved there six months ago and now, deliriously in love and pregnant, she hated to leave the town, even to check on her antiques store in Fort Lauderdale. Endlessly praising the quiet virtues of the place, Vicki had repeatedly invited Louise to come for a visit, but Louise never had time.

She turned away from her grossly mortgaged view and went into the apartment to call Vicki. *You've got plenty of time now, honey,* she told herself. *And if Bayberry Cove can't turn you from a lioness into a pussycat, I don't know of any place that can.*

TWO DAYS LATER, on a spectacular May afternoon, Louise drove her black BMW down Main Street, Bayberry Cove, North Carolina. To her right was a row of two-story buildings with granite cornerstones proclaiming each of them to be over a hundred years old. To her left, a typical town square with ancient trees dripping shade over brick sidewalks and cast-iron benches. A perfect place for people to stop and enjoy the simple pleasure of a picnic lunch or lazy afternoon chat.

The only problem was that while Louise could admire the pastoral solitude of a leafy town green, she wasn't a picnicker, and she wasn't much for small talk. She was a woman to whom every minute was precious and not meant to be squandered. She pulled into a parking space and approached an elderly man seated on the nearest bench.

As she came closer, he shielded his eyes from the sun and grinned with obvious interest. Accustomed to such blatantly admiring looks, Louise settled her ball cap low on her forehead and flipped her long black ponytail through the opening at the back. Then, since she could plainly determine the focus of the old guy's attention, she tugged her halter top so it covered the slash of midriff above the waistband of her Liz Claiborne stretch capris.

"Hi there," she said, flashing the man a sincere smile. "Can you tell me where I might find Pintail Point, the home of Jamie Malone?"

He looked her up and down with appreciative scrutiny, murmured directions and gestured into the distance with a gnarled finger.

Louise thanked him and headed out of town to a two-lane road he'd identified as Sandy Ridge. She turned right and in three miles spotted the causeway that would lead her to where Vicki lived with her husband.

The tires crunched on loose gravel as she drove across the narrow spit of land. Dust settled on the wax on her car. When she parked at the end of the point, she got out and walked toward a neat little houseboat with geraniums in the window boxes. She heard a welcoming squeal before she actually saw her best friend.

"Oh, my God, you actually came!" Vicki crossed the wooden bridge from the boat and ran toward Louise.

"It's me," Louise stated unnecessarily. "Now slow down or you'll pop that baby out four months ahead of schedule."

Vicki threw herself into Louise's arms. "Don't worry about him. He—or she—is as protected as the gold in Fort Knox, and not going anywhere." Keeping her hands on Louise's shoulders, Vicki stepped back and fired questions. "How was your trip? How long can you stay?" She darted a glance over her shoulder where her husband, the totally gorgeous and charmingly Irish Jamie Malone, was approaching at a leisurely pace with his odd-looking dog beside him.

"Cover your ears, Beasley," Jamie said to the dog. "All this squealin' and squawkin' is typical women-folk jabber."

He placed his hands on his hips and grinned at Louise. "Well, well, Miz Lady Attorney. Fancy seeing you on Pintail Point."

She sent him a smug look. They'd had their disagreements in the past, especially about the divorce Vicki had claimed she wanted from the virtual stranger she'd married thirteen years before when he'd needed a green card and she'd needed money. Thinking she was doing her friend a favor, Louise had had the mysterious Mr. Malone investigated and subtly intimidated—until Vicki had fallen head over heels in love with him and shredded the divorce papers once and for all.

Louise took a step toward him. "Come on, Jamie. I know you're glad to see me." She angled her cheek toward his face. "Give us a wee kiss now."

He laughed and obliged her.

"So this is the love nest?" she said, walking to the boat. "The famous *Bucket O' Luck* I've heard so much about."

"This is it," Vicki said, keeping pace with her. She stopped and pointed across Currituck Sound to a hill rising next to Sandy Ridge Road. "And that's going to take her place in a few months when it's finished."

A partially completed house crested the hill, its bare timbers rising toward the afternoon sun. "Very nice."

"It will be. But for now, it's the *Bucket* or nothing." She opened the door and waited for Louise to precede her inside. "So talk, Lulu. What's the real reason you're here? You were very vague on the phone. I never thought you'd come."

Like the true friend she was, Vicki listened to Louise's tale and sighed at the injustice of it. "What are you going to do now?" she asked when Louise finished her story.

"Well, this looks like a nice place," Louise said. "I'll probably stay here for a while. Maybe Oppenheimer is right. Maybe I do need some downtime."

Vicki shot a glance in Jamie's direction. He hunched his shoulder in male confusion. Louise laughed. "I don't mean *here* here," she said. "I'm not moving in with you, for heaven's sake. I meant here in Bayberry Cove."

Relief washed over both faces. "Oh, well…" Vicki said. "If our house was ready, there'd be no problem, but we only have one bedroom on the *Bucket* and…"

Louise waved her hand to dismiss her friend's concern. "Enough, Vic. I don't want to stay with you two any more than you want me to. Just direct me to a motel. Anything in town will do."

Vicki shook her head. "That's a problem."

"Why?"

"There are no places to stay in Bayberry Cove."

"What? Nothing?"

"Nope." Vicki looked to Jamie for a suggestion.

He thought a moment and finally said, "There's always Buttercup Cottage. I could ask Haywood if he'd rent it."

"There you go," Louise said. "Of course, I've never churned butter or made my own candles…."

Vicki laughed. "It's not like that. It has indoor plumbing and electricity."

"Good. Show me the dotted line I sign on."

"You'll have to talk to Haywood Fletcher," Jamie said. "His family owns the place. I think you probably recognize his name."

Louise winced. "How could I forget the attorney who claimed he'd found flaws in that perfectly executed divorce decree I wrote for Vicki?"

Jamie laughed. "Don't blame Haywood for that. It was a stall tactic I used to buy time until Vicki admitted she loved me. Haywood will treat you fairly, but there might be one problem.''

''What now?''

''My mother used to work for Haywood. She told me that his son is coming home sometime soon. He's a semi-retired commander from the navy, and there's a chance he might want to move into the cottage.''

Vicki groaned. ''Oh, no. That place would be perfect for you, Lulu. When is Wesley due to arrive?'' she asked Jamie.

''Ma didn't say. Probably not for a while. And anyway, he'll most likely stay at the mansion in town with his father.''

''So, where is this cottage?'' Louise asked. ''I'm going to check it out so I know it's worth grappling with the town's only attorney over a lease agreement.''

''That's the best part,'' Vicki said. ''It's right next to us, just a mile farther down Sandy Ridge. You can't miss it. It's stained a delightful color, like—''

''Don't tell me,'' Louise said. ''Buttercups.''

TEN MINUTES LATER, Louise drove onto the pebble driveway of Buttercup Cottage. Besides the identifying color, a wooden placard above the front door confirmed that she was at the right place.

She stopped in front of the entrance and got out of her car. ''This looks fine,'' she said, imagining the hypnotic effect of raindrops on the sloping tin roof, lightning bugs twinkling outside the double casement windows. The sound of waves lapping the shoreline behind the house reminded her that she was only steps away from the protected bay.

Louise walked around the side of the house. "I suppose I could look through the windows. No one's living here now."

She peered into a bedroom. A double bed covered by a bright quilt looked cozy. The ceiling fan, dormant now, would stir up a nice breeze on warm evenings.

The next window provided a view of a compact bathroom with a porcelain vanity under a small medicine cabinet. "Adequate," she said, and proceeded to the back of the house.

Pleased to see that the rear door had a window in the upper half, she walked up to get a look at what was no doubt the kitchen. She was just leaning into the glass when a man appeared in her view, and the door swung open. Louise jumped back a step, but not far enough. Without warning, she was doused from chest to ankles with the grimy contents of a large pan.

She hollered, swore a little and shook her hands free of water mixed with unidentified substances. Then she watched in horror as rivers of rust permeated her new white capris. She stared at the open door where a man in a cap emblazoned with a gold insignia stood with the now-empty pan dangling from his hands. Plucking her halter away from her chest, she glared into bright aqua eyes and snapped, "Look what you've done."

CHAPTER TWO

HE STOOD THERE gawking at her as if she'd descended out of the sky. "Wow, look at you," he finally said. "I'm sorry about that. I didn't see you out here."

She glanced down at her pants again. "That's comforting. It's nice to know you weren't lying in wait...."

He disappeared into the house. Gone.

She leaned across the open doorway. "Hey!"

He came back with a roll of slightly soggy paper towels. "Here. Dry yourself."

She unwound about a dozen squares and began patting her clothes. When she swiped along her arms, she jerked her face away. "This stuff stinks. What is it?"

"I don't know. It's been in the pipes for something like five, six years. I can't remember when somebody last stayed here." He ran a sympathetic look down her legs. "I'd say it contains a good bit of rust, though."

She scowled at him. "Obviously you're a chemistry wiz."

He almost smiled. "Hardly. Unfortunately, I'm not

much of a plumber, either. The pipes under the kitchen sink are winning this battle.''

''Look, while you're joking about skirmishes with copper pipes, I'm fighting real germ warfare. Do you think I could come in and use the universal antidote to all this grime?''

''What's that?''

''Soap, Mr. Chemist. Plain old bacteria-eating soap. There is soap in this place, right?''

He moved aside. ''Oh, sure. Plenty of soap.''

She stepped through the door while digging her car keys out of her pocket. Her first look at the interior of the small kitchen confirmed the plumber's story. Sections of old pipe and numerous tools stood in puddles of murky water on the floor in front of an open cabinet, along with various lengths of shiny new PVC tubes waiting to replace their worn-out predecessors.

Louise picked her way across the disaster area and turned around. ''Can you do me a favor? My car's out front. Would you bring in the smaller of the two suitcases from the trunk?''

''Bring in a suitcase?''

She almost laughed at the expression on his face. ''Don't panic. I won't disturb your work. I'm not moving in this minute. I haven't even signed a lease yet. But I do need to change clothes.'' She tossed the keys, and he snatched them in midair. ''Good reflexes, chemist. I'll be in the bathroom.''

WESLEY FLETCHER DIDN'T like chaos in his life. He'd spent years eliminating as much of it as possible from his daily routines. He started every day with the same rituals. He ate his meals at the same times. He hardly ever watched a new show on television, preferring a select number of tried and true ones.

That's why he was determined to fix the pipes in Buttercup Cottage before it was time to prepare dinner. He glanced at his watch as he walked around the side of the house. He had only two hours left to accomplish the task, or after eating his thick, juicy T-bone, he'd be cleaning the broiler in the bathroom sink. This day would have gone so much better if the one plumber in Bayberry Cove hadn't told him it would be forty-eight hours before he could make a house call.

And now Wesley was carting a suitcase weighing at least twenty pounds back to his home, where a half-crazy lady was occupying his bathroom and making claims about moving in. That was chaos of a sort that could turn his already cockeyed day upside down.

It wasn't that he didn't owe her a favor. He did. Nearly drowning her in liquid muck was a pretty nasty thing to do to a woman. A woman whose clothes and demeanor indicated she was not from around here. And that was the biggest mystery of all. Who was she and where had she come from?

He entered the house and set the suitcase by the bathroom door. Tapping lightly to get her attention, he realized he didn't even know her name. "Ma'am?"

She opened the door about ten inches and, now hatless, presented him a view of a face that could rival any movie star's. "Call me ma'am one more time, chemist, and I may have to slug you. The name's Louise.''

Through the opening he saw her reflection in the small mirror over the bathroom sink. For the last twenty years he'd lived by a code that, had this particular situation actually been in the books, would surely have demanded that he look away. But he didn't. His gaze was riveted to a smooth ivory spine that curved delicately to what was no doubt a well-proportioned posterior. Unfortunately, verification of that hypothesis was impossible, since that body part was abruptly cut off by the end of the mirror.

''So what's yours?'' she asked him.

He snapped his attention back to her face. ''My what?''

''Name,'' she coaxed. ''I should at least know who to send the bill for my new pants.''

Maybe she wasn't kidding. He couldn't tell. Maybe he should buy her new pants. He didn't know the protocol for this circumstance. But he did know his name, and he told her. ''Wesley Fletcher.''

''Okay, then, Wesley. Move away from the door so I can open it and get my case inside.''

He went back to the kitchen and scowled at the sink. His first day back in Bayberry Cove was certainly not going according to plan.

LOUISE TWISTED THE TAILS of her floral print blouse into a knot at her waist and zipped up her peach-colored shorts. She brushed her hair, gathered it at her crown and whipped the mass through a thick elastic band. In her mind she listed all the details she should consider before contacting Haywood Fletcher about renting the cottage. "Obviously some repairs are needed," she mumbled to herself, and then froze with her hand on the doorknob.

"Haywood Fletcher!" she said aloud. "The guy just said his name was Wesley Fletcher. He's no clumsy, blue-eyed plumber. He's Haywood's son, the navy man who Jamie said might have his sights set on my cottage."

She left the bathroom prepared to negotiate for Buttercup Cottage. Finding her adversary flat on his back under the sink, she tapped the sole of his sneaker with her big toe. He pushed himself out and sat up, leaving his cap behind collecting drops of water from the faucet above.

Draping well-muscled arms over bent knees, he looked at her for a second and then ran tapered fingers over close-cropped, wheat-colored hair.

"Damn." He groped under the sink and retrieved his cap. The gold insignia had taken on the same rusty hue as Louise's capris, and he frowned at the ruined embroidery.

"Looks pretty bad," Louise said, allowing herself a little smile. "I know how you feel."

"I have others."

"Navy officer issue, right?"

He nodded and stood up. "You look better."

"I think I washed off anything that might enter my bloodstream and communicate a fatal disease."

He smiled. "I apologize again. I really didn't see you. The back door was just the easiest way to dump the corroded water, and I never expected anyone to be outside.''

"Isn't this the type of town where folks just pop up on their neighbors' doorsteps for a piece of apple pie?''

He smiled again, revealing even, straight teeth. "In town I suppose that's true, but out here on the sound, visitors are pretty rare. Besides, nobody knows I'm here. This place has been vacant for so long there's not a soul who would have a reason to stop.''

"Except for me, you mean.''

"I guess except for you, and I'm a little curious about why you're here.'' He went to an old wooden kitchen table and lifted the lid on a red cooler. He pulled a can of Coke from a pool of melting ice and held it out to her.

She sat on one of the four spindle-back chairs—the one with all its spindles—and popped the top. "I wouldn't have snuck up on you except I didn't see a car when I drove up.''

He opened a can for himself, sat across from her and nodded toward the backyard. "My Jeep's in the shed. I put it there because the salt in the air can be rough on the paint.''

They each took a few sips of soda before Wesley spoke again. "So...why *are* you here? And even more important, I suppose, who are you?''

She set her Coke down and folded her hands. "My name's Louise Duncan. I'm a friend of Vicki Soren—'' She stopped when she realized she was about to give Vicki's maiden name, the one she'd used until six months ago. "Make that Vicki Malone.''

"Malone?" He nodded in recognition. "Jamie's wife? The one who married him so he could get a green card all those years ago?"

"That's the one."

"My dad told me those two found each other after something like thirteen years. He said he had a hand in keeping them together after all that time."

Louise scoffed. "I guess you could say that. I was Vicki's lawyer, and I drafted the faultless divorce settlement she presented to Jamie. And then your daddy took it upon himself to concoct a number of loopholes. No offense to your father, but he's a crafty old buzzard."

Wesley chuckled. "None taken. In the Fletcher family, that's a compliment." He eyed her over the top of his can as he took a long swallow. "So you're a lawyer?"

"That's right." She looked directly at him. "And I've heard every shark and bottom-feeding joke you can think of, so you can keep them to yourself."

He affected an innocent shrug. "Believe me, I wasn't going to make any cracks."

She relaxed. "Okay then. Now as for why I'm here in Bayberry Cove, I'm on vacation, sort of." Seeing no reason to delay the inevitable, she announced, "And I've come to Buttercup Cottage because I want to rent it for a couple of months."

He set the can down with a metallic thump. "Sorry. It's not available."

"Why not?"

"Because I'm living in it."

"But you could live anywhere."

"So could you."

She took a deep breath. Engaging in a war of words with Wesley Fletcher was not likely to get her anywhere, especially since the cottage she now obsessively wanted to rent was in his family's name. "Look, I might consider renting something else, but my friend told me there is nothing available in Bayberry Cove—no motels, no seasonal places even."

"That's true, but you could point that BMW down Sandy Ridge Road, and in ten or fifteen miles you'll hit some quaint little towns with enough gingerbread bed-and-breakfasts to make your mouth water." He picked up his can and pointed it in a direction roughly behind him. "Or head to Morgan City and get a room at the Comfort Inn. They have a free continental breakfast."

"That's almost twenty miles away." His answering shrug was impassive, and Louise had to struggle to control her temper. She drummed her fingers on the tabletop and watched for any sign of capitulation. Nothing.

"I think we can reach an agreement here," she finally said. "I'm only in your town for one reason. My friend lives a mile from this cottage and I want to spend time with her."

"That makes sense."

"And I know that your father lives in a big house in town. Jamie Malone told me. Couldn't you stay there for a couple of months? Then when I leave, you could move back to this place."

He shook his head. "I'd rather not. It's really not convenient."

Logic wasn't working, and now Louise wanted to rent Buttercup Cottage with a craving that was almost scary. She changed tactics. "I'll pay you, of course. And I know this time of year demands higher rates. Would you say a thousand dollars a month is a fair price?"

He barked with amusement. "For this little waterfront gem?" He leaned toward her across the table. "Here's what I think is a fair price. Assuming I can get the pipes fixed..." he glanced around the small kitchen "...and assuming these old appliances are in working order, which I haven't tested yet since you stopped by and interrupted me. And assuming that when I get up on the roof and walk around I won't find any leaks...then I'd say a fair price might be about four hundred a month."

Now they were getting somewhere. In fact, Wesley was turning out to be a decent guy. "You'd do all these repairs and only charge me four hundred a month?"

"No. I said that would be a fair price. Actually, I'm not going to charge you anything because I'm not renting you this house."

She stood up, sending her chair scooting along the worn linoleum floor. "I see what's happening here," she said.

"You do?"

"Absolutely. Don't move. I'll be right back."

He looked at his wristwatch. "Can I at least move back to the sink? I'm behind schedule already."

She glared at him, then picked up her keys from where he'd left them on the counter, and stomped through the kitchen to a parlor, where a few old pieces of furniture were haphazardly arranged. She picked her way through a clutter of old magazines and knick-knacks and stepped out the front door to her car. Opening the passenger door of the BMW, she snatched her purse from the front seat. When she went back to the kitchen, Wesley was under the sink again.

"Excuse me," she said.

He scooted out and stood up.

Louise moved to within inches of him and waved her checkbook in front of his eyes. "How much? Name your price."

He stared at her and slowly shook his head. "Are you crazy?"

"I want to rent this place, Wesley Fletcher. And I mean to have it. I've played games with your father in the past, but I'd rather not play games with you. Can't we just settle this here and now?"

His blue eyes turned flint-gray, and Louise took a step back. *Be nice, Lulu,* she said to herself. *Be compassionate and caring like Roger says. Don't intimidate.* She took a deep breath. "Please, Wesley. I'll pay whatever you say."

He crossed his arms over his chest and regarded her with serious intent. After a moment he turned his hands palms up. Louise experienced a gratifying rush of victory at the obvious gesture of surrender.

And then he said, "The place isn't for rent. That's final."

His was as resolute a face as she'd ever seen in her life. It was a granite and steel countenance that would be perfect at a peacemaking summit between world powers. Or above the green felt of a high-stakes poker table. And it was a face that wasn't going to change.

Louise marched into the bathroom, stuffed her soiled clothes into her suitcase and her feet into her ruined sandals and wheeled the bag back to the kitchen. Wesley was under the sink again, but his shadowed gaze snapped from the gaping pipes and remained fixed on her face.

''I suggest you let the local postman know you're living here, Wesley,'' she said. ''The bill for my clothes will arrive in the mail. Since I don't have an address, you may send your check in care of the Malones.''

The corner of his mouth lifted in an odd little grin that might have been endearing on a young boy, but was simply maddening on Wesley. ''Aye, aye, Counselor,'' he said.

She stepped to the sink, carefully avoiding contact with his bent knee, and gave the old enamel spigot one quick flick of her wrist. The rewarding squeal and shimmy of old copper tubing filled her with satisfaction. Water spurted through the pipes, hitting Wesley Fletcher square in the middle of his smug face. Louise smiled down at him, grabbed the handle of her suitcase and exited Buttercup Cottage.

CHAPTER THREE

WESLEY DROVE HIS Jeep Wrangler onto the gravel road leading to Pintail Point, the home of his long-time friend and Bayberry Cove's resident artist, Jamie Malone. Wes had been home less than twenty-four hours and there were plenty of people he needed to see, but on this picture-perfect morning with the sun shimmering off the blue water of the sound, it was Jamie he wanted to talk to.

After he determined that Louise Duncan's black BMW wasn't anywhere in sight, Wes parked under a couple of tall, sweeping sea pines. He walked toward the houseboat, scanning the yard until he was convinced Louise wasn't there. Then he fixed his gaze on the picnic table where Jamie's dog, Beasley, was napping. The long-legged beast opened his golden eyes, crawled out from under the table and emitted a low-pitched bark of welcome. Then he plopped down at Wesley's feet.

Wesley scratched behind one of the animal's floppy ears. "Hey, Beas, how are you? Energetic as ever, I see."

Jamie burst out the door of the *Bucket O' Luck* and strode toward them. "Wes Fletcher, I heard you were home." He held out his hand. "Good to see you."

"Same here." Wes resumed a reconnaissance of the property while answering Jamie's questions about his retirement.

After a few minutes of conversation, Jamie snapped his fingers to get Wes's attention. "She's not here, buddy."

Wes was forced to focus on Jamie's face. "Who? I don't know what you're talking about."

"The heck you don't. I'm talking about Louise Duncan, who stopped by here yesterday after you doused her with what she described as some sort of sewage."

Wes scrunched up his face. "It wasn't sewage. It was rusty water from the kitchen pipes. And did she mention that she gave as good as she got?"

Jamie smiled. "Oh, yeah. That was the part of the story she enjoyed telling most."

Wes shook his head. "She's one strange woman. Bossy, pushy, demanding…"

"Don't forget drop-dead gorgeous," Jamie added.

Wes laughed. "I guess that's true, too. And determined. She wouldn't take no for an answer when it came to renting the cottage."

"We heard. Frankly, my wife, whom you haven't met, but who is the sweetest woman on this green earth, is a little ticked at you. She was hoping you'd move in with your dad."

Wes shrugged. "I've been given a grant from the National Oceanic and Atmospheric Administration to fund a project on marine ecology. I need to be on the water."

"Why didn't you tell Louise that? She might have

understood why living at the cottage was so important to you.''

''She didn't seem interested in anyone's motives but her own. And have you ever tried to get a word in with her?''

Jamie chuckled. ''A few times. Your point's well taken.''

''So where are the women now?''

''You just missed Vicki. She drove into Bayberry Cove to meet Louise at the Kettle. She stayed at a motel in Morgan City last night, but she's determined to find a place in town to rent for a couple of months so she can just sort of kick back.''

Wes pictured the Bayberry Cove Kettle at eight-thirty on a Saturday morning. The restaurant would be packed, and he had no doubt who in the crowd would be the center of attention.

LOUISE TURNED ONTO Main Street and looked at the digital clock on her dashboard. Already ten minutes late, she reluctantly slowed to a frustrating, but law-abiding, thirty-five miles an hour and scanned the street for available parking. She settled for a spot two blocks away from the Bayberry Cove Kettle, got out of her car and walked briskly to the entrance.

She threaded her way through the crowded restaurant to where her friend was seated. ''Sorry I'm late,'' she said, hanging her purse over the back of the chair and sitting down.

''Don't apologize. I only got here five minutes ago. I took my time, since I remembered it was you I was meeting.''

"Funny." A pleasant-looking waitress came to the table. "What's good here?" Louise asked Vicki.

"Everything's great, isn't that right, Bobbi Lee?" Vicki said.

Louise gave Vicki a knowing look. So this well-rounded waitress in the red-checkered dress was the notorious Bobbi Lee Blanchard she'd heard so much about, the woman who'd lusted after Jamie Malone for years.

"Not a bad choice on the whole menu," Bobbi confirmed.

"In that case," Louise said, "I'll have two eggs over light, hash browns, wheat toast and a side of bacon. And, of course, coffee—large."

Vicki ordered scrambled eggs and an English muffin and waited until Bobbi Lee had gone to place the order before she said, "What happened to yogurt and fresh fruit?"

Louise shrugged. "I'm in the country now. Fresh air makes me hungry." She pointed to Vicki's bulging belly. "It could be worse. Look what it did to you."

They chatted about Vicki's store in Fort Lauderdale, her new house, the wood carvings Jamie was sending to a Boston gallery for a summer showing. "Enough about my life," Vicki said when they'd finished their meal and were sipping coffee. "Be honest, Lulu. How are you going to stay in Bayberry Cove for two months? You're going to die of boredom."

"No, I won't. I like this town. It's cute and cozy. With the exception of Wesley Fletcher, the people seem nice. I'll find things to do. Maybe I'll help you shop for baby stuff.''

Vicki's eyes sparkled with amusement. "You? Baby shopping? One trip to Infants 'R Us in Morgan City and you'll be begging for mercy."

Louise nodded. "Maybe. But I'd like to give the town a try—if I can find a place to stay. I'm not driving nearly twenty miles each way to the motel."

Vicki set her mug on the table. "Sorry things didn't work out for Buttercup Cottage. And even sorrier that Wes gave you such a hard time. I've never met him, but Jamie's always told me what a super guy he is."

Louise arched one perfectly shaped eyebrow. "Believe me, Vic, there are things about him that definitely fall into the super category."

"Ah...so what Bobbi Lee just told me is true. Commander Fletcher is a hunk."

Louise smiled. "Close enough. He's way too clean-cut for my taste, but with a little roughing up, he could be the mountain man of my dreams."

"Somehow I can't see a career navy guy turning into Grizzly Adams."

Louise was about to respond when Bobbi Lee returned. "Can I get you anything else, ladies?"

Louise grabbed the check just as a customer approached the table demanding Bobbi's attention.

"Hi, Earnest," she said. "You want the usual?"

"That'll be fine, Bobbi Lee. Just wrap it up and I'll take it back upstairs to my apartment. I've got a whole day's worth of bookkeeping ahead of me."

Louise stared at the man's balding pate as he

walked behind Bobbi Lee toward the counter. "Vicki, did you hear what that man said?"

Vicki tucked a strand of honey-blond hair behind her ear. "Something about a take-out order."

"Right. An order he can take up to his apartment." She pointed to the ceiling. "His apartment upstairs."

Vicki was clearly baffled. "So?"

"This street is lined with two-story buildings. There must be living quarters on the second floor of most of them. All I have to do is find one that's empty."

"What are you going to do?" Vicki asked. "Check every building on the street?"

"If I have to."

"Would you like me to help? I promised Jamie I'd work with him on his exhibit today, but he'll understand."

"No. Go on home to that gorgeous husband of yours. I'll wait and pay the check." As Vicki stood to leave, Louise looked out the window to the park across the street and grinned. "I won't need your help anyway, Vic. I know just who to ask."

WES WAS LUCKY. He pulled into a parking place right in front of the Bayberry Cove Kettle just after a customer backed out. Glancing around at the spots nearest him, he confirmed the absence of a black BMW and couldn't decide if he felt relief or disappointment.

He opened the door to the restaurant, and Louise breezed through it wearing a midthigh sundress splashed with sunflowers and held up with inch-wide shoulder straps. A flurry of gastric activity began in

Wes's stomach that made him forget his earlier cravings for pancakes and bacon.

She stopped in front of him and locked her mesmerizing pale lavender eyes with his. A shock of recognition—no doubt as profound as Wes's own—shimmered in her gaze for mere seconds before mutating to an amused familiarity. Nothing seemed to faze this woman for long.

"Well, well, Commander." She placed a fist on her hip and gave him a self-assured grin. "You clean up pretty darn well."

His fingers twitched at his side. He resisted the ridiculous urge to salute. He literally *was* a commander, but he didn't feel in charge of this encounter. "Good morning, Louise," he said, reassured by the commanding tone of his voice, at least.

"You look refreshed, Wesley," she said. "I assume you slept well in your seaside retreat."

"Very well, thank you." That was a lie. The window air conditioner in the master bedroom had cranked and hissed in competition with the twenty-year-old compressor in the refrigerator. But outdated appliances weren't all that had kept him awake most of the night. He was staring at the main reason for his restlessness. "And you?"

"Like a top," she said. "The motel you so generously recommended had all the amenities of, well…a motel." She flipped a shimmering column of black hair over her shoulder. "But you'll be glad to know that I may have solved the problem of my living quarters."

"Oh?"

She raised her eyes to scan the tops of the buildings on Main Street. "I can't imagine that there isn't a room to let above one of these Bayberry Cove establishments. I can be quite comfortable here in the middle of everything that goes on in your little town."

"That is an interesting solution, Louise. I'm sure you'll find the nightlife in town quite stimulating. Have you checked with any of the shopkeepers yet about vacancies?"

"I don't need to go door-to-door," she answered smartly. "I've already made one friend in Bayberry Cove who will be helpful." She pointed to the park across the street, where an old man sat on a bench.

Wes smiled when he recognized the familiar figure who had occupied that particular bench for most of the last five years.

"He was kind enough to give me directions to Pintail Point yesterday," Louise continued. "I'm sure he'll help me find a vacancy. I'll bet he sees everything from that vantage point. And I'll bet he knows everyone in town."

"That's probably a good bet," Wes said.

Louise inclined her head toward the restaurant door. "You enjoy your breakfast, Commander. By the time you've finished, I'll have signed a two-month lease, and we'll practically be neighbors."

"I don't doubt it." Wes glanced at the old-timer in the park. Mason was a tough cookie in most of his dealings, but if anyone could talk him into the lease deal of the century, it was Louise. "Why don't we meet back here in, say, forty-five minutes, and you can let me know how you made out," Wes suggested.

"I'll even spring for coffee and promise not to pour any on you."

Amazingly, she seemed to like the idea. "Forty-five minutes it is." She gave him a grin and left.

"HI. DO YOU REMEMBER ME?" Louise said to the old man sitting under the sprawling oak tree.

He looked at her with surprisingly clear blue eyes that were still apparently capable of appreciating her obvious attributes. Sliding over to give her room on the bench, he motioned for her to sit. "I may be old," he said, "but my memory's as fresh as last night's dew for things that catch my fancy. Did you find your way to Pintail Point yesterday?"

She sat, then angled toward him with her elbow on the back of the bench. "I did. Your directions were perfect. I'm counting on you knowing every little thing about this town. That's why I've come back for your help today."

He layered his hands over a thick wooden walking stick and appraised her with an intensity that suddenly seemed strangely familiar. "What is it you need, young lady?"

Louise squirmed on the bench seat just a little, suppressing the feeling that she knew this man as more than just a passing acquaintance from the previous day. It was more than his eyes. Though his skin was creased with wrinkles and slack on his face, she detected a once-square jawline, punctuated by a strong chin that thrust forward with authority.

She told him about her search for living quarters and that she was hoping an apartment might be available in town. He nodded, asked her a few questions about her intended length of stay and her reason for being in Bayberry Cove.

She answered truthfully, and when she'd finished, he thought a moment and then replied. "There's a small house out on the sound about four miles from here," he said. "Has a sign above the door that says Buttercup Cottage. I think you'd like it there."

Louise laughed. "I would indeed, but it seems someone beat me to it. A man is already living there...."

His scraggly white eyebrows lifted in surprise. "Do you know his name?"

"Wesley Fletcher," she said.

The beginning of a smile curled the man's thin lips. "So, the boy's come home," he said. "I wondered when I caught a glimpse of him going into the Kettle."

"He has. I tried to bargain with him—"

"Oh, you can't bargain with Wesley. He's as stubborn as his father."

Louise nodded. "So I've experienced."

The old man chuckled. "You'd best leave the cottage to him." He pointed across the street. "Now, then, see that furniture store? McCorkle's New and Used?"

Louise nodded again.

"You try that place. I know the upstairs is vacant, and I think it's in pretty good shape. 'Course, all these buildings are showing signs of age. But I expect that one will do."

''And who should I see about renting it?'' Louise asked.

''Ask for Suzie or Evan McCorkle. They run the place. You tell them that Mason told you to inquire.'' He winked at her. ''You'll get the apartment. I guarantee it. Just have Suzie draw up a simple agreement saying you'll pay three hundred a month for the next two months. Tell her to give you a copy and that'll be that.''

''Really? It's that easy?''

''You run along and get your suitcase. It'll be that easy,'' he assured her.

And it almost was. Evan McCorkle, gray-haired, well-fed and a living, breathing folk-art archetype of middle-class virtues, was at first reluctant to rent to Louise. She determined from what she deciphered from snatches of his whispered debate with his wife that Evan thought Louise might play loud music or entertain guests at odd hours.

But Suzie McCorkle argued that she had a good feeling about Miss Duncan, and couldn't she always trust her feelings? In the end, it was Suzie's intuition and the mention of Mason's name that clinched the deal. By the time Louise entered the Bayberry Cove Kettle to meet Wesley Fletcher for coffee, she had a signed lease in her hand. ''The place is a bit dusty,'' she explained to Wes, ''but I can fix it up. And I bought a few pieces of furniture from the McCorkles. I'll be very comfortable there.''

Truthfully, it would take her a good two days to even make the place livable. The furniture needed sprucing up. The cobwebs alone would fill up a trash can, and the grime on the windows all but obliterated the view of Main Street. But Louise wasn't about to admit to Wes that any of those details were more than a passing inconvenience.

"Sounds like everything worked out for you even without Buttercup Cottage," he said, while filling her coffee mug.

"Absolutely." She stirred her coffee and let a smug grin convey her feeling of self-satisfaction. "And the best part is I got a great deal, and don't have to write any rent checks to the Fletchers."

He smiled down into his own cup before leveling a serious gaze on her face. "That's not necessarily so, Louise. If you look at that document carefully, you'll see that your rent payments should be made out to Mason D. Fletcher Enterprises."

Louise darted a glance out the window at the old man in the park. "His name is Mason *Fletcher?*"

"'Fraid so," Wes acknowledged. "Your landlord is my grandfather." When he noticed the puzzled look on her face, he added, "Mason Delroy Fletcher owns these entire three blocks of Bayberry Cove, Louise. So no matter what second-story apartment you chose, you would be supporting the Fletchers."

He took a long sip of coffee. "And we certainly do appreciate your patronage."

CHAPTER FOUR

VICKI MALONE CAREFULLY removed a china dinner plate from the packing box. She stacked it on top of others on an old wrought-iron and glass table in the kitchen section of Louise's apartment. "These dishes are really pretty, Lulu," she said. "I love the cherry blossom design."

"The best the Morgan City Wal-Mart had to offer," Louise responded. "And within the limits of the dollar amount I set to furnish this place."

Vicki swiped her finger through a layer of dust on the single kitchen counter. "Are you really going to sleep here tonight?"

Louise snapped plastic gloves onto her hands and dipped a cleaning rag into a solution of vinegar and water. "Absolutely. Two nights in a motel is enough for me. I'm looking forward to all the…" she paused, glanced around the room at the work that still needed to be done, and gave Vicki a rueful smile "…comforts of home. Have I mentioned how grateful I am to you two for your help?"

Jamie Malone, intent on turning an old oak bureau into a utilitarian work of art, shrugged off the comment. "Forget about it. What are friends for?"

"Besides, you've mentioned it about a hundred

times," Vicki said. "With the three of us working, we actually might have this place in order by this afternoon. It's going to be lovely," she added. "The curtains and linens and pillows you bought are adorable and will add a lot of charm to this room."

Louise stared at her dearest friend. Vicki loved pottery and flowers and chintz, so Louise allowed her to use words like *adorable* and *charm*. Louise's viewpoint was that a person needed towels. So what if they had a little lacy trim on the hem? So what if a plate had a cluster of cherries painted in the center? It would still hold a microwave dinner. "That's the look I'm going for," she said with a grin.

When she finished unpacking dishes, Vicki picked up a candle that had been sitting on the table, and examined it closely. "I didn't know you were into these things. Did you buy this at the Bayberry Cove Candle Company?"

"Hardly, since I've never heard of the place. The truth is, I didn't buy it at all. It was outside my door this morning when I got here."

"It's a beautiful shade of blue," Vicki said. "Did you read the tag taped to the side?"

"Tag? No. I didn't know there was a tag."

"It says, 'Look to the sky and look to sea for this tranquil shade of blue. Light it tonight and it will bring comfort to your home and you.'"

Louise walked over to the table and took the candle from Vicki. "Very touching," she said, "if not exactly poet laureate material."

"If you didn't buy it," Vicki said, "I wonder where it came from."

Jamie turned off the power to his electric sander and set the tool on top of the bureau. "I'd guess that Suzie McCorkle left it," he said. "She's interested in that kind of stuff. Candles, crystals, things like that. It's probably her way of wishing you domestic harmony."

Louise pictured the mousy woman with the shoulder-length gray hair neatly pinned back from her forehead with two barrettes. A New Age lady? Well, why not? Louise looked at the mattress and box springs and the "nearly new" plaid sofa she had bought from Suzie's shop the day before, and another explanation came to mind. "Maybe she's just thanking me for buying a few things."

Jamie ran his hand over the surface of the dresser and picked up the sander again. "Maybe. She would do something like that—quietly leave a candle without expecting recognition. She's a nice woman."

The origin of the candle solved, Louise returned to her struggle with the first of three windows that looked over Main Street. After scrubbing for ten minutes with the vinegar solution and following up with industrial strength glass cleaner, she was finally able to see the sun dappling the sidewalks in the square across the street. She yanked another batch of paper towels from a roll and feverishly wiped the stubborn glass with a circular motion. "Just have to eliminate a few more streaks," she huffed, "and then a bird with a bad case of cataracts might actually knock himself silly trying to fly into this place."

"For the love of Saint Pat, Louise," Jamie said

above the steady whirr of his sander, "you'd better quit now before you rub a hole in the glass."

"Jamie's right, Lulu. You're taking out your frustration on the window."

Louise laid her forehead against the nearly clean pane and sighed. "You're right. I still can't believe I didn't notice the name *Fletcher* on that lease. Four days ago, if I'd had a client who'd done something as stupid as sign a document without reading it carefully, I'd have seriously considered not representing him."

Jamie looked at Vicki and was unsuccessful at hiding a grin. "And what difference does it really make now? You have a place to stay at a reasonable rent— the *only* place available, as I see it. Why do you care who owns the building?"

"But they're so smug," she said. "Wesley practically crowed when he told me that his family owns this building."

"They own Buttercup Cottage, too," Vicki pointed out. "And that didn't bother you when you thought you could rent it."

"That was yesterday, before I knew them." She gestured out the window, where people in the square were now visible through the sparkling glass. "And that old guy over there…Mason Fletcher. Now that I think about it, he was smug, too. And I can just imagine Haywood. He's probably more smug than the rest of them."

Jamie hunched a shoulder in a sign of agreement. "Smug, clever…there's a fine line between the two if you ask me. You have to be clever first in order to justify being smug. And as for your signing the lease, my advice is to forget about it. You're on vacation from lawyering, so you might as well relax and enjoy yourself." He walked to the middle window and with his fist cleared a three-inch circle through the grime so he could see the street below. "Bayberry Cove is a really nice little town."

Louise let out a long breath and followed his gaze. It was Sunday morning, and families had gathered on the square. Fathers pushed children on swings and women chatted on benches.

"Yes, it is," she admitted. "And you're right. I'm going to relax just as soon as I get this place clean. And right after you tell me how old man Fletcher got all his money."

Jamie went back to the bureau, picked up a piece of sandpaper and began smoothing the edges by hand. "That's an interesting story," he said, his words a soothing accompaniment to the rasp of the paper. "Mason was in his early twenties when he took a small inheritance his father left him and traveled from Bayberry Cove to Arizona. He invested in a silver mine out there with some other fellas, and as luck would have it, they uncovered a rich vein that gave them each a good stake for their futures."

Louise dipped her rag again and attacked the middle window. "So he came back to North Carolina and bought Bayberry Cove?"

Jamie chuckled. "Not all at once. He made his real fortune in patents. Sold one to Henry Ford that revolutionized the assembly line process. And then, bit by bit, he started buying up property around here and dabbling in various ventures. He built Buttercup Cottage in 1935 for the love of his life, the woman he married.''

Louise stared down at the old man under the oak tree. She wasn't surprised to learn a romantic soul lurked behind his knowing blue eyes. Smugness aside, Mason Fletcher had a soft spot. ''Who was she?''

''An Arizona gal. He married her out there and took her away from all that soaring rock and desert and brought her to the sea. They say she loved being on Currituck Sound, and Buttercup Cottage was his gift to her on their second anniversary.'' He stopped sanding and looked first at Louise and then at Vicki. ''He called her Buttercup. He was a man very much in love, apparently. Still is, twenty-some years after her death.''

''Haywood was their only child?'' Louise asked.

''The only one who survived the polio epidemic of the late forties,'' Jamie answered. ''Haywood had two younger sisters, twins. They both died.''

Louise watched as Mason Fletcher rolled a colorful plastic ball toward a group of children in the square. ''That's sad.''

''And Haywood only had one child—Wesley.'' Jamie blew a film of sawdust from the top of the bureau. ''Can't say he didn't try for more, though. He's been married four times—which is why he shies away from wedded bliss today,'' Jamie added with a hint of bitterness in his voice.

Louise resumed scrubbing. ''So Haywood is quite the ladies' man as well as a renowned legal mind. I can't wait to meet this paragon of Bayberry Cove society.''

"You will meet him,'' Vicki said. "The only woman in his life now is Jamie's mother, Kate.''

"But didn't you tell me that Jamie's mother works for Haywood?'' Louise asked.

"We said 'used to,' as in she used to be his house-keeper. Now she's a bit more to him than that.''

"Yeah, but not his wife,'' Jamie said with that same edge of rancor in his tone.

Louise spritzed a generous amount of cleaner on the window and began rubbing it dry. As the solution evaporated, a group of men standing on the sidewalk in front of the Bayberry Cove Kettle came into her view. There was no mistaking the tall, lean figure waving goodbye to the others and heading across the street. She quickly cleaned a larger section and watched Wesley Fletcher walk toward his grandfa-ther. "Speaking of the Fletchers, the youngest one just appeared on the square.''

Vicki levered her pregnant body off the chair. She stood beside Louise at the window. "Is that him? Is that Wesley?''

"In the flesh.'' Louise admired the stretch of a snug T-shirt over his chest and his muscled thighs extending from a pair of gray jersey shorts. "Or the next best thing to it, anyway.''

"Ohh…'' Vicki's one syllable rolled into several seconds of blatant admiration.

"Don't stare at the poor man, ladies,'' Jamie said from the middle of the room. "You couldn't be more obvious.''

Vicki laughed. "You're just jealous because there's someone in Bayberry Cove who is *nearly* as good-looking as you are."

"Maybe a little," he admitted. "But Wes is a good friend. And he's the town's favorite son. He was born and raised here and all the locals followed his exploits through the naval academy and beyond. I'm content to stand in his shadow as the adopted son."

Louise drummed her nails against the pane. "I wonder why he's not married."

"He was, once," Jamie said. "To a girl he met while he was at Annapolis. She was a journalist in Washington, a couple of years older than him."

"What happened?"

"She went her way, covering stories around the world, and he went his, to wherever the navy sent him. Tough to make a marriage work under those circumstances. They divorced after a few years."

Louise drew her friend's attention back to the window. "Look, he's a runner."

Both women watched as Wesley stretched his legs and arms. He jogged in place a moment before taking off around the perimeter of the square.

"He runs a few times a week when he's in town," Jamie said, adding that he started the regimen at precisely the same time each day. "Now get away from the window and give the man his privacy."

"No way," Louise scoffed. "He doesn't want privacy. He's running in the middle of the town square!" Determined to raise the window, which probably hadn't been opened in a decade at least, she struggled until old paint finally cracked and the glass slid upward with a stubborn hiss. She waited for Wesley to sprint around to the street side again and then leaned out the window. "Ahoy, Commander," she yelled. "Good morning."

He looked up, shielded his eyes. "Good morning to you, Louise," he called. "How are the new digs?"

"Couldn't be better," she said, propping the window up with a yardstick.

He tossed her an offhand wave and jogged around the corner. Louise continued to watch. His legs churned with nearly effortless grace. His arms pumped rhythmically at his sides. He was all fluid, powerful motion, an image of focused elegance. She nudged her friend. "So, what do you think?"

"Oh, you're right, Lulu. I've never seen a man more outrageously..." Vicki fumbled for the right word and glanced over her shoulder at her husband "...sinfully *smug* in my life!"

Louise hooted with laughter. "See? I told you. But on him it does look good."

Louise's approach to life in Bayberry Cove was characterized by good intentions. First, she intended to take Jamie's advice. Once the apartment was in good shape, she'd kick back, relax, read a few good books. She'd definitely brightened the day of the owner of Books by the Bay when she'd walked out of the shop Monday morning with ten novels.

Second, she intended to stay a little bit angry with Wesley Fletcher. It was the safest way to combat a growing attraction to the good-looking ex–naval officer who seemed to be popping into her thoughts with alarming regularity. A man who lived his life according to regimens and schedules wouldn't complement Louise's more flamboyant style. More importantly, she wasn't staying in Bayberry Cove for long. Two months in this town was the only interlude she meant to have from her real life.

And last, she definitely intended to avoid legal matters of any kind. She was in the South, where everybody understood that the livin' was easy, and she was going to return to Oppenheimer Straus and Baker bathed in an aura of mint-julep cool if it killed her.

Unfortunately, each of these good intentions was blown all to hell on Tuesday evening.

Just two days after she moved into her little apartment, an unexpected event made her ignore every promise she'd made to herself.

Tired of reading, bored with dusting and totally disinterested in popping a frozen dinner into her microwave, Louise wandered down to the Kettle, where she'd eaten most of her meals the last couple of days. There was a good supper crowd gathered in the diner, but she found a small table and sat down.

After a few minutes Bobbi Lee came to take her order. "Hey, girl, how's it going?" she said, her red lips curving into a welcoming grin. "How's that place of yours working out?"

"Just fine, Bobbi Lee," Louise said. She and Bobbi had established a friendly relationship. In fact, Louise was now beginning to worry about how this steadily increasing bond with the waitress might translate into fat grams.

"What'll it be tonight?" Bobbi asked.

Louise folded the menu so she couldn't see the words *sausage gravy*. "Just a salad."

Bobbi sauntered off to place the order and Louise sat back and watched the people around her. Four women at a nearby table caught and held her attention. Each lady had a full bottle of Budweiser in front of her. Twice the number of empties sat waiting for the busboy to take them away.

Occasionally the women's conversation was interrupted by boisterous laughter. But without fail, they quickly resumed a serious discussion once the joviality passed. Other sounds of the restaurant faded as curiosity made Louise tune in their voices. The ladies were obviously close acquaintances even though there was a wide range in their ages.

"All I know is that I couldn't afford to give up another day's wages at the factory to stay home with my son," a young, olive-skinned Hispanic woman said. "Thank goodness he was well enough to go back to the baby-sitter today."

"Did you tell Justin why you needed to stay home?" an older woman with a long gray ponytail asked.

"I did, hoping he'd be sympathetic. He said, 'Go ahead, Miranda. Take all the time you need, but come payday—'"

"Wait, don't tell us," a slim woman with short blond hair interrupted. "He said, 'Come payday, your check might be a little less than you expected.'"

Empathetic laughter erupted around the table until the older woman lifted her bottle into the air. "Let's drink one to Justin Beauclaire, in honor of his unending compassion for his employees and his sense of fair play,'' she said.

Something of an expert herself in the subtle deployment of sarcasm, Louise appreciated the old gal's admirable use of it. She smiled and raised her glass of iced tea in silent commiseration.

Four bottles met and clinked above the center of the table, and each woman took a long swallow of beer. The older woman set down her bottle, wiped suds from her mouth with a napkin and gave her friend a serious look. ''You know, Miranda, you could have brought Lorenzo to my house yesterday. It was my day off, and I would have watched him.''

Miranda smiled in gratitude. ''Thanks, Bessie, but you've got enough to handle just taking care of your husband. Besides, who knows what germs Lorenzo could have brought into your house? If Pete had caught something from him, his emphysema might have gotten worse.''

''How's Pete doing, anyway?'' a woman with coffee-brown skin asked.

''Not too well, Yvonne,'' Bessie said, ''but thanks for asking.''

''You've got to get some help,'' Yvonne said. ''Between work and Pete, you're wearing yourself out.''

''Without health insurance, I can't afford to get outside help,'' Bessie said. ''Even if I could afford insurance, I doubt I could get coverage for Pete at this stage of his illness.''

Not an individual policy, Louise agreed to herself. *But it would have been nice if you'd had family cov-*

erage provided by your employer when you started working.

Yvonne, the African-American woman, shook her head slowly. "That's a shame. My sister's husband over in Raleigh got coverage for the whole family when he went to work for the paper mill...."

Louise nodded. *Right. That's the way it should be.*

"...and tight ol' Justin Beauclaire won't even provide coverage for his employees," the woman continued.

The blonde, the youngest by several years, downed the rest of her beer in one long gulp and curled her lips into a catlike grin. "Yeah, but we get all the candles we can steal," she said.

Candles? These women must work for the Bayberry Cove Candle Company, which Vicki had mentioned a couple of days ago. The factory was the town's largest employer.

The young woman unzipped a huge canvas purse sitting on the floor beside her chair and pulled out an eight-inch pillar candle. "I figure this pretty one will set the mood when Luke and I are alone at his place later."

"Shame on you, Darlene Jackson," Bessie said. "You took that from work?"

Darlene shrugged. "Why not? I haven't had a raise in three years. I figure the company owes me."

Bessie sighed. "The last thing I want to see when I leave the factory every day is another candle."

"Yes, girl," Yvonne said, and then shook a finger at Darlene. "Especially when you're wasting it on

Luke Plunkett. When are you gonna wise up and find yourself a nice fella?''

Darlene stuffed the candle back in her purse and frowned. ''As soon as Justin Beauclaire pays me a wage that allows me to put a little away each week so's I can walk outta that factory for good. And you all know that's not likely to happen.'' She set her elbows on the table and cradled her chin in her hands. ''Until I can afford to get outta here, Luke is about all I got to look forward to each night.'' She gazed at the ceiling, avoiding eye contact with her friends. ''Besides, he can be nice.''

Yvonne stared at Bessie and said in a conspiratorial voice, ''Is it snowing in hell, Bess?''

Darlene stood up, dug into the pocket of a pair of skin-tight jeans and tossed a few bills onto the table. ''I heard that, Yvonne,'' she said. ''But even you've got to admit that a girl can't sit home with her momma and daddy every night on a big, lonely farm. And like I said, Luke can be nice.''

She draped the purse strap over her shoulder and pushed in her chair. ''I'm off to the Brew and Bowl. Luke will be wondering where I am.'' She straightened her spine defiantly and lifted her chin. ''See you all next Tuesday night, I guess. And tomorrow at work.''

Louise munched on the last of her salad and watched with the three other women as Darlene strutted from the restaurant.

''I don't know what will become of that girl if she stays with Luke,'' Bessie said with a shake of her coarse gray ponytail. ''She's got a big heart, but I don't think that boy will ever appreciate the goodness in her.''

Miranda ran a hand through her long dark curls and sighed. ''I worry that Luke will get drunk and really hurt her. Deputy Blackwell has broken up a couple of fights between them, but one day Darlene won't be so lucky. She needs to get away from that devil before it's too late.''

Yvonne smirked. ''Not much chance of that as long as she's working for Beauclaire and earning minimum wage. She can't afford a place of her own.''

Louise had heard enough. The problems at the candle factory were issues she understood well in her capacity as a corporate lawyer, though she'd never really studied them from the employees' point of view. Her promise to avoid work-related entanglements abruptly abandoned, Louise stood up and went to the table.

''Pardon me, ladies,'' she said. ''I couldn't help overhearing. I'm Louise Duncan, attorney. Do you mind if I sit down?''

None of the women spoke, apparently too surprised to respond. Finally, Bessie pressed her booted foot on the leg of the chair Darlene had just vacated, and pushed it away from the table. ''It's a free country,'' she said.

Miranda narrowed her dark eyes suspiciously. ''Not to an attorney it isn't.''

Louise dropped onto the chair and scooted close. She waved off the Hispanic woman's comment with a flutter of her hand. ''Don't concern yourself with what you've heard about lawyer fees,'' she said. ''If you ladies and I come to an agreement about some things, and I decide that I can help you, I'll take on this project strictly for the experience—and the fun of it." She smiled at the women.

"I know a little about corporate law, ladies," she continued. "And a thing or two about labor regulations." She looked at each woman. "If you three have a little more time this evening, I'd like you to tell me all about the factory and your employer, Justin Beauclaire."

The two younger women looked to Bessie, who chewed her bottom lip a moment and finally said, "Girls, I can't see as it would hurt to talk to her."

CHAPTER FIVE

WESLEY CAME AROUND the third corner of the town square jogging path and slowed to an easy trot, just as he'd done the last two mornings. He looked up at the three windows above McCorkle's New and Used Furniture Store on Main Street—just as he'd done the last two mornings. He knew his actions must be conspicuous, and he felt like a fool. If Louise were looking out one of the windows, she'd surely notice that he altered his pace each time he passed this particular part of the track.

She wasn't there. In fact, she hadn't shown her face since Sunday when, in front of half the population of Bayberry Cove, she'd hollered a greeting from her window and cheerfully wished him a good morning. And now it was Wednesday, and he hadn't felt nearly as cheery since. He waved at his grandfather, seated, as always, on a bench, and picked up his speed, heading into his second lap. "Forget about her, Wes," he puffed to himself on short, choppy bursts of air exploding from his laboring lungs. "Louise Duncan is the last woman on earth you should be interested in."

At the next corner, he ran faster. Louise was still in town. He'd heard that from several sources, including Jamie Malone. In fact, Jamie couldn't seem to talk about her without aiming a knowing grin at Wes.

Surely Jamie didn't think he was interested in Louise. She was about as alien to Bayberry Cove as nouveau cuisine was to the Kettle. If Wes ever did settle down with one woman again, it wouldn't be with an independent, wisecracking, sexy-as-hell city girl like Louise Duncan.

Jamie wasn't the only one in town who'd taken a liking to Louise. Bobbi Lee referred to her as "the princess" without the slightest hint of malice in her voice. Lots of folks in town seemed to like her. Wes wasn't at all sure how he felt about her, but as each day passed, he found himself wishing the warning bells in his head would cease their clamor so he could have the opportunity to decide how he did.

And then opportunity knocked—or dashed—right smack into his exercise regimen. In the middle of the long section of track opposite Main Street, Louise suddenly appeared next to him, jogging with all the vigor he had begun to lose. Long, lean legs extended from clinging midthigh shorts and ended in sparkling white running shoes. A form-fitting tank top revealed a slash of creamy abdomen each time her fists pumped away from her body. The material stretched tightly across her breasts, permitting just enough of a subtle bob to make his throat feel as if it were stuffed with cotton. A brazen red baseball cap completed her outfit. She wore it low on her forehead, and a swath of raven hair swung from the opening at the back, reminding him of the tail of a Thoroughbred twitching at the starting gate.

"Nice day for a run, isn't it, Wesley?" she said, her voice even and controlled, and irritatingly unlabored.

He huffed out an answer. "A beautiful morning, Louise. I haven't seen you run before."

"I've indulged in entirely too much Southern cooking at the Kettle," she said, patting a tummy which, now that he looked, might be straining her zippers a little. "I run three days a week at home." She smiled at him. "Can't let myself go just because I'm on vacation."

Ordinarily Wes might have slowed as he approached the third curve for the second time. But he wasn't about to exhibit a lack of endurance in front of Louise. He sucked in his diaphragm, straightened his back and kept up the pace that somehow in the last minute he'd let her establish. "So how's that vacation thing working out for you?" he asked.

"Fine, but I'm counting on you to help make it better."

He stumbled on absolutely nothing. In disciplined military fashion, he covered his blunder and kept running. But he knew from the quick upturn of her lips that she'd seen him falter. "Oh?" It was all he could manage to say.

"I figured, who better to show me the sights than one of the town's most respected citizens." She cast him a sideways glance. "And from all I've heard, that's you, Commander."

The sun glinted off a silver medallion that bounced against her chest above the scooped neckline of her top. Wes couldn't take his eyes off it.

Her voice jolted him back from a dangerous place. "Wes? Are you interested?"

He snapped his eyes to hers. "Well, okay. Where would you like to go?"

"I thought we'd start with the candle factory."

The candle factory? He'd expected...deep down he'd *hoped* she would request a boat ride on Currituck Sound. In fact, he could picture her in his speedboat or the lively little skiff he'd brought out of dry dock and kept by the shore at the cottage. Or he thought she'd ask to see Bayberry Park with its thirty-foot waterfall, an anomaly in an area that boasted few attractions above sea level. But no, she wanted to see the candle factory.

As if sensing his confusion, she elaborated. "I love candles. I have dozens in my condo in Florida. What about this afternoon? I want to see the factory from the inside out, how candles are mass-produced, all the details I wouldn't get if I didn't go with someone who knows the territory."

Of course he could accommodate her. His father and the candle factory president, Justin Beauclaire, had been friends, fishing buddies and poker-playing rivals for years. The factory was certainly a safe place to take the bewildering Miss Duncan, but Wes's thoughts kept returning to a vision of a more intimate afternoon at the park or skimming over the crystal water of the sound. "Okay, the candle factory it is," he said, trying to hide a disappointment that surprised him with its intensity. "I'll pick you up behind the furniture store at two?"

They'd reached the path by Main Street again, and

Louise veered off toward her apartment. "Great. See you then."

As soon as Wes was certain she couldn't see him, he stopped running, bent his knees and placed his hands on his thighs. He expelled a long, exhausted breath and heard his grandfather chuckling. Wes looked over his shoulder, frowned and said, "What's so funny?"

"I'm just sympathizing with you, boy," Mason said. "That woman can knock the wind right out of you."

HER LEGS ACHING, her heart pounding and her breathing as ragged as if she'd climbed a hundred steps instead of eighteen, Louise flung open the door to her apartment, grabbed a bottle of water from her small refrigerator and collapsed onto her sofa. "You idiot," she said. "Are you trying to kill yourself?"

Running a mile-long track around the square was nothing like hitting the treadmill for fifteen minutes at her Fort Lauderdale gym before getting a smoothie and a massage. She gulped the water and lay on her back, propping her head on the arm of the couch. Her gaze connected immediately with her coffee table and the single item sitting there, the blue candle.

"I just love candles," she said in a sing-song voice that mimicked her previous comment to Wes. "I have dozens in my condo." She flung her ball cap and hit the candle dead center, hiding it from view. "Candles, my ass," she groaned.

The only ones she'd ever bought in her life had been skinny little things to stick into birthday cakes, and those she'd bought for someone else. Louise was a firm believer in electric light—bright, soft, sexy, whatever. As long as it illuminated without threatening to set the house on fire. But what the heck? She was getting inside the candle factory, and she was going in on the arm of Wesley Fletcher.

BY TWO O'CLOCK that afternoon, Louise had showered, applied makeup and slipped into a coral shirtwaist dress with what she considered a respectable hemline. On impulse, as she went down the back staircase from her apartment, she popped open the top two buttons and spread the yoke of the dress just enough to distract Wesley from the questions she intended to ask.

He was waiting at the bottom of the stairs, wearing a pair of khaki shorts and a tan knit shirt that fit his military-sculpted chest as if it had been molded to him at the factory. He leaned on the hood of an immaculate dark green Jeep.

"Nice car," she said, figuring a compliment to his vehicle would go a long way with a guy like Wes.

He opened the passenger door, and she slid onto a spotless tan leather bucket seat. "It gets me where I need to go," he said.

He bolted to the other side, got in and started the engine. With one wrist draped over the steering wheel, he turned to her and asked, "You sure about this? You really want to see the candle factory?"

She swiveled toward him so her knees were mere inches from his thigh, and stared at the handsome, rugged face that had invaded her thoughts for the last few hours. "I've been thinking about this excursion all day." That was the truth. "I can't wait to see how candles are made." That was a lie. "I hope you can take me behind the scenes—you know, introduce me to the movers and shakers at the factory."

He laughed. "I'm afraid the only moving and shaking you'll see is when Justin Beauclaire walks across his office to the bar and shakes the martini pitcher." He pulled out of the lot and headed down an alley. "But whatever your pleasure…"

The factory was located a couple of miles outside of town on a two-lane county road that curved past the Brew and Bowl Alley, a few blue-collar businesses and three trailer parks. Louise recognized the name of the mechanics garage where Miranda Lopez's husband, Pedro, worked, as well as the Lazy Day Mobile Home community where the family lived.

Louise knew she might see the women she'd talked to the night before at the Kettle. They'd all agreed that if they encountered each other at the factory, they would pretend to be strangers. Their association would be public soon enough, but for now, Louise was concerned with getting information, and her guise of being a tourist interested in candles was the best way of doing that.

Wesley parked near the double doors of the two-story colonial offices. This part of the building resembled a modest but gracious Southern mansion. The rest of the business, the production area extending behind the offices, was a long, single-story metal building with windows along the roofline.

Wes and Louise entered a lobby furnished in Wedgwood-blue wing chairs, Queen Anne tables and peaceful pastoral prints. And of course, candles. A half-dozen mahogany shelves displayed the products, which came in many shapes and sizes. The receptionist, a middle-aged lady, gushed over Wesley while Louise scanned the racks, picking up samples. One fact was abundantly clear. This company didn't miss a holiday sales opportunity or the chance to permeate the world with all sorts of intoxicating smells, from light floral to exotic spice.

After answering questions about where he'd been, how long he'd been home, and thanking the receptionist for expounding on what a handsome young man he'd become, Wes waved for Louise to follow him through a door that led from the lobby. "I called ahead," he told her. "Justin Beauclaire, the CEO of the company, is expecting us."

Louise walked beside him down a short hallway to an elevator. This was exactly what she'd hoped for. She whistled in appreciation. "Wow, are we getting a tour from the president?"

"Looks like it."

"I'm impressed with your contacts, Wesley."

"Don't be. This is a small town. Justin and my dad go way back."

They exited the elevator on the second floor and were met by a portly, balding man. He shook Wes's hand and introduced himself to Louise as Justin Beauclaire. While he openly admired his visitor, Louise gave him her sweetest smile, slipped her hand into her shoulder bag and discreetly turned on her tape recorder.

BACK ON THE MAIN FLOOR, Justin Beauclaire took his guests past offices on either side of a long hallway. They ended at a metal door. "Through here lies the pulse and energy of the factory," Justin said. "This is where tons of paraffin is turned into the beauties I hope you saw on display in the lobby."

"I did indeed," Louise responded. "I was truly amazed by the number and variety of candles produced here."

"We're trying new designs all the time," Justin said. "We have a research department entirely devoted to market analysis, product testing and nationwide sales." He opened the door and held it for Louise and Wes to precede him. "Ordinarily I don't allow any visitors into this part of the business," he explained. "Insurance issues, you understand."

She stopped just inside the warehouse and waited for Justin to close the door.

"'Course, I don't mind breaking the rules for old Wes, here," he said. "Even if I do remember wiping his nose a few times when he was just a little sprout."

Wes, clearly embarrassed, forced a snicker.

"We have a lot of expensive and sensitive machinery in here," Justin added. "Plus nearly every employee inside this building is working with wax in one form or another. In the beginning stages of candle production, wax can be tricky to handle. We melt ours to one hundred eighty degrees." He gave Louise a sly grin. "Can't have any novices poking their pretty noses, or fingers, into a vat of hot wax, now can we?"

Louise *tsked* in sympathy. "Certainly not. I promise to stay safely away from any bubbling cauldrons." She studied the huge metal tanks across the warehouse. Suspended above each were large circular racks, each holding dozens of taper candles of varying thicknesses. "Has anyone ever gotten badly burned?" she asked.

Justin waved off the question. "No. The wax isn't hot enough to cause blisters. Just smarts a little if it gets on the skin. Besides, we have all the required safety measures in place." He frowned. "Got no choice in the matter. We have government inspectors from OSHA breathin' down our necks every time we turn around." He clarified in case she didn't understand. "That's the Occupational Safety and Health Administration."

Louise nodded. "I see." She gestured toward one of the wheel racks that had just begun lowering its candles into a vat. "What's happening there?" she asked.

"That's one of our dipping wheels," Justin explained. "We have six of them operating sixteen hours a day. Each candle is dipped fifty times and cooled in between each lowering."

Louise remembered that Bessie referred to herself as a dipper. She'd worked in that position for fifteen years. As if to validate that thought, the older woman walked out from behind a wheel and glanced at the trio of onlookers. Louise gave her a hint of a smile. A hairpin held between her teeth, Bessie nodded at her behind a pretense of rewinding her long gray mane into a knot at the crown of her head.

Justin next took them to where wax was molded into various shapes. Several women poured the thick substance from large tubes into metal forms, reminiscent of cake decorating on a grand scale. When Justin had explained the procedure, Louise asked how many people the candle company employed.

"We're the largest employer in the county," he said proudly. "Got one hundred and thirty-three on the payroll. We're just one big happy family here at Bayberry Cove Candle Company," he added. He poked Wesley in the ribs. "Even had Wes working for us at one time. Remember the summers after your junior and senior years of high school, boy?"

The question produced an involuntary flinch, as if Wes was trying to erase the memory from his mind. "How could I forget?" he said. "I left here every afternoon smelling like a bouquet of roses."

Justin hooted before explaining to Louise, "Wes worked in the scent department. He was a good employee. We could have made a junior chemist out of him if he'd stuck around."

Louise cast a sideways grin at Wes. "You mean instead of the junior plumber he's become?"

Wes rolled his eyes. "Never mind, both of you."

"How many positions are there in the candle factory?" Louise asked.

Justin stared at the ceiling. "Let me see, now. We've got dippers and packers, cutters and polishers, dyers, mixers, machine operators...too many to list. And then, of course, we've got our office, research and sales force in the main building, where you first came in.''

As they'd walked the hall earlier, Louise had glanced into each office. "I noticed mostly men behind the desks," she said. "Don't you have any women in management positions?"

"Not really," Justin answered unabashedly. "We mostly hire women for the production jobs." He walked ahead of her to a rear entrance and turned around before leading the way outside. "Women seem to take to the repetitive tasks better than men. Guess it comes from all that diaper changing."

Gratified to hear Wes blow out a breath of air in a quiet whistle, Louise bit her lip before answering. "Well, of course, all that diaper training is good preparation for employment."

Justin held the door as she stepped into the paved lot of the factory's loading area, the apparent end of the tour. "You're right there, Miss Duncan. You got any young 'uns yourself?"

"No, not yet. Got to find me a good man first," she said with a flippant tone she figured Justin wouldn't notice even though his narrowed eyes were giving her a close scrutiny.

"From where I'm standing," he said, "there's probably a few fellas in this town who wouldn't mind applying for that job. You staying here long?"

"As long as it takes," she answered. "Now, if I can just ask you a few more questions…"

TWENTY MINUTES and at least as many questions later, Wesley walked around from the passenger side of the Jeep, climbed behind the wheel and slammed his door. He was angry. He'd been had. Duped. Plain and simple. This woman who'd professed with a saccharine smile to love candles had taken him on a merry chase.

He stared across the space between them and scowled. Fiddling with the contents of her shoulder bag, Louise pretended not to notice his emotional state. Or maybe she really didn't notice, and that was probably worse. One thing was certain. This lady, with her sexy dress, her high-heeled sandals and a body that practically made him drool, cared as much about seeing candles made as she would digging oysters out of the muck of Currituck Sound.

He started the engine, thrust the gear shift into reverse and backed out of the parking space, spitting gravel from his rear tires. And then, because that was childish and stupid, he reined in his anger and put the Jeep through its gears until they were retracing their tracks to town at a safe speed.

But he'd gotten her attention. Out of the corner of his eye he saw her arch her eyebrows in question. "Something wrong, Commander?" she said.

He clenched his teeth, tightening his jaw muscles. "What were you doing back there?"

She concentrated on her purse again. "What do you mean?"

"I mean that you grilled Beauclaire like he was in front of a congressional hearing."

"I did no such thing," she said. "I was merely trying to learn as much about candles—"

"Let's cut through the scum and get to the clean

water underneath," he said. "What are you up to, *Counselor?* And why did you feel it was necessary to involve me?"

Her shoulders sagged as she sighed deeply. "You already are involved, Wesley," she said. "You live here. You worked there. Nearly everyone in this town is involved to some degree."

"In what, Louise? Do you see some sort of conspiracy that no one else has noticed in the last thirty years?"

"No, not a conspiracy." She emitted a most unladylike snort. "That almost makes it worse. What's happening at the candle factory is out in the open for all the world to see…and ignore!"

He gripped the steering wheel and stared at her. "What are you talking about?"

"The injustices perpetrated by your buddy, Justin Beauclaire, every day. The man virtually laughs in the face of the EEOC…that stands for Equal Employment Opportunity—"

"I know what it stands for," he answered curtly.

She had the decency to blush. "Sorry. I don't mean to be condescending. But Beauclaire simply doesn't give two hoots for his employees."

"That's ridiculous. There are people who have worked in that factory since I was a teenager. If conditions were so horrible, why are they still there?"

"Why are they still there? Why, in this depressed economy with our nation facing the highest unemployment rate in decades, would anyone stay in a dead-end job?" She expressed her dismay in an openmouthed stare. "Have you truly been in the navy all these years, Wesley, or have you been on the moon?"

He yanked the wheel to the right, pulled off the road and jerked on the emergency brake. His anger was palpable. He felt it beating in his heart and trembling in his hands. "You know something, Louise?" he sputtered. "You've got a mouth on you. And something of an attitude."

Her cheeks turned the color of her dress and she looked up at the overhanging tree limbs. "So I've been told," she answered with something resembling genuine contrition. "I'm sorry. That was uncalled for."

The boiling in his stomach became a slow simmer. "It sure was."

She turned to face him. "Do you know Bessie Granger? She works at the factory."

He thought a moment. "I'm sure I'd know her if I saw her."

"You did see her. About a half hour ago. She was standing by the candle dipping rack she's operated for fifteen years. In all that time she's had three pay raises, and she now earns a whopping seven dollars and thirty-five cents an hour. Would you like to know why she stays at the factory?"

He shrugged, refusing to admit he was curious.

"Because she's fifty-seven years old, and her husband has advanced emphysema and diabetes. That's why she stays. She has no health insurance because the company doesn't offer any, so she maintains his well-being as best she can at home. The state of North Carolina pays for his insulin."

"I see."

"And there's Miranda Lopez. She and her husband are Mexican immigrants who ran out of money in Bayberry Cove before they reached New Jersey and relatives who have since reneged on a promise to help them. They're lucky to have jobs at all. Miranda has two little boys she sends to a private baby-sitter who charges her more than Miranda can afford. She makes minimum wage.

"And Yvonne Richardson, a single mom who barely makes do, and Darlene Jackson, who actually loves candles and would be a great sales rep if only—"

"Okay, I get your point," Wes interrupted. "It's not a perfect world. But why single out the candle factory in this campaign of yours to right the evils in society?"

"Because I can," she said. "I have the time, the expertise, and I don't need the money these women can't afford to pay me, anyway. For once in my life I can do something for purely altruistic reasons." She looked out the windshield, her gaze focused on a butterfly fluttering in front of the Jeep. "I might have reconsidered and kept my—" she lowered her voice and slipped into Beauclaire's Southern drawl "—*pretty nose* out of this town's problems. But then I realized that Justin Beauclaire is a self-indulgent chauvinist and a braggart.

"I think my mind was made up when he boasted about the golf vacations three times a year to Hilton Head. He charters private planes to take his front office people for three days to one of the most expensive resorts in the country.''

Wes winced inwardly. He'd known about the lavish expenditures for years. In fact, his father often went along.

''Do you realize,'' she continued, ''that even a small percentage of the money from one of those weekends would keep Miranda's two boys in private schools until they were ready for college, and there would still be enough left over to pay their tuition?''

Wes checked his side mirror and eased the Jeep back onto the road. He couldn't very well argue with Louise against motherhood and education. But he knew darn well she would be butting her head against a brick wall if she tried to take on the candle factory.

In a few minutes he pulled behind the furniture store to let her out. ''I don't suppose you'll take any advice,'' he said.

''I've never been particularly good at it. But maybe someday I'll take yours.'' She looked at him, her expression unreadable. ''I'm sorry I used you today, Wes. It was dishonest. But unfortunately, I've got to do it again.''

He gave his head a quick shake. Had he heard her correctly? ''What?''

''I need an appointment with your father. He's the only attorney in town, and I can't pursue this case on a legal level without aligning myself with a recognized North Carolina attorney. Haywood Fletcher seems the logical choice.''

Wes might have laughed out loud, but Louise wouldn't understand the depth of the irony in her request. Instead he gave her his most sincere look. "Here's my first piece of advice, Louise, whether you're ready to accept it or not. Consider it a warning of sorts. Don't even think about seeing my father."

She lay her hand on his arm. He stared at slim fingers tipped in polish. "You're sweet to worry about me, Wes, but don't. I think I can convince him of the validity of my commitment." She squeezed his arm. "Please, just call him and tell him I'd like to see him in the morning. And tell me how to get to that mansion of his."

She was just a bit too cocky. Too self-assured. She'd ambushed him this morning and now she was completely ignoring his warning. So he wouldn't explain the folly of her decision to visit his father.

Instead, he nodded and gave directions. "I'll tell him to expect you at ten o'clock tomorrow."

"Good. Now, what about dinner Friday night?"

"Dinner?"

"Sure. I owe you for today and tomorrow. And besides, Commander, you're not half-bad to be with. Dinner would be a bonus for both of us." She took a small tablet out of her purse. "What's your number? I'll call you."

A voice inside him warned that spending more time with this woman would only lead to disaster. The emotional kind, and the physical kind, because after she'd seen his father, she might end up lacing the bonus dinner with arsenic. Despite all that logic, and the fact that Louise wasn't his type at all, Wes heard himself recite his phone number.

She got out of the Jeep. "Okay. See you Friday."

She was halfway to the building when the back door opened and Suzie McCorkle came out. The woman's surprised expression changed to one of sincere enthusiasm as she took a couple of steps toward the Jeep. "Hi, Wesley. Welcome home," she said.

That was about all anyone could expect from Suzie at any one time, and Wes called back an equally succinct greeting.

"How are you, Suzie?" Louise asked.

The woman looked up over her wire-framed glasses and stuck out her hand. "Fine. I was going to leave this candle by your door."

"How nice," Louise said. "I did enjoy the blue one you gave me."

Suzie gave her a beatific smile. "See, this one is violet and meant to soothe your inner spirit. When you light it, a sense of calm permeates the room and encourages peaceful self-development. The scent is very delicate."

Wes listened to the exchange with a sense of awe. He'd never heard Suzie speak more than one sentence.

Louise took the candle. "Thank you, Suzie. I'm sure I'll love it."

Wes pulled out of the parking lot. *You'd better enjoy your soothed inner spirit tonight, Miss Duncan. Your peace and calm is about to be blown to hell when you visit Haywood tomorrow morning.*

CHAPTER SIX

SECTIONS OF Haywood Fletcher's house appeared through groves of budding trees as Louise drove down a curved driveway from the ornate front gate. She caught glimpses of angled rooflines, fieldstone exterior walls, sweeping multipaned windows. But none of these architectural hints prepared her for the mansion that sat with all the splendor of an English country manor in a sea of green grass and expertly manicured shrubs. "The pride of Bayberry Cove. Yes indeed," she said to herself.

At precisely ten o'clock, the exact time she was expected, the new, never-tardy Louise Duncan stopped in front of the massive double doors and cut the engine of her BMW. "So this is where you could be staying, Wesley," she said to his imaginary presence. "Instead, you chose that dinky little cottage, *my* cottage. To each his own, my friend, but it seems to me that years of living on destroyers and battleships would have sent you scurrying to Daddy's humble estate."

Walking to the door, she smoothed her navy-blue midthigh skirt and buttoned her hip-length tailored jacket. The deep V neckline was accentuated with a simple white silk scarf. Louise was thankful this morning that she'd packed one of her designer business suits. The argument that she wouldn't need it in North Carolina had been proved wrong.

She lifted the impressive brass knocker, but the door was opened before the lion's head ever sounded against its heavy metal plate. Louise looked into the chestnut-brown face of an older gentleman whose halo of coarse peppered hair matched straight, evenly groomed eyebrows. Dressed in an immaculate black jacket and charcoal-gray pants, the butler lacked only a pair of white gloves to complete the picture of Southern elegance.

"I'm Louise Duncan," she said simply.

He took her offered hand and introduced himself as Rudy Williams. "Mr. Fletcher is expecting you," he said. Opening the door to its fullest extent, he admitted her to a large entry hall. "If you'll follow me, please…"

Haywood's office was in the rear of the house. Louise's first impression of the dark-paneled room was that it was saved from dreariness by wide windows overlooking a terraced back lawn interspersed with colorful gardens.

The butler's voice drew her from the picturesque scene to a large desk in the corner. "Mr. Fletcher, this is Miss Louise Duncan."

Haywood stood up, slipped one pudgy thumb under a wide suspender and came around the desk to shake her hand. She looked into Wesley Fletcher's blue eyes, but all similarity between the two men ended there. While Wes was tall, lean and wiry, his father was medium height with most of his weight centered at his waistline. His abundant white hair was combed back from a prominent forehead and tamed with oil. His eyebrows were thick, with errant hairs spiking over a narrowed, keen gaze.

"How do you do, Miss Duncan," he said.

"Just fine, Mr. Fletcher. I appreciate your taking an appointment on such short notice."

He dismissed her gratitude with a flick of his fingers. "No thanks necessary. When my son called and said you wanted to see me, I was happy to honor the request."

He excused Rudy and indicated Louise should sit in a plush upholstered chair. Then he returned to his position behind his desk. "I assume this has nothing to do with that bit of unpleasantness you and I found ourselves in a few months ago with regard to Jamie Malone's divorce papers."

Good. The sly old fellow had brought their past involvement into the open right away. He knew he'd fabricated a reason to keep Jamie from signing the perfectly executed divorce settlement she'd drawn up for her friend Vicki. And he knew Louise was well aware of his bluff. There was no reason to pretend otherwise. "Certainly not," she said. "All's well that ends well, and I think we would both agree that Jamie and Vicki's relationship has ended quite satisfactorily."

"Indeed it has," he declared. "So what brings you out here this morning?"

Louise sat back in the chair and crossed her legs, noting that Haywood watched her movement with masculine interest. "I've decided to represent a group of workers in Bayberry Cove," she said. "I've discovered some inconsistencies with regard to certain federal labor regulations in one of the businesses in town. I think I can help my clients to better their positions within their working environment."

He rubbed his thumb and forefinger along a slack jawline. "Would this business be the candle factory, Miss Duncan?"

She wasn't surprised that the news of her visit to the candle company had reached him. "Yes, it is. Some of the policies of the EEOC seem to have been ignored or at least manipulated to suit the purposes of the company's president, Justin Beauclaire. I'm willing to represent the employees on these issues, but I need to align myself with an attorney in town."

Haywood nodded slowly, exhibiting what she took to be astute interest. "As you know," she continued confidently, "an out-of-state attorney can be admitted to practice locally on a temporary basis for a particular case. But for me to be admitted pro hac vice, I need to be sponsored by a North Carolina attorney. Naturally, knowing your son, I came to you first."

"Naturally. Besides, I am the only practicing attorney in this town."

"Yes. That too."

He stared at her over the wide expanse of the desktop and finally grinned in an almost fatherly way. "Let me tell you something, Miss Duncan. You don't want to do this."

"What?"

"This employer-busting campaign isn't necessary in a town like Bayberry Cove. It isn't necessary and it isn't suitable." He picked up a pencil and rolled it between his hands. "You're only visiting our town, isn't that correct?"

"Yes, but I don't see what difference—"

"I'd advise you to forget about legal matters and find something else to occupy your time while you're here."

She sat up straight. "Forget? I will not, Mr. Fletcher. I would advise *you* to reconsider. There are serious issues…"

The pencil twirled, clicking against a thick ring on Haywood's right hand. "I don't need to reconsider," he said. "I'd made up my mind even before you stepped into this office." The grin was back, but now it lacked any warmth. "Truthfully, it didn't take much internal debate on my part."

"How did you know why I was coming here?" She had the answer as she asked the question. "Of course, your son told you."

Haywood cocked his head to the side. "You're wrong. He didn't say anything besides asking me to meet with a visiting attorney. Though from your obvious distress at his possible betrayal, I realize that he knew why you were coming." He sighed. "I must speak to that boy."

"Then how did you find out?"

"Justin Beauclaire and I are old friends. He called me right after Wesley did. Justin may not be the brightest firefly in the park, Miss Duncan, but he did, eventually, suspect an ulterior motive on your part. When he told me about your extensive questioning, I put two and two together. And then Wes called. He's a well-intentioned fella, my son, but he should have advised you against pursuing this.''

Louise frowned. Okay, she couldn't blame Wesley. ''He did advise me against it,'' she admitted. ''But I refused to listen to him, just as I'm going to refuse your counsel.''

He shook his head. A low chuckle came from his throat. ''Well, you won't get any sponsorship from this office. No, ma'am. You seem like a nice enough gal, but you shouldn't get involved with this.'' He stared at her expensive suit, her pricey shoes, and swept that stupid pencil in an arc that encompassed her entire appearance. ''You aren't what folks around here are used to. We're simple, uncomplicated citizens who are comfortable with the status quo. If you come into town making all manner of insinuations with your big-city whereases and heretofores, all you'll end up doing is antagonizing a lot of good people.''

Louise's fists clenched around the arms of the chair. How dare this self-righteous bag of wind attack her appearance, her credentials? She stood up. ''I'm sorry I took up your time, Mr. Fletcher. It's obvious we're on opposite sides of a fence that runs right down the middle of your status-quo-loving town.'' She headed for the door but turned around before leaving the room. ''But if I may leave *you* with one piece of advice. You might want to warn certain *good* people that there will be some antagonizing in the near future.''

LOUISE'S PLAN TO EXIT Haywood Fletcher's house as quickly as possible was thwarted when she ran into a plump, redheaded lady who was lurking in the hallway.

The woman took her elbow and forced her to assume a more modest pace toward the front of the house. "My goodness, dear. You act as if the devil himself is chasing you."

Louise glanced over her shoulder. "He wouldn't dare," she said. "Surely even *that* devil knows he's done enough evil for one day."

The woman laughed, a soft tinkling sound like ice in a crystal glass. "Oh, he's not really so evil, once you get to know him. Though I admit that's not such an easy thing to do."

Louise stared at the pleasant-looking woman. Her Irish accent was almost musical, soothing to Louise's offended sensibilities. "I know who you are," she said. "You're Kate, Jamie Malone's mother."

"That I am."

Remembering her conversation with Vicki and Jamie the other day, Louise couldn't help adding, "Your son and daughter-in-law told me about you and Haywood. And, Kate, you have my sympathy as well as my admiration."

Kate looped her arm through Louise's and guided her down the hall to an expansive kitchen. "I've just put the kettle on. Would you like some tea?"

Louise wasn't a tea drinker, but she knew that Vicki considered the brew something of a miracle. "Sure, why not." She sat in one of eight sturdy chairs surrounding a thick pine table and watched as Kate prepared two cups and brought them over. Louise thanked her and added, "You are the only evidence I've seen that Haywood Fletcher has a heart. According to your son, you have somehow managed to snag it."

"He does indeed have a heart, though he tries his best to hide it, even from me sometimes. But after seeing you in such a state, I'm wondering what happened to his manners." Kate took a sip of tea. "I apologize for his behavior, Miss Duncan...."

"Call me Louise." She raised her cup, swallowed and released a deep sigh. "You and I could be friends, Kate."

"I'm sure we'll get the chance to find out," she said. "Jamie tells me you're staying in town awhile."

"That's right."

"And from what I heard through the opening in the door just now..." She winked at Louise. "It's the way I keep abreast of things around here. Anyway, I heard that you've found a way to keep busy."

"Yes, and your fella didn't discourage me one little bit."

"Good for you. A woman should be true to her convictions." Kate appeared to concentrate on her tea for a moment and then said, "There is something you should know, however."

"Oh? What's that?"

"The real reason Haywood refused to sponsor you." Kate fisted her hand, settled it under her chin and leveled a green-eyed gaze on Louise's face. "He owns thirty percent of the candle factory. Next to Justin Beauclaire, Haywood is the least likely person in

Bayberry Cove to want to see any changes in the way things are run down there.''

Louise felt her jaw drop at the information. "You don't say? Well, that explains a lot, but it doesn't change my mind.''

Kate shrugged. "I didn't expect it would. I just thought you should know.''

Louise suddenly remembered an earlier conversation she'd had with Wesley. Her hand shaking, she set her teacup on its saucer. "Does Haywood's son know that his father has an interest in the factory?''

"Of course. Wesley is the executor of Haywood's will. He's knowledgeable about all of his father's holdings.''

So Wesley wasn't above exacting a little revenge himself, Louise thought. He'd warned her not to meet with his father but he hadn't explained *why* the old guy wouldn't be receptive to her suggestion. *I'll bet he's having a big laugh thinking of me....* Louise forced the thought from her mind and stood up. "You'll have to excuse me, Kate. I have an important errand to run. And it involves a visit to Buttercup Cottage.''

KATE MALONE MARCHED down the hallway to Haywood's office, letting the sound of her determined footsteps announce her arrival. The door was still open, so she crossed the threshold and stopped just inside. Haywood looked up, frowned and returned to the document on his desk.

She headed toward him. "Haywood Fletcher, I'll have a word with you,'' she said, crossing her arms on her chest.

He peered up at her over the clear lenses of his reading glasses. "Now, Kate, don't start—"

"I'm not thinking of *starting* with you, Haywood. I'm thinking of finishing."

He took off his glasses and stared at her. "You don't mean what you're saying...."

"I'm saying that it's time you put a stop to rude, bullish behavior."

"Listening at keyholes again, Katie?"

She shook her finger at his smug face. "Never mind that, mister. Have you no manners at all? The way you treated that young woman. You ought to be ashamed."

He scowled. "It's a legal issue, Kate. You should stay out of matters that don't concern you."

"Decency concerns me, Haywood. And fair play. You could at least have told her why you can't involve yourself in the candle factory's problems."

He raised his bushy eyebrows in shock. "What problems? There are no problems at the factory. Beauclaire has things running like a fine Swiss clock down there."

Kate placed her palms on the desk and bent at the waist until her face was very near Haywood's. "You think that, do you?"

"I do indeed."

"You sit here in your ivory tower, collectin' your profits without ever knowin' how they come to you. What do you know of matters at the factory? What do you know of the lives of the people who help you to live like a king up here on the hill?" She sat heavily in a chair and took a deep breath. "I'm just sayin', Haywood, you could have heard the woman out instead of suggestin' that because she's not like the women from around here, she's somehow unsuitable for the task. I'm surprised at you, I am.''

"I was merely giving her some good advice, Kate. You heard her. She has a big-city attitude that doesn't play well in Bayberry Cove, along with a cocky, take-charge air that doesn't suit folks around here. And you saw her. A skirt so short I could have seen a tattoo on her fanny.''

Kate narrowed her eyes. "I see you did give the woman a second thought, or look, after all.''

Haywood chuckled, stood up and came around the desk. "Yes I did, Kate. And a third, if the truth be known." He walked to her and nuzzled her neck, letting his mustache tickle her ear. "And found her wanting when compared to you.''

She swatted him away. "Don't try to sweet-talk me into letting this go, Haywood.''

"I wouldn't for the world, Katie. I know you too well.''

She rose and faced him squarely. "You mind what I say. That girl is not about to give up. She believes there's more to that factory than candle glow and sweet smells. And my guess is she'll make Justin Beauclaire sit up and take notice.''

Haywood wrapped his hands around Kate's arms. "She wouldn't be the first pretty face to make a man do that." He grinned with something very much like boyish mischief. "As you darn well know, Katie, the men of Bayberry Cove are especially susceptible to fine-looking women.''

Despite the thirty pounds she wished she could shed, and despite the fact that her last birthday cake had sixty-two candles, Kate knew that she still blushed like a young girl whenever Haywood tossed her an admiring phrase. She couldn't help loving him, though one of his faults was a stubborn refusal to make her his lawful wife.

She reached up and straightened the knot of his already perfect tie. "Enough of your blarney, Haywood. It's time for you to go to court. But you show those other men down at the factory that you're better than they are. You're willing to listen to your woman."

He picked up his briefcase and headed for the door. "I wouldn't dare not listen to my redheaded Irish girl." He glanced over his shoulder. "We'll see what happens, Kate. Miss Duncan wouldn't be the first woman who's all smoke and no fire."

Kate watched him go and shook her head. Speaking softly to herself, she said, "There's fire comin' all right, and maybe it's due."

LOUISE ROARED OUT OF Haywood Fletcher's driveway and sped down the county road that led back to town. She spotted a pay phone in a parking lot. On impulse, she parked, entered the booth and began flipping through the yellow pages. In South Florida, the Attorney section took up about a hundred pages. In this part of the country there were only about fifty listings total.

She started with the A's and held her finger under the name of Lawrence Aaronson. He listed labor regulations as one of his specialties. She dialed his number on her cell phone, spoke to his secretary and was put through to his office.

"What can I do for you, Miss Duncan?" he asked.

It was a short conversation, and considering the random selection process, a lucky conclusion. She told him about her interest in helping the women at the candle factory, and mentioned her unsuccessful meeting with Haywood Fletcher. Mr. Aaronson agreed unconditionally to sponsor Louise in her representation of the workers. He knew very little about the factory or its policies, so his decision was not influenced by any convictions. But he did know a good deal about Haywood Fletcher.

It seemed that two weeks previously at Spring Tree Downs in Raleigh, a three-year-old Thoroughbred named Lightning Strike, owned by Haywood Fletcher, had bested Larry's Luck, owned by Aaronson. In addition to the generous purse that went to Fletcher, the gloating winner collected an additional five thousand dollars from a costly side bet he'd goaded Aaronson into making five minutes before the start of the race.

Louise smiled as she disconnected the call. Amused by this very personal aspect of small-town politics, she said, "Let's see how we do in this contest, Haywood. I can't wait to see which one of us turns out to be the horse's ass this time."

She pulled out of the lot and continued toward Main Street. She wasn't going to stop at her apartment, however. As she'd told Kate, she had an errand to run. Her confidence restored, and her desire for satisfaction at its height, she drove toward Sandy Ridge, the road that led to Buttercup Cottage.

WES CHECKED THE WATER temperature in the third of his large aquariums, as well as the salinity, sediment textures and nutrient balance. Once he'd recorded his findings, he adjusted the air conditioner he'd installed in the shed behind the cottage so the temperature closely resembled actual outdoor conditions.

This morning, as always, he'd headed out from shore in the trim twenty-two foot Aquasport powered by a smooth-running two hundred horse Mercury outboard. The National Oceanic and Atmospheric Administration had provided the boat to facilitate his research. Once he'd gathered semi-salty samples from Albemarle Sound, brackish water from Currituck and fresh water from the heads of the North and Pasquotok Rivers, he'd returned to his dock and added his newly collected specimens to the tanks in the shed. Then, as he routinely did, he had a light breakfast before going into town for his run.

Wes had spent most of his life adhering to strict regimens, so he found this routine of living in Bayberry Cove on the edge of the sound well-suited to his needs. And today, as he'd jogged, he'd been able to concentrate on the track instead of the second-story windows of McCorkle's Furniture Store. He knew Louise Duncan was meeting with his father.

Now with a last look at the sea life populating his tanks, he closed the door to the shed and slid the bolt across. Immediately he heard the sound of an engine racing and tires spewing gravel on his driveway.

Coming around the corner of the cottage moments later, he saw—and heard—Louise rapping on his front door.

He halted several yards away and watched her draw her shoulders up rigidly with an impatient breath. It didn't take a psychologist to read the woman's body language. She was angry, and he was probably the reason.

"Nobody's in there," he said before she could split her knuckles on the weathered wood of the old door.

She spun around and glared at him. "Are you hiding from me, Wesley?"

He tried to fight a grin and lost. "No. If I were hiding, you wouldn't see me right now. I'd be somewhere else. I'm better at hiding than this."

"Very funny."

He continued to the front door, wiping his damp hands on the soft jersey of his shorts. "This is a nice surprise, Louise," he said. "I thought our date was for tomorrow night."

She smirked. "I'm starting to think that it's less of a date and more of a second round."

"Oddly, they both have a certain appeal." He stepped around her and turned the knob. "The door's hardly ever locked. You might want to remember that the next time you try to break it down." With a sweep of his arm, he invited her in.

She marched ahead of him, stopping to notice the arrangement of the items in the room. Wes tried to see the place through Louise's eyes. It was significantly different from when she'd been there a week ago. Two easy chairs were spaced an equal distance from the sofa. The desk occupied a spot exactly in the middle of the window to catch the best sunlight. The chair fit neatly between the double pedestals. Writing utensils were arranged in rows on the surface. Magazines that had been scattered haphazardly around the room were now stacked in squared-off piles on the coffee table.

As much as he appreciated uniformity, Wes found himself thinking that it looked a bit sterile.

With a toss of her head, she said, "I love what you've done with the place. So cozy." She ran a finger along the top of an end table, leaving a slight smear in the fresh polish. "If I'd been lucky enough to descend from Mason Fletcher's family tree and gain possession of this cottage, I'd at least have left enough dust to write my initials on the furniture." She gave him a hint of a smile. "I'm very territorial underneath my easygoing exterior."

He chuckled at her obvious misrepresentation and walked toward the kitchen. "You're probably going to hate my cupboards," he said. "My canned goods are in alphabetical order."

She followed him. He opened the refrigerator door, revealing an assortment of drinks lined up like little soldiers on one shelf. "Soda?"

She glanced at her watch. "What the heck? It's eleven o'clock. Give me one from the second row. It starts with a *C.*"

He tossed her the Coors Light and opened one for himself. She sat in the chair she'd occupied during her first visit. He sat opposite her. She took a long swallow from the can and licked her lips before an amber drop could fall to the lapel of a navy-blue jacket that was probably standard business attire in the city. It had a low enough neckline to be as sexy as lingerie in Bayberry Cove.

She leaned toward him, the gap in her jacket widening. He wiggled in his chair. "I suppose you know why I'm here," she said.

Right then he wished he could suggest a reason without getting slapped. "It'd probably be better if you told me," he said.

"I just came from your daddy's." She tapped the beer can with a long nail. "Nice guy, that Haywood."

"All the Fletcher men are known for their charm. I'm glad Dad didn't disappoint you."

She grinned in a feline way, without showing any teeth. "Actually, I plan to disappoint *him*. But I didn't come here to tell you that. I came to make a simple accusation. You could have told me."

Wes pretended ignorance. "Told you what?"

"That your father owns a third of the candle factory. We did spend a couple of hours yesterday ambling through the quaint little business. Did that fact skip your mind?"

"No. Facts rarely skip my mind."

She snorted. "That I believe. So, you could— *should* have told me."

He leaned back in his chair and matched her grin with his own. "Fair is fair, Louise. You should have told *me*."

"What, exactly?"

"That we were going to the factory to put poor old Justin Beauclaire on the hot seat. That up your pretty pink sleeve yesterday you were probably packing a tape recorder and a detailed report intended for the EEOC.''

She had the decency to blush. "That's different. I…'' She paused as if she'd started an argument that she knew couldn't be defended.

He lifted his beer in a toast. "So why don't we call it a draw, and you can tell me how your meeting went with Dad.''

Her gaze drifted from the can to his hand and up his arm to his bare shoulder. He'd put on a T-shirt with the sleeves cut off. It wasn't like him to wear nonregulation clothing, but now that he saw such blatant interest in Louise's eyes, he wasn't sorry.

She tapped her can against his and leaned back in her chair, depriving him of the view of shadowy cleavage he'd had a moment before. "Okay, it's a draw. And since you asked, the meeting went pretty much as you expected, I'm sure. Haywood didn't want any part of sponsoring me. He even had a few choice words of advice.''

Wes nodded. "Tough break.''

She idly revolved the beer can between her hands. "Not really. I found another attorney to sponsor me. Quite an enthusiastic supporter, I might add.''

Once again she'd surprised him. She worked fast. "Are you going to tell me who? Dad's the only attorney in town.''

"But not in the county. Lawrence Aaronson is my sponsor.''

Wes whistled in admiration. "Top drawer. Does he believe in your case?''

"He doesn't have to. It's enough that he dislikes your father. Besides, I don't know exactly what my case will be yet. Maybe I won't find anything significant to submit to the EEOC." She took a swallow of beer and set the can down. "On the other hand, maybe I'll really shake things up in candle land."

"Maybe you will." He slid his can around in the little water spot on the table. "What about dinner tomorrow night? Is that still on or have you passed the sins of the father onto the son?"

She finished her beer and stood up. "Of course it's still on, but I've decided on a change of plans. I'll bring dinner here."

"Here?"

"Sure. I want to see what the sun looks like setting over the cottage that was almost mine. And I want to see you freak out when your kitchen counters get a little messy."

"Okay. Buttercup Cottage it is."

His cell phone rang, and he dug in his pocket to retrieve it. "Sorry."

"No problem. I've got to go, anyway. I have a shingle to hang next to the entrance of the furniture store." She gave him a little wave and left through the front door.

Wes read the number on the digital screen of his phone and punched the connect button. "Yeah, Dad, what is it?"

The voice that responded was gruff and impatient. "Wesley, I want to see you this afternoon."

"What about?"

"I'll tell you when you get here. Make it three o'clock."

"See you then." He disconnected and went into the living room. From his front window he watched Louise's car pull onto Sandy Ridge Road. "Something tells me this meeting has everything to do with our town's new lady lawyer," he said to himself.

CHAPTER SEVEN

HAYWOOD FLETCHER SET DOWN his glass of bourbon, glanced around the room to make sure the other three men were paying attention, and smiled at his son. "At ease, Wesley. I'm not going to give you a demerit."

The others chuckled, no doubt because they were expected to. "That's right, Wes," Justin Beauclaire said. "This is your father's house, not a court-martial."

Realizing he had been standing at attention, Wes allowed his shoulders to relax and his knees to unlock. It wasn't that these men intimidated him. He'd known Justin for more than thirty years and Hatch Winslow, vice president of personnel at the candle factory—or human resources, as it was now called—almost as long. The youngest of the trio, Warren McGovern, had been VP of marketing for nearly five years. Still, Wes thought, as he took the last remaining chair, he'd not been summoned here to engage in a friendly father-son chat. These men obviously had a serious matter on their minds.

"So what's this all about, Dad?" he asked, though now that he'd seen the cast of characters, he knew the answer.

"We need to talk, Wesley, about that little foray you instigated into the candle factory yesterday."

Wes shook his head. "Foray? Come on, Dad, it wasn't a military maneuver."

"Maybe not to you. But your participation's upset ol' Justin plenty. I think you owe all of us an explanation as to why you cooperated with Miss Duncan's snooping around the business." He put his grin back in place and added, "'Course, now that I've seen her assets face-to-face I can understand your interest in playing along with her scheme—to a degree." He snickered and waited for responses from his companions. "Since any red-blooded man can understand what you hoped to gain by helping her, I'm just wondering how much you knew about her motives beforehand."

Wes crossed his ankle over his opposite knee and tried to appear casual. His father's insinuation about Louise, and Wes's hormonal reaction to her, rankled, but he supposed the best way to handle the situation was to tell the truth.

"What did I know of her motives?" he repeated. "Nothing. She told me she wanted to see the factory, and I took her there. What did I hope to gain?" He smiled. "Community goodwill. You gentlemen can understand that. Two of you are on the town council, aren't you?" He stared pointedly at Justin and Warren.

"Then you didn't know she was a lawyer?" his father asked.

"Well, yes, I knew that. But I believed she was a lawyer on vacation who was fond of candles." He shrugged one shoulder. "Now, like all of you, I realize Louise Duncan is much more than that."

Haywood raised his hands palms up and looked at each of the factory executives. "Now there, you see? I told you Wesley wasn't a party to this woman's shenanigans. He knows where his loyalties lie..." he patted the breast pocket of his jacket "...and his bank balance."

Wes sat forward and curled one hand over his knee. "Thanks for the vote of confidence, Dad, but right now my loyalties lie with the National Oceanic and Atmospheric Administration and a shedful of experiments I'm conducting thanks to their generous funding. So if all you gentlemen are satisfied, then I guess I can get back to business."

He started to rise, but his father's outstretched hand stopped him. "Not so fast, Wes. It's good to know that you were an unwilling party and that you were taken in by this city lawyer just like Justin here, but..."

Wes looked at Beauclaire. "No offense, Justin, but I actually had her figured out by the time we got to the specialty candle department. I just wanted to see how far she'd go."

"But," his father repeated more emphatically, "our meeting is not concluded. It occurred to us—" his hand swept toward the group of men "—that this female could possibly stir up something of a ruckus. Not enough to matter, really, but enough to cause an interruption in the operation of the factory."

"I understand what you're saying, Dad." Wes

scanned all four faces. "You guys are scared of her. Maybe you should be."

Haywood scowled. "We're not scared of her, son. But I've never been one to underestimate an opponent. And she identified herself to me this morning as just that." He blew out a breath. "That was a mistake on her part, but Miss Duncan's got moxie, and we've got to be ready with a counterattack if need be."

This time Wesley did stand up. "That's up to you, Dad. I think Louise can handle her end, so you gentlemen plan whatever you need to. I'll be interested to see how it all turns out."

Haywood leaned forward and pounded his fist on the desk. "Damn it, Wesley, you're not taking this seriously. We need a lawyer on our side, and you're it."

He dropped back into the chair. "What?"

"Well, I can't represent the factory. Because of my shares in the company, it'd be seen as a conflict of interest."

"Then get somebody else."

Justin Beauclaire took a step forward. "We don't want anybody else, Wes. You're a hometown boy. You care about Bayberry Cove. You're one of us."

"Oh, sure. Justin, just because my current address is within two miles of your house does not mean you can still wipe my nose."

Haywood's eyebrows knitted in warning. "Son…"

His father was right. The remark was uncalled for. "Look, Justin," Wes said more calmly, "I can't represent the factory in this. I just told you that I'm working on a grant from the NOAA. I have responsibilities to that organization."

"This won't take much of your time," Haywood argued. "A few hours at most. You know we can't let that woman come here and turn everything upside down. You've worked at that factory. You've seen that nobody's mistreated. Everybody gets honest pay for honest work."

"Even if that's true, I'm not your man. I served in the Judge Advocate General's Corps. I look at everything from a military perspective."

"Your specialty was civil cases," Haywood pointed out. "And you're still recognized by the North Carolina Bar Association. This little matter would be a piece of cake for you."

"And we'd never find another lawyer who would care so much about Bayberry Cove and the values we believe in," the aspiring mayor, Warren McGovern, said.

"Mostly, son, this will just be a matter of signing your name to a few documents," Haywood added. "I'll be advising you all the way. It'll take hardly any time away from the fish and seaweed you've got down in the shed."

"It's a matter of principle, Wes," the previously quiet Hatch said. "We can't let this woman come in and tell us how to run our business. We've been doing a bang-up job of it till now and it wouldn't be right if some big-city lawyer came in and made us look bad."

Wes gazed at the ceiling and gathered his thoughts. He truly didn't know what Louise had in mind. But he figured she had enough confidence and old-fashioned grit to pursue her goals.

He addressed the four men waiting for his reaction. "What if she's right?" he asked. "What if things do need fixing down at the factory?"

"Aw, hell, son, you don't believe that," Haywood said.

"I don't know...."

"Tell you what. If she finds a thing or two that we can change without much fuss, then we'll do it. But once you start digging into labor regulations you'll see that we follow the letter of the law."

Wes sensed the trap closing. "Once *I* dig into regulations?"

"You, me, whoever," Haywood corrected. "Come on, son, make me an even prouder father than I already am. Come to the aid of your community. Don't let this thing get out of hand. Tell us we can count on a Fletcher to stand by us. Show this community that you're thankful for all the support these people have shown you over the years."

Wes sighed. When he'd decided to take partial retirement from the navy, he certainly hadn't planned to enter the legal game again. He thought of his aquariums, his experiments, his plan to keep Currituck Sound safe from development. And then he looked at the men who represented the people he'd grown up with. "And you'll do most of the work?" he said to his father.

"You'll be a consultant, that's all. It's just your name instead of mine on the paperwork, to keep things aboveboard."

"And you'll change a few things if Louise is successful in pointing out some shortcomings?"

"I said we would, didn't I?"

Even as he stood and said the words, Wes feared he would regret them. "All right. But—"

He never had the chance to finish. Four hands simultaneously slapped his back, and he began to cough.

Haywood beamed. "Wait till that gal hears we got the best damn lawyer in all of North Carolina."

Wes cringed. He'd already thought about how she would react to hearing the news. "Actually, Louise doesn't know I'm a lawyer," he said. "At one point she thought I was a plumber, and not a very good one."

Haywood hooted. "She doesn't know? Then this will be a real sweet surprise."

Wes walked out of the office thinking of his date the next night. It would probably be the last one he would have with Louise Duncan, and that was really for the best, especially now that they were on opposite sides of a legal debate.

BEFORE MCCORKLE'S New And Used Furniture opened for business on Friday morning, Louise was in the shop. She climbed over a pair of tapestry living room chairs, skirted around an end table and two floor lamps and got down on her knees in the front display window.

"Here now, what's going on? What are you doing up there?"

Startled, she retraced her steps and jumped down

from the platform. She clasped a plastic document holder to her abdomen so Evan McCorkle couldn't see what was inside. "Good morning, Evan. I'm just waiting for Suzie. She's bringing some decorations...."

"Here they are," Suzie called from across the room. She waved a garland of silk pansies as she traversed the aisles of sofas and dinette sets.

"What are you doing with that thing?" her husband asked.

Suzie presented the string of flowers to Louise. "I told Louise that these would make her sign stand out in the window."

"Sign? What sign?"

"Her lawyer sign, of course."

Louise tried to smile to combat the frown on Evan's lips. "It's just a small sign, Evan. Just so people know I'm here. I'm putting one in my window upstairs as well." She showed him the clear plastic frame she'd picked up at Cove Stationers that morning. The shop owner had used her computer to print the sign that identified Louise Duncan as an attorney. And when Louise had paid her bill, the woman, who'd said she was a friend of Bessie Granger's, had wished her luck.

Evan groused at his wife. "Now, Suzie, this is a furniture store. Our windows advertise our own stock. I don't think I like announcing to everyone who walks by that we've got a business operating right upstairs. As you know, I don't even like putting up notices of the Girl Scouts Jamboree."

"I know you don't, Evan, you old grouch. But this

sign hardly takes up any room at all. And besides, I told Louise she could put it here. How else will all the ladies know exactly where her office is located?''

His cheeks flushed scarlet. He apparently wasn't used to chastisement from his wife. ''All what ladies?''

Louise climbed back into the window. She chose a spot for the frame and began arranging the garland around it. The flowers were strictly Suzie's touch, but Louise wasn't about to tell her they weren't necessary.

''That's the other thing I was going to mention, Evan,'' Suzie said. ''Louise is having a meeting in her apartment tomorrow morning. Several of the women from the candle factory are coming.''

Evan belched, the evidence of his distress. ''Now, see here, Suzie…''

''I don't think there will be too many ladies,'' Louise offered. ''And why don't you give me a bunch of those flyers advertising this week's specials in the shop? I'll hand them out to everyone who comes and encourage them to stop downstairs and look around before they leave.''

Suzie clasped her hands under her chin. ''How thoughtful of you, Louise. See, Evan, isn't that nice?''

''I don't like this, Suzie,'' he said. ''I've heard grumbling around town about this woman shaking things up. Some of the men don't like the sound of it.''

''Oh, who cares, Evan?'' Suzie said. ''If you ask me, those fellas down at the hardware store need some shaking up.''

He huffed loudly. To preserve his dignity, however, he straightened his spine and nodded. "I'll let it go this one time," he said, "and I'll just get those flyers."

Louise's hastily prepared shingle sat in the morning sun in the window of Bayberry Cove's only furniture store with a string of colorful spring flowers drawing attention to its existence. Out on the sidewalk with Louise, Suzie sighed. "It's beautiful. All we need is a candle garden to set it off." And she scurried inside to get one.

AT NOON ON FRIDAY, Jamie Malone copied statistics onto a tablet as Wes relayed them from the detailed charts by his tanks. "Do you really know what all this means?" Jamie asked when they'd finished.

"I hope it means that I can intelligently argue in front of the North Carolina State Legislature this fall that the high-rise construction slated for this county needs to be reconsidered."

Jamie set the tablet on a counter and leaned over to study the fish and plants in the largest of Wes's tanks. "I know you think Currituck Sound is being affected by increased building, but these guys all look fine to me," he said.

"Yes, they do, right now, but subtle changes are happening in our waters that will only get worse if contractors continue tampering with the shoreline." He looked at Jamie. "I can explain it in more detail if you're really interested. A lot of variables are involved, including wind speeds, current changes, even the flow of the Gulf Stream...."

Jamie laughed. "Hey, buddy, you've got my vote if it ever comes down to it. I'm trusting your brain to sort all this out. Right now I'll settle for a beer and a sandwich."

"Sure. It's the least I can do after that dinner you and Vicki fixed Wednesday night." He smiled. "Have I mentioned that you've got a great girl there?"

"I think she was worth fighting for," Jamie said.

The two men left the shed and walked to a pickup where Jamie whistled for Beasley. The dog jumped from the cargo area and lumbered toward them. He then flopped down in the middle of a patch of sea oats by the shore, curled himself into a pretzel and fell asleep.

"That's some dog," Wes said. "I might actually consider getting one to share the cottage with me if I thought I'd find one as uncomplicated as Beas."

Jamie followed Wes into Buttercup Cottage. "Yeah, he's pretty easy to please most of the time. But he sheds. I can't see you fighting the battle of dog hair every day."

Wes pulled pristine plastic bags of salami, cheese, tomatoes and lettuce from his sparkling refrigerator. He set two hoagie rolls on a cutting board and two cans of beer on the table. "Why does everybody think I'm such a neat freak?" he asked.

Jamie raised his eyebrows, glanced around the kitchen and said, "Duh."

Wes laughed, washed his hands and began slicing the rolls. "Point taken."

Jamie sat in a chair, popped the tab on his beer and

said, "So Vicki tells me you've been seeing a lot of Louise."

Wes looked over his shoulder. "It depends what you mean by 'seeing.' I've run into her a couple of times, and she suckered me into taking her to the candle factory under false pretenses."

"I heard about that. My guess is you're not the first guy to be led down the primrose path by that gal. Vicki thinks Lulu's serious about representing the workers over there."

Wes snickered. "Oh, she's serious all right. But that's not the worst part."

Jamie picked up the thick sandwich Wes set down in front of him. "Oh? What's the worst part?"

"Louise doesn't know it yet, but she's not the only one who's suckered me into something lately. My dad and his cronies from the factory talked me into representing their interests if Louise actually files complaints with the EEOC."

Jamie stopped the sandwich halfway to his mouth. "You're kidding? You said yes?"

Wes nodded.

"Couldn't you think of a way out?"

"Actually, I tried and then I figured maybe it wouldn't be so bad. Dad assured me the factory will make some changes if the issues warrant it. And I really do owe something to this town. Those old boys down at the factory gave me jobs, wrote letters of recommendation to the Academy when I was applying, sent me Christmas cards every year no matter where I was. And besides, I don't think conditions are all that bad at the factory. I think Louise may be stirring up trouble where none exists.''

''Maybe so, but buddy, siding with the enemy is no way to further a blossoming romance. Louise is not going to like hearing that you're the counsel for the opposite side.''

''That's no problem,'' Wes replied. It was time to set Jamie straight. ''There's no romance between Louise Duncan and me.''

Jamie grinned. ''Yeah? Vicki seems to think there might be. I don't mean to pry into your business, Wes, but isn't Louise coming over here for dinner tonight?''

Sudden heat infused Wes's neck. Damn this small town. ''Yes, she's coming here, but only to make up for tricking me into taking her to the factory.''

''That's what she said, huh?''

''Yes, exactly.''

''Okay, buddy, but if you ask me, a combination of good food, wine, moonlight on the water and a great-looking woman like Louise means anything can happen.''

Wes had been having those same thoughts all morning, and liking them too much. But, emotionally and intellectually, he'd made up his mind that he was strictly opposed to any sort of relationship with Louise. He just wished he could get his physical components to go along with the decision. Maybe convincing Jamie would be a good start. ''I'm not interested in anything like that with Louise.''

He stared at Jamie's skeptical expression for several seconds before emphasizing again, "I'm not. Not in any way. And you know why."

His friend slowly nodded his head. "Donna."

"Right. I've been down this road before with a woman like Louise. And it was too bumpy a ride."

"Louise isn't your ex-wife, Wes."

"No, but she's close enough to sound alarm bells in my head. She's independent, determined, bossy...."

"Yes, she's all those things. But Donna, from all I've heard, was self-serving, conniving and ambitious. You were lucky she took off."

All that was true—and the reason Wes hadn't had a serious relationship with a woman since his divorce fourteen years ago. And part of the reason he'd come back to Bayberry Cove. If he ever hoped to find a woman suited to him it would be here, where he'd grown up, where Mason Fletcher had made his fortune and given his beloved wife a cottage by the shore.

Wes wasn't opposed to marrying again. In fact, he often thought it would be nice to have a future with the right woman. But this time he'd pick a simple girl, straightforward and honest, who'd put their life together above everything else. Wes's wife—if he was lucky enough to find one—would have roots as deep as his and wouldn't spend the better part of their marriage trying to dig them up.

She certainly wouldn't be Louise Duncan, who manipulated the world to suit her needs.

Wes snapped out of his reverie when Jamie waved

his hand in front of his face. "Wes, come back, buddy."

"Sorry. I was just thinking about what you said."

"I've been thinking, too," Jamie said. "And I think I've figured out why you took your dad's offer, why you're representing the factory."

"I told you. I owe these guys—"

"Nope, that's not it. Deep down you agreed because accepting that job is a sort of insurance policy for you."

"Insurance policy? For what?"

"To keep the biggest natural hazard in your life from attacking you on all vulnerable sides. You agreed to be your daddy's lawyer because you knew Louise wouldn't like it and she'd lose interest in you immediately. It's a sure way to keep the boundaries clear between you."

Jamie stood and pushed his chair under the table. "And buddy, I hope you know what you're doing, because it just might work better than you anticipated. You might have maneuvered yourself into a position that is a whole lot safer than you really want it to be."

Wes smirked, but for a moment he didn't trust himself to speak. His mouth had suddenly gone dry. "You're a psychologist now?" he finally managed to say.

"Nope. Just a man. I know how we think when we're scared. I know about the walls we build. And I've also been scared of Louise. Pleasantly so, but scared just the same—until I realized that anyone Vicki would care about so deeply must have a whole lot of soft spots beneath her sharp-edged exterior. She's a lot of woman to handle. But I think you may have found the way to avoid having to do so.''

Jamie headed for the back door. "I'd tell you to have fun tonight, but I don't think the odds are in your favor. But, hey, that's what you want, isn't it?''

Jamie left, and Wes sat in the silence of the empty kitchen for several minutes. Damn. His old friend might just be right. Maybe those charitable reasons about community loyalty were nothing more than smokescreens hiding the real reason Wes had agreed to his father's demands. Maybe he *was* protecting himself from letting his feelings for Louise get out of control.

He stood up and took the dirty plates to the sink. "Well, so what?'' he said. "I can't imagine a worse combination than me and Louise Duncan.''

LOUISE SPENT PART of the afternoon preparing for her meeting with the women factory workers the next morning. She drove into Morgan City to consult with Lawrence Aaronson and to use his extensive legal library. Her research on federal labor law provided factual material she was anxious to share with the Bayberry Cove ladies.

She accomplished what she needed to in order to have a successful meeting despite the fact that her mind kept wandering to the dinner plans she'd made with Wesley for that evening. She couldn't stop thinking about him. He was a fascinating combination of inflexibility and unpredictability. He built his life around schedules and order; yet he somehow amazed her with his ability to adapt to situations that might catch other men off guard.

He'd refused to give in on the cottage issue, and he'd stood his ground when she'd accused him of withholding information about his father's investments in the candle factory. He seemed interested in her as a woman, yet only marginally affected by those characteristics that usually enabled her to win any contest between the sexes. He didn't appear uncomfortable around her as many men did. Yet he hadn't made any advances that would indicate he wanted to pursue her. Maybe all that would change tonight.

It was no secret that Louise liked men, but she usually gravitated toward bold, assertive types. However, since meeting Wes, she was finding the quiet, yet indisputably confident man more appealing. Handsome, well-built, intelligent, Wes piqued her interest on almost every level. She could certainly envision having a romantically satisfying relationship with him once she broke down his barriers. She didn't doubt for one minute that underneath that crisp, disciplined military exterior, Wes Fletcher could be wild and fun in bed and quite a pleasant diversion for the next two months.

CHAPTER EIGHT

WHEN LOUISE KNOCKED, Wes took a fortifying breath and mentally rehearsed his plan to keep the evening short and uncomplicated. Then he opened the door, and Louise waltzed in, leaving a trail of gardenia fragrance in her wake to assail his senses and send his thoughts on a course far different from his goal. She gave him a bright smile and said, "Hi. I figured you for a seafood man."

"You figured right."

"Good. I'll just fire up your oven so I can warm some things."

She strode into the kitchen, set a basket on the table and began familiarizing herself with the contents of his cabinets. "I hope you're hungry," she said.

"Starved." He watched her remove foil-covered dishes from the basket. His mouth was watering, but he wasn't at all sure it was the food producing the pleasant sensations in his body. He tried to find something he didn't like about her appearance. It wasn't her hair, which fell in a glistening black wave below her shoulders. It wasn't that face with expressive lavender eyes framing a cute little nose. It wasn't lips tinted light coral and just full enough to tempt any man to kiss them. It wasn't a body that filled out a pair of shorts and a top so perfectly, all he could think about was what lay under them.

"You're going to be impressed with this meal, Commander," she said, sliding dishes into the oven. "I debated about telling you I prepared it myself, but I decided to put my best foot forward, and not tell any more lies. Our relationship is strictly on the up-and-up from now on."

The ex-plumber-turned-candle-factory-attorney tried to ease a smile onto his face. It probably came across as a smirk. "Honesty between us. That's quite a change."

She passed by him on her way to the table and tweaked a button on the shirt he'd just picked up from the dry cleaners that morning. "I'm hoping honesty will have its rewards," she said.

He gulped. "Wine?"

She produced a bottle from the basket, then another. "Fine idea. Open this one and I'll chill the other for later."

Later? She planned on a later? That was great, since he'd definitely anticipated only an earlier. His plan had been to eat, talk a little about not much at all and say farewell. Of course, he could still make that happen. All he had to do was wait until she'd had enough wine to mellow out a bit, and then tell her he was legal counsel for the candle factory. That information would ruin this evening like a bomb dropped in the middle of the kitchen.

"Where's your corkscrew?"

He snapped his attention back to her and was reminded of the famous line that started, "The best-laid plans…'' No, he would not be led astray by one very sexy woman pretending with an oven mitt and spatula to be a domestic goddess. Goddess, yes. Domestic, hardly. ''In the drawer to the right of the sink.''

She skillfully opened the bottle, filled two glasses and handed one to him. When she raised hers in the air, she said, ''To an evening that begins with the score tied between us and ends with…well, no one can predict the future, right, Commander?''

Wrong. He knew how the evening would end. If he stuck to his guns.

''We have to wait a half hour or so for the food to heat,'' she said. ''What kind of music do you have?''

He thought of his limited CD collection and was suddenly self-conscious that his tastes weren't more éclectic. ''Mostly 1970s stuff.''

''Jim Croce? Eric Clapton?''

She had him pegged. ''Yeah. My CDs are in a box in the living room. You can pick out something while I hook up the player in here.''

A couple of minutes later they were listening to the blended tones of Simon and Garfunkel crooning ''Bridge Over Troubled Water.'' Louise walked to the back screen door and looked out on the sound. ''It's nice here.'' She smiled over her shoulder at him. ''I would have liked living in this cottage.''

''No, you wouldn't have. The electricity only works part-time. Water pressure's terrible. Most days they forget to deliver my mail. And sand gets into everything.'' He looked at his Jeep, which sat under a pine tree and was protected from the elements by a bumper-to-bumper canvas cover. There had been no room in the shed for the vehicle once he set up the tanks.

She tucked a windblown strand of hair behind her ear. "Sorry, Wes, but you haven't discouraged me." Then, as if reading his mind, she said, "What's in the shed over there?"

"Nothing you'd be interested in. I've set up some experimental biology tanks. I'm keeping track of water conditions, marine life, things like that."

She moved away from the door, picked up the wine bottle and refilled their glasses. "Show me."

"You want to go to the shed?" He'd figured the words *biology* and *experimental* would have been a sure turnoff.

"Absolutely. I'm a sucker for any dark, mysterious place, including a…" she gave him a seductive smile accompanied by a horror-movie growl "…la-bor-a-tory." She flounced away from him, burst through the door and took a direct line to the shed. She knew he'd follow, and he did—wordlessly.

He slid back the bolt and ushered her inside. Lights on top of each tank illuminated the water with what approximated a soft infusion of moonlight. The fish seemed to glow as they darted among plants that had taken on an olive hue in the artificial dusk he'd created.

Louise stood in the middle of the room between tables that held jars, thermometers, testing equipment, all the tools of his current trade. Aerators emitted their continuous subtle hiss. Bubbles squirted from air lines under the floor of his manmade sea beds and plopped softly at the surface. All teasing now absent from her voice, she whispered, "Wow."

He stood behind her, close enough to put his hands on her shoulders if he'd let himself. He didn't. "It's kind of overwhelming, I guess."

"It's amazing. What do you do out here, Wesley? What are you trying to accomplish?"

How could he tell her what he'd spent years studying, exploring and now attempting to safeguard? How would anyone comprehend the depth of his commitment? How would this woman, especially, understand why he would give up everything else to live a solitary existence by the sea in the company of creatures with scales? "It's complicated," he ended up saying. "I couldn't explain it in the little time we have."

She teased him with a flutter of dark lashes. "Come on, Wesley, in a hundred words or less. Try me."

And so he told her about the unique characteristics of the marine habitats of Currituck Sound and the Outer Banks. He explained about coastal swamps and estuaries and barrier islands, and how the distinctive qualities of each combined to create one of the most intricate and unusual marine environments on the planet. And when he determined that her eyes had not glazed over, he told her that it was vital to the North Carolina coastal region to preserve the wetland and the essential fish habitat.

She actually asked questions, interesting ones, and he answered with more detail than he was sure she expected or needed. And when he paused and looked at his watch, forty minutes had passed.

He gave her a guilty smile. "I'm afraid your dinner might be blackened by now."

She leaned over and watched a small fiddler crab burrow into the sand. "I wouldn't worry about that. I suddenly feel guilty offering you anything fishy at all. You're going to feel like you're eating pets."

He laughed. "Not at all. That's what I was going to explain to you. We need to safeguard this environment so that the fishermen and—"

She put a finger to his lips. "Wes, if it's really okay that we eat the food I brought, then let's do it."

She removed her finger but did not step away from him. She remained in close proximity to his body, her face inches from his, her eyes like amethyst crystals in his manufactured moon glow. Her lips turned up in an insinuating smile that any normal man would recognize as an invitation to kiss her—and only an idiot would resist. He clenched his hands at his sides until the blunt nails bit into his palm. He swallowed, retreated. "Well, then, let's go eat," he said, and went to open the door.

The idiot was saved.

TAKING DOWN THE WALL around Wesley Fletcher was going to be harder than she thought. During dinner conversation, he'd been attentive, complimentary and polite. The problem was, he'd shown more enthusiasm for a tankful of fish than he had for her.

When they'd finished one bottle of wine and the gourmet dinner, Louise picked up the dishes and stacked them in the sink. She turned on the hot water and let it run while she reached under the counter for detergent.

Wes came up behind her, took the plastic bottle out of her hand and set it beside the sink. He turned off the water. "No way. You fixed the meal. I'll do the dishes."

"Well, okay. Shall I open the other bottle of wine?"

He waved his hand. "None for me, thanks."

"Coffee?"

"I guess coffee would be all right."

She plugged in his automatic drip machine while he took a canister from the cupboard. Then he slid a Bee Gees CD into the player.

She found the cream and sugar, asked him if he wanted either, and prepared his coffee. He remained distant, but she was convinced he watched each move she made. What was with this man? she wondered. Was he shy? Or just afraid to express what was on his mind? She could read the interest in his eyes, see it in the anxious way he kneaded the back of his neck. So why did he avoid getting close to her?

She handed him a mug. "Let's take our coffee outside. I'd like to look at the water, listen to the waves."

He raked his fingers through his hair, which had grown since he first arrived. "I don't know about going outside," he said.

"What's wrong with that?"

"It's late. There could be mosquitoes."

"Wes, it's nine-thirty. And there's a breeze. Mosquitoes don't land when it's windy." He still looked so uncertain she almost took pity on him. "Do you want me to leave?"

"No!"

The conviction of his answer startled her, and she blurted out a bark of laughter. "All right, then, I'll stay."

"Unless you have something you have to do," he countered.

"I don't."

He walked to the back entrance and looked out. "I guess it won't be too bad out there." He held the door for her. "You might as well see what Currituck Sound looks like at night."

She stepped over the threshold and smiled back at him over her shoulder. "My thoughts exactly. Everything's different at night, don't you think?"

They walked down to the water's edge, where an outcropping of boulders provided a convenient platform for viewing the waves. Louise climbed over the first one with Wes's help and settled on the higher rock next to it. She set her mug down and slid over to make room for him.

A half-moon winked down at them and shimmered on whitecaps that rolled to shore. A few feet away from her canvas shoes, waves crashed on the smaller boulders and retreated back into the sound. Louise leaned against Wes's shoulder. "It's beautiful."

"Yeah, it is. No matter where I've gone, I always come back. And always with a sense of anticipation that's hard to explain. This part of the country calls to me somehow."

She looked to her left a few yards down the beach,

where a dock jutted into the sound. She identified vague shapes bobbing in the scant moonlight. "Are those boats yours?"

"One is, the little Hobie with the single sail. I've had it since I was a teenager. The other one is a speedboat. It's on loan from the National Oceanic and Atmospheric Administration."

She gave him a quizzical look and he explained. "They're funding my experiments. They have an office in Norfolk where I was stationed for a couple of years. I visited there a lot and talked about Currituck Sound and what I wanted to do here. I suppose I made a pest of myself."

"I doubt that," she said. "I'd say you made an impression."

He smiled. "Maybe."

"So where do you go in the speedboat?"

"All over. To the head of the sound, up the Pasquotok River, into Albemarle Sound. Sometimes when I need especially salty samples, I go all the way to Pamlico, where there's a major inlet from the ocean. All the bodies of water feed into each other. Yet, at their heart, they each maintain their own unique characteristics."

She looped her arm through his. His biceps contracted and relaxed. "Will you take me with you sometime?"

"Those are working trips I make out there," he said. "I have cages in certain locations so I can retrieve live samples. So, I would take you—"

"Good. When?"

He laughed, the first truly relaxed sound she'd

heard him make since he'd played professor in the shed. He knew she wasn't going to be put off, and he seemed okay about it, and even pleased. "You don't take no for an answer."

She smiled up at him. "Sometimes I have to. But mostly I just don't let other people say it." She smoothed the palm of her hand along his bare forearm, then wrapped her fingers around his wrist. "Tell you what, Wesley. I'll give you a chance to say no to me, and I'll accept it."

He glanced at her out of the corner of a narrowed eye.

"Your skepticism is showing," she teased.

"A little, I suppose. But go ahead, ask what you want to."

"Okay. Do you like me, Wes? Even a little?"

He blew out a slow, long breath and looked out at the water.

"Is it that hard to answer?" she said.

"No. Sure, I like you."

She moved her fingers and grazed the palm of his hand with her nails. The tendons in his wrist flexed. "But?"

"No *buts*. Despite the fact that we don't have much in common, and despite the fact that you tricked me the other day into taking you to the factory, and even though you soaked me with dirty water from the cottage faucet, I still like you." He grinned a little. "Now that I think about it, I probably shouldn't, but I do. Still, you are a little pushy."

Everything he'd just said was negative, and yet Louise's spirit soared. He did like her. She heard his affection in his tone of voice, saw it in the smile he tried to hide. And she planned to take full advantage of that affection now. "Some men need a little pushing," she said.

"What do you mean?"

"Wesley, we've been together a lot lately." She picked up the silver medallion that lay against her chest and slid it back and forth along the chain she wore around her neck. She was pleased when he followed the movement with his eyes. "In case you haven't noticed, I've put forth considerable effort to make you aware of me. And deep down I think you are. But it's time for you to act on your feelings."

He drew his eyebrows together in a frown and looked away from her. "Louise, in all fairness, you can't possibly know what my feelings are."

"No, but we have connected on a level that goes deeper than just friendship. I can feel it, and I'm pretty sure you can, too. Are you going to say that you aren't attracted to me? That you haven't wondered what it would be like to, well, to get to know each other a little better?"

He exhaled, rubbed the back of his neck again. "Louise, even I have to admit that you are damn hard not to notice. But frankly, while you've crossed my mind a time or two, I've been too busy with my experiments, catching up with family and old friends, trying to make the cottage livable."

She removed her hand from his arm, laced her fingers together and angled her body so she faced him squarely. Despite the limited confines of the rock ledge, he managed to put a few more inches between them.

"Wes, you said the other day that we should cut through the scum and get to the clear water underneath. I think that was good advice, and we should follow it right now."

"Okay. And?"

"I think you should kiss me. I can't think of a better time or place than right now, in your backyard with the surf rolling in and moonlight filtering through hazy clouds. As you say, I can't possibly know what your feelings are, but I can tell you that kissing you is what I want right now. And I'm hoping it's what you want as well."

His gaze moved over her face. He seemed to study each of her features one by one until he let himself stare overlong at her mouth. He moistened his lips.

Her breath hitched in her lungs. If ever a man was preparing to take a woman in his embrace and kiss her senseless, it was Wesley Fletcher. Louise leaned close to him, so close her mouth nearly touched his. Her skin tingled as she anticipated his arms around her. She closed her eyes, breathed deeply and waited. And waited.

After a moment she forced her eyes open and looked into cool blue eyes that had lost their desire and had assumed a steely resolve.

He turned away from her and focused on the far horizon. "We shouldn't be doing this," he said. "It's not as simple as it may seem to you."

Louise's appetite for Wes Fletcher evaporated as if she'd just eaten a seven-course meal of humiliation.

"It's not brain surgery, Wes. It's not even plumbing. It's a kiss. And you're making too much out of it. Either you want to kiss me or you don't. And it's obvious now that you don't."

He drew his knee to his chest, threaded his fingers together and wrapped his clasped hands around his leg. "I agreed to something yesterday, and I think you should know what it is."

She felt almost dizzy from this abrupt change in conversational direction. "Okay."

"I agreed to represent the factory in the event you bring charges against Justin and the executives with the EEOC."

This made no sense at all, and Louise felt herself lose patience. How could Wes represent anyone? "What are you talking about? Beauclaire is going to need a lawyer if I decide to do this, not a marine biologist—"

Oh no. She halted midsentence, suddenly struck speechless with the significance of his confession. Then she stated the obvious conclusion. "You're not a marine biologist, are you, Wes?"

He gave her a serious look that quickly mutated to a sheepish grin. "No. Not technically. It's an avocation only."

"And your vocation?"

"I was a naval lawyer."

Louise struggled with a range of emotions that ran from shock to betrayal to a condemnation of her own naiveté. She should have known that Wesley, smart, knowledgeable, well-spoken, was more than a career navy man who sailed the seven seas studying radar screens and thinking about fish in Currituck Sound. Of course, in her own defense, he'd failed to mention that rather important detail of his life. She bit her bottom lip and tried to gather her thoughts. Finally she said, "Those gray bars and embroidered gold leaves on that cap you were wearing the day I found you at the cottage…?"

"Judge Advocate General's Corps. Sixteen years."

"I see. No wonder your repertoire of lawyer jokes was lacking that day."

The corner of his mouth lifted in a small grin. "I still know a few."

"That's not all you know, Wes," she said, standing up and dusting off her shorts. "You're an expert at spoiling a perfectly wonderful evening, and at dashing a woman's expectations."

She turned away abruptly and climbed from the rocks without any help from him.

NOW WHAT WAS HE supposed to do? Go after her? Let her vent her anger by stomping back to the cottage alone? He'd done the right thing. He'd been honest and told her that he was counsel for the candle factory.

And he'd saved himself from stepping onto the dangerous quicksand that would never have supported a relationship between him and Louise. It hadn't been easy for him. She'd been close enough for him to smell the citrus scent of her hair, see the swell of her breasts, feel the heat from her body.

Even when she'd offered him the taste of those full coral lips, he'd survived the challenge of giving in to a gorgeous, sexy woman who was all wrong for him. He should be patting himself on the back. Instead, like a crab on steroids, he was climbing over the rocks to reach her.

He caught her arm at the back door. She whirled around and glared at him. "Let me go."

He didn't. "Look, I'm sorry," he said. "I shouldn't have blurted it out like that."

"Why not? Would the significance of the moment been any different if you'd told a joke first to soften me up?"

"Well, no, but you were so..."

She stared at him while he struggled for words, and then she finished his sentence for him. "So what, Wesley? I was so willing to see if a human heart actually beat under that solid chest wall of fine, up-standing military bearing?" She twisted her arm free. "Don't apologize, Commander. You did us both a favor. You pulled the bandage off quickly. In the end, that's the best way."

She stormed into the house, grabbed her purse off the kitchen table and kept going. At the front entrance, she yanked on the knob, but he slammed his hand against the door. "Come on, Louise, don't go like this."

She spun around. "Like what, Wes? Like a woman scorned? Like a lawyer deceived? Like a friend be-trayed? Well, sorry, but that's what I feel like and that's how I'm going." She pushed at his hand. He kept it right where it was. She exhaled loudly. "Be-sides, I really do have things to do tonight. I have an important meeting with my clients in the morning."

It was subtle, but it was definitely a threat. "This business with the candle factory doesn't have to get ugly, you know," he said.

She stopped pushing at him and leaned against the door. He placed his other hand on the wood panel beside her face, trapping her between his arms. She ducked. He lowered his arms in a childish game of cat and mouse. She rolled her eyes to the ceiling.

"I don't intend for this business to get ugly at all," she said. "I know the difference between what's business and what's personal, and right now it's the personal stuff between us that's not very pretty."

Her chest rose and fell with each labored breath. Her breasts flirted with the front of his shirt. Her face was flushed, just as it would have been if he'd kissed her the way he'd wanted to out on the rocks.

His hands curled into fists and it was all he could do not to pull her to him. He felt his reaction to her all the way to his toes, though it was definitely centered halfway down his body. He tried to look away from her but his eyes wouldn't move. And so he said, ineffectually, "I know you're upset...."

"That's right, I'm upset. But not as upset as you're going to be."

She was threatening him again? Only this time it was ridiculous. He had her pinned to the door. She couldn't budge, and yet she was trying to intimidate him. "What do you mean by that?"

She reached out with one arm, wrapped her hand around the nape of his neck and pulled his face down to hers. Their lips met with a blinding, crushing force that nearly buckled his knees. It was the most terrifying, exquisite kiss he'd ever experienced, full of fire and passion and anger. His blood rushed to his ears. His lungs felt as if they might explode. Even when she drew back, he forgot to breathe. And he dropped his arms.

She yanked the door open and stepped effortlessly outside. ''Think about *that* when you go to bed tonight, Commander.''

CHAPTER NINE

THOUGH SHE'D HAD a restless night, Louise was ready for her meeting at eight forty-five Saturday morning. She felt relaxed and comfortable in jeans and a white T-shirt with Key West Florida printed across the front in glittery pink paint. She gathered her hair into a multicolored elastic wrap at her crown and then lit the lime-green candle Suzie had brought upstairs to the apartment fifteen minutes before.

"Lime candles are known for eliminating discord," Suzie had said. "It's the color you use when you're facing obstacles to settling a dispute."

Louise regarded the flame flickering on her coffee table. "You've got your work cut out for you, Candle," she said. "After last night, I feel like my whole world is in discord. Luckily for the ladies of the Bayberry Cove Candle Company, I'm infinitely more qualified to handle the problems at the factory than I do the ones in my own life." She waved her hand as if the gesture would put Wesley Fletcher out of her conscious thoughts once and for all, but she knew it was hopeless. His obstinate, handsome face refused to go quietly to a dark corner of her mind.

A knock at the back door sent her scurrying to answer it. Bobbi Lee waltzed inside balancing two large boxes in her hands. She was followed by a bus-boy who carried a tray loaded with six thermal jugs and packets of cream and sugar. "I've got your order," she chirped.

"Thanks a lot, Bobbi," Louise said. "I know Saturday mornings are busy at the Kettle. I hope you didn't get in any trouble bringing all this stuff up here."

"Trouble? Are you kidding? Max is as happy as can be with this order. He'd have carried each pastry up one by one himself and presented you a tab dipped in gold leaf for this kind of money."

Louise pictured the congenial owner of the Bayberry Cove Kettle and smiled. "I hope he's not the only person in town I can help this morning," she said.

Bobbi Lee opened the boxes and placed a stack of napkins on the table. "I know you'll help the girls at the factory," she said. "I've been friends with most of them for years, and it's about time somebody stood up for them."

After the busboy left, having received a tip from Louise, the waitress sidled up to the kitchen counter, leaned her hip against the sink and gave Louise a sly grin. "But I'm interested in more than candle company news this morning," she said. "So tell me. How'd it go last night?"

The fiasco at Buttercup Cottage was the last topic Louise wanted to discuss, but since she couldn't be rude, she settled for evasive. "You were right. The food from the Seafood Station was wonderful. Thanks for the recommendation, Bobbi."

"You're welcome, but that's not what I'm asking about and you know it. How did things go between you and the sexy sailor?"

Louise knew Bobbi wanted to hear some gossipy news about a budding romance. Well, heck, Louise wished she could fulfill her expectations. Unfortunately, the truth still hurt. She shook her head slowly. "Not so well. It looks like Commander Fletcher and I have many more differences than similarities."

"So what? That just makes gettin' to know each other all the more interesting." Bobbi smiled. "Don't you get discouraged. And don't give up on Wesley. I've known him since we were kids, and he's always let his codes and his morals get the best of him. That fella never cut up once in his life that I know of." She chuckled at a memory. "We used to call him Mr. Stick in the… Well, you know the rest. 'Course, we all liked him and admired him just the same. Even when he married that out-of-towner, Donna VanFleet. We all knew she wasn't right for him."

That was the second time Louise had heard a negative reference to Wes's first wife. She couldn't deny her curiosity. "You and I need some girl time together," she said to Bobbi. "There's a lot I don't know about the commander, and I'll bet you could fill me in."

"Anything you want to hear, I'll tell you," she said, and headed for the door. "Now have a good meeting. I figure you're going to find out that Wesley isn't the only mule-headed man in Bayberry Cove. The gals comin' up here today will give you an earful."

Bobbi left and a few minutes later Bessie Granger arrived with five middle-aged women from the candle factory. "Looks like I'm the official shuttle service for us blue hairs," Bessie said with good humor. "I saw to it that we arrived first so we wouldn't have to subject our old bones to sitting on the floor."

"How's Pete doing?" Louise asked, after she'd been introduced to Bessie's co-workers.

"Pretty well right now. I'm taking him into Morgan City for his treatment after the meeting."

Miranda Lopez arrived next with two other women, both young, and both with children at home. Yvonne and four others came next. Darlene was the last of the original group at the Kettle to show up. She ambled in, grabbed a pillow off Louise's bed and plopped down on the floor near Bessie. A huge yawn served as her greeting when Louise welcomed her. "I don't know why we had to start this meeting at the crack of dawn," she said. "Besides, I don't see what any of this can do for me."

Bessie reached down and patted the girl's arm. "You won't know until you listen to what Louise has to say." She frowned, cupped Darlene's chin and angled her face to get a good look at her. "Darlin', were you out all night with Luke Plunkett again?"

"Where else would I be? And you can quit examining me like you were Doc Penderghast. Luke was a gentleman."

"That'll be the day," Bessie snickered.

Three others came to Louise's apartment though none of them were directly involved with the candle factory. Suzie arrived, grinning jubilantly. Louise remembered her promise to Evan and handed out the flyers advertising the week's store specials.

Vicki Malone came to show moral support for her friend, and introduced herself to the women she hadn't yet met. Then she sat to the side, looking very feminine in a ruffled maternity top.

The last woman to appear—and the one who created the biggest stir—was Kate Malone. She breezed in under her cloud of bright red curls, kissed her pregnant daughter-in-law and pretended to ignore the murmured comments about her unexpected attendance. She grabbed a Danish and sat in the middle of the group.

Louise was delighted to see Kate. Bessie Granger, however, was skeptical. "What are you doing here, Kate?" she asked. "This isn't your fight. I hope you're not going to run back to Haywood with information."

Kate bristled. "What a thing to say, Bessie. I'm here as a woman of Bayberry Cove who wants to see fair play down at the factory." She gave Bessie a chiding glance. "If it's spies you're expecting this morning, you'd best take your search elsewhere. You'd easier find one of your own husbands on a ladder outside these windows." She smiled up at Louise. "Do you think I'm a spy, dear?"

"Kate stays," Louise said. "I trust her."

And so the first meeting of the Bayberry Cove Women's Movement for Employment Opportunities officially began. And of all people, it was Suzie McCorkle who came up with the lengthy name and volunteered to make a BCWMEO canvas banner on the old sewing machine she used to repair seams in sofa cushions.

TWO HOURS LATER, the coffee carafes were dry, the pastry boxes were empty and Louise had taken fifteen pages of detailed notes.

"So what do you think, Louise?" Bessie asked. "Do we have legitimate complaints that you can file with the EEOC?"

"Oh, I have enough here to bring a representative from that organization to Bayberry Cove on the next bus," Louise said. "But I have to address Bessie and Miranda and Darlene first, since I've spoken to you three more than any of the others."

The three women sat up with attention. "What more do you need from us?" Miranda asked.

"I've heard a number of violations from all of you today," Louise said. "Many of them are repetitions of the ones you three ladies have encountered, and are indicative of the ways the company has kept some employees from advancing. But I can't possibly expect the EEOC to consider each and every instance where a violation has occurred. I need test cases that will represent the company's infractions."

Bessie looked at Miranda and Darlene. "And you think the three of us will make good test cases?"

"Yes, I do." Louise flipped through her notes to the appropriate page. "Bessie, you have clearly been the victim of age discrimination according to the Equal Pay Act. You reported that recently a man who'd never worked a day at the candle factory and who is half your age was hired to supervise your department after you repeatedly applied for the promotion yourself. And he is being paid half again as much as you currently make.''

''That's right,'' Bessie declared.

''And Darlene, every year you've filled out the proper paperwork to be considered for the marketing and sales apprenticeship program.''

The blonde nodded. ''Yes, I have. And each time I've had to go back to the personnel office to ask why I wasn't picked. And each time ol' Hatch Winslow tells me to apply again next year and that somebody with 'more potential' was chosen for the program. This year Newt Parker got in over me. A slug has more potential than Newt if you want my opinion.''

There was a titter of laughter as all the ladies agreed with Darlene's evaluation of the man.

''That's also discrimination,'' Louise confirmed. ''Title VII provides for equal opportunity in training programs.''

''And Darlene would be great at marketing and sales,'' Bessie stated. ''She could go to trade shows all over the country and sell candles better than any other employee I know of. She actually likes candles more than anybody else in Bayberry Cove—'' Bessie broke off and fixed a guilty grin on Suzie. ''Except maybe you, hon.'' Turning back to the group, she continued, ''And Darlene would love to travel, and, in my opinion, needs to get out of this town.''

Louise understood the implication. Everyone who cared about Darlene wanted her to get away from her destructive relationship with Luke Plunkett.

''And Miranda, you say that Justin Beauclaire

made you take a leave of absence six months into your last pregnancy?''

The Latino woman shook her head, sending her dark, spiral curls dancing. "Yes, he did. He said I was a safety hazard, that I might fall or catch my loose clothing in the scent vats. I told him I would switch positions, but he told me to stay home. I lost three months pay, not counting the time I nursed Mateo after he was born.''

"And you've been at the candle company for four years without a raise in pay?''

"That's right. None of the female Mexican workers have had raises.''

Louise folded her tablet and laid it on an end table. "I have plenty to take to the commission, ladies. I'll use these three cases as examples of violations that occur regularly at the factory. And hopefully, by bringing these issues to light, we can initiate changes that will improve conditions for everyone.'' She looked at each of the three women and raised her eyebrows in question. "So, are we agreed? We'll go forward?''

Miranda squirmed on the rug, where she sat on a pillow. "Will our names be used?'' she asked.

Louise wasn't going to make these ladies think their fight would be an easy or an anonymous one. "Yes, Miranda. That's a condition of filing.''

"Could I be fired?''

"I don't think so. If there is any harassment or retaliation as a result of you coming forward, it would be another case to bring before the EEOC, or even take to court as a full-fledged lawsuit. I can't guarantee there won't be some type of retribution, something petty, perhaps. But I don't think the executives at the factory would risk a lawsuit.''

Bessie was the first to speak out. ''I say let's go for it.''

''I'll stick with Bessie,'' Darlene said. ''She's got the most to lose, and if she's got the guts to do this, then I do, too.''

Miranda chewed her lip. ''I have children to think about. I can't get fired....''

Bessie reached down and took her hand. ''Think about those kids now, Miranda. Think what you getting a raise could do for them. I think we should take the chance Louise is offering us.''

Louise studied her worried expression. ''Tell you what, Miranda. If it's okay with Bessie and Darlene, I'll concentrate on their complaints first and use yours only if we need it.''

Miranda managed a small smile of relief. ''Okay. Then count me in.''

There was a round of applause before Bessie asked, ''What's the next step?''

''Bring me any documentation you have,'' Louise said. ''When you were hired, the approximate dates you were denied promotions and apprenticeships, recent incidents of salary loss due to personal emergencies, pay stubs from the last few years and written reports of the violations, in your own words. I'll take it from there and file the appropriate papers.''

''Wow, this is the most exciting thing that's ever happened in this town,'' one woman said as the group filed out of Louise's apartment. "Imagine taking on Justin Beauclaire and the candle factory!"

When everyone but Vicki had gone, Louise smiled at her friend. "The excitement's just beginning," she said.

Vicki scraped icing from the bottom of one of the pastry boxes onto her finger and licked off the sweet confection. "You know, Lulu, I was impressed seeing you in action this morning. You're a terrific leader."

Louise swept around the room picking up empty cups. "You've seen me in court before."

"Yes, but this was different. More personal, I suppose. You seem committed...."

Louise laughed. "Maybe I should *be* committed, you mean."

"Not at all. I'm amazed by you, my friend. You could be sitting at the beach in Fort Lauderdale doing nothing, or drowning your resentment every night at a bar, but you're not. You're helping these women. You care about them and their problems, and I'm proud of you."

Louise halted her cleaning spree and stared at Vicki. Her friend's words just then meant as much to her as any hefty retainer from a corporate executive. "Well, thanks," she said with a humility that felt alien, but good.

Vicki smiled and abruptly changed the direction of the conversation. "But speaking of commitments, how did it go with Wesley last night?"

The adrenaline rush Louise had experienced during the meeting vanished. She had to address the Wesley issue one more time, and it wasn't any easier to discuss now. "Not well. It turns out the sailor I'd set my sights on is actually an attorney. And he's going to represent the candle factory if I submit violations to the EEOC."

Vicki frowned in sympathy. "I heard. Jamie told me last night. That really stinks, Lulu, but maybe you can't blame Wes. I hear his father can be pretty convincing."

Louise stuffed the cups into her trash can, tied the ends of the bag and carried the garbage to the back door. "His father is a lot of things. Convincing is only one of them. Anyway, I'm not thinking about Wesley today. I've got more important things on my mind."

"But you're not giving up on him?"

There was his face again, with its strong chiseled features and bright blue eyes, popping into her mind with all the clarity of the sun in a cloudless sky. Louise settled a fist on her hip. "When have you ever known me to give up after one defeat? I'm simply shelving the subject of Wesley Fletcher until I can truly concentrate on what to do about him. But one more evening like last night, and I may switch him to the hopeless column."

Further discussion of Wesley was forgotten when shouting from the back parking lot drew the attention of both women. "What's going on out there?" Vicki asked.

"I don't know, but it sounds like Darlene's voice."

Louise opened the back door and stepped onto a wooden platform that led to the staircase. The parking lot was empty except for her BMW, an older model Japanese car and a black pickup truck. Darlene and a tall, rangy man in a cowboy hat were standing near the pickup. He had his hand wrapped around her upper arm, and she was struggling to get free.

"Let me go, you big ox," she shouted. "You had no right to come here."

"I've got every right," the man hollered back. "Especially when you lie to me. You said you were going to your sister's this morning. I don't like being lied to, Darlene."

She yanked her arm away and took several steps back from him. "You make me lie to you, Luke, by always telling me what I can and can't do. I'm sick of it."

He closed the distance between them and held up a fist. "Get in the truck, Darlene. We're going for a ride."

"I'm not going anywhere with you when you act like this…."

"That's right," Louise shouted from the platform. "You come up here with us, Darlene. And you—" she shook a trembling finger at Luke "—you make tracks, buster."

Luke stomped over to the stairs and glared up at her. "Who the hell are you? Oh, wait, I know. You're that lady attorney who's been creating a ruckus around here."

"I'm also Darlene's friend. And it's your misfortune that I happen to be the one friend who can put you behind bars for a few years if you lay a hand on her."

Luke put one booted foot on the first step. "You don't scare me, lady."

Darlene grabbed Luke's arm and pulled him away. "Just go, Luke, please. I don't want any trouble. And you sure don't need any more."

For one long, frightening moment, the man appeared to weigh his options. He narrowed his eyes first on his pickup, then Darlene and finally Louise. She held her breath and stared back at him.

And then a Jeep Wrangler came down the alley and pulled into the parking lot. Wesley stepped out, looked at all the parties, who were now standing in silence, and said, "What's going on here? Luke, what are you up to?"

Luke yanked his hat off and slapped it against his thigh. "Nothing's going on, Wes. Nothing at all." He delivered a last blazing look at Louise and Darlene and said, "I was just leaving." He stomped to the truck, climbed in and sped out of the parking lot. Darlene got into her car and drove off in the opposite direction.

And Louise let out the breath she'd been holding.

"Thank goodness," Vicki said from behind her.

Wesley watched the dust settle from the pickup's wild departure and then approached the stairs. "Good morning, ladies," he said. "Do either of you know what got into Luke?"

Louise smirked. "Gee, I don't know, Wes. Maybe the men of Bayberry Cove just don't know how to treat their womenfolk." After experiencing a slight jolt of satisfaction at seeing him cringe a little, she said, "But more to the point, what are you doing here?"

He went back to the Jeep and lifted her picnic basket from the passenger seat. "I was just out for a drive and thought I'd drop this off. You forgot it last night."

"How thoughtful of you, Counselor," she said. "But I can't see myself using it again in the near future. Suddenly I don't have much interest in picnicking, and I know I won't have the time."

He brought the basket to the stairs, acted for a moment as if he might ascend to the second floor, but stopped before climbing up. Instead, he set the basket on the bottom step. He rubbed his hand along the nape of his neck and said, "So how'd your meeting go?"

She gave him a stiff smile. "Swell, thanks."

"That's good." He shifted from one foot to the other, as if waiting for an invitation. When none was forthcoming, he added, "I guess I'll be going then."

Louise nodded. "Bye."

"Nice seeing you again, Vicki," he said.

"Same here, Wesley."

"I'll see you later, Louise."

She flicked her fingers in an offhand wave. "No doubt."

Once he was in his vehicle and heading away, Vicki released a long, audible sigh.

"What's that for?" Louise asked.

Vicki gave her a silly grin. "I just get all squishy inside when I see love in bloom. That guy's crazy about you, Lulu."

"Right." She retrieved the basket, carried it upstairs and put it on her kitchen counter. "He probably thinks I left it at his house on purpose so I'd have an excuse to see him again."

When Vicki didn't respond, Louise turned around to look at her. The silly grin was still in place. "What now?"

"Did you?" Vicki asked.

"Leave the basket on purpose?"

"Yeah. Because if you did, I'm proud of you for the second time this morning. It's a little obvious, but that's all right. It still shows that never-give-up determination of yours that I've grown to admire."

Louise started taking items from the basket. Everything had been washed and packed carefully, and she smiled at one aspect of Wes's personality that was truly predictable. "Of course I didn't mean to leave it there. Don't be ridiculous."

But had she? Louise remembered how she'd picked up her purse from Wes's table, never once thinking of the picnic basket. The subconscious worked in strange ways.

ONCE SHE SAW Haywood's car in the driveway and realized he'd returned from his golf match, Kate drove around to the back of the house and walked into the kitchen through the rear entrance.

"That you, Katie?" Haywood hollered from his office. "I've been waiting for you. What's for lunch?"

"I don't know yet, Haywood," she said, regretting that she hadn't made her usual Saturday-morning trip to the grocery. "How does a can of soup sound?"

"Like we're running a nursery school," he called back. "A man needs real food, Kate, not something he can slurp with a straw. What did you buy today?"

"I didn't go grocery shopping," she said.

Relieved when he didn't comment, she found some stew and inserted the can into the electric opener. And then she squealed in fright and leaped away from the counter when she heard Haywood growl right behind her, "What do you mean you didn't go shopping? You always go to the grocery store on Saturdays."

She whirled around and shoved him away. "You scared the wits out of me, Haywood. Don't sneak up on me like that."

"Okay, but where were you this morning?"

"I went to a flea market in Wrightsboro." Though she knew her anger was mostly unreasonable, she dumped the stew into a pot and snapped, "If that schedule doesn't suit your needs, you can drive yourself to McDonald's!"

He raised his hands. "Whoa, Katie. I was just asking."

She tried to be more pleasant. "I'm sorry, dear. I'm a little jumpy I guess."

He sat in the large chair at the head of the pine table. "I could do with that stew, I guess."

She realized she was feeling more guilty than angry. She'd never lied to Haywood before.

"So what did you buy?" he asked as she handed him the stew.

"Where?"

"At the flea market. You always come back with an oddity or two when you go to one of those."

What was this? An inquisition? Kate dipped her hands under the spigot of running water and spritzed drops of water onto her warm face. This was no time for a hot flash, or a guilt flash, or whatever it was. "Well, not today, Haywood," she said. "Didn't see a thing I wanted."

"Did you happen to get downtown this morning?" he asked around a mouthful of beef and potatoes.

She turned the water on full force and filled the dirty pot. "Downtown? Why would I go downtown? I told you I didn't go to the supermarket."

"Yes, I know, but the strangest thing happened. My father finally learned to use his cell phone. He called me from the square today and said there was a flock of women going into that lady lawyer's apartment."

Kate scoured the pot until she feared the Teflon lining might come off. "My, that is strange. I didn't think Mason would ever catch on to that cell phone."

"That's not the strange part, Katie, and I think you know it. He said he saw your car on Main Street."

She slammed the clean pot loudly on the drainboard and faced him. "What's this, Haywood? Now you've got your father spying on me?"

"No. I'm just curious about why you lied to me."

She threw up her hands. "All right. I was at that meeting. And I'm not sorry I went."

He stood up, came to the sink and completely surprised her by wrapping her in a huge bear hug. "Neither am I, Kate. I'm pleased as punch to hear it." He kissed the tip of her nose. "Now tell me what you found out, you clever woman."

"I'm not going to tell you anything."

He stepped back from her as if she'd suddenly grown a forked tail. "What?"

"I went there to support the women in this town, Haywood. Anything that happened at that meeting you'll find out soon enough, but you won't hear it from me."

His eyes bulged under bushy white brows. "You can't be serious."

"I'm all that and more. I'm proud of the women I was with this morning. They're showing great courage in the face of…the bullies at the factory. And I admire that young lawyer who's standing up for them."

Haywood pounded his fist on the counter—just once, and just loudly enough to command attention. "Kate, I demand you tell me what those females are cooking up. Your loyalty is to me and this house, and by God, I *own* this house!"

He had gone too far. Kate knew it and read in his eyes that he knew it, too.

"I'm well aware that this isn't my house, Haywood," she said. "I've lived in it for more than five years without benefit of license or title. I guess that makes me a guest, by your own definition. Well, by Saint Pat, I'll be a guest in your house if that's the way you want it. Tonight I'll sleep in a *guest* room until I can find more suitable accommodations elsewhere."

"Aw, Katie, come on now…"

He took a step toward her, but she stopped him with one look. She tore off her apron, crushed it into a ball and shoved it into his hands. "Here, you'll need this when you fix your supper."

On the way out of the kitchen, she ripped the grocery list from the magnetized tablet on the refrigerator door and thrust that at him as well. "And you can do your own shoppin'. Won't you be the dandy fella down at the Piggly Wiggly squeezin' melons!"

Haywood sank into the nearest chair and stared at the doorway. A few seconds later, Rudy entered the room with a backward glance over his shoulder.

"What's goin' on with Miss Kate?" the butler asked. "What did you do?"

Haywood shook his head. "Damned if I know, Rudy. All I said was, 'What's for lunch?' I think the women in this town have all gone mad."

CHAPTER TEN

FOR THE NEXT FOUR DAYS Wesley successfully avoided Louise. He jogged along the shore of Currituck Sound instead of the town square track even though the uneven, sandy terrain was not kind to the soles of his feet. He stayed away from the Kettle except for breakfast on Monday morning, when Bobbi Lee acted as if taking his order was as unpleasant as getting a root canal.

"You won't see her here this morning," Bobbi Lee had smartly informed him.

Of course he pretended he had no idea what she was talking about. "Won't see who?" he'd asked.

"Don't play ignorant with me, Wes Fletcher," she'd snapped at him. "I remember your high school grade point average." And then she'd smugly told him that Louise was in Morgan City conferring with her legal team, which included one Lawrence Aaronson. Wes had laughed at the whole idea. He was quite certain that Louise didn't need a team of any sort nor any help beyond her sponsorship.

During his infrequent trips to town, Wes realized something else as well. The ladies of Bayberry Cove had obviously heard who was acting as counsel for the factory. The cold shoulder he'd received from

Bobbi Lee was pretty much the same reaction he got from most of the women in his hometown. People who normally waved and smiled at him from passing automobiles now pretended they didn't see him. Even the checker at the supermarket swept his purchases over the scanning window without so much as a "How are you today?"

He found out that circumstances weren't much better for his father. By Wednesday night, when the isolation of Buttercup Cottage was making him stir-crazy, Wes accepted an invitation to eat with his dad at a chain restaurant on the freeway a few miles from town. Besides questioning Wes about what he knew of the secret meeting on Saturday morning, Haywood complained that his relationship with Kate had turned as cold as a winter frost.

"That blasted lady attorney is turning my life upside down," he grumbled. "So what has she got on us, son?"

"I don't know, Dad. Maybe you should tell me."

Haywood covered a belch with his napkin and dipped his twelfth chicken wing in spicy barbecue sauce. "Nothing. She's got nothing. Justin Beauclaire tells me we're clean as a scrubbed blackboard."

"That's not the impression I get from half the women in town. I feel like my female neighbors have suddenly taken sides and I've assumed the identity of a damn Yankee."

Haywood leaned over the table and spoke in a whisper. "Do you think she's filed any complaints with the EEOC?"

Wes took a long swallow of beer. "Well, Dad, she

said she would, and I don't think she's the type to make idle threats. She's not afraid of any of you boys, and she's set herself up with Aaronson. So, yes, I'd say she probably has, or will as soon as she gets enough documentation.''

''Hellfire. This is just what I need to hear with Kate treating me like a flea off a dog's hiney.'' He stared down at his empty plate with a look of disgust. ''I haven't had a decent meal in nearly a week. And that's not even mentioning what else I haven't had!''

Wes held up his hand. His father's sex life, or lack thereof, wasn't a topic he wanted to discuss. Wes didn't need to hear how a few days deprivation was making his father grumpy. ''Let's keep to the legal issues, okay?'' he said.

''So what are you going to do? How are you going to handle this situation?''

Even after forty years association with Haywood Fletcher, Wes could still be knocked over by the sheer nerve of the man. ''How am *I* going to handle this? Dad, have you forgotten that I'm just your consultant? I'm supposed to sign my name on the paperwork *you* prepare, remember?''

Haywood brandished his fork in the air. ''Don't throw my words back at me, Wesley. I'll help you, but you're the legal eagle in this case. You've spent the last sixteen years studying contracts and inter- preting civil law. I'm counting on you, son.''

Wonderful. Wes should have known that his father would pass the whole job of defending the factory on to him. ''I'll do what I can, Dad. But I can't promise anything. If it looks like Louise has chosen obscure, even insignificant violations, then I can argue on the side of the company. Admit to innocent negligence if I have to. But if—''

''Well, hell, of course she's scraping the bottom of the barrel! Petty stuff. That's all she's got. The kind of things that every company in America gets away with.''

Leaving his steak half-eaten, Wes searched the restaurant for their waiter. The first signs of indigestion rumbled in his stomach as he waved the boy over and asked for the check.

BY THURSDAY MORNING Wes gave up pretending to himself that he was enjoying every minute of his simple, uncomplicated life at Buttercup Cottage. He was in this quagmire of a legal dilemma up to his waist and sinking lower. The case of the women candle workers versus the factory executives wasn't going to go away. And neither were the nagging thoughts of the dynamite attorney who represented the other side.

Circumstances being what they were, he'd have to see her again. To keep this candle factory business from getting out of hand, he decided to try and make things right with Louise. He was a grown man with a firm control on his emotions and actions. He could see her in social situations and act like the gentleman he'd always been. After all, they were on opposite sides of a legal debate, which meant that they couldn't engage in bedroom activities no matter how appealing the idea.

Besides, Wes wasn't a casual-sex type of guy. So he could see Louise again now that he'd admitted honestly that she fascinated him on several levels. One of those levels was a safe, intellectual one. She was interested in his studies of the wetlands, and he could keep their personal relationship grounded on that common interest.

He'd invite her to go out on the Aquasport. She'd said she wanted to, and it would be the perfect way to break the ice that sat between them like a polar glacier.

After tending to his experiments on Thursday morning, Wes drove over to the Malones' houseboat. He accepted the cup of coffee Vicki offered him, talked a little with Jamie and then stated bluntly, "Vicki, I need her phone number."

A smile spread across her face. "Lulu's?"

As if there was any other phone number on the face of the earth he could possibly be asking for. "Yes, Lulu's."

"She only has her cell phone. It's a Florida number. Long distance."

"I'll figure the added expense into my budget," he said.

Vicki jotted the number on a piece of paper and handed it to him. "It's about time."

Jamie gave him an enigmatic smile and a shrug that seemed to say, *Why resist the inevitable?*

Wes went home and dialed the number.

She answered on the third ring. "Louise Duncan."

Her voice was crisp and cool. Businesslike. No doubt the majority of her phone calls were related to her business affairs these days.

"Louise. It's Wes."

There was a pause, and for a moment he thought she might hang up. "Well, my goodness. Wes. What can I do for you?"

To the point, slightly aloof but thankfully not antagonistic. "I'm calling to see if you're still interested in going out on the boat with me. I thought you might like to learn how I collect my samples. I'm going all the way to Pamlico Sound tomorrow. It would be a good chance for you to experience our marine environment."

Geez, Wes, could you make it sound any more boring? "It's supposed to be a beautiful day," he added, hoping that extra perk would compensate for his lackluster invitation.

"I see." She paused again, showing a command of the element of suspense. "Will I need a life jacket?"

"I have them in the boat already. I always recommend—"

"It was a joke, Wes. Though subtly aimed at determining if we're going as friends."

He smiled. "Absolutely." *Friends who can have a platonic relationship despite the legal issues between them.*

"Okay. I'll go. Shall I drive to your place?"

"That would be great. Can you be here by seven? I like to visit my collection sites before the waterways get too crowded with pleasure craft."

"All right. Seven o'clock it is."

"I'll have a thermos of coffee."

"And I'll bring doughnuts from the Kettle."

Wes stared at the phone for several seconds after they disconnected. He felt energized, more enthused than he had in days. Since Friday night's dinner if he were truly honest—even though that experience had ended disastrously. Louise was fun. And didn't he deserve to have a little fun? It didn't have to lead to more. He was a man of conscience, control. Master of his own destiny.

WHEN HE HEARD THE SOUND of a car engine on Sandy Ridge Road, Wes looked up from the deck of the Aquasport where he was readying the boat for the morning's trip into Currituck Sound. Louise's dark BMW slowed and turned into the drive of the cottage.

Wes noted the time on his wristwatch. Six-fifty. A guy had to admire a female who didn't keep him waiting. She came around the corner of the house and Wes decided a guy had to admire even more a woman who looked like she did at this hour. Dressed in shorts and a sleeveless top, her hair bound in a kerchief, her stride eager, her face luminous in the morning sun, Louise was so striking he nearly lost his grip on the thermos he was stowing in a cup holder.

"Hey, Commander," she called. "Everything ship-shape?"

He noticed the white sack from the Kettle. "It will be once I have a doughnut."

She tossed him the bag and climbed into the boat as if she'd been sailing every day of her life. "Any particular place you'd like me to sit?" she asked. "I wouldn't want to throw off the balance of this thing and send us toppling overboard."

With that statement he realized she hadn't been sailing much at all. He indicated the seat next to the captain's position. "That will be fine. Your life vest is stored under the seat cushion."

"Good. That answers my next question."

He laughed. "You can put it on now if it makes you feel better."

"No. Just promise you'll give me enough time to fasten it before we capsize."

"No problem. I'm known for my slow rollovers." He filled a marine-style coffee cup hinged at the sides to keep liquid from spilling over, and held it out to her.

She took the warm mug, settled in her seat and slipped on a pair of dark-framed sunglasses. "I'm ready when you are."

He turned the ignition key with the engine in neutral and felt the steady, assertive vibrations. Louise stowed her cup in a holder and grabbed the sides of her seat.

"You're going to love this," Wes said, thrusting the throttle to its forward position. The boat shot away from the dock, banked in a tight turn and raced into Currituck Sound.

She squealed before shouting through a cool, brisk wind that whipped her hair around her shoulders, "If you say so, Commander."

HE WAS RIGHT. She loved it. Once her breathing returned to normal and she decided they weren't going to become an artificial reef for future scuba divers to explore, Louise reveled in the performance of the speedboat.

She'd been on cruises, of course. She'd sailed on

large, lavish ocean liners fitted for two thousand passengers. She'd taken dozens of pictures of glass-enclosed elevators outlined in sparkling white lights, and buffet tables that stretched the length of a basketball court. But none of it compared with the exuberance of racing across the sound with the sun at her back and the watery world shimmering to the horizon.

After about fifteen minutes, Wes slowed the boat as it approached a red plastic ball bobbing in the current. "We're here already?" she asked.

"This is only our first stop. I identify my research sites with these floats so I can find them again." He dropped an anchor over the side and let the boat drift to the marker. Then he reached under the ball and pulled on a chain.

"I know we talked about your experiments a little the other night," Louise said, "but what is it exactly that you hope to prove?"

"I'm trying to show that development of Currituck Sound in any major way, such as with high-rise apartments, luxury hotels and so on, will upset the delicate balance of the North Carolina marshes and wetlands. I gather specimens from the various water types—salt, fresh and brackish—and demonstrate in the tanks in my shed what would happen to sea life if waters with such diverse salinity levels intermixed too rapidly."

"And development would do that?" she asked.

"It already has." He continued coiling the chain onto the deck of the boat until he pulled up a wire cage with a funnel-like device on one side. He left the cage in the water while he finished explaining.

"Development causes change in the salinity of the water from such things as dredging, waste material dumped from the shore, even, believe it or not, human viruses being introduced. Changes in salinity affect aquatic vegetation, which in turn affects the life cycles of the creatures who feed on it. All these changes would be disastrous to our water industries like fishing and shrimping."

He lifted the cage, causing water and sand to run from the sides. When he settled the contraption on the deck of the boat, Louise observed several creatures scurrying or flopping about on the bottom tray. "How do they get in there?"

"That's what the funnel's for," he said. "Fish and crabs go in the wide opening but can't find their way back out."

"Are you taking these guys back to your shed?"

"Yep." He raised the lid on top of the cage and began transferring the creatures to a larger tub of water inside the boat. He seemed pleased when he picked up one fish behind its gills and held it up for close inspection. "This is an interesting specimen."

"How so?"

"This is a shortnose sturgeon. He spends most of his life in saltwater, only going to fresh to reproduce, which he shouldn't be doing at this time of year. You're kind of lost, aren't you, buddy?" he said to the fish before putting it into the tub and returning his attention to Louise. "He's a perfect example of specimens who get comfortable in an environment that's exactly where they should be, and then new stimuli move in when the salt levels become inconsistent.

The sturgeon loses his way and doesn't know if he's coming or going.''

An interesting analogy, Louise thought. "You'll pardon me for saying so, Wes," she said, "but it seems as if you understand what this fish is going through.''

He closed the lid of the tank and leaned back on his haunches. The look he gave her was both thoughtful and amused. And incredibly intense. After a moment he said, "Maybe you've got something there, Counselor. Maybe I do understand this guy's dilemma.'' He stood up and returned to his task. "It will be interesting to see if he survives the new environment of my tanks as I alter the salinity and nutrient levels.''

She smiled at him. Poor Wes. Nineteen years in the navy characterized by regimens and codes and a lifestyle that didn't change much from day to day. And all he'd hoped for was a simple life of scientific accomplishment in Bayberry Cove, perhaps with an uncomplicated woman in blue jeans and a gingham shirt waiting by the back door of Buttercup Cottage. But what did he get after a week of retirement? A major legal role in an EEOC investigation, and quite possibly some weird, unwanted attraction to a woman who was about as far from his ideal as anyone could be.

"I have a prediction about that fish, Wes," she said. "He seems like the hardy sort. I think he'll figure out what he has to do to stay alive…and swim happily along.''

"You could be right, Louise," he said as he secured the cage again and dropped it over the side. Back in business mode, he returned to his seat and pushed the throttle into gear. "Keep your eye open for the next red float," he said. "We've got four more cages to find."

LOUISE HAD BEEN A GOOD sport about everything. She'd even picked up a couple of blue crabs from one of the cages and, with their jointed appendages wiggling madly, had transferred them to the temporary tank in the boat. At one point in Pamlico Sound she took over controls of the boat, punched the speed up to its maximum and whooped with the enthusiasm of a rodeo rider. But when they returned to Buttercup Cottage around noon, she was the first one out of the boat, racing toward the house and the conveniences inside.

Wes introduced his new specimens to the aquariums in the shed and secured the boat and its equipment. When he entered the cottage a few minutes later, he found Louise standing at the kitchen counter with various utensils spread out in front of her. She'd abandoned the kerchief around her hair, which hung straight and long, past shoulders that were tinged pink from the sun.

"You hungry?" she said.

"I could eat an octopus."

She grinned. "Sorry. You're fresh out. But I did find some ham and cheese in the refrigerator, and I'm making sandwiches." She found a tomato and a head of lettuce in the crisper and slathered mayonnaise onto thick slices of bread.

She looked so natural performing this domestic task that Wes sat down at the table and simply watched her. Many times the last few days he'd wondered what she'd been doing, but he'd never pictured her in a kitchen looking as if she belonged there. He stretched his legs under the table and said, "Do you like to cook?"

Keeping her attention on the tomato she was slicing, she said, "Sorry again, but no. I bought my current condo in Fort Lauderdale based on the variety and accessibility of take-out food in the neighborhood."

The answer disappointed him, though logically it shouldn't have. Why would it matter to him if Louise enjoyed cooking? "So what do you do in your spare time?" he said. "Do you garden?"

She laughed. "Wes, I said 'condo.' As in 'no lawn, no flowers, no shrubs.' I have a beautiful silk tree in the corner of my living room that I tend lovingly with a feather duster and a damp cotton swab." She set two plates and two beers on the table and sat across from him. He took a large bite from his sandwich.

"Now that your mouth is full I guess it's safe for me to ask if you have any other questions," she said.

Maybe he was probing a bit too much into her personal life, but now that he'd gone this far, he decided to plunge ahead. He washed down the sandwich with a swallow of beer. "I don't mean to be nosy, but—"

"Yes, you do."

He grinned. "Well, maybe. You must have a hobby. Do you knit? Do needlework? Make things?"

Her eyebrows shot up in amusement. "Make

things? No, Wes, I don't make tea cozies or twig wreaths. But I can file efficiently, and I type sixty words a minute. So if this is a job interview, you might want to consider me for any position other than that of the next Mrs. Wesley Fletcher.''

He choked on soggy bread and took another gulp of his beer. ''What in the world are you talking about?'' he said when he'd caught his breath. ''I wasn't even remotely suggesting—''

She shook her head, took a dainty bite of sandwich and swallowed. ''Calm down, Commander. I know I'm not a suitable candidate.''

He stood up, walked to the door and looked out at Currituck Sound. ''You really amaze me with the things you say sometimes.''

''Just like you amaze me with the ones you *don't* say.'' Her voice came from directly behind him, and he spun around to see her standing within inches of him. ''I know you and I would make a terrible old married couple, Wes. But I'm still tickled that you're searching for some little facet of my character that might make me even moderately acceptable to your Bayberry Cove standard of womanhood.''

His skin started to heat up. ''That's ridiculous.''

''I don't think so. The other night you said you liked me. You couldn't understand why exactly, but you did. I was happy to hear that—despite how the evening turned out—but now I think I need a few specifics. I don't grow things or sew or bake.'' She took a step closer to him.

His knit shirt suddenly felt too tight. He pulled at one sleeve, trying to stretch it out around his biceps.

."So what *do* you like about me, Wes?"

"This is silly. You've put me on the spot."

"Good. It's where you should be. Name one thing you like about me. My hair? My figure? My brain?"

He rolled his eyes. Actually, he liked the first two a great deal. The third was a little scary.

She clasped her hands behind her back and lifted her face up to his. At the same time other tempting body parts came dangerously close. "I play a pretty fair game of tennis," she said, "and believe it or not, I once bowled a perfect three hundred. I'm an excellent driver and I have a double-jointed thumb." She gave him a tight-lipped grin that came across as a dare. "Have I mentioned anything yet that you really like?"

If she meant to intimidate him, it wasn't working. If her goal was to fire every red-blooded cell in his body, she was doing a damn good job. At the same time, he was beginning to figure Louise out.

He flexed his shoulders, answered her grin with one of his own and stared down at her until she was the one who seemed uncomfortable. Amazingly, his voice was calm as he said, "Yes, there is something. I like the fact that you bowl. I think we can build on that."

Her eyes grew so wide that for a moment all he could see was the sheer lavender brilliance of them. And then a deep, rich chortle came from her throat. "Now we're getting somewhere," she said. "But know this. I will never, *ever,* let you win. We'll go all the way to the tenth frame each time if we have to."

''I don't doubt that you'll make it a worthy contest, Counselor.''

She unclasped her hands and crossed her arms in front. The gesture lifted her breasts until Wes could see a slash of white skin below her recent sunburn. Her puckered nipples, visible through the soft fabric of her top, nearly brushed his shirt. The first admonitions from his damnable conscience echoed somewhere in the back of his brain. *Watch yourself, Wes. Not with this woman. You're about to step off an emotional cliff, and while the fall may be a thrill, you still have to face hitting bottom.*

But, damn, he was allowed to look, wasn't he? To savor? His fingers twitched. To feel?

''Just so we understand each other, Wes,'' she said. ''We're not just talking about bowling anymore, are we?''

She was testing him to the limit, and it was inhuman to try and resist her. For right now, just this once, he would silence the controlling forces in his head and deal with the consequences later. He grasped her elbows and pulled her into close, intimate contact. ''No, Louise, I don't think we are.''

He lifted her to her toes and crushed her against his chest. When his mouth covered hers, his blood raced through his veins until the voice of his conscience was erased by the hum of his desire. He'd wanted to feel her against him like this perhaps from the first moment he'd seen her. And now she was soft, pliant and willing in his arms. She bent to his demands, parted her lips to let his tongue probe the warmth of her mouth.

He tasted every inch of her face, relishing the salty tang of her sun-warmed skin. He held her hair away from her neck and nuzzled her throat, nipping his way to her ears. She moaned, wrapped her hands around his nape and flattened her breasts against him. She returned his kisses, holding nothing back. Maybe Louise Duncan was the last woman he needed in his life, but right now, she was the one he most desired, and to hell with everything else.

SHE'D KNOWN IT ALL ALONG. Underneath that polished military exterior, Wes Fletcher was an amazingly passionate man, and she was enjoying discovering this far more than she should. *You've got to stop, Louise,* she said to herself. *If you're not careful this could turn dangerous.* But she didn't stop. Instead, she arched her body against his, twined her fingers into his hair and held on, reveling in a ride that was more thrilling by far than the one across Currituck Sound. He made her skin tingle, her body tremble and her appetite for what he promised soar. But she should stop him. And she would—soon. What they were doing couldn't lead to the ultimate conclusion—not today.

He backed into the wall, taking her with him. She half stumbled and he grabbed her leg, wrapping it around his waist. He curled one strong, capable hand over her breast and kneaded her flesh. He kissed her again until her body longed to melt against his, to merge with the hard angled planes of his chest, the probing evidence of his desire between his legs.

He breathed into her ear. ''Louise, we can't stay like this.'' He inched away from the wall toward the living room…the bedroom. *Now, Louise. You've got to stop this now.*

She made herself listen to the ticking coming from above her head. She looked up and saw an old school-house clock mounted to the wall. Two o'clock. She squeezed her eyes shut and released a long, frustrated groan against the mouth that still threatened to send her over the edge.

Wes leaned away from her. "What's wrong?"

She lay her forehead against his chest. "It's two o'clock."

He kissed the top of her head and rubbed his hand down her back. "So? I can't think of anything else I have to do."

"Well, I can, and you're not going to like it." And neither did she. All morning she'd been aware of her afternoon appointment. She hadn't intended for a little playful flirtation to get out of hand. After the first fun kiss, she'd meant to be the one to stop before Wes could call a halt to the activities as he had the other night. Plus she knew that he wouldn't be comfortable fooling around with her once he discovered she had to leave to meet with a representative from the Equal Employment Opportunity Commission.

Louise didn't have a problem separating the activities of her legal life from the activities of her personal one, but she knew Wes would. She sighed, admitting to herself that putting his feelings first was something new to her.

She walked away from him, picked up the dirty plates and carried them to the sink. That way she didn't have to face him as she said, "I have a meeting at two-thirty."

"With anyone I know?"

"His name is Christopher Tenant, and he's with the EEOC."

There was a moment of uncomfortable silence until Wes said, "He's coming to Bayberry Cove to meet with you on a Friday afternoon?"

"Yes, but I didn't know about it until late yesterday. He received my paperwork on Thursday, and since I mentioned that I'm pressed for time on these cases, he made an adjustment in his schedule and called me right away."

She turned to face him. "I'm sorry, Wes."

He stared as if he weren't really seeing her. His eyes were as bleak as a winter sea. "Don't be sorry. You were right to put the brakes on what was happening here. It was crazy. I don't know why…" He stopped, rubbed the back of his neck. "I guess you'd better go, then."

"Yeah." She picked up her purse and headed for the living room. "It was a lot of fun," she said as she left the kitchen.

He went to the sink and picked up where she'd left off, putting his tidy world back together. "Right," he said. "Fun. We'll do it again sometime."

CHAPTER ELEVEN

LOUISE STEPPED HARD on her brakes and swerved into a parking space a few yards from her apartment. She'd made the trip from Buttercup Cottage in six minutes flat, which was not nearly as much time as it should have taken. She'd never looked at her speedometer. Wouldn't have cared if she'd gotten a ticket. She felt that lousy about what had just happened, and more confused than she'd ever been about her feelings for Wesley Fletcher.

And now she only had fifteen minutes to pull herself together for the meeting with Christopher Tenant. "At least I've got one thing going for me," she said as she got out of her car. "Tenant's a government employee. He won't be early."

She hurried up the sidewalk. Her foot was on the first step to her apartment when she heard her name being called. "Miss Duncan? Young lady?"

Turning away from the stairs, she peered across the street to the town square. Mason Fletcher was waving at her. She and the old guy had gotten to be pretty good friends. She could always count on him being at his familiar bench, and he always seemed eager to talk to her. "Hi, Mason," she called back. "I don't have time to chat now. I'm running late."

He pointed to a man sitting next to him, and Louise noticed the stranger for the first time. "I know ya' are," Mason said. "And this young fella's waiting for you."

Christopher Tenant. It had to be. The guy whose head was the target of Mason's pointer finger was definitely an out-of-towner. In tan chinos, a dress shirt and tie, he was Raleigh all the way.

"Well, nuts," Louise said under her breath. She made a quick repair to her appearance, tucking her blouse into her shorts, smoothing her windblown hair and pressing her lips together before she remembered that any lipstick that might have remained from this morning had been thoroughly kissed off. She plastered a smile on her face and crossed the street, wishing she could make a better first impression on the man who would decide the fate of the women candle workers.

She stuck her hand out when she reached the bench. "Mr. Tenant?"

He stood up and shook her hand. "That's right."

"Louise Duncan. I'm sorry you had to wait."

He appraised her with cool gray eyes that probably assessed her none-too-proper business attire. "It's no problem," he said. "I'm early, and I've only been here five minutes." He glanced at Mason, who was studying Louise with equal intensity. "This gentleman has kept me entertained, and informed."

She narrowed her eyes at Mason. "I'll just bet he has. I hope you didn't prejudice the case against my clients, Mason."

"He couldn't do that, Miss Duncan," Christopher

said. "It's my job to judge each case with an unbiased eye, and I take it very seriously."

So Mr. Tenant was all-business. When Louise returned her attention to him, he was still staring at her, holding her hand and smiling. She noticed that his tie was loosely knotted and hung at an awkward angle on his chest. He wasn't perfection, after all. She extricated her hand and smiled back. "Call me Louise. And if I could ask a favor of you, Mr...."

"Chris. And ask anything at all."

"There's a café just down the street called the Bayberry Cove Kettle. Could I buy you a cup of coffee while I run up to my apartment and change? I don't normally conduct business in the same clothes I wear on a speedboat."

"You look fine to me, Louise," he said. "But sure, I could go for a cup of coffee. You take your time."

She pointed the way to the Kettle and Chris set off. Before she'd taken two steps toward the furniture store, Mason chuckled and said, "You've been out with my grandson, haven't you?"

She shot him a stern look over her shoulder. "That, Mason, is none of your business."

"All right, young lady, you can sass me all you want. I'll just ask someone else."

She shook her head and kept walking. *Small towns!*

LOUISE SHOWERED and changed in record time. She and Christopher Tenant ended up conducting their meeting in a corner booth of the Kettle. The EEOC rep reacted to Louise's findings pretty much as she'd anticipated.

"I think you've got some legitimate charges," he said over his third cup of coffee. "After some in-depth research, I'll take my conclusions back to Raleigh and see where we should go with this. I'm sure that mediation will be suggested at the very least."

Louise sipped her iced tea. "What other research do you have in mind?"

Tenant's professionalism slipped a notch as he flashed her what she figured was supposed to be a winning grin. "I'll need to go over these reports again for starters. Are you free for dinner?"

"I've got to eat," Louise said, her feminine instincts on alert. "If you'd like to make it a working meal, I have no objection."

"Great. Is that your apartment over the furniture store where I saw you earlier?"

She indicated it was.

"I'll pick you up at seven. You choose the restaurant."

Louise gathered her papers together. "Fine. Obviously we'll need one with a good source of light."

"IT'S LOVELY OUT HERE," Louise said Saturday evening when she and Vicki sat on the front porch of the houseboat. The women had returned from a shopping trip to Morgan City. Louise had been amazed at how much stuff a baby needed. Now she was enjoying the cool, dry air that drifted off the sound and stirred the flames of citronella torches that kept the insects away. From the living room, a sportscaster's voice droned on about scores of the day's baseball games. Jamie was inside, giving the women the privacy they needed.

Vicki poured tea from a china pot into two cups and slid containers of sugar and milk to her friend. "Now, what's going on with you and Wes?" she asked.

Louise swirled cream into her tea. "It's hard to explain. Wes isn't like anyone I've ever dated."

Vicki responded with a knowing grin. "I thought so. Our handsome commander is getting under your skin."

"I'm not sure. Maybe."

"But you are dating?"

"That's just it. I'm not sure about that, either. We're like two dogs growling across an alley at each other one minute, and sharing the same string of spaghetti the next."

Vicki smiled at the Disney reference. "Except that Wes is no tramp, and most of the time you, my good friend, are no lady."

Louise accepted this honest appraisal from her closest friend without feeling insulted. "That's true, Vic, and it's part of the problem. From the first minute I saw Wes, I was attracted to him. Tall, muscular, with enough earthiness to hold my interest... He was definitely a target for my libido, if you know what I mean."

"So what's the problem? He's obviously attracted to you, too."

"Yes, I think he is, reluctantly so. Ordinarily, if this were Fort Lauderdale and if Wes were any other guy, I'd be pursuing him with every feminine weapon

I possess. But this is homey little Bayberry Cove, and I have to tread more carefully. Each time I start to, well, get close to him, I get this horrible attack of guilt.''

Vicki huffed an incredulous breath. ''You, my take-no-prisoners friend, feel guilty?''

''Yes, and it's the pits. I can talk myself out of any kind of guilt most of the time. Except not now. Wes is just too…'' The right word failed to come to mind.

''Noble?'' Vicki suggested.

''Okay, yes, and…''

''Trustworthy?''

''Yes.''

''Uptight?''

Louise laughed. ''Definitely that, though maybe not as much as when I first met him. It's just that he's so…good. Every instinct I have screams at me to tear his clothes off, but my conscience butts in and tells me to behave myself.'' She sighed. ''What am I going to do, Vic? This man isn't just a romp in the sack.''

Vicki put her elbows on the table and gave her friend an earnest look. ''Lulu, I can't believe I'm saying this, since for the last fifteen years you've continually shocked me with your outrageous behavior, but I honestly believe you're analyzing too much. You're letting Wes Fletcher intimidate you, subtly but surely, and the Lulu I know and love wouldn't let that happen. You're who you are, and despite some of the things I've said to you in the past, I've always admired the woman you dare to be. And a lot of men have responded pretty favorably, as well.''

Dear Vicki. She could always find the best in any

situation. And she was right. Men usually reacted to Louise in positive, flirtatious ways that she normally encouraged. But it was time to clear up a misconception that Vicki had been living with for too long. Louise leaned forward and clasped her hands on the table. ''I've got to tell you something, Vic, and I hope it won't burst any bubbles you may have about me.''

''There's nothing you can't tell me,'' Vicki said with a little grin. ''Though maybe there are still things that could shock me.''

''This probably will. The truth is, Vic, where my exploits with the opposite sex are concerned, I've often talked a bolder game than I've actually played.''

Vicki's eyes opened wide with surprise, but Louise sensed it was mostly for show. ''You mean you've lied to me?'' her friend asked.

''Not lied so much as exaggerated a few times. I decided long ago that when you work in a man's world, it's best to create an aura that makes them think you have the upper hand, both in and out of the workplace. But,'' she added, ''to my knowledge, I've never really hurt anyone. I've always maintained certain ground rules where men were concerned, and I played fair.''

That's why this relationship with Wes, whatever it was, had become so disturbing, she thought. Maybe her rules no longer applied. Maybe her attitudes were changing since she'd come to this quirky little town where everyone knew his neighbor's business and really cared about it.

Now it was time to tell Vicki what was really troubling her. ''Here's the truth, Vic,'' she said. ''Deep down I know that Wesley Fletcher doesn't really want me. I'm not his type and I never will be.''

Vicki jumped to her friend's defense. ''That's silly, Lulu. How do you know what Wesley's type is?''

''Because he practically told me so yesterday. He actually questioned me about my domestic skills. What a laugh, huh? He asked if I cooked or quilted or did anything homey.''

Vicki sat back in her chair. A look of genuine shock crossed her face. ''He didn't!''

''Yeah, he did, the poor guy.''

''Well, then, that proves it. Wesley Fletcher doesn't know his type himself. Because, Lulu, I've seen his eyes when he's talked about you, and honey, you're his type.''

''But he doesn't want me to be. And even if he did, he knows that anything that might happen between us can only last a few weeks. I'm not staying, remember? I'm going home once I figure I've become the nice person Roger Oppenheimer wants me to be.''

A mischievous twinkle lit Vicki's eyes. ''Then I'm not worried, because that will never happen. Besides, look at me. Six months ago I never thought I'd be living in Bayberry Cove.'' She rubbed her belly. ''And living for two.''

''And it's fine for you.'' Louise laughed softly. ''But imagine *me* living in Bayberry Cove!''

''Well, what if it works out between you and Wes?'' Vicki asked.

''It won't. That's what I've been telling you. I've never been really serious about any man. I live by my own standards, which certainly aren't anything like

Wes's. And besides, we're on opposite sides of a legal battle. This is probably not the best time for us to get involved.''

"Oh, pooh," Vicki said. "I know you're committed to helping the women at the candle factory, and that's fine. But it's not like you and Wes are arguing Roe versus Wade here. You probably won't even go to court over these issues.''

"No, but I'm pretty sure that if it ever came down to seriously sliding between the sheets, Wes's ethics would kick in at the last minute and he'd run like the wind. Remember, he is solid, moral, not to mention what you said—uptight.''

Vicki reached across the table and covered Louise's hand. "My dear Lulu, Wes Fletcher is forty years old. He's responsible for his own decisions, and if he gave in to temptation with you, it would be because he wanted to. I'm sure he's quite capable of bearing the consequences of his actions." She smiled with a coyness Louise hadn't seen before. "Here's what I think, my friend…''

Louise smiled back at this woman who had been her confidante and support for more than a decade. "What *do* you think, Vic?''

"I think it's time to loosen Wes up a bit. The candle factory case won't last forever, anyway. Maybe he needs to learn that it's okay to separate business from pleasure. And who better to teach him than you? My guess is he'll thank you for it.''

Jamie came around the corner of the houseboat. "I hear you ladies plotting to snare Wes.''

"We're not plotting anything," Vicki said, giving Louise a knowing look her husband couldn't see.

"Don't get me wrong. I'm all for it," Jamie said. "Wes has been running from women since he broke up with Donna. It's time he let one catch him." He jerked his thumb down the side of the houseboat. "You can start chasing right now. He just drove onto Pintail Point."

CHAPTER TWELVE

As WES DROVE UP THE causeway, he was relieved to see lights still burning in the Malones' houseboat. It was almost ten o'clock, late to be calling on friends even if it was a Saturday night. And too, married people seemed to live by a different clock than single ones.

He pulled his Jeep alongside Jamie's pickup, got out and walked to the boat. Beasley lumbered around from the bow and stood staring at him from the cat-walk.

A few feet from the narrow bridge that connected the boat to land, Wes crouched down and whistled softly. "Hey, Beas, how ya' doing?" The dog crossed over and rolled to his back. Wes took the hint and scratched his belly.

Jamie came out to greet him. "Wesley, my lad, what brings you to the *Bucket O' Luck* tonight?"

Wes stood, followed Jamie and Beasley onto the boat. "I hope it's not too late," he said. "I have a favor to ask."

"Of course it isn't too late. Wait here." Jamie ducked inside the boat and returned with a couple of beers. "Let's go on the porch."

Jamie walked ahead to the deck at the bow. Just

when Wes rounded the corner, Jamie made the announcement he should have made before there was no turning back. "Vicki and I have company tonight," he said, as if that simple statement weren't designed to rattle Wes to his toes. "I'm sure that's all right with you." He held out a beer.

Wes stood like a statue, the cold bottle sweating in his hand. Both women stared at him, Vicki with an amused expression on her face and Louise with something near horror on hers. Vicki scooted a chair to the table with the toe of her sneaker. "Hi, Wes. Sit down."

The scowl he leveled on Jamie was wasted. His friend was enjoying this. Still, he showed a modicum of commiseration by handing him the second beer. "Here, I figured you could use both of these," he said under his breath.

Wes set one bottle on the table and screwed the top off the other. Seeing no alternative, he settled into the chair next to Louise.

"Jamie, why don't you see what's in the kitchen," Vicki said. "Are you hungry, Wes?"

He took a drink and set the bottle down. "Couldn't eat a thing. I just came from that big Italian restaurant by the interstate. My dad bought one of everything on the menu."

"I'm surprised," Jamie said. "My mother doesn't usually eat Italian food."

Wes frowned. "Kate wasn't there, and I wish to heaven she had been. This separation or whatever it is she's forced on my dad is driving me crazy. He's probably gained ten pounds since Kate quit cooking for him. And I've gained five.''

Vicki nodded dramatically. ''Isn't it silly how this whole candle factory business is making everyone in town so edgy?'' She took a sip of tea. ''Pure nonsense if you ask me. Anyone should be able to see that whatever happens at the candle factory shouldn't affect personal relationships.''

Wes gaped at Vicki while Louise coughed and seemed to shrink in her chair. Jamie affectionately patted his wife's hand. ''Didn't I get me a wise ol' gal here,'' he said, and then turned his attention to Wes. ''Now, then, what's that favor? Assuming you can ask it in front of the ladies.''

Grateful that the conversation was now on a safe topic, Wes drew a normal breath. ''I need you to check on my aquariums in the shed for a while. I won't ask you to do anything too complicated. Just see that the temperatures remain at a constant level, check a couple of gauges, that type of thing. I'll leave a chart.''

Louise sat forward in her chair. ''You're going away?''

''For a few days. I've been called to Newport.''

''Why?'' Jamie asked.

''When I took semi-retirement, one of the conditions was that I'd be available to teach classes in civil law at the Naval Justice School in Rhode Island. One of the regular staff is ill, so they called me in.''

Out of the corner of his eye he caught Louise staring at him. ''When are you leaving?'' she asked.

''Monday. I'll be back next Saturday night.''

"Oh." The single syllable was soft, almost childlike. Wes rolled his bottle between his hands. "You're not sorry to see me go are you, Counselor?"

She put her confident grin back in place, and he felt a little disappointed. "You know what they say about small towns, Wes. The loss of one person diminishes us all."

"Funny. I've never heard that one." He looked at Jamie. "So, can I count on you?"

"You can indeed." He winked at Vicki. "Remind me to buy extra tartar sauce at the market this week, love. With me watching the gauges, I've a hunch we'll be having fried fish."

Louise stood up. "Now that that's settled, I have to be getting home."

Without thinking, Wes blurted, "Your car's not here." *Idiot! Now she knows you actually looked for it when you drove up.*

"Very observant," Louise said. "Vicki drove tonight. We were in Morgan City doing some shopping." Louise picked up her purse from the deck. "Ready to take me home, Vic?"

Jamie gave Wes a pointed stare. "I won't have you two women driving along Sandy Ridge in the dark. I'll take you myself."

"Don't be ridiculous, Jamie," Louise said. "It's perfectly safe—" She stopped abruptly and frowned down at her friend. Wes had seen the exchange under the glass-topped table. Vicki had just kicked Louise's leg.

Several seconds went by before Wes said the line

he supposed had been scripted for him by the Malones. "Never mind, Jamie. I'm leaving, anyway. I'll take Louise home."

Louise gave them all a look that would have made the most stubborn jurors quake in their boots. "Well, gee, I don't mean to put anyone out."

Jamie jumped up and tugged on the back of Wes's chair. "You're not putting Wes out. Like he said, he's got to go, anyway. Why have two cars out on Sandy Ridge, when one will do quite nicely?"

Wes stood, swept his arm toward the catwalk of the boat. "Okay, then. Miss Duncan?"

He followed her to the Jeep, marveling at how he'd been roped into this. And thinking how much he'd rather be taking her anywhere but home.

LOUISE WAS THANKFUL the top was down on the Jeep. The vast expanse of Carolina night sky gave her plenty of excuses to keep her eyes off the man beside her. She glanced through the front window, then out the side toward Currituck Sound. She laid her head back and pretended to study the stars. Despite the spectacular panorama of nature, it was still difficult to ignore the rugged profile of Wes Fletcher just a couple of feet away.

They drove slowly down the half-mile causeway. "So you and Vicki were shopping," Wes said after a moment.

"For baby things." She focused on the gravel roadway. "Not that I was much help."

He didn't respond. Of course he wouldn't. They

certainly couldn't repeat a conversation about her lack of domesticity.

"So what did you do today?" she asked.

"Actually, I did something I haven't done in months. I played golf."

She stared at him then. Yes, she could picture him on a golf course, his long, lean body silhouetted against a background of carpet-soft green grass and moss-draped willow trees. She could visualize the subtle arc of his muscled right arm as he raised the club over his shoulder, the power of his left arm, straight and sure as he drove the ball confidently down the fairway. She almost shivered at the image of athletic perfection.

"I'm really lousy at it," he said. "I never could get the rhythm of the swing."

She burst out laughing as her vision shattered.

He gave her a self-effacing grin. "What's so funny?"

She waited while he braked at the end of the causeway in preparation for the turn onto Sandy Ridge Road. "I guess you should have gone bowling," she said, knowing he would remember their conversation from yesterday.

He thrust the gearshift into first while he gripped the steering wheel with his other hand. His gaze never wavered from her face. "I thought about bowling today. Too much, probably. A guy shouldn't think about bowling when he's trying to smack hell out of a golf ball to impress his father's cronies."

She looked down at her clasped hands, away from his penetrating blue eyes. "No, I suppose not."

They sat at the juncture of the Pintail Point cause-way and Sandy Ridge Road. The Jeep's engine rum-bled patiently, waiting for direction. If Wes turned left, they would be heading toward Buttercup Cottage, and soothing sounds of the sea cloaked in the sweet-scented darkness of isolation. If he turned right, they would go to Main Street of Bayberry Cove, populated with folks feeling the energy of a small-town Satur-day night.

She squeezed her hands together until they hurt. *Turn left, Wesley, please turn left.*

He turned right. Okay, so she wasn't telepathic. Maybe Suzie had a candle for that.

Ten minutes later he pulled into a parking place in front of the furniture store. Several doors down, the Kettle bustled with late-night activity. A small group of people came out and strolled by the Jeep. A few of them stared into the vehicle, and then mumbled in reaction to seeing Wesley and Louise together.

"I probably should have pulled around back," Wes said.

"It doesn't bother me," she stated. "But then, I'm not really one of them."

"Lately I've been wondering if I am, either."

"Look, Wes, there's something I should tell you."

He curled his arm over the steering wheel and stared at her. "Louise, every time either one of us starts a sentence that way, it turns out badly."

"I know, but that's not going to stop me."

"I didn't think it would."

"Christopher Tenant. Remember that name. He's the rep from the EEOC...."

"Okay. What about him?"

"He's going to request personnel files from the candle factory records. He's doing an in-depth study on a couple of cases, specifically Bessie Granger's and Darlene Jackson's."

"Then I suppose I should warn my golfing buddies."

"Probably, although this is standard procedure."

"I know that, but the old boys still should be given the chance to stock up on antacids. Plus I'll have to tell them that a sudden unexplained fire would look a bit suspicious."

"I'm telling you this so you can go in tomorrow and make copies of the files for yourself. You should know what you're up against."

"Well then, thanks for the heads-up, Counselor."

"It's only right, Wes." She unbuckled her seat belt and reached for the door handle. "Thanks for the ride, and you take care of yourself up there in Newport, Commander. Don't let those JAG students leave a toad in your desk drawer."

"You take care in Bayberry Cove, Louise."

She got out and closed the door. Before she walked away, he said, "And don't go bowling without me."

THE NEXT MORNING, Wes walked into his father's office at the Fletcher estate, eyed the imposing man who was just hanging up the telephone, and wished he were anywhere but here. This wasn't going to be easy. "Got a few minutes, Dad?"

Haywood stood up from behind his ornate rosewood desk, placed his hands on his hips and said,

"What a coincidence, son. I just happen to have a question for you."

"Oh? What's that?"

The old man glowered at him. "Have you gone crazy, Wesley Fletcher?"

Wes strode across the room and sat in a plush leather chair. "Good morning to you, too, Dad," he said. "And to answer your question, before I took semi-retirement, a naval doctor gave me a psychological examination, and he didn't find anything particularly disturbing."

Haywood pointed an accusing finger at the telephone. "Then he hasn't heard the rumors I've been hearing lately." He came around the desk and stared down at Wes. "You've been cavorting with that lady attorney, haven't you?"

It was all Wes could do to stifle his laughter. Yet when he recalled that magnificent kiss Louise had delivered at his front door last Friday night, and this past Friday when he'd nearly lost his head over her in the cottage kitchen, he decided he probably had been guilty of a little "cavorting." And those incidents didn't take into account the wild dreams he'd been having about her, as well. He smiled. Fantasy cavorts, he supposed they were. But since he wasn't about to admit any of this to his father, he said, "It depends what you mean by cavorting, Dad."

"Dudley Boggs's son Chester was on the shrimp boat Friday morning, and he saw you and a brunette take off from Buttercup into the sound. And then last night, Hatch Winslow's wife was escortin' her grandkids out of the ice-cream parlor in town, and she saw you and Miss Duncan sittin' for all the world to see in front of the furniture store.'' Haywood's bushy eyebrows came together in a scowl. ''What do you have to say to that, Wesley?''

''I'd say that ten-thirty at night is awfully late to have two little kids at the ice-cream parlor.'' Wes settled one leg over the opposite knee and matched his father frown for frown. ''And I'd say that where I was last night is none of your business.''

Haywood huffed in frustration. ''You're going to ruin us, son. You can't make nice with the woman who's trying to tear down the very fabric of this community.''

''Oh, come on, Dad. Where are the dramatics coming from? If you want to look at Louise as the enemy, that's your problem. As I see it, I drove a lady home last night. Big deal. It just so happens that lady is trying to help out the female employees down at the factory. I hardly think that constitutes the total annihilation of everything we consider sacred in Bayberry Cove.''

Wes's explanation was amazingly simple, and he surprised himself by believing for a moment that his relationship with Louise could actually be viewed in such an uncomplicated context.

Haywood pounded one fist into his opposite palm. ''That's because you don't own one-third of the candle factory. And at this rate you likely never will! Once those women get their grips between our trouser legs, they'll never let go. They'll be pushin' for day care centers and birthday parties, and who knows what all.''

Despite Haywood's vulgar language, Wes knew his father was genuinely concerned. While the Bessie Granger and Darlene Jackson cases wouldn't change the course of history, they likely would have a noticeable effect on Bayberry Cove. As far as Wes could remember, there hadn't been any significant change in town for years. Bright red geraniums still bloomed all summer in the town square flower beds, and the same people still worked the same jobs at the candle factory and elsewhere. He'd just never realized that not everyone was happy with the situation.

His father gave him a pleading look. "Tell me you're not getting serious about that woman."

"Relax, Dad. No, I'm not serious about her. And even if I were, she's not the least bit interested in staying in Bayberry Cove. This is just a stopover for her."

Haywood's expression grew even more grim. "That's right. You don't need another gal like Donna who'll put her career above everything else. This one's cut from the same cloth. She's stoppin' by long enough to wreak havoc, and then, like that hurricane last year, she'll breeze off, leavin' the mess for the rest of us to clean up."

Hurricane Louise. That was an impression Wes's imagination could grab on to. He'd certainly considered that Louise had the power to leave his life in a mess when she took off. And like a hurricane, she sure created a thrill while she was around.

He was about to tell his father that he hadn't come to talk about his past marital mistakes when Kate scurried by the open door, her bright red hair a blur in her determination to avoid the office. Nevertheless, she'd obviously noticed Wesley, because she reappeared a second later, keeping her hand on the door frame.

"Hi, Kate," Wes said.

"Hello, Wesley. I didn't mean to ignore you. As we all know, I can't abide rudeness in any form."

"Except when you direct it at me," Haywood mumbled.

"What's that, Haywood?" Kate asked.

"Where you off to now, Kate?" he replied, ignoring her question.

"I'm going to Bessie's." She held up a canvas sack. "I went to the movie store today and selected a number of rentals for us to watch. I'll let Bessie and Pete pick what they want to see."

Haywood snorted in displeasure. "Hellfire, woman. That beats all. When's the last time you rented a movie to watch with me?"

"I honestly can't remember, Haywood. We've seen all the John Wayne movies at Blockbuster." She dangled the sack to irritate him. "There's not a war movie or western in here."

He waved her off with a flick of his hand. "Then go on and watch your sissy movies. I'll just fend for myself *again*." He gave his son a slap on the back that was apparently meant to seem jovial but practically knocked him out of the chair. "Where do you want to eat tonight, Wes? How 'bout that build-your-own-burger place? They hand you a half pound of raw meat and you cook it yourself."

Wes's stomach did a flip. "Actually, Dad, I thought I'd go back to the—"

"Yessir, the burger place it is," his father announced with finality. Kate frowned at the two of them and flounced off.

Wes stared up at his father with a look meant to convey his impatience. "Why don't you just ask the woman to marry you? You're obviously miserable without her."

"Am not. I wouldn't ask her now, anyway, not the way she's been acting. She treats me like the flea—"

Wes sighed. "I know. You told me. She's only doing that because she's trying to get through to you. She wants permanence in her life. She's tired of living—"

"I know what she wants." His father leaned against his desk and released a long sigh. "And I've given her an option in that regard. She knows I'm never going to marry again without having safeguards in place…"

"What kind of safeguards? You can't mean a prenuptial agreement."

Haywood's cheeks flushed with what might have been uncharacteristic embarrassment. "You know my track record of picking the wrong women," he said. "I've lost small fortunes!"

"Dad, Kate's not the wrong woman. I know that and so do you. Just trust her and you won't be sorry." When another thought occurred to Wes, he added, "Or maybe you're afraid she'll turn you down after all these years."

Haywood scoffed at the notion. "Shoot, no. She'd

grab my hand in marriage quick as a glowworm's twinkle…'' he strode to the window and looked out ''…despite being the finest piece of Irish frippery ever to come across the Atlantic.''

''Then swallow your pride, or whatever it is that's holding you back, and ask her.''

Almost as if he'd stopped listening, Haywood's voice became calm, reflective. ''That Kate…she's pretty as a shamrock, feisty as a Thoroughbred and sexy as a siren. And what made her perfect was that she needed me. She was grateful for every little thing I did.'' He turned back to Wes as the ends of his mustache lifted in a suggestive grin. ''And she showed it in the most interesting of ways, if you catch my meaning.''

Haywood paced in front of his desk. ''And now, since that damn lady attorney came to town, Kate's acting like the Queen of Sheba—givin' orders and steppin' out. It puzzles me, Wes. It puzzles me something fierce.''

Wes suppressed a grin. ''So, she's the queen, and all of a sudden you're something less than king.''

Haywood grimaced at the reference. ''I suppose.''

''You'll figure it out, Dad. You're a smart man.''

''I won't figure anything out on an empty stomach. Let's go eat. You drive.''

''Wait a minute, Dad. I came here to tell you something.''

''Well, out with it.''

Wes told him about his upcoming trip to Newport to fill in at the Naval Justice School. Once he'd convinced Haywood that, yes, the navy really could com-

mand his presence in spite of the controversy in Bayberry Cove, Wes delivered the next bit of bad news.
"There's a man in town," he said. "His name is
Christopher Tenant, and he's with the Equal Employment Opportunity Commission in Raleigh."

"And he's trouble."

"Maybe. I don't know. But he is going to request
some specific personnel files from the factory. And
Justin Beauclaire has to give them to him."

Haywood shook his finger as if it were a metro-
nome. "Justin won't do it. He'll burn the damn things
first. I know how he thinks."

"Well, he'd better not. If I hear that Mr. Tenant
encountered so much as a 'No sir' or a 'Can't find
them' from anybody at the factory, I'm off the case.
And tell Justin not to tamper with anything in those
files. I made copies of them today, which I'm taking
with me to Newport to study, so I'll know if he
changed even a decimal point."

Haywood scowled. "Whose side are you on, Wesley?"

"Not to sound corny, Dad, but I'm on the side of
justice. And if I can achieve that and still save the
factory's reputation, then I'll have done my job.
We're going to have some wiggle room on some issues, but you've got to let me handle it."

"Like you're handling that Duncan woman, I suppose."

"Dad…"

"Okay, okay. Have you met this Tenant fella?"

"No, but he's probably just doing his job, too. Remember, give the guy a break while he's here."

"All right. I'll behave myself. Now, can we eat?"

MERCIFULLY, the restaurant Haywood chose offered a grilled chicken breast sandwich, fully cooked. It was still early when Wes dropped Haywood off at the estate, and he didn't especially want to go back to Buttercup Cottage. His packing was all done. The aquariums had been set up so Jamie could monitor them. If he went home, there was nothing to do but try to find a decent television show among the twelve channels he could pick up with the cottage antenna.

He drove toward town and let an impractical thought take root in the often-ignored part of his brain that resisted logic and common sense. He actually considered stopping by Louise's apartment. Thank goodness reason prevailed and he avoided making the worst possible decision a lonely guy could make. Instead he pulled into the parking lot of the Brew and Bowl and went inside.

It wasn't crowded on this Sunday evening. Wes spoke to a few Bayberry Cove old-timers and took a seat at the bar. He'd have one beer, watch a little baseball and head home. Unfortunately, the game didn't keep him from thinking about Louise. He figured she'd have a laugh if she knew he was at the bowling alley thinking about her.

He pushed Louise to the back of his mind and tried to imagine what the EEOC rep, Christopher Tenant, was like. Probably a methodical, middle-aged government geek who was even more compulsive about his habits than Wes himself was.

Nothing at all like the thirty-something fella in blue jeans and a golf shirt sitting next to him. Wes noticed the man because he was talking on his cell phone, and making no attempt to keep his voice down.

''Don't expect me back in Raleigh anytime soon,'' he said into the phone. ''If you could see this lady attorney who's filing for the workers, you'd understand.''

Wes's ears perked up instantly. He glanced at the man's profile and watched a huge grin form on his face.

The guy took a sip of what appeared to be a gin drink and said, ''Hot? You bet she's hot. Star quality all the way.'' He cupped his hand at his own chest as men do when they're describing a certain female attribute. ''I can just picture her in one of those bikinis like the models in *Sports Illustrated* wear.''

Mr. Subtle glanced over at Wes and kept the grin in place. If he expected a fellow male to appreciate his hormonal tirade, he was going to be disappointed. Wes smirked at him, took a swig of beer and stared at the television.

Undaunted, the man continued his conversation. ''Right now she thinks I'm all-business, but I'm having dinner with her again tomorrow night. If I have my way this time, we'll give the case studies a quick going-over, and spend the rest of the night with a bottle of wine, good music and the pursuit of happiness.''

Wes hadn't been tempted to punch anyone's lights out since his senior year in high school. But his right hand itched to knock a few teeth out of Christopher Tenant's stupid grin. Not that Louise needed his help.

She could wipe the floor with a guy like Tenant, just as she'd nearly done that day with Luke Plunkett. But would she want to? That was the question that would bug Wes for the next week.

Going to the bowling alley had turned out to be a bad idea. So had telling his father to cooperate with the jerk the EEOC had sent from the capital. Wes gulped the rest of his beer and left the bar. Getting away from Bayberry Cove was the best thing he could do right now. And the worst.

CHAPTER THIRTEEN

LOUISE TURNED ONTO Route 17 North and reached
for the handwritten directions lying on her dashboard.
"The costume shop is on Lansing Street in Norfolk,"
she said.

Vicki took the sheet of paper from her hand. "I'll
read. You drive." After a few seconds she said, "It's
easy. Lansing is just inside the Norfolk city limits."

Louise wiggled in her seat, adjusted the rearview
mirror, tugged on her seat belt and fidgeted in general.

"Will you relax?" Vicki said.

"I still can't believe I'm doing this," Louise responded. "And I can't believe that you encouraged
me."

"Are you kidding? This is about the best idea
you've ever had."

Allowing a hint of pride to influence her response,
Louise said, "I suppose it is, and it's not like it's
totally out of character...."

Vicki let out a snort of laughter. "I should say it
isn't."

Louise tried to appear offended. "I was about to
say that it's not *totally* out of character...but playing
dress-up is a little crazy—even for me."

"Quit worrying. Wes will love this."

"I hope you're right."

"I am right. Wesley is the kind of guy you need to jolt into motion, and this plan will do that. And remember what I keep telling you, Lulu. Wes is a big boy. He can handle himself and make his own decisions—even about having sex, which means you are wasting good energy worrying that you're somehow trapping him. Trapping implies action that is cunning and calculating. You're seducing, and that's fun. Big difference. And Wes is a guy. There's no guy alive who wouldn't be totally flattered by what you're going to do. So don't even think about backing out."

"I'm not going to back out," Louise assured her. "Wes Fletcher is driving me crazy, and he's not even here. I can't sleep, because I'm always thinking about him. I can't eat. I've never let a man invade my space like this, and it's only Thursday. He left three days ago, yet it feels like he's been gone forever. And I'm not even related to him."

Vicki gave her a coy smile. "Not yet, anyway."

"Not ever, and you know it."

"I don't know any such thing, and neither do you. But any major decision along those lines can't happen until you get this particular event out of the way. You're both mature adults. You're obviously enormously attracted to each other. But you need to know if you're compatible in every way."

What was happening here? Louise always advised Vicki in matters of the opposite sex. Now the tables were turned. "This from a woman who was married for thirteen years before she ever made love with her husband," Louise said.

Vicki frowned. "No fair! You promised you'd

never bring up the marriage-of-convenience issue again. And besides, when I found Jamie after all that time, I knew at once he was worth waiting thirteen years for.''

''You get no argument from me on that.''

''And you could be just as happy with Wes.''

''Not when I'm litigating in Fort Lauderdale and he's collecting fish in Bayberry Cove.'' Suddenly uncomfortable with the topic, Louise said, ''Can't we talk about something else?''

''Sure. How are you going to get into Buttercup Cottage?''

''That's not another topic, Vic, but I'll tell you anyway. Wes hardly ever locks the door, but when he does, he told me he hides the key under a rock by the front steps.''

''Okay, so that's solved. Now tell me, how'd everything go with Chris Tenant?''

Louise wasn't too keen on this subject, either, but at least it was a change. ''He's a strange guy,'' she said. ''Professionally, I guess everything went well. He requested some files from Justin Beauclaire on Monday, and we met to discuss them over dinner Monday night.''

''Again?'' Vicki said. ''I can tell there's more to this story.''

''Right. We ate and came back to my apartment to discuss the particulars of the cases. A few minutes after he arrived at my place, I swear he was coming on to me.''

Vicki gave her a blasé look. ''There aren't too many guys who don't come on to you, Lulu.''

''But this particular guy shouldn't have. He's here

to perform a government service. And besides, he was much too obvious about it. When he got out of his car and came up the stairs to my place, he had a bottle of wine in each hand.''

"What did you do?''

"I thanked him for the wine and put it in a cupboard. And then I offered him a cup of coffee. About an hour later he moved over to the sofa where I was sitting and snaked his arm over the back cushion. I got up to get a glass of water. When I came back, I spread out the papers we were studying on the coffee table and handed him a pencil. Then I sat on the floor.''

"The poor guy," Vicki said.

"Poor misguided guy, you mean," Louise said. "I would never prejudice a case by fooling around with the person who decides its outcome. That really would be misconduct.''

"So where is Tenant now?''

"He went back to Raleigh. He said he would put together the appropriate charges against the candle factory once he checked his statutes. I just hope that when I poured cold water over his libido, I didn't extinguish his enthusiasm for settling this quickly.''

"I hope you did," Vicki said. "If Tenant stalls, that means you might have to stay in Bayberry Cove longer than you anticipated.''

"I'm afraid that's not going to happen," Louise said. "I'm going back to Fort Lauderdale in five weeks, assuming Oppenheimer calls me. Tenant knows that. If everything's not wrapped up by then, I'll handle it from my home office.''

"But you have to be here for the Fourth of July.

Jamie says Bayberry Cove goes all out for the holiday. There's a parade and banners on the downtown shop windows, and a picnic...."

The flippant remark Louise might have tossed out a few weeks ago never came because she actually agreed with Vicki that an old-fashioned Fourth did sound appealing. "We do celebrate the holiday in Fort Lauderdale, too," she finally said, "even though I've never participated."

"Well, we'll see," Vicki said smugly. "The first step is getting to Norfolk and making our purchase at Sophie's Costume Shop."

LOUISE HADN'T HEARD from Wes all week. But she hadn't expected to. They weren't in a call-me-from-out-of-town relationship. They weren't in any definable relationship at all. But he had phoned Jamie to inform him when he expected to be back in town. He was driving all day Saturday and would arrive about eight o'clock. That schedule gave Louise a lot of time to prepare.

At five o'clock on Saturday she packed a few gourmet goodies and a bottle of Chris Tenant's wine into her picnic basket and put the food, her costume and a few decorations into her car. She was about to leave when—on impulse—she entered the furniture store and waited for Suzie McCorkle to finish with a customer.

"Hi, Louise," Suzie said. "You look real nice. Going out tonight?"

Going out? More like breaking in. She certainly couldn't tell innocent Suzie what her plans were. It was enough that she was going to shock Wesley in a few hours. "Thanks," she said. "I am going out and that's why I stopped to see you."

"What can I do for you?"

"I thought you might have a candle that's meant to stimulate…" She stopped and stared at Suzie's beatific features. How could she explain to this sweet-natured woman what she wanted this candle to do?

She tried again. "I'm looking for a candle that encourages a man and woman to, well, take their mutual attraction to the next level. What I mean is…"

"Passion!" Suzie clasped her hands under her chin. "You want a passion candle."

Louise tried to conceal her surprise. "Ah… exactly."

"Wait here." Suzie scurried into the back room and returned with an eight-inch pillar candle wrapped in black cellophane and tied with a silver cord. She slipped the knot on the ribbon to expose the top of the candle. "I don't let just anyone see this color," she whispered. "Not everyone can handle it." She tipped the candle so Louise could see it. "Look for yourself." Suzie breathed deeply, sucking the essence of the candle into her lungs. "Experience the redness."

Louise looked. This candle was no ordinary red. A person would never find this color hanging from an apple tree or painted on a child's wagon. No, this was a color to make the devil jealous. This red dazzled, bewitched, burned the cornea of anyone who dared steal a peek at it. And it smelled of passion. Rich, deep, a smoky, sinful Far Eastern scent that clung to the nose and swirled in the head. Louise gasped in awe. "It's perfect."

Suzie leaned in close and giggled. "And it works, believe me. I light one every year on New Year's Eve. Evan and I have never failed to ring in the holiday with a few fireworks of our own." She retied the cord and slipped the candle into Louise's purse.

"Suzie, you're making a candle convert out of me," Louise said.

"Not me, dear, the candles make their own magic. Have fun."

LOUISE CALLED VICKI on her cell phone when she passed by the causeway to Pintail Point. "I'm almost there," she said.

"On my way," Vicki responded. She met Louise at the front door of Buttercup Cottage ten minutes later.

"Where'd you park your car?" Vicki asked.

"I left it on the side of the road just around that curve," Louise explained. "Is Jamie ready?"

"Yep. He's going to call Wes in a little while to determine his true ETA. He took the letters from Wes's mailbox and is going to pretend he did it by mistake and Wes should stop by the houseboat and get the mail before coming home. Then, as soon as Wes leaves the *Bucket,* Jamie will call us, and I'll get outta here. The rest is up to you."

Louise found the rock, retrieved the key, and the two women went inside. Vicki looked around at the furnishings. "Sheesh, this guy *is* a neat freak."

"Tell me about it," Louise said. "I'm just hoping he doesn't get upset when he sees I'm wrinkling the bed linens."

"No man is that big a freak," Vicki murmured

encouragingly. "And something tells me Wes Fletcher is capable of twisting a few sheets himself when the right woman is involved."

"I guess we'll find out."

For the next two hours Louise and Vicki turned Wes's compact, clean little world into a scene of seduction. They hung nets from the bedroom ceiling and decorated them with crab trap buoys and colorful plastic sea creatures from the party store. They replaced Wes's hundred-watt bulbs with softer ones and hung wispy blue scarves over the lamp shades. They plugged in the CD player and inserted a disc of soothing ocean sounds. They exchanged Wes's percale sheets for aqua- and cream-colored satin ones. And last, they displayed Louise's snacks on silver trays and uncorked the bottle of wine.

At seven-thirty Louise took her costume from its plastic bag and laid it on the bed. She surveyed the room and smiled. "It looks good, Vic. I'm starting to believe I won't regret the two hundred bucks I spent for this outfit." She wiggled into the tight bottom and hooked the bra top. She draped her throat with a shimmering mother-of-pearl shell necklace and attached silver seahorses to her ears. She was trying different positions on the bed when Vicki's cell phone rang.

"He's on his way," she said. "I'm gone." Vicki picked up her purse and rushed to the exit. Before she crossed the threshold, she turned to admire their efforts one last time. "It's perfect, Lulu, and you look like dynamite."

"Wait!" Louise hollered as Vicki started to leave. "The candle. We forgot it."

Vicki came back and lit the wick. "Now then, remember what I told you. Just be yourself."

They both stared at the sparkling scales that slithered down Louise's legs and the large, fan-shaped fins that covered her feet and draped across the foot of the bed. "Be myself?" Louise repeated, and they both burst into a fit of laughter.

After Vicki left, Louise decided that seducing could indeed be fun—unless the seducer totally misread her target.

WES TURNED OFF the causeway from Pintail Point and headed toward Buttercup Cottage. *That was the strangest meeting with Jamie just now,* he thought, glancing at the stack of envelopes beside him. *What was so important in this batch of ads and bills that couldn't wait until tomorrow?*

"People are just funny I guess," he said aloud, and rolled his shoulders to relieve the stress of driving for hours. He was halfway to the cottage when he noticed the headlights of another car. He glanced at the driver as they passed each other. Even in the darkness he recognized Vicki Malone. What was she doing driving on Sandy Ridge at this hour?

Of course, seeing Vicki reminded him of Louise. Not that he needed any outside stimulation to bring her to mind. He'd been thinking of her for weeks, and never more so than these last six days while he'd been out of town. He'd gone over the chance encounter with the EEOC rep in his mind dozens of times and always with an unsatisfactory conclusion. Louise and Christopher Tenant had had dinner together on Monday night. But was that all they'd done together? Had

Tenant been successful in his attempts to lure Louise into bed?

Wes's hands tightened on the steering wheel. All right, so he had no claim on Louise, but surely she wouldn't, she *couldn't* succumb to the sleazy play of a guy like Tenant.

But what if she had?

Wes turned into the driveway of Buttercup Cottage, parked around back and lifted his suitcase from the rear seat. He hadn't bothered to change after leaving his class records with his commanding officer this morning, and after the long drive, his dress whites needed a good pressing. He'd drop them off at the cleaners on Monday. Even if he didn't need them again for a while, he liked knowing his uniform was ready to wear at all times.

"You can take the boy out of the military," he said as he opened the back door of the cottage, "but you can't take the military..."

He stopped just inside the door. What was that sound? It was lyrical, like muted chimes in a gentle breeze. And waves, swishing and receding in soothing repetition. But it wasn't coming from outside. It was coming from his... No. It couldn't be coming from his bedroom.

He dropped his suitcase on the kitchen floor, passed through the living room to a short hallway that led to the two bedrooms. As he approached the larger of the rooms, he noticed a soft aqua glow coming from the partially opened door. And an unusual smell. It reminded him of the market in Marakesh. He hadn't thought of that exotic place in years.

"What the hell...?" he said aloud. Having no idea

what to expect, he slowly pushed the door open the rest of the way. Part of him tingled with the prospect of getting to the bottom of the strange stimuli assaulting his senses. Another part shuddered with the thought that he should return to the living room for the fireplace poker in case he needed to defend himself against an intruder.

He stood on the threshold, his legs spread wide, his hands clenched at his sides, and stared into the darkened room lit only by a blue glow shimmering under silken scarves. His mind absorbed many details at once. Nets hanging from his ceiling. Starfish, glass balls, sea life dancing along his walls. And those chimes. Delicate, seductive. And that scent. Cloying, mysterious.

And that intruder!

The woman who had haunted him for the past six days leaned slightly forward from pillows piled against his headboard. Her long black hair spilled over one shoulder and curled at the top of a scanty bra-type thing that revealed enough ivory flesh to set his blood boiling. And her legs…whatever she was wearing covered all of her gorgeous legs in glittering sequined splendor that hugged her hips and molded to her calves like a second skin.

He took a step closer, half expecting the strange, alluring image to fade. It didn't. In fact the very real vision moved again, gliding with grace and elegance along satin sheets.

"Louise?" he whispered hoarsely. The word was nearly lost in the elusive melody of tinkling chimes.

She smiled. "Welcome home, sailor."

She shifted on the bed, and the strangest sight stole

his breath. Her feet—no, her *fins* lifted from the mattress and fluttered in a brazen salute. "I'll bet you've never caught anything like me before," she said.

He was rooted to that spot just inside the bedroom door. His eyes took in all of her while his feet refused to lead him closer. She was perfection. She was glorious. His mind careened in so many directions he didn't quite know what to do next. "Damn," he said. "You're a mermaid."

"And you're a commander in the U.S. Navy." Her lips curled seductively. "Doesn't that give you any ideas?"

One. It gave him one great big, magnificent idea. Yet he didn't voice it. He was forty years old, a graduate of the Naval Academy, a nineteen-year veteran who'd served his country, and he truly thought that if he said aloud the idea that was about to burst his blood vessels at this moment, it would come out as an ineffective squawk.

She placed her fists on her bare waist, just above the hip-hugging band of her costume. Her eyes narrowed, became serious. "Wesley, this isn't that hard to figure out. You've heard of people playing doctor and nurse? Housewife and pizza-delivery guy? This is our version. Mermaid and naval commander."

He nodded his head. "That was the idea I had."

"Well, good. For a minute I thought you were considering taking me to a laboratory for blood and organ testing."

He smiled. Finally. "No, ma'am, Miss Mermaid. I assure you. I don't have any interest in taking you from that spot right there to any other place on earth."

She patted the silvery-aqua bed. "Then come on over and test the water."

He'd never in his wildest dreams expected to be this lucky. Other guys were lucky. Wesley Fletcher sometimes found himself in favorable situations. But never in his life had he been this out-and-out damn lucky to be in his skin at this place for this wild, wonderful moment of time. He completely abandoned his rules about not having casual sex. There was nothing casual about this night. What Louise was offering him was intense, unprecedented and spectacular. And certainly not casual.

He left a trail on the bedroom floor. His polished shoes, his dark socks, his belt with the shiny brass buckle.

And, like the lucky, grateful man he was, he savored his sea creature, every touch, smell and sound of her, starting with the rattle of her seashell necklace when he unfastened it and let it drop to the floor.

He hardly recognized his own voice when he said, "Louise, how did you—"

"Don't ask for explanations, Wes," she said. "I learned today that sometimes you just have to accept the magic."

She unbuttoned his shirt, slowly enough that he thought his chest would burst through the fabric before she'd completed the job. He raised his arms, and she slipped his T-shirt over his head. His arms came down and encircled her and he pulled her close. He held the back of her head and kissed her until he was senseless and she was moaning against his lips. Damn right. It was magic. He'd analyze it later. Or maybe he wouldn't analyze it at all.

He reached around and found the hook to her bra, slipped it off and let his hands explore her breasts. He kneaded the nipples gently with his thumb and forefinger until he moved his mouth to take in one puckered tip. When that wasn't enough, he slid his hand down her slinky scales searching for the way to get to the most intimate parts of her.

"It's a zipper," she whispered in his ear. "On the side."

He found it, and the metal teeth rasped softly as he exposed her hip. Slowly, by inches, he slid the silky fabric over her thighs, down her calves to her ankles. When he'd removed the costume, his mermaid was gone, but Louise was there—all beautiful, seductive flesh and womanly desire trembling against his hands. He explored every inch of her, stopping only to return to her mouth to taste her again and again.

She worked at his remaining clothing, tugging his trousers and underwear off and flinging them to the floor. One hand splayed on his chest, teasing his nipples. Her nails rode the ridge of his back to the base of his spine. His muscles flexed in delicious antici-pation.

His tongue left a warm, damp trail between her breasts and over her abdomen while his fingers sought her inner thighs and the hot, moist center that waited for his touch. When his thumb caressed her, she arched her back and twisted her fingers in his hair. "Now, Wesley," she murmured into the spicy scented air.

He reached out, away from the bed. His hand slapped the nightstand. "Oh, God, Louise. I've got to find—"

He was only vaguely aware of her hand slipping under a pillow. She handed him a small foil square. "Is this what you're looking for?"

As he tore open the package and prepared himself to enter her, he knew that this night would be forever etched in his memory. His last lucid thought was that his fantasy cavort had become an even better reality.

LOUISE LAY IN WES'S ARMS and munched on a cracker mounded with crab dip. Never in her life had she felt so utterly satisfied—both with the company and the sexual experience. Of course, she didn't know if Wes felt the same. He wasn't the type of man who'd talk about his grocery list, much less sex. But she knew he'd enjoyed himself and that he'd willingly come to the bed of a mermaid and ended up making love to a woman.

She turned in his arms, offered him a bite of cracker, and decided to risk prying the truth out of him. "So, Commander, what are you thinking?"

He smiled down at her. "If you have to ask, Louise, then I guess everybody's been right all these years, and I truly need to work on expressing my emotions."

"No, no. You expressed them very well. But I was a little worried that you might have some regrets. Vicki called our plan a lesson in separating business and pleasure." When she noticed a strange twinkle in his eye, she added, "I guess you figured out that Vicki and Jamie were somewhat involved in what went on here tonight."

"Oh, yeah, I figured that out."

"Anyway, I have no problem in accepting the difference. I think it's entirely possible to have two independent lives, the public, business one and the private, pleasure one. But I'm not so sure you agree."

"I'll admit I had my doubts. Maybe I still do to a degree. It's hard to accept ethically that we can be on opposite sides of a legal debate and still…" He stopped, blew out a breath.

"Be lovers?" she suggested, filling in for him.

"Yeah."

"Wes, I'm ninety-nine percent certain that this case will be settled by an impartial third party. If I thought that you and I would have to face each other across an actual courtroom, I'd be a bit cautious about our relationship myself."

She ran a fingertip down his chest. "Wesley, we're both lawyers. I'm a darn good one, and I assume you are as well. So when I speak for the women at the candle factory, I'm going to do the best job I can. And I expect you to do the same for the men you're representing." She picked up his hand and kissed his palm. "I'd be terribly disappointed if you didn't."

She nestled closer to him and felt his heart beat against the side of her breast. "While this case is being settled, we're both going to do our jobs. But when we're together like this, I plan to be the best lover I can. And I'll be terribly disappointed if you don't do the same…now that I know how very *very* good you can be."

He tightened his arm around her. "You present a convincing argument, Counselor. But I wonder how this scenario will play out in Bayberry Cove."

It was understandable that he would be concerned about gossip and small-town attitudes. This was where he grew up. These people looked up to him, supported him, cared about him. She was beginning to understand how citizens of small towns felt. And it was nice.

"What we do in this room, Wesley, will be witnessed only by an audience of two," she said. "And I won't ever tell, though I may have a hard time explaining the glow that will be part of my aura from now on." She leaned up and kissed him. "In short, Commander, I know how to close a bedroom curtain and button a lip."

He stroked his hand down her waist, over her hip. "But where do we go from here, Louise?"

That was the question that had no answer...at least not yet. Louise still intended to return to her life in Florida, and she knew Wesley wouldn't give up his research for the NOAA's Fisheries Department. But in the last hour she had begun to wonder about the frequency of flights to North Carolina.

"No answer to that one?" he said.

"You want to know where we go from here?" She draped her arm over his chest and subtly moved her hand lower. When she felt the evidence of his arousal, she said, "I think you've already figured out the answer."

AT EIGHT O'CLOCK Sunday morning Louise, wearing Wes's robe, came into the bedroom with two cups of coffee. He sniffed the air, opened his eyes and sat up. "You're an early riser," he said, taking a steaming mug from her.

She sat next to him. "It's a curse. It comes from being raised by two obstetricians who've never kept normal hours. Besides, I've always done my best work in the mornings.''

He sipped his coffee and grinned suggestively at her. "I might take exception to that, but I'd like to run a personal comparison."

She reached for her purse on the floor and withdrew her cell phone. "There's nothing I'd like more, but I'd better check my messages." She turned on the power and recognized the persistent beep indicating someone had tried to reach her. She scrolled through the list of missed phone calls recorded on the small screen and frowned.

Wes leaned toward her. "Something wrong?"

"I don't know. Probably not, but I have four messages from women in town. Two are from Darlene. One is from Kate. And the other is from the Bayberry Cove Kettle, so I assume that's Bobbi Lee."

His eyes widened with amusement. "You have the Kettle's number programmed into your cell phone?"

She shrugged. "What can I say? A girl's got to eat."

She listened to the first message. Kate Malone's voice was urgent, almost desperate.

"Louise, dear, I'm trying to find you. It's midnight on Saturday. I'm at County Hospital. Pete Granger has taken a bad turn. They don't expect him to come out of this. Can you come?"

The other three messages were similar in content. Louise jammed her phone into her purse and went to the closet for her clothes. In the mirror she saw the concern on Wes's face.

"Is there something I can do?" he asked.

"It's Bessie Granger's husband, Pete. He's…" She

paused, as if time would alter the facts. "He's dying. I'm going to the hospital."

Wes set his cup down. "I'll drive you."

"No you won't." She headed for the bathroom. "I appreciate the offer. Really I do. But this concerns our public lives, Wes. It's eight o'clock on Sunday morning. Why in heaven's name would you be driving me to the hospital?" To soften her tone, she padded to the bed and kissed him. "It's time to shut the curtains, Commander. Remember?"

He didn't argue. "I hope Bessie's okay."

She was showered and dressed in ten minutes and found Wes in the kitchen. "I'll call you," she said. "And all that mermaid stuff I left in the bedroom…" She threw him a smile over her shoulder as she walked to the front door. "You can keep it here. I don't think I'll be wearing it anyplace else."

CHAPTER FOURTEEN

LOUISE TOOK THE EXIT off the interstate that led to County Hospital. Despite the serious circumstances of this journey, she was experiencing a strange sense of satisfaction that had nothing to do with the night she'd just spent with Wesley, although that had been truly fantastic. This odd contentment, or whatever it was, began right after she'd checked her messages, spoke to Kate and realized that these women thought enough of her to include her in the tragedy unfolding in one of their lives.

For well over a decade, Louise had had only one true friend in her life: Vicki Malone. She knew many other women, of course, ones in the South Florida business community, saleswomen who appreciated her patronage, female members of her health club. But she'd never been part of a family of women who cared for and looked out for each other. Since coming to Bayberry Cove, she felt as if she belonged to a kind of sisterhood.

She arrived at the hospital and found the intensive care waiting room. Kate and Darlene met her at the door. Their faces were drawn, their eyes tired, their clothes wrinkled. They embraced Louise.

"Is there any news?" she asked. "How's Bessie?"

"She's in with Pete," Kate explained. "The doctors can't do any more for him. They've just made him comfortable, but it's as if his system just shut down. They're calling it congestive heart failure, but I think Pete's just tired of trying."

"Can I do anything for the two of you? Get coffee?"

Kate smiled. "We've had enough of that to float a shrimp boat. Just sit with us awhile." She took Louise's arm to escort her to a chair, but stopped when Haywood Fletcher burst into the room.

Concern was etched on his features as he walked up to her. "Katie, what's wrong? I got up this morning to find a note that you'd gone to the hospital. I checked the names of every patient when I came in here to determine why you'd come. Thank goodness your name wasn't among them." After finding her in good health, he scowled at her, but his eyes were still shadowed with worry and relief. "You could have been more explicit to keep me from blowing my cork, you know."

"I'm sorry, Haywood. I guess I wasn't thinking. When Bessie called, I just scribbled a few words and ran out. I didn't realize how the note would sound."

"You took about ten years off my life, woman," he said, and moved as if he might take her in his arms until he realized they weren't alone. "Miss Duncan, what are you doing here?"

"Same as you, Mr. Fletcher," Louise said, and then couldn't resist a little jibe. "When a member of the community, and its largest business, is in need, we all want to lend support."

"Well, you can go. I'm here now, and I'm capable of providing the support these people need in this time of trial—"

Kate administered a jab to his ribs. "Leave off, Haywood. Now's not the time for preaching. Now's the time for praying."

He clamped his lips shut, but seemed about to speak again when Bessie Granger came out of her husband's room. Everyone stood silently as she moved toward them. In answer to the unspoken question, she nodded her head once. "It was a peaceful passing."

Kate hugged her. "Pete's with the angels now, love."

Louise told her how sorry she was.

Haywood mumbled a message of sympathy.

And Darlene marched right up to him and spewed all the frustration and anger of a tense situation and a sleepless night right in his face. "You didn't even know him, did you?" she challenged.

Haywood blustered, cleared his throat. "I knew who he was. A fine man—"

"Stuff it, Mr. Fletcher," Darlene said. "*And* your thirty percent of the candle factory. Don't think you can march in here while poor Bessie's grieving and make a few empty comments about the man Pete was. He would still be alive if Bessie'd had health coverage. If she'd been home with him more. If Justin Beauclaire had allowed her more personal time...."

Louise reached for the young woman's hand. "Darlene, don't—"

Bessie waved Louise back and put her arm around

Darlene's shoulder. "Shush, now, honey," she said. "None of that's true. Pete had the medical help he needed, and I was there for him during those times when he got real bad." She ran her hand over the girl's short blond hair. "Pete was just real sick. You know that. The factory's not to blame. Pete's time was up."

Darlene broke into tears. "But what are we fighting for? We're trying to make things better...."

"For the living, Darlene. For the future and women like you." She looked at Louise. "And we will, won't we, Louise?"

"We're sure going to try," she vowed.

Bessie grasped Darlene's shoulders and stared into her eyes. "You're exhausted. All of us are. I want you to go home and get some rest. Everything's going to be all right. We'll go ahead with our plans, just like we talked. And, honey, if you really want to do something for me, you stay away from Luke Plunkett, you hear?"

Darlene's sobs subsided and she nodded her head. "Okay. I am pretty tired." She turned around and glared at Haywood. "But don't expect me to apologize to that—"

"No, no, darlin'," Kate said. "Nobody's expecting you to do any apologizing." She kissed Darlene's cheek while gesturing behind her back for Haywood to leave.

He stalled a few seconds and looked as if he might actually try to say something. But to his credit, he backed toward the door, turned and left. A few minutes later, Darlene followed.

Kate, Bessie and Louise sat in the waiting room and discussed plans for Pete's funeral. When they'd come up with a preliminary schedule, Bessie thanked them and rose from her chair. "I'm going home myself," she said. "There's much to be done. And Louise, you might have heard what I said to Darlene. We've come up with a plan, and we need to talk to you about it." She sighed with fatigue. "But not today."

She left, and Louise studied Kate's closed expression. "Do you know what Bessie's talking about?" she asked.

"I might have an inkling," the Irishwoman answered smartly. "You probably should call a meeting of the candle factory workers again in a few days, but I'll tell you this much. The folks in Bayberry Cove, especially those boys down at the factory, are going to know that the women who make the candles are a strong and clever lot."

Louise studied the resolution in her features. "Tell me something, Kate," she said. "Why are you so involved in this? You've lived in Bayberry Cove for five years, most of it in the Fletcher mansion. It's no secret that Haywood and I are at swords' points most of the time, but you and he are apparently a good match. Why would you risk your relationship with him to stand with the factory workers?"

Kate took a deep breath. "Don't get me wrong, Louise. I do love that ornery man. And you're right. My life here has been pretty good. But for all I mean to Haywood, I've always been just on the fringe of his life, as if I'm forever standing at a door he won't open all the way.''

Louise understood. ''The door to matrimony, you mean?''

Kate nodded. ''I've been Haywood's *partner* for years now, and I thought I had to accept that I'd probably never be his wife. Then you came along and opened my eyes to the possibility of women getting what they want and deserve. Now I'm not so sure I'm willing to settle for Haywood's terms.''

Louise wasn't at all certain she wanted to take the credit, or the blame, for Kate's revelation.

''I see myself in the women at the factory,'' Kate continued. ''We want what we've been denied. Our goals may differ, but our will is the same, and we mean to be heard.'' She smiled. ''And you know? For the first time, I think Haywood may actually be ready to listen.''

''I hope so, Kate. I hope you get what you want.''

Kate patted her hand. ''Now, then, let's you and I get out of this hospital. We can't do anything more for Pete, and like Bessie said, there's much to be done elsewhere. Oh, by the way, Wesley was supposed to be home yesterday. In all this sadness, I forgot to check if he made it back from Newport. Have you seen him?''

Louise looked for some sign of duplicity in Kate's expression, some evidence that she was fishing for information she already suspected. Finding none, she said, ''Jamie's seen him, I believe.''

''Fine. Wes is a grown man, but I still worry.''

The two women walked out of the waiting room.

When they reached the hospital exit, Louise stopped Kate. "Whatever the ladies are planning, Kate, is it legal?"

"I never heard of a law against it. And even if there were, I wouldn't want to be the sheriff who tried to arrest any of us."

THE TOWN TOOK SEVERAL days to grieve for Pete Granger. At Bessie's tidy little bungalow, the dining room table overflowed with casseroles and baked goods. The garage refrigerator was pressed into service to keep cold dishes from spoiling. Included was the pasta salad Louise prepared with her own two hands and a *Good Housekeeping* recipe.

The funeral was held on Wednesday, four days after Pete's death. More than one hundred people attended, an impressive number to show respect for a man whose life had been decent and good, if not remarkable. Haywood and Wesley came, the only representatives from the so-called upper echelon of the candle factory. Despite tensions between factory workers and executives, Bessie's friends accepted the Fletchers' presence with good grace.

"What did you expect, Wes, a public flogging?" Louise teased later that night when she was nestled in his arms on her sofa. "People tend to behave themselves in the presence of ministers, coffins and a couple dozen gigantic floral displays." She traced a nail down Wes's forearm. "Don't be lulled into a false sense of security, though. I don't think you or your father will be invited to any cookouts with my friends."

"No, I suppose not. By the way, on Monday Justin Beauclaire received notification of charges filed by the women workers concerning violations of EEOC laws. As I'm sure you know, the charges involve the Equal Pay Act and the Age Discrimination Act. I'm anticipating Christopher Tenant's next step in the filing process."

"You'd better warn Justin about what is to come," Louise said. "Chris already reviewed employee records, but he may request interviews with the head of personnel and Beauclaire himself. And he'll likely visit the factory and talk to people there."

"You should know, Louise, that I filed papers requesting that the charges be dismissed."

"I expected you would. It's what a competent lawyer should do." She shifted in his arms and looked into his eyes. "You don't think that's going to happen, do you?"

"No, I don't, but I've got to earn this big salary Dad and the guys are paying me."

She smiled. "I guess our salaries are about equal on this case." Then, more seriously, she said, "This will likely go to mediation, Wes. I hope you can convince your clients to consider that as a way of bringing the issues to a close. As we discussed before, neither one of us wants to see this go to court."

"I'm all for mediation, Counselor, but if you're expecting us to give in on every issue without a fight, I have to tell you a lot depends on what you ladies throw at us. Are there going to be any curve balls?"

"Truly I don't know what my clients have in mind, but they've asked me to call another meeting, so you can anticipate something in the near future. But either way, this will soon be over.''

''I look forward to that.'' He kissed the top of her head. ''But in the meantime, I left my Jeep parked behind the ice cream shop. Do you think anyone will notice it and wonder where I am?''

''They'll just think you've popped into town for a triple fudge sundae.''

''Then they'll be wrong.'' He turned her to face him and captured her mouth with his. ''I've popped in for something much sweeter than that.''

THE SECOND MEETING of the Bayberry Cove Women's Movement for Employment Opportunities began at nine o'clock Saturday morning in Louise's apartment, with thirty-two women in attendance. She began the session by explaining the steps that had taken place so far. ''The initial facts I presented to Mr. Tenant from the Equal Employment Opportunity Commission appear to support violations of the law,'' Louise said. ''From this point on, the investigation will proceed according to the schedule of the EEOC rep.''

One middle-aged woman who was attending for the first time stood up. ''When do we go to court?''

''We don't really want to go to court,'' Louise replied. ''And we shouldn't have to. But you should know that Wesley Fletcher has asked that the charges be dismissed—''

A hoot of indignation rose in a chorus of women's voices.

''Wait a minute,'' Louise urged. ''That won't happen. His request is merely a matter of form. And he knows that the commission has already assigned an investigator to our cases.''

The woman plopped her fists on her hips and scanned the crowd with a stern eye. ''I want to go to court. Nothing can happen unless we get a judge on our side.''

''Sit down, Goldie,'' Bessie said. ''Let our attorney speak.''

Louise continued. ''The only way this will go to court is if conciliation efforts conducted by the EEOC are ignored by factory officials. That isn't likely to happen. When an EEOC representative becomes involved, mediation is almost always successful.''

''So all we're going to do is talk?'' the woman asked.

''What did you want to do, shoot everybody?'' Bessie said.

Darlene raised her hand. ''I have a question.''

Grateful to be discontinuing the court discussion, Louise gave her the floor. ''Okay, Darlene.''

''I understand that we want the company to answer to the age discrimination and equal pay charges....''

''Right.''

''But can we ask for more?''

Louise considered the question carefully. She hadn't intended to involve herself in other issues, although she did understand that health and child care concerns were important in this community of growing families. ''Any employee can petition an employer for *anything*,'' she finally said. ''You can ask the administration of the candle factory to consider any suggestions, but unless there is a specific statute governing the request, the company is not required to provide it.''

"Like health care, you mean?'' Darlene said.

"Yes, like health care. Employers in this country are not required by law to provide universal health coverage for their employees.''

Darlene reached down and withdrew some papers from a canvas sack on the floor. She stood up, thrust her shoulders back and began speaking again. ''I went to the library last week and did some research on the computer.''

"What did you find?'' Louise asked.

"I looked up the top ten companies in this country who treat their female employees with the most consideration.''

Several ladies nodded in approval of Darlene's innovative step.

"Some companies offer child-care facilities right there where the mothers work. Some even offer in-home care when it's needed.''

A few women chuckled. One said, "Can you imagine Justin comin' to the house to baby-sit?''

"Some offer paid leave to new mothers, and—'' she looked at Miranda Lopez ''—none of them make a pregnant woman give up her job when she's in her last trimester.'' She flipped through her pages of notes. ''One company has programs for women so they can learn new skills and advance themselves. And another one gives college scholarships to employees' children.''

The woman who was eager for a court battle spoke

again. "We should get some of those things." A few backed her up with encouraging comments.

"Ladies, please," Louise said. "Darlene is telling you about the top ten companies in the nation with regard to women's employment opportunities. Naturally they are going to have stellar programs, but the fact is, most companies do not." She looked around the room, capturing each woman's attention. "You can't expect the executives at the candle company to give in to demands that only the top companies in the nation subscribe to.

"And remember, until a few weeks ago, you were working under conditions that clearly violated basic government standards. We will do well to correct the most blatant violations we picked as examples without trying to change the entire structure of company operations."

Darlene dropped her papers to her side. "You mean we can't get any of this stuff?"

Louise sighed. "As I said, you can ask for anything, but you won't…" She stopped. *Wait a minute. What is mediation for, anyway? It's a give-and-take process.* "I have an idea," she said. "Which of these issues do you think is most important to you?"

After considerable debate, it was decided that health coverage and child care were most vital to the majority of women at the candle factory.

"Okay, those aren't covered by the Equal Employment Opportunities Commission, but let's try for them," Louise said. "How do you plan to make your wishes known? Will one of you appoint yourself spokesperson and meet with Justin Beauclaire?"

The women exchanged puzzled glances around the room. It seemed no one wanted to take on the responsibility of arguing their case. "We thought you would, Louise," one lady suggested.

"I've agreed to follow the mediation process with regard to Bessie's and Darlene's age and pay discrimination charges. I can't represent you on issues not covered by the EEOC. So any requests for further benefits should first come from you all. You're the ones with small children and medical bills, and I don't see anything wrong with asking the company to consider these needs."

"She's right," Bessie said. "And we've got a plan that will catch their attention."

Louise looked to the corner of the room where Kate Malone sat with a cool smile on her face. She slowly nodded her head, warning Louise that she was finally about to discover what this mystery plan was all about.

"You're absolutely right, Louise," Darlene said. "It's up to us to get those boys down at the factory to listen to us, and we know the way to do it." She grinned. "We think Wednesday night just after dark ought to be a good time...."

HAYWOOD WALKED TO the sink and ran hot water into a steaming pot. Then he added a few drops of detergent, hoping to loosen the scalded milk stuck to the bottom. "Damnation! I never knew a stove was so hard to operate. Medium ought to mean 'medium,' not 'boil over.'"

He took the glass of milk he'd salvaged and walked

toward the den. Maybe he could find a good book
that would take his mind off the fact that it was nearly
midnight on Saturday night, and he had no idea where
Kate was. He knew Louise Duncan had called a meeting of her ladies' brigade this morning, and he figured
Kate had probably attended. He'd been waiting all
day to give her a piece of his mind. A man could take
only so much, and Kate had driven him over the edge.
He was going to lay down some ground rules and get
his life back in order, or else…if only she'd come
home.

He entered the dark den and turned on the lamp
sitting on the desk Kate used to pay bills and write
letters. How many nights he'd sat close to her in this
room while she composed page after page to her two
boys, who'd been in prison in Ireland for more than
a decade. She never gave up on those two, always
planning for the time they'd get paroled and come to
America. He didn't have the heart to tell her that any
militant Irishman who'd been imprisoned for setting
bombs and blowing up businesses loyal to British rule
wasn't ever going to be given a visa to enter the
United States.

He smiled now as he perused the books lining the
den walls. "Never underestimate Katie," he chuckled
to himself. "She's got enough old-fashioned grit to
take on the entire immigration service and get those
boys over here, after all."

He turned away from the bookshelf to settle into
his favorite chair with a copy of *Ivanhoe* in his hands.
Instead he found himself staring into soft hazel eyes

that looked up at him from a face sad with weeping. "Kate! I didn't know you were home," he said.

She wiped a tissue under her eyes. "I've been here awhile," she said. "I was thinking about my lads, just as you were now, about the way their paths ended up. Thank goodness Jamie never got caught up in their rebellion. They never hurt anyone, you know that, don't you, Haywood?"

"You've told me, Kate."

"They destroyed property, and that was wrong. They were angry boys with fire in their hearts. But everything they did was for a cause they believed in." She shook her head. "Believing in causes can sometimes break a heart."

Haywood set his milk and book on an end table and sat in an uncomfortable straight-backed chair close to the one she occupied by the cold fireplace. "What is it you want, Katie?"

"I want to see my sons again."

"I'll send you to Ireland then. Whenever you want to go."

"That's not all, Haywood. I want you to ask me to marry you and go with me as my husband."

He squeezed his eyes shut, not daring to look at her. "Ah, Kate, you know how I feel...."

"Yes, and you know how I feel."

"You've told me before, woman. And we've always disagreed. I'm not going to marry again without a prenuptial agreement. Four mistakes is enough for any man...."

She sat straight and faced him squarely. "So, that's how you see me, Haywood? As another mistake?"

"I don't know, Kate. It wasn't how I saw the others until it was too late. Until I'd lost—"

"Back to your money again, is it?"

"Kate, be reasonable. We've both been down the rocky road of marriage."

"If you're referring to what I had with Frank Malone, you're wrong. It wasn't marriage. It was bondage. I never had the real thing with Frank—the trust, the pledge of faith, the true meaning of words spoken at an altar."

Her eyes pleaded with him so much he could barely look at her. "I want it now, Haywood, without your fancy legal document meant to destroy the union of a man and wife. I want your pledge to me, and mine to you, in the eyes of God, to be all we ever need. And I want it before I'm too old and gray...and bitter."

He reached for her hand. She let him hold it, but her fingers were limp, unresponsive. He couldn't really blame her, but he'd had four wives, and all of them had stripped him of his pride and half his bank account. He thought he'd done it right with Kate. He'd kept his assets while being generous to her. "I never meant to hurt you, Kate," he said. "But you know I won't marry you unless it's on my terms. Ask me anything else." He smiled at her, squeezed her hand. "Ask me for the moon, Katie, and I'll deliver it on a sterling platter at your feet."

"I have no use for the moon, Haywood." She stared into his eyes with an intensity he found almost too much to bear. "I don't want your money. You can keep every cent of it. And I won't sign a paper saying our marriage is based on mistrust. I only want your name and your word, spoken in front of our friends and family, that you believe my pledge to you is true.''

''But you have my love, Kate. It has to be enough.''

''Not anymore, dear.'' Her gaze wandered to the window, which looked out over the front drive and from there to Bayberry Cove. ''I want what they have out there.''

''Who, Kate? What who has?''

''The people who live in Bayberry Cove, in little houses with platters made of crockery, not sterling. They're women with husbands who've not signed a thing but a marriage license.'' She turned to look at him again. ''I want to be like them.''

His world had been so perfect. He'd been in charge of it, and Kate had let him rule. If she'd been unhappy—and he supposed she had been sometimes—she'd mostly kept it to herself. She'd brought up the marriage issue a time or two, and he'd thought they'd discussed it logically. She'd always dropped the subject when he wouldn't budge. Until now. Until this lady attorney had come to town and upset his perfect world. He supposed that Louise Duncan was going to have her way about some things. But not this.

He stood up. ''I'm sorry, Kate. I want you to stay here with me, but on my terms. They're the same terms you've lived with for five years. And I'm the same man.''

Her lips trembled, then curved upward. It was a sad, accepting kind of smile. ''Yes, Haywood, you are. I'm going to bed now.'' She left the room and Haywood knew that, once again, Kate's bed wouldn't be his.

He didn't find out until the next morning that she'd moved in with Bessie Granger.

CHAPTER FIFTEEN

WES SAT AT A TABLE by a window in the Bayberry Cove Kettle and scowled down at his plate of cottage cheese, pineapple, and green salad. He should have ordered the Philly cheesesteak. That's what he really wanted, not this rabbit food. And then he thought of his expanding waistline and resigned himself to doing the right thing.

He scooped a mound of lumpy cheese onto a fork, looked out the window and spied a familiar face. Thank goodness. At least he wouldn't have to consume this miserable lunch alone. He rapped on the glass, catching Jamie Malone's attention. Jamie smiled and headed for the restaurant entrance.

"What's up?" he said as he plunked himself down in the chair on the other side of Wes's table. "And good God, what are you eating?"

"No comment. Have you had lunch?"

"Nope."

"Then order something wonderful that I can at least smell," Wes insisted.

Jamie called Bobbi Lee over. "What's good today, Bobbi?" he asked.

"Same as every Wednesday, Jamie, as if you didn't

have the menu memorized. Corned beef hash, and Max is piling it on pretty thick today.''

"Okay, I'll have that. And a Mountain Dew.''

Bobbi wrote the order on her pad and then curled her hand over one well-rounded hip. "So, you boys gonna be around tonight right about dark?''

"Hadn't planned to be," Jamie said. "But you're not the first female who's hinted that there's something going on in town tonight. You want to provide more details?''

Bobbi arched her penciled brows. "Nope. Don't care to at all. But I think you should be here, and spread the word, too.'' She gave a pointed look at Wes. "And since I've gotten over being mad at you, I'll advise you specifically to be here.''

Wes waited until she had left before he said, "You know what's going on?''

"Haven't a clue.''

"Where did the girls go this morning?''

"I don't know that, either." Jamie set his chin on his fist and glanced out the window. "Wherever two women go to spend money when one of them is pregnant and the other one is chasing a man." He dropped his hand and gave Wes a guilty half grin. "About that chasing thing, I hope you're not steamed over the part I played in that little stunt a week ago Saturday.''

Wes laughed. "I have to admit you confused the heck out of me when you pilfered my mail, and I was a little concerned when I walked into the cottage and realized I wasn't the only one there.''

Jamie chuckled. "I'll bet you weren't half as scared as when you recognized exactly *who* had broken in.

A burglar is easier to handle than Louise when she's on a mission.''

Wes purposely picked at his food and pretended nonchalance. "I handled her just fine," he said. "I've even left the net and all those plastic starfish hanging on the bedroom wall to remind me of Lulu's Big Adventure."

Bobbi brought a platter of corned beef and set it in front of Jamie. He dug in with all the gusto Wes lacked.

"So where do you and Louise go from here?" Jamie asked between bites. "It must be hard to meet in secret so folks in town won't know what's going on."

"It's tough, but I've come to terms with it. We're taking it day by day right now. In a few weeks Louise is going back to Florida, and I'll have collected enough data to start preparing my reports to a congressional committee."

Jamie's jaw dropped. "Whoa! So it's going to be back to square one with the two of you? Like this whole thing has just been a spring fling?"

"I guess so." Wes took a swig of coffee and found it bitter. "I don't have to like it, but all along I've known that Louise and I are about as different as two people can be. And she's been forthright in telling everyone her future doesn't include a life in Bayberry Cove. She would never be happy here, and since I've been back, I've come to accept that I'd never be happy anywhere else."

"Have you asked her?"

"Asked her what?"

"If she could be happy here? She might surprise you."

"I don't have to ask. She's told me a lot about her practice in Fort Lauderdale. She's a very successful attorney with a long list of corporate clients. She came up here to see Vicki and to mellow out, as she puts it, but she fully expects to go back to her job. And she should. She's invested a lot of time and skill in that position."

Wes pushed his plate aside. "Even if she flat-out said she loved me, which she won't because I don't think she does, I couldn't ask her to stay here. It wouldn't be fair. There's only enough work for one attorney in this town, and Dad's got it covered. And we all know how Dad feels about Louise. He's not about to share the town's legal dilemmas with her. He blames her for everything from the split between him and Kate to the crabgrass in his backyard."

Jamie shook his head. "That's another mess, isn't it? Your father and my ma going their separate ways."

Wes nodded. It definitely was a mess. Kate Malone was the best thing that had ever happened to Haywood, and in Wes's opinion, his father was a damn fool not to do whatever it took to keep her in his life.

"My faith in the course of true love is being tested in this town lately," Jamie said. "I almost regret helping to set you up with Louise. Maybe it wasn't such a good idea."

Wes had pondered that very thing several times. And he'd always come to the same conclusion. He wouldn't have missed a minute of Louise's amazing company for anything. She'd revitalized him, challenged him, made him laugh and made him happy. She wasn't at all the kind of woman he'd pictured for himself when he came back to Bayberry Cove with semi-serious thoughts of settling down and starting a family. Now, though, he had no problem envisioning lazy summer days and long winter nights with her nestled in his arms at Buttercup Cottage.

But that wasn't her dream. She would never be a stay-at-home wife. She was big-city excitement and sophistication.

He leaned over and squeezed Jamie's shoulder. "It was a great idea, my friend. The best one you've ever had—next to going after Vicki." He motioned for Bobbi Lee to bring the check. "In fact, I'm going to buy your lunch, even though I'm jealous of every bite you took."

Wes left several bills on the table and walked to the door with Jamie. "So what about tonight? You going to be here?"

"I wouldn't miss it," Jamie said. "Something tells me this is going to be a night for us lads to stick together."

IT WAS JUST AFTER DARK when Wes noticed a glow coming from the square. He found the last parking space down the street from the shops, got out and started walking. Not only were all the parking places taken, but cars lined the entire perimeter of the square and filled the side streets. The light from the square grew brighter as he came closer. When he reached the furniture store, he looked up at Louise's windows. Dark. She was out here someplace.

He crossed over, captivated by a flickering glow that permeated the entire two acres of the park. The dusky saffron hue was produced by hundreds of candles! Candlelight was everywhere. On the benches, in the bandstand, hanging from tree limbs. And scattered across the green lawn as if the clover had caught fire.

He stopped at his grandfather's bench and regarded the old man. Mason had a huge grin on his face. His foot was beating time to the strains from a trio of guitars and women singing an old Bob Dylan song, "The Times They Are A-Changin'."

"Good evening, Wesley," Mason said. "Looks like we're having a good old-fashioned country jamboree."

"It does at that, Grandpa." If he didn't know that trouble was brewing in Bayberry Cove, Wes might have tapped his foot along with his grandfather. He might have strolled down the row of concession wagons and tasted a candy apple, or bought himself a hot dog and a soda. That's what the kids were doing. But all this laid-back charm was masking the very real purpose of this night's events. The true meaning could be read in banners stretched between trees and flags waving from women's hands.

We Love Our Children. Keep Our Babies Close. We Support a Child Care Center. Justin Beauclaire, Open Your Eyes. A few signs advocated universal health care as well. Wes read one message after another as a steady procession of women passed by in an organized demonstration.

"Don't this beat all?" Mason said. "I wish Buttercup was here to see it."

The reference to his grandmother made Wes smile. From what he remembered of the outspoken lady, he believed if she were still alive, she might be carrying a sign of her own.

"Hope they don't burn down the town, though," Mason added.

It didn't seem a credible threat. The women had thought of everything. The candles Wes could see were elevated on metal platforms or tucked into punched tin boxes, keeping the flames out of the wind. And for extra precaution, the town fire truck was positioned just off the square.

Though he feared the answer, Wes leaned down to speak into his grandfather's good ear. "Gramps, where did they get the candles?"

The old man cackled with genuine good humor. "Been stealin' 'em for weeks, from what I heard. Right out from under Beauclaire's nose."

"I was afraid of that," Wes said.

"Wes! Wesley Fletcher! Don't you move!"

Wes heard the voice and flinched at the commanding tone that could only belong to his father. He turned around and saw the powerful figure of Haywood Fletcher bearing down on him. He wanted to ignore his father's warning and move as fast as he could, but naval commanders stood their ground, even if it was littered with miniature fires and flowery scents.

"Hi, Dad. How you doing?" he said when Haywood practically barreled into him.

"How am I doing? What kind of a question is that? How do you think I'm doing? These crazy women are burning up profits left and right."

"Excuse me, Mr. Fletcher, but that's not exactly true."

All three men gawked at Bessie Granger, who'd silently come up behind them.

"You didn't steal these candles from the factory?" Haywood challenged.

"Well, yes, we did, but they're mistake candles."

Haywood's face turned crimson, a fitting color for a night consumed with fire, even harmless twinkling little blazes. "What are you talking about?"

"Surely you know about the factory's policy with regard to mistakes, Mr. Fletcher," Bessie said.

"Of course I know it. We do, don't we, Wesley?"

Wes shrugged. "I don't know it."

Bessie smiled patiently. "Bayberry Candles are known across the nation for their quality and reliability. If anything goes wrong in production, if a dye is slightly off, if the wicks aren't completely straight, if the pillars are slightly tipped, if the scents—"

"Go on," Haywood said irritably.

"Well, those candles that don't meet the rigorous standards of our executive inspectors are thrown into giant bins and are either recycled into wax slabs that must be removed of color and scent, or, if they're not reusable in any form, are tossed into the Dumpsters. I've always thought it quite a wasteful practice, really."

Haywood snorted. "So you're saying you ladies have been filching the mistake candles?"

"Exactly. Every day for weeks, a few at a time in our lunch buckets or purses." She smiled sweetly. "Your profits are safe, Mr. Fletcher."

"Hardly safe, Mrs. Granger," he bellowed back. "You women are causing enough of a ruckus to upset candle factory operations in a much larger way than the loss of a few mistake candles. You've got the whole town buzzing about what's going on at the factory."

"In all honesty, Mr. Fletcher," Bessie said, "that is exactly what we intended. We felt this was an appropriate way to draw attention to our cause, in an orderly, law-abiding way. Mr. Beauclaire has never listened before...." She gazed off across the square to where Justin was standing close to a van with an antenna reaching high into the night sky. "I think he's being forced to consider our wishes tonight."

Haywood squawked in mortification. "That's a Channel Six News truck next to Beauclaire!"

"Oh, hell," Wesley said. "And that's Louise with him."

Haywood cupped his hand over his eyes and squinted hard. "That woman in the pink suit is a reporter for the eleven o'clock news. Wesley, you get over there and do damage control. We don't know what Beauclaire is saying. And I don't even want to think about what that attorney friend of yours is spouting off about."

Wes took off at a jog. "I'll do what I can, Dad." As he closed in on the group at the van, he was caught in the glow of a spotlight running off the van's generator. The reporter, Justin Beauclaire and Louise were in the center of the beam. The reporter held a microphone.

"So it's your contention, Miss Duncan," the woman said, "that the Bayberry Cove Candle Company has been guilty of Title VII labor and employment violations for a number of years?"

"Exactly," Louise answered. "We intend to prove that female employees at the factory have been consistently overlooked for pay raises and promotions."

Justin was growing red in the face, and he actually grabbed for the microphone. Wes stepped up in time to stop him, but was unsuccessful in silencing his verbal outburst.

"Tarnation!" Justin said. "There's just not a word of truth to what this lawyer is telling you. We're all a happy family at the Bayberry Cove Candle Company. There's never been a day when our employees weren't treated with respect and dignity."

"So there have been no pay raise violations, and women have advanced according to their merit?" the reporter asked.

"Absolutely—"

Wes cleared his throat. "Excuse me, Justin, if I may…"

"And you are?" The reporter shoved the microphone at Wes's jaw.

The light swerved to his face, and he blinked at its intensity. "I'm Wesley Fletcher, legal advisor to the candle factory."

"And what is your take on these proceedings tonight, Mr. Fletcher? Did you know the women had organized a public demonstration?"

He darted a glance at Louise, who responded with a slight nod and an almost imperceptible rise in one shoulder, as cocky a shrug as he'd ever seen. Was she enjoying this or regretting the fact that she hadn't warned him?

"No, I wasn't aware of the activities in the square tonight, but I certainly have no objection to the women expressing their opinions in an open forum such as this one."

"And do you agree with Mr. Beauclaire, that no violations have occurred?"

"Of course he agrees with me," Justin interrupted. The reporter quickly switched the microphone to pick up Justin's comments. "Wes here is a hometown boy." He jabbed a thumb in Louise's direction. "This lady attorney's come from Miami or someplace. What she knows about Bayberry Cove wouldn't fill a thimble."

Wes discreetly stepped in front of Justin. "Whether or not violations have occurred is not for me to say. This matter will undoubtedly progress to the mediation stage, at which time I'm sure a conciliatory agreement will be reached between both parties."

"And what about the women's desires to have a day care center at the factory and health care provided by the company?"

"Those are not issues regulated by the Equal Employment Opportunity Commission," Wes said. "The women are of course within their rights to voice any of their suggestions to the owners of the candle factory. But the owners are under no obligation to comply with demands not covered by Title VII and the EEOC.''

The reporter turned away from the group and commanded the attention of her cameraman. ''There you have it, folks. It's almost a festive atmosphere in little Bayberry Cove tonight. But aside from all the candlelight, music and refreshments, issues of extreme importance to this community are taking center stage. Is this a case of some good old boys ignoring federal labor statutes for years? Or are we looking at an example of the age-old animosity between the sexes? Either way, I'd say the ladies have the advantage tonight. We'll keep you posted. This is Rochelle Vassar, 'Channel Six Nightly News.'''

Ms. Vassar flashed a dazzling smile at each of the people she'd interviewed. ''Thanks, folks. You can catch this story tonight at eleven.''

Louise walked off to join a group of women who'd been watching events unfold. She was soon swallowed up by the enthusiastic females, whose expressions clearly indicated that they thought they'd scored a victory in the interview.

Wes escorted Justin away from the news van. ''I think we did pretty good, Wes,'' Justin said. ''Came across like real men who aren't going to lay down and roll over just because a few women are trying to scare us.'' He grasped the lapels of his jacket and practically strutted to the bench where Mason and Haywood Fletcher—and about a dozen other men with worried expressions—waited.

''It'll be on at eleven,'' Justin announced. ''Can't wait to see what I look like on TV. Wes sounded real good using all that legal lingo. And I managed to say a few choice words about that lady attorney from Florida.''

Haywood looked as if his last meal was about to stage a revolution. He stared at Wes, obviously searching for some sign that Justin hadn't single-handedly inspired the citizens of Bayberry Cove to come after the factory executives with tar and feathers.

Wes rolled his eyes. It was the best he could do.

WES TUCKED THE BAG he was carrying under his arm and left the town square. It was eleven o'clock, and the banners and flags had been taken down. The concession trucks were gone. The determined demonstrators, curious onlookers and baffled men had gone to their homes. And as Wes walked down the dark, deserted street he knew that in the next few minutes Bayberry Cove was going to be in the spotlight, at least for the area serviced by Channel Six News in Raleigh.

He smiled, something he'd managed to do quite often this evening as he'd encountered the people he'd grown up with, and tried to explain that the events at the factory weren't signaling the downfall of civilization as they knew it.

He glanced up at Louise's windows again as he passed by McCorkle's. Still dark. She was probably watching the news with her clients. He felt a stab of disappointment that he wouldn't see her tonight. In spite of everything that had happened, he'd come away with one significant conclusion. Louise looked darn good in candlelight.

His Jeep seemed lonely and forlorn in the last parking spot at the end of the street without even the glimmer of one streetlamp shining upon it. He opened the driver's door, slipped inside and immediately encountered two long, slim legs encased in denim stretched out along the passenger-side floor. He jerked back, nearly falling out of the vehicle, and dropped his sack between the seats.

"'Bout time you got here," Louise said.

"Good God, Louise, are you trying to give me a heart attack?"

"Sort of. But not in the way you're thinking."

She pulled the lever at the side of the passenger seat, raised herself from a reclining position and rotated her neck. "I'm glad you're here finally. I'm in pain from crouching down to avoid public detection." She scanned the deserted neighborhood. "It looks okay now, but you might want to start driving just in case."

He glared at her, but couldn't begin to come across as angry. He was simply too delighted to see her. "You beat everything, you know that?"

"I'm trying, but I'm not all that familiar with my competition. And speaking of competition, you pulled off the Channel Six interview quite well. I'm impressed."

"Gee, thanks. Need I tell you that it was totally impromptu? I didn't have a chance to prepare any comments."

"Yeah, I know. I couldn't give you a heads-up on

this one, Wes. Lawyer-client privilege. The girls wanted to catch Beauclaire off guard.''

"And they did.''

She smiled. "He sounded as pompous as I'd hoped he would.''

"As pompous as I'd hoped he *wouldn't,*'' Wes countered. He started the engine. "Where do you want to go?''

"I don't care. You'll think of someplace.''

He already had a destination in mind and headed west out of town.

"Have you checked your mail today?'' she asked.

"Yes, a lot of good it did me. The regular mail person was off, so naturally I didn't get delivery.''

"Oh. I'm sure you'll get a letter tomorrow.''

"From whom?''

"Christopher Tenant. Remember, he's the rep from—''

"I know who he is.'' Wes scowled out the side window.

"Anyway, he's coming on Monday with a federal mediator. We're meeting in the council room at city hall at one o'clock. You're supposed to bring Beauclaire, Winslow and McGovern.''

Tenant was efficient, Wes decided, along with other, less admirable qualities. He'd interviewed the factory executives by phone this week after requesting more company records, and now had already arranged the mediation. Wes wasn't kidding himself. He knew the men were going to have to give in on a number of issues. They were guilty as hell of good ol' boy management. But if he could keep them quiet, at least he might preserve the company's dignity and end the proceedings on a cooperative note. And keep the women from running away with benefits that would seriously threaten the company's finances.

As if reading his mind, Louise said, "So what did you think of the demonstration tonight?"

"The music was good."

She laughed. "I saw you talking to some of the men when it was over. Are they giving you a hard time?"

"Some of them. Guys like Evan McCorkle and a few of the older husbands of factory workers. They aren't too happy about Saturday meetings and Wednesday night carnivals." He smiled at her. "But they'll get over it. Pay raises will go a long way to smooth ruffled feathers. But Beauclaire and the boys—that's another story. Frankly, Louise, I'll just be glad when this is over and things can return to the way they were before this mess started. I need to forget about law and all the entanglements this case has brought to my life, and get back to my NOAA studies full time."

Aware of her sudden intense stare, Wes turned to face her. "What's wrong?"

"I was just thinking about something," she murmured. "It doesn't matter." She focused on the bag he'd dropped earlier. "What's in there?"

Feeling a little foolish because he hadn't expected her to discover his contraband, he smiled sheepishly. "What do you think? Candles."

"Really?" She reached for the sack. "May I?"

"Help yourself."

She opened the bag and dumped a half-dozen candles on her lap. "You took these?"

"Hey, they're only mistake candles, anyway."

"What are you going to do with them?"

"I'd planned to take them home." He watched her face for a reaction. "They're good to use when someone unexpectedly drops by. Someone who looks especially great in candlelight."

Whatever was bothering her seemed to fade from her features, replaced with a grin. "Why, Wes Fletcher, you *are* a romantic."

"That's me. But now I've changed my mind."

"You have?"

Was that confusion on her face? Disappointment? Whatever, he had her wondering what was on *his* mind for once. "There's this place about ten miles from town. It's something you should see."

"Oh?"

"It's our very own waterfall, in Bayberry Park. Quite an attraction for an area that's at sea level. It's a real waterfall with rocks and a babbling brook at the bottom. A result of some prehistoric earth burp, I imagine."

She looked out the window, seemingly aware for the first time that they'd been driving for a while. "Is that where we're going?"

"Yep. It's after eleven o'clock on a school night, so I figure the teenagers who usually hang out there have gone home. I've got a blanket in back. I thought we'd sit awhile, watch the moon on the falls, light some candles and have a little demonstration of our own."

She pretended to be stunned at his announcement, a good acting job, since he doubted Louise was ever truly shocked about anything. "Ohh... Are you saying that you're taking me to a make-out spot?"

"That's what I'm saying. Unless, of course, you want to go home and see yourself on TV."

She carefully replaced the candles in the bag. "Would I have been in this Jeep if I wanted to do that?"

CHAPTER SIXTEEN

JUST BEFORE ONE O'CLOCK on Monday, Louise stood in front of her dresser mirror and adjusted her silver medallion so it lay against her skin in the exact center of the open placket of her blouse.

"I've always admired that piece," Vicki said from the sofa. "Didn't you tell me it was an old family crest?"

"That's right. My mother inherited it from her grandmother, who originally brought it from Scotland. I've always thought of it as sort of a good luck charm. Anymore, I don't think that's so true."

"Why not?" Vicki asked. "Don't you think the mediation will go your way today?"

"Yes, I think it will. I was referring to a matter that is more personal. And frankly, I believe my luck has run out in that regard."

Vicki was thoughtful for a moment before she said, "So this has nothing to do with the career side of your life. I can only assume, then, that you think your luck has run out with regard to Wes Fletcher."

"How'd you guess?" Louise asked sardonically. "By the end of the day, the women at the candle factory will have opened some very significant doors. Unfortunately, Wes and I will have closed some."

"What are you talking about? You and Wes see each other nearly every night, don't you?"

"Yeah. I guess I like long goodbyes."

"Goodbye? This is June fourteenth. You're not leaving till the end of the month."

"That was my original plan, but things have changed. I've decided to return to Fort Lauderdale by the end of the week. I called my cleaning lady this morning and told her to give my condo a good going-over, that I would be sleeping in it on Thursday night."

"No!" Vicki sat forward on the sofa and gaped in shock at her best friend. "You're telling me that we've only got a couple more days together? Has Roger Oppenheimer called you to come back?"

Louise sighed. "No, he hasn't, and that is something of a problem. But he did suggest I take a couple of months off, and it's only been six weeks." She picked up the navy-blue jacket of her business suit she'd brought from home, and slipped her arms into it. "I have to believe that I'm going to hear from him soon, and that I still have a place at the firm."

Vicki's expression turned angry. "You have a place here, Lulu. Don't you know that?"

Vicki's words stung. "As what, Vic?" she snapped back. "An attorney without a license to practice in North Carolina? A sometimes-companion of Wes Fletcher's, someone to keep him occupied while he searches for a proper wife who cooks and cleans and waits for his boat to return from Currituck Sound every day?"

"He doesn't want that in a woman."

Louise stared hard at her friend, trying to make her see what she herself already knew. "Yes, he does, Vicki. And he should. He has a right to settle down with the woman of his dreams and accept nothing less."

"But you're that woman."

"I'm the woman of his fantasies, honey—not his dreams. And I've been happy to play that role while I've been here, but now it's time to accept reality and go home."

"What makes you so certain that Wes wants this classic homemaker you're describing? You could be wrong."

"We talked last night, a lot. Mostly he told me about Donna, his first wife." Louise picked up her purse, rummaged through it to determine she had her wallet, cell phone, the essentials. Doing something so mundane kept her from thinking too seriously about last evening's conversation. "And now I understand what he didn't come right out and say. I am a lot like Donna. I'm driven, competitive, independent." She smiled when she remembered Roger Oppenheimer's assessment of her character. "But I am nicer now," she admitted. "Bayberry Cove has brought out the compassion in me, I think. But I'm still not Suzie Homemaker." She laughed, though it sounded cold, like breaking ice. "Hell, Vic, I'm not even as domestic as you are, and you're the busiest woman I know. You keep tabs on a business in Fort Lauderdale while you light up the life of a doting husband, and build a house and a baby at the same time."

Vicki blushed, something she did more charmingly

than anyone Louise had ever known. "Of course you're not me. You're uniquely you. There's no one else like you, though many women would like to be. And I don't care what you say. You're the woman Wes Fletcher wants."

"He wants me in the bedroom," Louise admitted. "But he wants someone else entirely in every other room."

"Have you asked him about this, Lulu? You're very analytical and usually right about your instincts. But in this case I think you're trying to get into Wes's head, and coming up with the entirely wrong conclusions."

Louise snapped her purse closed and picked up her briefcase. "That's where you're wrong, Vic. Wes told me he couldn't wait for this whole candle factory situation to be over. That all he wants is to get back to his old life with his fish and his aquariums and his one-man show to save Currituck Sound. He wants the peace and quiet he came back here for."

"He said that?"

"Yes, indeed. And it's okay. He had a satisfying life before he met me, and I don't blame him for wanting to go back to it now. And I had a satisfying life, as well. And I'm going back to it. Square one, Vicki." Louise forced a smile. "There's nothing wrong with solidly planting your feet on square one. For many people it's where they belong."

"Have you told him you're leaving?"

"No. I just decided a couple of days ago. I'll tell him today." She smoothed her jacket over her skirt. "How do I look?"

"Like you're going to win, at least at the mediation," Vicki said. "But then, you always do."

"Nobody wins all the time, honey." She patted Vicki's tummy. "Except maybe you. So don't mess up now."

The women went downstairs. Vicki got in her car and headed toward the *Bucket O' Luck.* Louise looked down Main Street toward city hall. It was a short walk. She didn't need her car. As she passed the BMW, she couldn't help noticing that Bayberry Cove dust had settled on the normally pristine black exterior. She smiled, thinking how the small town had worked its way into her life in the strangest of ways.

She'd only gone a few feet when she heard Mason Fletcher call out to her from his bench in the square. "Today's the day, isn't it, Louise?"

Having a few minutes to spare, she crossed over. "This is it, Mason."

He chuckled. "Don't make my grandson look too bad."

"Nobody could. Least of all me."

He smiled a bit, crinkling his eyes. "What'd you think of the demonstration last Wednesday night? Imagine those gals from the factory takin' all those mistake candles and lighting them all over the town square. Damn clever if you ask me. Put them to good use, too."

Louise consulted her watch. "That they did," she said. "Well, I'd better go." She started to walk away, Mason's words replaying in her mind. *Put them to good use...* She stopped suddenly. An idea had popped into her head, as if some serendipitous fate had struck a deal with her common sense. She turned, hurried back to the bench. "Mason, will you still be here in a couple of hours?"

"Can be." He slipped his cell phone out of his pocket. "That fussy nurse of mine doesn't come for me till I call her on this gadget."

"Great. I have a business proposition to discuss with you."

That settled, Louise strode purposefully to city hall.

KATE MALONE TOOK her powder-blue sweater out of the bureau in Bessie Granger's guest bedroom and folded it over her elbow. It would look fine with her white blouse and gray skirt in case the temperature was a bit chilly in city hall. Besides, her gray jacket, which would have been preferable in this instance, was still at the Fletcher estate, so she had to make do without it.

She walked down the short hallway of Bessie's bungalow and stepped into the living room.

Bessie came out of the kitchen looking confident and very un-Bessielike in black slacks and a red blouse. "Too much for an old denim gal?" she asked, plucking at the satiny fabric of the shirt.

"Absolutely not," Kate assured her. "Red is a power color. That's what you need today." She glanced with some embarrassment around the parlor, which was brilliant with flower arrangements, none of which had anything to do with Pete's funeral now twelve days past. Those bouquets were on his grave site.

"How long are you going to make him suffer?"

Bessie said, leaning over to smell a particularly resplendent arrangement of pink roses.

Kate had moved out of Haywood's house nine days ago, and now, an equal number of floral arrangements occupied every flat surface of Bessie's living room. The first to arrive—a modest little bouquet of white carnations and baby's breath—was currently turning brown in the sunlight coming through the bay window. The card, a simple white vellum, had succinctly stated Haywood's demands. "Kate, come home." Since then, the arrangements had become more elaborate and so had the flowery sentiments expressed on the cards.

"I don't know," Kate answered honestly. "Until Haywood stops letting flowers speak for him and says the words I want to hear himself." She gave Bessie a sympathetic look. "But I will start clearing out some of the older bouquets tonight. It really is an excessive display."

"He has apologized on many of these cards, you know," Bessie pointed out.

"Oh, yes, I know." Kate picked up her purse and marched to the door. "I'm just not convinced he knows what he's apologized for."

Bessie followed her outside. "I appreciate you going with me today, Kate, but I doubt they'll let you into the mediation room."

"That's all right. I'm content to be your moral support in the hallway." Kate squeezed Bessie's hand. "You'll know I'm there."

Once they were in Kate's car, Bessie presented an interesting challenge. "What if Haywood is there in the hallway providing moral support to Justin Beau-claire?''

Kate carefully backed out of the driveway, put the car in drive and shot down the narrow street. ''That's his right, of course, but it won't make a bit of differ-ence to me. Besides, he won't be. Wesley told me that Haywood has more or less washed his hands of the whole affair.'' She grinned with a small show of victory. ''It seems he wasn't too pleased with Justin's performance on the news the other night, and has de-cided to remain in the shadows for once and let Wes handle everything.''

''That doesn't sound like Haywood Fletcher,'' Bes-sie observed.

Kate nodded. ''And that, my dear friend, is a good sign.''

LOUISE MET BESSIE and Darlene in the hallway out-side the meeting room in city hall. ''How are you both feeling?'' she asked.

''Ready to go,'' Bessie said. ''Good or bad, I'm not afraid of the outcome.''

''Me neither,'' Darlene said. ''I'm ready to kick some corporate butt.''

Louise laughed. ''That's good, Darlene, but let me do the butt-kicking in there, okay?''

''You're the boss.'' She took Louise's elbow and leaned close to her. ''We are going to win, aren't we? And if not, you're going to help me get another job?''

Louise patted her hand. ''We're going to win, Dar-lene. Not everything, but enough. And if this turns out the way I think it will, you are going to like your new job at Bayberry Cove Candle Company.''

After an encouraging word from Kate, the three women entered the meeting room. Wes was already there, seated between Justin Beauclaire and Hatch Winslow. Along with Warren McGovern, head of sales and marketing, they occupied one side of a conference table. The ladies walked to the opposite side.

''Hello again, Mr. Tenant,'' Louise said to Chris, who sat at one end of the table. In this formal situation she would never have considered using his first name. And from the scowl on his face, she doubted she'd ever use it again.

''Ms. Duncan.'' He gestured to a man at the other end of the table. ''This is Harold Freeman, a federal mediator who works for the Equal Employment Opportunity Commission.''

Louise shook the man's hand and introduced her companions. After the ladies were seated, she spoke to the three executives from the candle factory. ''Nice to see you again, Mr. Beauclaire,'' she said. He mumbled a guttural response.

And then she allowed herself a good long look at Wesley. Despite her years of experience and normally cool demeanor, Louise was thankful she was sitting. Otherwise her knees might have buckled with the flush of heat making her body feel limp and tingly at the same time.

In a charcoal suit, white-and-gray pin-striped shirt and a tie with a dash of royal blue, his sandy-colored hair neatly parted and spiked onto his forehead, this ex-navy man was a model of civilian sophistication.

And sexy as hell. She arched her brows in a silent message she was certain Wes would understand and said, "It's good to see you looking so well, Mr. Fletcher."

He gave her a little grin. "Ditto, Ms. Duncan."

The mediator took over. "All right then. All participants are present, so let's begin." He tapped a pen on a fan of papers spread out in front of him. "I've had a chance to look over the charges by Mrs. Granger and Miss Jackson as they've been presented by Mr. Tenant, our investigator. So let me start by giving you my conclusions."

Mr. Freeman's conclusions coincided with Louise's expectations. Personnel records supported Bessie's claims that she had been passed over for promotions a number of times, the most recent being when a relative of Hatch Winslow's had been hired as supervisor of candle-making operations. Also, pay raises had been denied her without substantiation.

Wesley argued that Bessie had never made her expectations known through proper channels, and the company had perhaps acted negligently but without malice. Therefore the board should not be expected to award any back pay for punitive damages. In accordance with Freeman's suggestions, Wes agreed that company executives would appoint Bessie to the next supervisory position. Mr. Freeman then established a time frame of six months for the promotion to occur and further stated that Bessie's salary should double effective immediately.

Louise agreed to those terms when she looked at

Bessie and realized the woman was beaming with satisfaction.

They moved on to Darlene's complaint. Louise pointed out the characteristics demanded of a marketing/sales associate according to the candle company's own specifications. And she proved with results of personality and employable skills tests that Darlene met nearly all of the criteria the factory required to hire someone on this level. Darlene's personnel records supported her claim that she had been passed over for a sales position repeatedly without ever being given follow-up interviews with regard to her application.

"In direct violation of Title VII's job description policies," Louise said.

The mediator strongly suggested that Darlene's application be considered at once, and that she should be awarded a sales position or be placed in an apprenticeship program to acquire skills needed for the job. Since Hatch Winslow had nothing to say in his defense on this issue, the matter was settled.

Freeman referred to a last charge in his stack of papers, the one that concerned an anonymous Hispanic worker and her claim that she had been forced to miss work during the latter stage of her pregnancy for unspecified safety reasons. The mediator regarded both attorneys. "Would either of you care to address this issue?"

Hoping to avoid using Miranda Lopez's name, as she'd promised, Louise said, "I would, sir. My client isn't here today. But she is willing to drop her case against the candle factory if the executives would consider providing licensed day care at the facility.''

Justin Beauclaire pounded a fist on the table. ''Babies at the candle factory! We won't have that. We can't!'' He looked to Wes, who had laid a placating hand on the older man's arm. ''I told you all hell would break loose after that demonstration the other night.''

''In all fairness, Mr. Freeman,'' Wes began, ''this isn't an employment issue, and the candle factory is under no obligation to provide child care. Besides, the current facilities are not conducive to such a program.''

Louise held up her hand. ''Actually, Counselor, they are. In the office structure in front of the warehouse, there is a large sunny room that, according to my studies, is hardly ever used.''

''The executive lunchroom!'' Justin bellowed. ''She's talking about turning the executive lunchroom into a playground.''

''The executives rarely use that room, Mr. Freeman,'' Louise said. ''I've kept a record of the noon eating habits of the office staff at the candle company. Almost without exception, the executives go out to lunch.'' She handed the mediator a sheet of paper. ''This is a list of the restaurants the men choose, a different one for each day of the week. As for the secretarial help in the office, the women I spoke to said they are not permitted to use the lunchroom facilities, anyway, and they will continue eating their lunches at their desks.''

Freeman looked at the list. ''These are all fine eating establishments I noticed myself on the way into town," he said to the men. "I wouldn't mind an extended lunch hour at any one of them." Then he leveled a serious stare on Louise. "However, as Mr. Fletcher pointed out, this is not an employment issue, Ms. Duncan, and therefore—"

"Don't you think it's just a matter of time before child care will be mandated for female employees?" she said. "Many companies with large numbers of women workers are providing some type of care for their staff's children now. I don't think it's out of line to discuss it today in preparation for the time it becomes an employment issue. And I would very much like these men to consider it."

Wes cupped a hand over his mouth, but she detected a smile of respect for her argument. "Mr. Freeman," he said, "since none of us in this room has a crystal ball, I suggest we table this discussion for now until we see where future legislation leads us."

The mediator looked at Louise.

"Fine," she said. "But I do have one other issue, the matter of health benefits."

"Again, Ms. Duncan," Freeman said, "while I sympathize with employees nationwide over this matter today, it is not within my mandate to mediate an agreement."

"And, Counselor," Wes added, "I've done a little fact-finding of my own. To offer health care to the employees at the Bayberry Cove Candle Company at this time would cost the business a minimum of fifteen thousand dollars a month. The expense is simply prohibitive. And, as you know, health care is not a mandatory benefit in the United States." He looked at Freeman. "Frankly, I don't see this as anything to discuss."

"I have to agree," Freeman said.

Louise had known she would lose this argument. Wes was right. The company was under no obligation to provide coverage. However, she had one more card to play.

"Mr. Fletcher, would your clients consider health care symposiums at the factory? Scheduled times when professionals in the field of providing coverage could come in and speak to the employees about their options? Perhaps if my clients knew about modestly priced individual policies, or about state-funded coverage for children under the age of eighteen, this issue could be tabled for now with no hard feelings."

Wes switched his attention to Beauclaire. "Justin? Any objections?"

The older man ran his hand down his jaw and looked very much as if he wanted to come up with a powerful objection, but Louise knew he couldn't. She wasn't asking for more than a little company time. To deny that would put him in a bad light with Freeman.

"No, I suppose not. I'll have someone look into it."

"Thank you," Louise said. "Now if I can just re-open the topic of day care…"

Mr. Freeman gave her a stern look. "Ms. Duncan, we have settled this matter, and I must warn you—"

She opened her briefcase and pulled out a number of folders. "Sir, what I have here are additional cases of Title VII EEOC violations perpetrated on factory workers by the Bayberry Cove Candle Company. I could file charges on each of them, but the women represented by these claims are willing to forgo personal gain and almost certain punitive damages for mental anguish and inconvenience *for the time being…*'' she switched her best no-nonsense courtroom stare on Beauclaire ''…if the gentlemen over there agree to abide by EEOC regulations from now on.''

She paused for emphasis, letting her implied threat sink in. ''And if the executives will consider establishing a day care center, which will ultimately benefit everyone in the community.''

She selected another folder from her briefcase and slid it across to Wes. ''These are statistics showing how child care centers across the country have decreased absenteeism while increasing employee performance. And exact figures on the cost of turning the executive lunchroom into such a facility, which will positively impact the future of candle-making specifically and Bayberry Cove in general. A modern, well-equipped center will cost less than one golf weekend at Hilton Head. Surely you gentlemen can give up one weekend?''

The company executives bristled at the implied condemnation of the long-standing company benefit. Out of the corner of her eye, Louise saw a look of surprise on Freeman's face. ''Do this for the children,'' she added. ''You won't be sorry. And your community will thank you.''

Freeman stared at Wes's team. ''While this issue is not within my jurisdiction, gentlemen, I will go out on a limb and strongly suggest you think about the ladies' request. Considering that stack of complaints Ms. Duncan has, I guarantee it will save you a lot of headaches in the future.'' He removed his glasses and set them on the table, making his gaze that much more penetrating. ''And besides, it's the right thing to do.''

Wes regarded his three associates. Each remained stone-faced. Obviously interpreting their reluctance to comment as capitulation, he stood up and extended his hand to Louise. ''I believe we've reached an agreement, Counselor.'' He smiled at her. ''The lunchroom will undergo the modifications to make it a suitable child care center.''

Bessie and Darlene hooted in victory and grabbed Louise for breath-stealing hugs. And if Louise had just won a case before the Supreme Court, she wouldn't have felt more pride.

''I guess this concludes our work here today,'' Mr. Freeman said. ''And I can make it back to Raleigh in time for dinner.'' He stuffed his papers in his case, stood up and headed for the exit. ''Good luck to all of you. And you gentlemen…'' He stared pointedly at Beauclaire, Winslow and McGovern. ''Your attorney, Mr. Fletcher, has kept you from facing more serious consequences. But I want you to remember that your employees are your most valuable assets. I urge you to abide by all legislation in the future. This is a nice little town you have here, but I don't want to come back.'' He smiled. ''Unless it's to buy a candle.''

Louise barely heard his words. As the mediator

walked out the door, her focus was on Wes. He tried to console his clients by restating the small victories they'd won. While the mediator's warning had been serious, the company hadn't been fined. The dignity of the corporation was intact, so long, Wes added, as no one else appeared before a television camera. As his clients grumbled, Wes flashed Louise a grin and a thumbs-up, making it blatantly clear he admired and respected her.

She knew that leaving Bayberry Cove was going to be the hardest thing she'd ever done. While she accepted the congratulations of Bessie and Darlene, she could only think that she would be saying good-bye to them very soon. For that reason the smile she gave was forced. And she was going to miss Wes…more desperately than she'd ever imagined. In two days she would head to Fort Lauderdale and get her life back in order as the more compassionate, people-friendly attorney her weeks in Bayberry Cove had made her. But she wouldn't have Wes, because admiration, and even mind-numbing passion, weren't enough.

WES WATCHED LOUISE FOLLOW Bessie and Darlene from the room. Thank goodness this business was over. Louise had been spectacular. Stunning. She belonged in a big city courtroom where other competent legal minds could be blown away by such superior ability coming from such a captivating package. What right did he have to ask her to stay in little Bayberry Cove? How could she give up what she'd worked years to achieve? What did this little town, and for that matter, this ex-navy biologist, have to offer her that could compare with what she would give up? Nothing.

But he still had two weeks to try, and by God, for the next fourteen days he was going to mount an all-out offensive to get her to stay. Because how could he let her go?

CHAPTER SEVENTEEN

OUTSIDE CITY HALL, Wes stood to the side while Louise, Kate, Bessie and Darlene celebrated. Their victory was well deserved. Wes was satisfied with the case he'd presented, but he'd known all along the ladies would come out ahead. The factory administrators had gotten away with a flagrant disregard for the law for a lot of years, and no lawyer could have spared them the embarrassment of the dressing-down they got today.

Louise shot him a glance over her shoulder and then spoke to the women. "Thanks anyway, but I'll catch up with you later, and we'll have that beer. You guys go on."

"Thank you for everything," Darlene said. "I'm sorry I had an attitude about all this at first."

"Forget it," Louise said. "A little attitude can be a good thing." She gave each woman a hug and watched them walk off together.

When she was alone, Wes came up behind her and whispered in her ear. "You were magnificent."

She leaned against him. "So were you. I only won because the case was so indisputable. I'd hate to face you in a courtroom when the scales were balanced."

He put his hands on her elbows. "Flattery like that

will get you a slice of pie down at the Kettle. What do you say? It's two forty-five, perfect pie-eating time in this part of the country, and we don't have to play hide-and-seek any longer. Besides, it's only fair that we give Bobbi Lee a chance to gloat.''

Louise laughed. ''You've got a deal.''

They were approaching his Jeep in the city hall parking lot when a mud-caked pickup roared by them. Instinctively, Wes sheltered Louise with his own body. When he recognized the driver, he said, ''That's Luke Plunkett. And it looks as if his truck's not the only thing gassed up this afternoon.''

Louise quickened her pace. ''And that's Darlene just ahead of us, going to her car.''

The truck careened to a stop a few feet from Darlene. Luke got out and slammed the door. He stood in front of her, his hands on his hips, his legs spread wide.

''I just saw Beauclaire,'' he said. ''You women got your way, didn't you?''

''Yes, we did,'' she answered. ''And you might at least congratulate me.''

''Like hell! There's no way I'd congratulate you for turning your back on me and pretending to be something you're not.''

''I'm not pretending anything. We deserved everything we got.'' She jabbed a finger at his chest. ''It might interest you to know, Luke Plunkett, that it took a lot of courage for me to be one of the test cases today.''

He let out a bark of laughter. ''Courage? Stupidity is more like it.''

"Don't call me stupid!"

He leaned over her. "I'll call you whatever I want. Stupid. Ignorant. A lying bitch. You've treated me like horseshit the last few weeks, and it's going to stop." He grabbed her. "We're getting out of here so I can straighten this mess out once and for all."

Wes lunged forward. "I've heard enough."

He'd gone a couple of feet before Louise reached for his arm. "Wait a minute, Wes. Let's see what happens."

In disbelief he turned to stare at her. "I know what's going to happen, Louise. I've seen Luke in action before."

"But not against this adversary," she said.

Against every instinct urging him to Darlene's rescue, Wes halted. He watched for any twitch of Luke's body that would indicate a renewed threat. But none came.

In fact, Darlene shoved him away from her with enough force to send him stumbling into the side of his truck.

He pushed himself up and dusted off the seat of his jeans. "What the devil are you doing, woman?" he shouted at her.

"Something I should have done a long time ago. You're not going to bully me any longer, Luke. I've got a future now. I'm going to be traveling around the country to shows and selling our candles."

He approached her, drawing dangerously near once more. "The hell you are. You're my woman, and that's not gonna change just because you won a stupid contest with Justin Beauclaire. You're staying right here where I can watch you.'' His arm shot out to snatch her again.

Wes flinched.

And Darlene stood her ground. "You come one step closer, Luke, and I'll scream at the top of my lungs.'' She stuck her arm out with a determined finger pointed at city hall. "Deputy Blackwell is just inside. He'll come running out and slap handcuffs on you so fast you won't know what hit you. I'll press charges this time, Luke, and I'll watch you go to jail.''

He stared openmouthed at her. "What kind of talk is that?''

"It's truth talking, Luke. I'm through with you. I've got a chance now, away from you and that miserable hopeless farm. I'm leaving here and you're not going to stop me.''

He narrowed his eyes as if seeing her for the first time. "Now come on, honey…''

"Don't 'honey' me, Luke. Climb in your truck and get out of here. Now.''

He turned, started to walk away, but whirled back around to face her again. She waited, unmoving, unyielding, unrelenting.

Luke paused for several seconds, then stomped around his truck, got inside and peeled out of the parking lot.

Wes shook his head. "Do I believe what I just saw?''

"I believe it enough for both of us,'' Louise said. She wrapped her hand around his elbow and tugged ?

him toward the Jeep. "It's a day of victories. Let's eat pie until we bust."

As soon as Louise and Wes entered the Kettle, Bobbi Lee raced over to seat them. "Well, how'd it go?"

Wes affected an injured look, nodded toward Louise and said, "Ask the lady who schooled me in the art of argument."

"Whoopee! That's the best news I've had all day."

Wes smiled. "Can you tone it down a little, Bobbi? There's a person here who's trying to heal an injured ego."

Bobbi nudged him between tables to a prime spot by a window. "You're a big boy, Wesley. You'll get over it. Now, Louise, tell me everything. What happened with Bessie and Darlene?"

"I'm so proud of them," Louise said. "They stood up to the executive board and achieved what they've worked for. Bessie's getting a big pay raise and a promotion. Darlene will soon be selling Bayberry Cove Candles at trade shows across the U.S."

"Go ahead, tell her the rest," Wes said, pretending the news really hurt. "You might as well give her all the humiliating details."

"Oh, yeah," Louise added. "As an added bonus, there's going to be a child care center occupying the executive lunchroom."

Bobbi Lee flashed her brightest smile. "You go, girl."

"Thanks," Louise said, "but the women of this

town should be given most of the credit. I was just the key that started their engines running."

Bobbi Lee leaned close, as if she were hiding her next comment from Wes. "Order everything on the menu, honey. I'll make sure Wesley gets the bill."

"We want pie, Bobbi Lee," Wes said. "Bring us huge slices of apple pie loaded with mounds of ice cream. And keep 'em coming until I'm drunk with sugar and my wounds are sufficiently licked."

Bobbi Lee chuckled and sauntered off. Wes stared intently across the table at Louise. "You are the star today. Especially in my eyes, and I'm the loser."

She felt her cheeks flush, a purely feminine reaction that warmed her all the way to her toes. "In that case, Wes, can I ask a favor of you before those fifteen hundred calories arrive and you forget what you just said?"

"Anything at all."

"Your grandfather is in the square. I need to speak to him. Would you mind going to get him and bringing him here?"

Wes stood up. "You and Gramps? That's an alliance I hadn't expected."

She grinned up at him. "Next to you, he's my favorite Fletcher." She watched him cross the street, speak to Mason and point toward the Kettle. A few moments later, both men came inside and sat down.

Wasting no time, Mason increased the pie order and said, "A business proposition, you told me earlier. Let's hear it."

Wes, clearly curious, looked from one to the other. "That's right," Louise began. "Did Wes tell you that the role of women at the candle factory will be expanding very soon?''

"He did. Congratulations, young lady. I'm not surprised by your success. The more I've gotten to know you, the more I've come to realize that you have the tools to get what you want. But I'm still amazed you couldn't talk Wesley out of Buttercup Cottage when you had the chance weeks ago.''

Louise put on a crestfallen expression. "Some battles simply can't be won, Mason. Your grandson taught me that.''

"Well, what can I do for you?''

Louise waited while Bobbi Lee set down plates heaped with the Kettle's trademark apple pie à la mode. She took a bite, savored its cool sweetness and continued. "Earlier you mentioned the mistake candles the ladies had at the demonstration. You said it was a clever idea to use them.''

Mason wiped his mouth. "I did.''

"It made me think.''

Wes concentrated on his pie, but Louise knew he was listening intently to every word.

"What if the company could sell those candles?'' she said.

"Who'd buy them?'' Mason asked. "As I understand it, the company won't ship candles that don't meet specific requirements. A business has to be mindful of the quality of its product or risk losing its reputation.''

"I agree,'' Louise said. "But what if the candles weren't shipped anywhere? What if they were sold as seconds right here in an outlet store?''

"An outlet store? Like the ones in that big shopping center off the interstate?"

"Yes. But it would be located in downtown Bayberry Cove. With a minimum amount of setup, a few shelves and supplies, plus a bit of advertising, a nice little outlet shop could be established on Main Street."

"And it'd sell only mistake candles?"

"Right. The ones with the imperfect colors or shapes, funky candles that came out of molds a little lopsided. Or close-out candles that were overproduced." Once she'd started, Louise's mind mushroomed with ideas. "Or out-of-season stock, like Christmas candles in June, or styles that for some reason never caught on and were returned." She leaned her elbows on the table and riveted Mason with a look she hoped would mirror her enthusiasm. "Even at half price, the candles would bring in a profit. Much better than throwing them out or remelting them into slabs."

"Could be," Mason said thoughtfully. "But what about operating costs? And where exactly do you have in mind for this shop?"

She leaned back, anticipating the first real resistance to her plan. "That's where you come in, Mason."

He sent her a skeptical glance and then focused on his pie.

She continued. "As you know, there's a vacancy coming up in two weeks right next to the furniture store. Mr. Adams is moving his realty company to Morgan City. It would be the perfect spot for the outlet store. And I have the perfect person in mind to run it.''

He nodded, tuned in to her idea. ''Suzie McCorkle.''

''She's a natural,'' Louise said. ''She loves candles. Who better to sell them in Bayberry Cove?''

Wesley had been silent during this exchange, but now he chuckled out loud. ''I told you she's amazing, Gramps.''

Louise gave him a smug look. ''And that's not all.''

''I didn't think it was,'' Wes said.

''But why involve me?'' Mason asked. ''I don't care if you gals rent the shop and set up your candles. Go see my accountant and have a lease drawn up, and—''

''Well, there might be a problem, at first....''

Wes sat back, leaned his arm on the table. ''Ahh, here we go.''

She shot him a warning look to which he responded with a grin. ''It would be a while before the operation could show a profit,'' she explained to Mason. ''There aren't any funds to start with, and even though I'm sure volunteers would get things rolling, it would be a few weeks, maybe months, before the rent could be met.''

Mason's eyebrows knitted over clear blue eyes. ''So you're asking me to float the rent indefinitely?''

''*Indefinitely* is such a vague word,'' she said. ''And I haven't even brought this up to the executives at the factory or the women who would contribute to the success of the shop, so nothing is decided yet. But my plan would have more appeal if you would agree to postpone the rent for a time.''

Mason threaded his gnarled fingers together and sat still as a stone. Finally, when Louise thought she couldn't stand his silence another minute, he said, ''It's a mighty poor businessman who sells, or rents, his product for nothing.''

''Or a truly generous benefactor,'' she countered.

He tapped his fork against the empty plate for what seemed an eternity. Then he looked at Louise and said, ''Three months. That's it. And you pay for my pie.''

Louise closed her eyes for a second and said a prayerful but silent ''yes!'' Then she thanked Mason for his generosity and assured him that if her plan met with approval, everyone involved would know the project was only going ahead because of Mason's help.

''But,'' she said, ''Wes has already agreed to pay for the pie.''

Mason swung his index finger in front of her face like a pendulum. ''No welshing,'' he said. ''You pay for mine.'' He turned to his grandson.

''We're done here, Wesley. Cooked like a Thanksgiving turkey. Walk me back to the park and I'll call Cora May to come pick me up.'' He stood and supported himself against the back of the chair.

''One more thing, Mason,'' Louise said. ''I believe this will please you. I'm anticipating that profits from the mistake candles could be applied to the company's sponsorship of a health care program for employees. If the firm covers even a percentage of the cost, that will give the workers another option for medical care. Your contribution today could have far-reaching effects.''

Wes slowly nodded his head while he took his grandfather's arm. ''You never give up, do you, Louise?''

She returned his gaze and suddenly was overcome with an intense sadness. The future of Bayberry Cove would take shape over the next few months. Hers would be determined in the next two days. ''Almost never,'' she said, and watched the two men walk away.

While Wes escorted his grandfather back to the square, she contemplated the best way to tell him about her plans to return to Fort Lauderdale. She decided to suggest a late-night dinner at her place, something simple that she could prepare herself. She was formulating a plan when her cell phone rang. She pulled it out of her briefcase, recognized the number and depressed the connect key.

''Hello, Roger,'' she said calmly, trying to mask her surprise.

''Louise. How are you? Enjoying your vacation?'' His voice positively chirped with good humor.

''Yes, very much. I'm so glad you advised me to take it,'' she added, with just the right amount of sarcasm.

''I knew it would do you a world of good, and that's why I've called.''

''Oh?''

''I know I suggested you take a couple of months, but knowing you, I figured you must be itching to get back behind your desk here at the firm a few days early. Am I right?''

"I don't know that *itching* is exactly the right word, and frankly, Roger, I would think you'd be more interested in my mental state than a skin condition.''

He laughed. ''Always the kidder, Louise. That's what I miss about you.'' He cleared his throat in preparation for a more serious topic. ''But tell me, how *are* you doing with regard to those little problems we spoke of before you left?''

"It must be the country air in North Carolina. It's made a pussycat out of me.'' As soon as she said the words, Louise knew her explanation to Roger was a gross oversimplification. True, she had changed while staying in Bayberry Cove, but not because of the country air. She'd encountered honest, hardworking people who cared about each other and who'd trusted a stranger enough to put their futures in her hands. And because of that, she now understood the deep-down gratification that comes from helping others.

"In fact, Roger,'' she added with a regretful sigh and a wish that it were so, ''everybody here loves me.''

"I knew you just needed some time away from the rat race,'' Roger said, his words sounding like a verbal pat on his own back. ''But it's time you came home.''

She'd already come to that conclusion, but hearing her boss say it with such conviction made the realization that she didn't belong here all too evident. ''Are you saying you need me at the firm, Roger?''

He paused, prompting her to think he was trying to decide on the right amount of enthusiasm to inject into his response. Should he admit honestly that she was essential to the firm or hedge a bit?

"Well, sure we do, Louise. I only meant for you to get away for a while. You know the intent was always for you to return here. As a matter of fact, some of your old clients have been asking for you."

So, the clients who'd found her too aggressive six weeks ago now wanted her back. There was some satisfaction in hearing that.

"It seems they miss that certain quality you brought to the settlement of cases," Roger added.

"You mean that quality that often won?"

He snickered. "Well, yes. So when can we expect you, Louise? I want to have your desk polished and your name entered in the race for the next promotion."

He was tempting her with the biggest carrot he had. The only problem was, Louise knew the next promotion might not come for years. Oppenheimer Straus and Baker was a firm with very little turnover.

She rested her forehead in her hand and closed her eyes, wondering why she found it so hard to answer his direct question. After all, she'd made this decision. She took a deep breath and said, "Coincidentally, I've already made up my mind, Roger. I'll be in Fort Lauderdale Thursday, and I'll see you in the office the next morning."

The sound of footsteps made her jerk back in her chair. She raised her head, opened her eyes and stared into the glittering ice-blue gaze of Wes Fletcher.

He'd heard. Roger continued talking. Louise didn't listen. "I've got to go, Roger," she interrupted. "I'll call you later."

She pressed the disconnect button on her phone and set it on the table. "Wes, sit down, please."

He gripped the back of a chair, leaned slightly forward. "Is it true? You're leaving Bayberry Cove soon?"

His voice was devoid of emotion. Cold.

She nodded once. "I'm leaving Wednesday. I was going to tell you tonight."

"Well, now you don't have to."

"Wes, you always knew… I always knew…" His granite features didn't change. "I have a good job in Florida. I've worked hard for it." This wasn't going at all as she'd hoped it would. Her words sounded shallow, meaningless. "We can talk about this, Wes. Tonight. I was thinking—"

He threw the same words she'd spoken to Roger back at her. "I've got to go, Louise. I'll call you later."

He turned away and strode from the restaurant.

ALL RIGHT, he'd been childish when he'd walked out of the Kettle, but thinking back now, a half hour later, it seemed more sensible to have left than to have started breaking plates. Trying to reason with himself, Wes paced back and forth inside the kitchen of Buttercup Cottage. What did he expect? He knew she was going to go back to her old life. She'd never once indicated that her plans would change.

But so soon? He'd planned on two more weeks,

two weeks when he could… What? Charm her? He'd tried that with what he'd thought had been some success. But it obviously wasn't enough. Cajole her into staying? No way. Louise was stubborn and determined. Promises? What could he possibly offer her that she didn't already have in Fort Lauderdale—except himself, a poor second to a lucrative law career?

He strode to his back door, looked out at Currituck Sound, which was glass-calm in the fading glimmer of dusk.

Damn. He loved her. That was the only explanation for the way he felt now—hopeless, helpless, panicked. This was a fine time to have that bolt of realization slice into his consciousness and blow all to hell his theory about Louise being too much like Donna. The truth was, Louise was like no other woman in the world. And she was the woman he wanted. He would have realized it in time. What he was feeling was too strong to be denied, and was worth fighting for. But he'd thought he had two more weeks!

And then an idea came to him that was so bold, so intriguing, that he was momentarily convinced it might actually work. A military man was never without strategic tactics. And Wes had thought of a good one. All he needed was a small army.

IT WAS NEARLY DARK when Wes knocked on Bessie's front door. She opened it, stepped back in shock and then peered intently. "My goodness, what's wrong? Does this have anything to do with the proceedings today?"

"Who is it?" Kate called from the living room.

"Believe it or not, it's Wesley," Bessie said.

Kate came to the door.

"No, this has nothing to do with the mediation," Wes assured the women.

Kate grasped his arm. "Is it Haywood? Has something happened?"

"No. Dad's okay. I need to talk to both of you."

Bessie stepped aside. "Come in. Sit down."

He entered what looked like the showroom of a florist's shop and drew the correct conclusion. "I hope this means Dad's been courting you, Kate."

"In his way," she answered.

"Now, tell us what's wrong," Bessie said when they were all seated.

After Wes explained that Louise was leaving town in a couple of days, Kate made an assumption of her own. "You love her! I knew it. You and Louise are perfect for each other!"

He blew out a long breath. "Actually, everybody seems to have noticed except us. And that's been the problem. But I want her to stay right here. With me."

Bessie looked at Kate. They both nodded. "Well, so do we," Bessie said. "All the women down at the factory are grateful for everything she's done. Why, it's like Louise has lived here for years."

"That's what I wanted to hear," Wes said. "Now, here's what I think we should do...."

He explained his plan, and with each approving murmur and exclamation from Bessie and Kate, he grew more confident. When all the details were in order, he stood up and went to the front door. When he opened it, he saw his father striding up the sidewalk.

Haywood stopped at the bottom porch step. "Wesley, what are you doing here?"

Wes was able to smile for the first time in hours. "If I'm not mistaken, Dad, I think we're both here for the same reason. Because we're miserable failures in the romance department." He walked by his father and patted him on the shoulder. "I'm trying to do something about my blind side. I hope you can, too."

Believing he was on the right track, and with more people to see, Wes left.

"KATE, HAYWOOD'S HERE!" Bessie called.

Kate had already changed into one of Haywood's favorite dresses. She twisted a few springy red curls onto her forehead for a youthful look, dabbed cologne behind her ears, and walked into the living room.

"What can I do for you, Haywood?" she said, sitting herself in a Victorian mahogany chair flanked by two of Haywood's bouquets.

Bessie excused herself with a story about a cake baking in the kitchen.

"I heard everything went well for the ladies today," Haywood said when he was alone with Kate.

"Quite well, yes."

He brought a chair to within touching distance of her and sat. "I'm glad."

"You are?"

"Yes. I can't deny any longer that there were cases of injustice at the factory. And I've come to see Justin Beauclaire in a new light."

"It's about time."

He raised his eyebrows and stared at her. A smile lurked at the corners of his mouth. "You're a corker, Katie," he said. "Those lips of yours can speak a sharp word, but I've come to know I can't live without them."

She sat primly, waiting.

"So…" He reached into the inside pocket of his jacket. "I've brought you a peace offering." Scanning the floral extravagance around him, he added, "Aside from the fortune I've already invested in posies." He handed her an envelope. "Open it."

She lifted the flap and withdrew two airline tickets to Ireland. All pretense of coyness fled from her body. She pressed her hand against her chest and squealed, "Ireland! I'm going to see my boys!"

"Yes, Katie. In two weeks."

With a great deal of effort, she managed to rein in her excitement when she realized the tickets might be nothing more than what he'd called them—a peace offering. "There are two tickets, here. Is one of them for Bessie?"

Haywood grinned like a boy. "No, but I'll buy her one if you want her to come with us on our honeymoon."

Kate pretended to search the envelope again, though her hands were trembling so she could hardly keep up the ruse.

"What are you looking for?" Haywood asked.

"Just checking that you didn't slip in a prenuptial agreement for me to sign."

"Yes, indeed, a corker," he said again. "There's no agreement of any kind in there, Kate. It'll be you, me and a marriage license to seal the deal. If you say yes.''

He took a black box out of his pocket, lifted the lid and showed her a brilliant diamond ring. ''Will you be my wife, Kate, in every way, for every day of the rest of our lives?'' He took the ring out of the box and slipped it on her finger.

''Oh, Haywood, are you sure?'' Kate kept her eyes on his face.

''I'm sure as I've ever been about anything. I don't want to spend another day without you.'' A teasing grin curled the ends of his thick mustache as he looked at the ring on her finger. ''Besides, we no longer have to worry about money problems. I spent every last cent on that damn bauble.''

Kate bounded onto his lap with the joy of a young girl. She let her gratitude flow from her lips to his in one long, satisfying, coming-home kiss.

CHAPTER EIGHTEEN

VICKI MALONE PACKED the last of Louise's dishes in a plastic carton and closed the door of the empty cupboard. "I really feel bad about taking these dishes home with me, Lulu," she said. "You just bought them six weeks ago, and now you're giving the set to me."

Louise secured the zipper on her largest suitcase and sat on the bed. "Easy Come, Easy Go, Vic. And Pack Light. Those are my mottoes."

"But you can easily fit this carton in your car. Why don't you take the dishes back with you?"

"Why? So I'll have three sets in my two-bedroom condo? Don't be silly. Besides, when I bought them, I thought of giving them to you when I left. You can see they're not my taste. I'm hardly the cherry blossom type."

Vicki looked toward the rear entrance of the apartment, where two other filled boxes sat by the door. "But those linens you're giving me. Surely you can use those in your condo."

"But I don't need them. And you do. You're the one building the new house." Louise rose, went to Vicki and put her arm around her friend's shoulder. "Quit trying to find reasons not to take this stuff.

They're gifts. Accept them with good grace.'' She swept her arm to encompass all the cartons. "Besides, I told you at the time I didn't pay more than two hundred bucks for these things.''

Vicki capitulated with a sigh. "What are you going to do with the furniture?''

"It's all taken care of. Have Jamie come by for the oak dresser he sanded. It'll look adorable in the baby's room. The rest will go into Suzie McCorkle's shop. She promised to buy everything back from me at half what I paid for it, which wasn't much in the first place considering it's all used.'' Thinking fondly of Suzie and her candles, Louise smiled. "I'm not going to ask her for the money, though. Suzie's been a good friend, and all her candle prophecies have come true.''

"Not the one about you and Wesley,'' Vicki said. "You're leaving and Wes hasn't done a darn thing to make you stay.''

Louise gave her a fond smile. "In all fairness, Vic, Suzie never gave me a candle that promised a long-lasting love. She gave me one for passion, and Wes and I definitely made that candle burn bright. And, in his own awkward way, Wes did suggest that I stay.''

Vicki's expression brightened. "He did? You mean you've seen him since yesterday when he overheard you on the phone to Roger?''

Louise wished she could say what Vicki wanted to hear. Vicki had found her own happiness in Bayberry Cove, and wanted the same for her best friend. But there wasn't going to be that happy ending for Louise.

"Yes, I saw him today,'' she said. "He called this

morning and offered to take me to lunch. We went to a nice place by the river in Morgan City.''

"Well, what happened?"

"He apologized for walking out of the Kettle yesterday without giving me a chance to explain."

"Okay, that's a start. Did he ask you to stay?"

Louise tried to smile, but her lips trembled. "He said he wished I wasn't going. Is that the same thing?"

Vicki tried to look hopeful. "Maybe. It depends how he said it."

"He said it gallantly and politely, and even with meaning, but, honey, it wasn't enough." Louise busied herself by packing shoes into the last of the cartons. She couldn't stop to think now about Wes's hand over hers on the linen tablecloth, about his blue eyes reflecting the sun through the restaurant window, about his commander-perfect deportment slipping just a little when he asked for two more weeks.

She couldn't give him two more weeks because she knew that all the time in the world wouldn't change what they both knew to be true. They were two different people living two completely different lives. Yes, she had changed, but not enough. She'd never be the woman Wes wanted. In two days, or two weeks, or soon after, Wes would come to accept that. In the end, he would never be able to overlook the differences and love her for who she was.

Unfortunately, Louise had come to an entirely opposite conclusion. What she'd realized in the last two days was that they could have made it work. And if Wes had believed that too, she would have offered him more than two weeks. She would have given him the rest of her life.

She brushed a tear away and tried to ignore the burning in the back of her throat. Damn Bayberry Cove and all the people who'd let her sample their joys and sorrows, victories and defeats while spinning a web of honesty and compassion around her heart. She wasn't the same woman who'd showed up here six weeks ago. Roger Oppenheimer would be pleased.

She drew a deep breath and blew it out slowly. "I guess that's everything," she said.

"I can't believe you're leaving tomorrow morning," Vicki murmured. "I'd really hoped… I thought that Wes…"

"Don't," Louise warned as she fought the urge to release a flood of emotion in her friend's arms.

You're made of sterner stuff, Lulu, she said to herself, and straightened her shoulders with the semblance of a smile.

"Hey, Vic, come on now. It's only a two-hour flight, a two-day drive. It's not like we're on opposite sides of the world. I'll be back when your baby's born, to make sure that if it's a girl, you don't stick it with a name like Lulu." Louise felt tears threaten and she turned away so Vicki wouldn't notice.

Much as she loved Vicki, she knew she wouldn't be coming back for the birth of the baby. Her broken heart was going to take much longer to heal.

THE NEXT MORNING at seven o'clock, Louise went into the Kettle for a cup of coffee, a Danish and a last goodbye to Bobbi Lee. The restaurant was empty except for the owner and the cook, who were both lounging on bar stools at the counter. And Bobbi Lee was nowhere to be seen. Louise swallowed her disappointment with a few gulps of coffee and nibbled at the sweet bun.

After ten minutes she left money on the table and walked back toward her apartment. She passed by the door to McCorkle's New and Used Furniture Store and knew she would miss its quirky, warmhearted owner. She climbed the steps to her apartment, thinking about her dealings with Mason and Wes before she'd rented it, and accepted that this would be the last time she would climb these stairs.

She opened the door and realized that she'd neglected to lock it. This was the first time she could remember ever leaving a door unlocked. But then, this was Bayberry Cove. She felt the tears threaten to overflow onto her cheeks.

"Get a grip, Lulu," she said to herself as she looked around the room that had been her home for six weeks. It was still furnished nicely, but lacked the little details that had made it her own, the cherry blossom dishes, which she truly did like, the flowery bed linens, the candles. All gone now.

She picked up her canvas bag, the one piece of luggage she hadn't packed in the car last night, crossed the hardwood floor and turned around for one last look. The three windows that faced Main Street still shone with the scrubbing she'd given them when she'd first arrived. She remembered watching Wes jogging around the square, so fit, so strong, and now when he'd become vital to her existence, so lost.

Shaking off the malaise, she opened the back door, stepped onto the platform of the stairs and froze in disbelief.

There, eighteen feet below her in the parking lot, were dozens of Bayberry Cove citizens all looking up at her as if she'd just stepped from behind a curtain, center stage.

Standing at the bottom of the stairs were Vicki and Jamie, Bessie and Darlene, and many others from the factory. There was Mason Fletcher, and Kate and Haywood, holding hands like a couple of young lovers. And Suzie and Evan. And Bobbi Lee.

And in front of them all, with his foot on the bottom step, was Wes Fletcher, staring up at her with a devilish expression on his face and one hand hidden mysteriously behind his back.

Louise dropped her bag, let her purse slide from her shoulder to the porch and gripped the rough lumber of the railing. She swallowed and reminded herself to breathe.

Wes looked up at her and spoke in a clear, strong voice. "Louise Duncan, this is an intervention."

She blinked, pursed her lips for a second and said, "Wh…what?"

"An intervention," he repeated. "It's what concerned citizens do for one of their own when that person doesn't have the good sense to know what's best for her."

Her hand clutched the soft fabric of her T-shirt. *One of their own?* "What are you talking about, Wes?"

"We're here to persuade you to stay, Louise." He

CHAPTER 2

Tyler Hadley's friends had pieced together that he'd been having a tough time lately—he seemed to be grounded all the time, and he was clearly depressed—but they never really worried about it. He was a jokester, mostly, albeit with a pretty dark sense of humor. If you believed everything he said, well, you'd have to buy that he was capable of killing his parents, after all. How could he say that and mean it, especially if he followed it up with a laugh? But overall he was a good guy despite his macabre tendencies, and he was fun to hang out with, so when he announced on Facebook on Saturday afternoon that he was having a party, his friends—and their friends—started making plans.

His first note read simply: "party at my crib tonight . . . maybe." A friend replied, "lmk"—Internet slang for "let me know." Wrote another: "partypartyparty." Another

called them all fags and accused them of breaking a bed
in half. In a direct message to another friend, Tyler bab-
bled in nearly incoherent teen web speak, saying he had
an "open crib for a lil bit" and asked if the buddy wanted
to chill. Translated into English, the back-and-forth went
something like this: Tyler's parents were leaving, he wanted
to smoke some marijuana, and he asked the friend to come
over—but not quite yet because his parents "aint left yet"
(sic). The friend, in on the "I'm going to kill my parents"
jokes, teased, "if i kill ur mom will u put the lincoln in my
name," and then he followed with a mistyped message that
he was only joking. Tyler replied, "no im gonna do it." Then
Tyler complained about his mom. She's been "bitchin," he
said. She didn't want him to go out and was trying to take
his car keys away so he'd be forced to stay home—"cuz
shes a cunt." At this point, it was about 1:45 p.m., and Tyler's
parents were still gone, having headed to Fort Pierce for
some errands and lunch. Michael, his girlfriend Morgan,
and Danny were still there about this time, too, and they
were expecting to party later that night. They just had to wait
until Mary Jo and Blake came home, packed their stuff,
and left for their trip to Orlando.

The anticipation over the party grew all afternoon, with
Tyler posting more messages and confirming that, yes, he'd
indeed have people come over to chill around ten o'clock
that night. But when friends first arrived, Tyler wasn't
there. They called the number he'd posted on Facebook,
and he told one who reached him to sit tight, he'd be over
soon. About half an hour later, a group of ten or fifteen
kids loitered on the lawn, where Tyler told them to wait
while he picked some things up inside. It didn't seem all
that odd to the wannabe partygoers; after all, a lot of people
were going to be in the house, and maybe Tyler was worried
that things might get smashed. When Tyler finally opened
the door, their suspicions seemed validated: The walls

were devoid of artwork or photos, but naked nails and picture hangers jutted from the plaster.

Tyler was a polite, if quiet, host, and he was stocked up on beer and food. What's mine is yours, he conveyed. His friends accepted the invitation, downing dozens of cans and bottles of beer and smoking cigarettes and marijuana. Some sat down at the family computer and played music, apparently oblivious to the dried blood that had crusted around the desk legs.

Tyler didn't do much socializing at first. He called a crew of his closer friends into his bedroom and sat on the floor smoking weed and drinking beer. When one buddy left the room to check on the party, only to come back and report that the house was getting trashed, Tyler just shrugged. So what? He didn't care. He had his blunt and his beer and a plastic bag with Percocet, a potent painkiller. The house filled with music as tunes from the home computer in the living room competed for attention with the jams Tyler played on the laptop in his bedroom—until the family computer screwed up and quit playing, anyway. And Danny had said the Hadleys had nice things. As if.

The party was fairly tame until about midnight, when a crush of newcomers arrived. That's when things started to get messy. It wasn't a huge house, and people filled every nook. Some sat in the family room, others surrounded the desktop computer in the kitchen, more still stood in front of the door. People coming in and out could barely open the door.

Michael Mandell was Tyler's best friend, had been for about a decade. Michael figured he knew Tyler better than he knew his own parents. They told each other everything. And on this night, that would become Michael's burden. Tyler approached Michael about an hour into the party with a secret. At first, Michael assumed his friend was just pulling him aside for a heart-to-heart. Tyler did that often. He was usually depressed—"depressed Tyler" was "normal Tyler," Michael would later tell a detective. But that's not what this chat would be about. The two left the house and walked to the stop sign at the end of the street. They'd made this walk before. Nothing was amiss. Tyler said he'd done something stupid. That didn't seem too worrisome, either, Michael thought.

"I killed my parents," Tyler said.

Michael scoffed. How ridiculous. "No, you didn't," he said.

"Michael, I'm being real. I'm not lying to you."

Tyler told him to look in the driveway: Both of his parents' cars were still there. Michael admitted that was odd, but shook it off. Tyler insisted. He said that he and his father had gotten into a fight and his dad had punched him in the nose. Michael didn't know what to say and insisted that he and Tyler go back to the party. This nonsense he was spewing couldn't be real anyway. Tyler was already drinking; maybe he was on some other drugs as well, and spouting off.

After they went back inside the house, Mike started to walk around. Before long, Tyler circled back to him, determined to make him believe. He told Michael to look for bloody shoe prints. Mike spotted one in the garage. Tyler told him to look closely at his parents' bedroom door and he would see the signs. Michael did and saw blood on the door frame, on the walls, on the ceiling. It wasn't obvious if you weren't looking for it, but it was plain as day if you were.

The two stood together inside the garage, the door shut to the other partiers. Tyler began to pace, chewing on his fingernails, and as he walked back and forth, the details began pouring out of him. He'd hid both his parents' cell phones in advance so they couldn't call for help. Then he stood over his mother for about five minutes as he readied himself for the first blow. He swung once, and Mary Jo whipped around. She managed to get out a single question before he bashed her again: "Why, Tyler, why?" When Blake walked into the room, father and son locked eyes— and then Tyler attacked. His dad screamed at him: *Why are you doing this?* Tyler replied, "Why the fuck not?"

For just a moment, Mary Jo and Blake screamed at the tops of their lungs. Then they were quiet. The younger dog, the Lab named Sophie, started growling protectively, so Tyler locked her in his parents' bedroom. Molly, the beagle, was too deaf and blind to sense that anything was off. Tyler let her be.

As Tyler described the killings, he swung his arms to mime the attacks. The hand gestures stuck with Michael, as did so many other descriptions. Tyler hadn't been able to do it sober, he said, so he'd taken three pills of ecstasy first and pumped himself up by listening to the rapper Lil Boosie in the garage. There was far more blood than he'd ever imagined there would be, and the cleanup took a good three hours. Afterward, Tyler climbed into the shower, washed off, then looked into the bathroom mirror and laughed. He was barely finished with the cleanup in time for the party.

Tyler rambled, too, about money: He said he stole eleven thousand dollars from his parents. It was money his grandparents had put in a trust fund. Mary Jo and Blake had it available through a credit card, Tyler claimed, and he'd stolen the card. As for the bag of Percocet, he'd had that for a reason, Tyler told Michael. After the party was over, he'd just down some pills. He'd end it. *Poof.* No prison. Michael protested—you can't kill yourself, he insisted, why don't you just run away?—but nothing seemed to resonate with Tyler, so when Michael later spotted the bag of pills jutting from Tyler's pant pocket, he filched it. He expected Tyler to whip around and catch him, but

Tyler didn't even notice. Michael thought about flushing
them down the toilet but figured he didn't have time, so
he dumped the bag out onto the floor of the bedroom
closet and hoped Tyler wouldn't figure out where the pills
were before it was too late.

Tyler told Michael that if he stayed until after the
party, he'd show him the bodies. Michael walked away,
stunned. He sat on the couch in the living room. Were
Tyler's parents really dead in their bedroom? He wandered the house some more. Tyler had described his mom
sitting at the computer, so he looked at the desk. Sure
enough, there was blood there, and a lot on the floor. It
was dried and brownish, seeming more like dirt to someone not looking closely enough. Michael knew the house
well, so he walked in the backyard and found the outside
door that led into the Hadleys' bedroom. It was unlocked.
He tried to open it, but it seemed stuck, as though something was in the way. Finally, he pushed it hard enough to
see partially inside the room. It was dark, so he used his
cell phone as a light and peered inside. He saw a man's
blood-covered leg, and he could tell from the cargo shorts
and a decade's worth of knowing him that it was Blake's
leg. He'd been buried beneath mounds of clothes and furniture, this giant of a man entombed in a heap of debris
on his own bedroom floor. Michael's head began to swim.

When he'd first walked into the house for the party,
he'd noticed the naked walls but dismissed it. Maybe
Tyler didn't want stuff broken, or maybe he was embarrassed by his family and didn't want people to see photos
of them. Now he realized that those mementos were
likely torn from the walls after a murderous rampage.
Tyler described smashing the family photographs over his
parents' dead bodies. It seemed like he'd emptied the entire
house on top of their corpses.

Michael again met up with Tyler in the garage.

"You really murdered your parents. You did it," he said.

Tyler nodded.

"I guess I won't be seeing you for a while. I guess I should take a picture."

"Take a bunch of pictures," Tyler said.

Michael held out his cell phone and snapped one photo alongside his childhood friend. Both wore stern "don't fuck with me" faces. Tyler held a red plastic cup in his hand.

Later, Michael would say that he should have done something. He should have called police or left the party or done anything at all besides roam the house in a near stupor as teens partied it up without a clue. But he was too shocked. He didn't know what to do. Soon panic started to set in. Tyler was in some deep shit, and many of the kids at the party already were on probation—including Michael. He'd served time for trespassing and was nearing the end of his sentence. He wasn't supposed to be at parties with booze and drugs. On top of that, what he'd seen—the lifeless leg, pools of blood amid the trash—was starting to weigh on him. And for the first time in their friendship, he was afraid of Tyler. If the guy could do that to his own parents, his flesh and blood, and seem so cool about it, what was to stop him from attacking his best friend?

Michael approached his friend Jesse Duryea. He struggled to find the words, and then told him bluntly: "Tyler might have killed his parents. *But don't tell anyone*." He told Jesse about the blood he saw, the leg, and what Tyler had told him. Jesse, freaked out, decided it was time to bounce. He didn't know if Michael was just screwing with him, but he didn't want to hang around to find out. Jesse approached Tyler and said that his mom was mad at him and he had to get home. He dragged a friend to the front yard and told her what Michael had said. She didn't believe him, but once a story like that starts circulating, it's probably time to bail. She called a buddy for a ride for herself, Jesse, and another friend.

More time passed. Michael still couldn't keep quiet. How could he? There were dead bodies inside the house. He spotted his friend Dustin Turner, who immediately sensed something was off. *I have to tell you something, and it's serious,* he said. He took Dustin to the back porch and approached the door that Tyler had showed him. He opened the door about a foot and used the light of his cell phone to illuminate the leg. Dustin took one look and stumbled away from the door.

"I was never here," he said. He wanted nothing to do with the shit that was about to go down, and he quickly left the party.

Around 3 a.m., as people were leaving, Michael noticed that another buddy, Ryan Stonesifer, seemed to be straggling. Like Dustin, Ryan probably didn't want any part of this, so Michael told him he should leave. Ryan protested. He'd planned on helping Tyler clean up after the party. He'd prefer to stay. So Michael told him what he saw and what Tyler had said. Ryan scoffed. "Don't fuck with me," he said. Michael announced their departure to Tyler, but Tyler said they should stay, and then walked quietly into the kitchen to make some food. There was a knock at the door. Someone had called the police about the party, about the noise wafting down the street. Tyler went to answer it. Michael saw the opportunity to bolt, so he grabbed Ryan's arm and the two ran away.

Michael decided he had to tell someone who mattered. He couldn't call the police and rat out his friend directly, so he dialed the number to a Crime Stoppers tip line. No answer. He found another number based in Orlando and left a panicked message, packing in as much information as he could: Tyler's name, his address, what he'd said, the sight of Blake's leg, the comment Tyler made about using the back of the hammer, the insistence that it was no joke, no prank, someone needed to check this out now. Michael described his friend as clean-shaven with light brown hair and a fade cut.

A woman charged with listening to incoming tips recognized the gravity and called Port St. Lucie's emergency number within minutes.

"We got a call from our call center." The woman's voice was almost quizzical. "There's a seventeen-year-old kid there, Tyler Hadley. He's claiming he killed his parents."

"He did what to his parents?" the 911 dispatcher replied.

"He's claiming that he killed his parents at about 5 p.m. last night and they're dead in the house . . . They're supposed to be in their bedroom."

The woman didn't have many more details, just that the message left—she didn't know by whom, but soon the world would know it was Michael Mandell—indicated he'd used the back of a hammer.

"Okay," the dispatcher replied. "We'll have somebody go out and check it."

Soon after Michael called the tip line, another call came in to 911. It was from Jesse's girlfriend, who'd heard from Jesse that Tyler might have killed his parents and insisted they call police. *But Mike already called Crime Stoppers,* he protested at first. Maggie insisted: Call 911. *Now.* So they did, together, and said maybe it was just a sick joke, but police should check it out.

Maggie's voice came first: "Someone had a party tonight, and someone reported that this kid had killed their parents, and I don't think they were playing about it. So if you guys want to go by and check . . ."

Jesse got on the phone next and broke it down further. "I was at a party with one of my buddies. He said his parents went out of town so he was throwing the party. And I'm at the party, and we're all hanging out, everything's cool, he's acting fine."

That changed when "mutual friend" Michael approached, he said.

"He told me the gist of it, that he did something to his parents," Jesse said. "I'm like, 'Bro, I don't want to know anything' . . . My understanding of it was he killed them. The bodies are supposed to be at his house . . . I'm really scared and confused, you know. I don't think they're joking about it . . . I think he needs help. I think he has mental issues and he needs help."

The dispatcher promised to send someone to check on the house. Within minutes, her voice reverberated throughout the city's squad cars: "371 Northeast Granduer. We're getting an anonymous tip from a crime line in Orlando that a Tyler Hadley at this location, 17 years of age . . ." The voice let out a sigh, as though to steel itself for the words to follow. "The anonymous tip advised that he killed both of his parents last night at 5 p.m., he used the back of a hammer, and that the parents can be found in bed at this location."

A male cop's voice responded, confused: "The parents are going to be there, or he's going to be there, or both?"

"He may or may not be 97," the dispatcher responded. *Ninety-seven* is cop code for "at the scene."

Police pulled up to the house. Through the windows, Officer Charles Greene could see Tyler pacing inside. The teen seemed to be talking to himself and had a bizarre look on his face, his eyes wide and unblinking. Police called in descriptions and license plates for the three vehicles parked outside. A gold Lincoln parked in the swale was registered to Tyler, a black Toyota truck to Blake, and a red Ford Expedition to Mary Jo.

Officers checked the backyard and readied themselves

for a confrontation. They knocked on the front door and rang the bell. No answer. Peering through a crack in the blinds of the bay window, they saw Tyler pacing still, this time grabbing a handful of books from the living room, then walking into a bedroom and tossing them on the floor. He appeared to say something as he pelted the books, though officers couldn't make out the words. Back and forth, he did this three times. He looked angry, deranged, and after he flung the third stack of books, he walked toward the front door. Greene braced himself and motioned for Officer Adrian Zamoyski to cover him in case Tyler opened the door to leave. But he didn't. Nothing happened. Greene approached again, knocked on the door, and again rang the doorbell. The lights inside the home abruptly flicked off. Greene repositioned himself closer to the garage and called for backup as Zamoyski stayed at the front door. Finally, Tyler opened the door.

The officers didn't know for sure what they were dealing with. His left hand was hidden behind his back at his waist. Worried that he was concealing a weapon, the officers ordered him to show his hands. They were empty, but something about Tyler's behavior was just off. He seemed agitated and incoherent. Greene leveled his gun at him and ordered him to the ground, placing the teen in handcuffs. The officers asked if Tyler was home alone. He said he was. They asked where his parents were.

"They're in West Palm Beach," he answered. But, no, he didn't know how to reach them. And, no, police couldn't enter the house.

The officers were immediately suspicious. He seemed nervous, frantic; while he spoke, his pupils were large. And his answers weren't jibing with the vehicles the officers saw in the front yard. If his parents had gone on a trip, why were their cars parked outside? And why wouldn't they have told their son how to reach them? The officers had been dispatched to check on the welfare of Mary Jo and Blake, and armed with that tip, along with Tyler's odd behavior and apparent lie about his parents not being home, they walked inside and called out to see if anyone else was in the house. No one answered. Then the officers heard a loud yelp from the back—apparently the family's beagle wasn't happy to be locked outside on the back porch. The officers started to explore the house.

"You can't go in there! Don't go in there!" Tyler yelled.

Every room inside the house was unlocked—except for one located just off the great room. An officer asked Tyler what room that was. His parents', he answered. The officer asked where the key to the room was, but Tyler said his parents had taken it with them to West Palm Beach. The officer peered harder at the door. The reddish brown dots along the frame worried him. Tyler mumbled something about going to "Rock Road"—slang for the local jail. One of the cops turned the doorknob hard, so hard it snapped open, and the door swung wide to reveal the hoarders-style mess inside. The room was strewn with furniture, pictures, and towels. And then the officers noticed the blood. Next, they saw Blake's leg and, after feeling that it was cold and unresponsive to the touch, called for medics. One of the officers crawled on top of the bed to check the closet and bathroom, which were otherwise inaccessible because of the mounds of junk on the floor. He found a black Lab locked away but unharmed. Then the officer removed a calendar from the floor, uncovering Mary Jo's arm. Greene read Hadley his Miranda rights, asked him if he understood, and led him to his squad car. Neither said a word about the incident as they headed to police headquarters. Hadley stayed calm and stared straight ahead.

CHAPTER 3

Detective Kristin Meyer of the Port St. Lucie Police Department got the call about 5:30 a.m. The details were gruesome and succinct: two people killed, one male and one female, found inside a home at 371 Northeast Granduer Avenue. Meyer was on the scene forty-five minutes later. By then, police had already found the bodies. Medics had gingerly waded through the mess in the bedroom to verify that the couple was dead, and the game of waiting for the proper search warrants had begun.

Meyer, an eleven-year police veteran, was on the shorter side with long blond hair. She had a no-nonsense approach to her work, especially when talking to teenagers. She'd dealt with a lot of them and she preferred to speak to them frankly, so she didn't hesitate to swear or tell them to cut the bullshit if they got uppity.

Usually, the detective's beat in the coastal Florida burg
was relatively quiet. The waterfront town of Port St. Lucie, lined with ocean-view restaurants and beautiful boats
docked along the Treasure Coast, had about 165,000 residents. In all of 2010, three people were murdered there.
The city battled it out for the title of Safest City in Florida
every year and was considered among the safest in the
United States. Police dealt far more often with nonviolent
crimes—burglary and the like—but even those rates
were on the low side. Port St. Lucie, a highlight of St.
Lucie County, wasn't a hoity-toity community but rather a
hardworking, blue-collar area that was somewhat afford-
able by Florida standards, though still ritzy when compared with much of the recession-pummeled country. By
the stats, the average income was about $50,000; the
median age, about forty; the average home value, about
$160,000. But picturesque views aside, Port St. Lucie suf-
fered from a problem common in so many communities,
suburban and urban alike: A lot of kids there liked doing
drugs. Some blamed the area for being too boring for
much else, so they threw parties. Dozens of young adults
would gather for one shindig around midnight, only to
pull up stakes and head to another across town at 3 a.m. It
wasn't unusual for the same group of friends to travel to
three parties a night, and at each there often was an ar-
gosy of alcohol and drugs: blow, beans, zannies, pot, you
name it. The prevalence led some to dub the city "Pot St.
Lucie" or "Port St. Lousy."

When Meyer pulled up to the house on Northeast
Granduer, she faced a typical Florida home—white, ranch-
style, pool in the backyard, big bay window in the front. It
had white trim and white window awnings and was built
of concrete block. The biggest difference between this
and other homes in the neighborhood was the yellow police tape that surrounded it. Outside, neighbors were al-

ready gathering, as were a couple of reporters who'd heard rumblings on the police scanner.

Meyer slipped protective booties over her shoes and stepped inside, careful not to disturb evidence on the floor. The place was slowly filling with officers and crime scene technicians. The entrance to the home was narrow and featured a California blue hutch bookcase that had seen better days. A couple of the slats on the lower facade were broken and dangling. A set of keys had been tossed on one of the shelves. On others sat empty beer bottles. In the great room, she saw the hodgepodge of furniture in disarray. Clearly, it'd been quite a party.

Meyer touched nothing. More beer cans and bottles were strewn across the floor. Ashtrays littered the countertops. Food remnants were everywhere. The dining room table, covered with a beige-patterned tablecloth, had almost a dozen red, blue, and green plastic cups filled with God knows how much booze, and cups of that same style spilled into the kitchen and the rest of the house. Even the sitting room, which clearly hadn't been the night's hot spot, was littered with cigarettes and beer. The whole place looked more like a college dorm room than the decades-long home to a rooted family of four.

It didn't help that the walls were devoid of the knick-knacks, photographs, and artwork that normally make a home feel, well, homelike. Clearly, that hadn't always been the case. Nails and picture hangers jutted naked from the walls—above the fireplace, in the hallways, near the dining hutch. This house hadn't always felt so cold; it had been stripped of its warmth and personality. Faint outlines could be seen around some of the nails—a sign that whatever had hung there had been on display for a long while.

To a casual observer, it might not have appeared like a crime scene at first—beyond, perhaps, a drinking-and-pot party designed for minors. It was mostly a messy house covered with spots of dirt and grime. But the law enforcement agents who would continue to descend on the home looked past the superficial clutter and crud to see clues—disturbing ones, like dried blood encrusted around furniture legs, and thin wisps of cast-off blood marring the white walls and ceilings. Evidence technicians were readying for the time-consuming task of photographing the entire house and labeling the blood to help forensic scientists determine from what direction the blood had come and how fast it'd been flying. They'd use adhesive labels scrawled with measurements in locations that would later be helpful to analysts: L. INT. DOOR would read one, indicating "left interior door," stuck beneath a nearly two-millimeter line of dried, reddish brown liquid. Another would be labeled M.D. for "main door," and it was placed beneath a reddish droplet about knee height on the front of the home. Crime scene technicians are always hesitant to declare a substance blood without definitive testing, but in this case, given the sheer amount discovered along the floorboards and in drip marks on door frames, it seemed unlikely that this was anything but. Still, they would photograph and swab, carefully securing samples in labeled bags that would be sent for genetic testing, first to verify that it was indeed human blood, and then to try to determine whose blood it was.

But this wasn't Meyer's job. Without moving anything, the detective walked through every room, examining without touching. As lead investigator assigned to a double homicide, she surveyed the still-undisturbed scene and made her way to the back bedroom, just off the kitchen and to the left of the dining hutch. She'd been debriefed already about the room's contents, but that didn't do much to prepare her. The room was so filled with items that she couldn't step past the doorway without risking an avalanche. The floor turned from off-white tile to a patterned faux wood, but the laminate was barely visible beneath the mounds of papers, photographs, dolls, clothes, towels, and magazines stacked so high that they nearly reached the mess of a bed—and the bit that was visible was smeared with blood. Dining room chairs sat precariously atop the bed, as did empty dresser drawers and overturned plastic storage containers. A roll of pink-and-purple polka-dotted wrapping paper looked cheerily out of place among the debris. But what was most immediately disconcerting was the bedspread. Its dated striped pattern was stained an unmistakable crimson. Not a foot away lay a red-handled mop atop a pile, as though it'd been tossed there last. Evidence techs zeroed in on the mop: used in a cleanup effort, perhaps?

By now, Mary Jo and Blake Hadley had been pronounced dead. Their bodies were only partially visible beneath the mess. As Meyer eyed the room, she noted that the leg of the dead man was still wearing a white sock. A few inches away, she spotted an elbow and a shirtsleeve stained with blood. As Meyer looked around the room, she saw that the personal belongings that had been missing from the home's main living areas had apparently been heaved in here. On the floor, just inside the door, was a spiral-bound book with an image of the Earth on a white background. Printed neatly beneath it was a name: MRS. HADLEY. A pair of paintings hung on a far wall, each depicting sweet-faced clowns in earth-toned colors inside matching white frames. In this room, the walls had been painted a Cambridge blue—more green than blue, really—and, wreckage aside, it was clear that this space at one time had been nicely decorated and comfortable.

Meyer noted the red spattering visible even five feet away on a large entertainment console that housed a sizable television set and outdated VCR. From the bedroom's entrance, she could see a bathroom door on the other side of the mess. A dog barked from behind the door. That was especially odd because another dog had been discovered on the back porch, clearly free to mingle with party guests. Officers would need to work quickly to reach the bathroom-bound black Lab. Later, Meyer would learn why the dog had been locked up rather than allowed to roam.

She made her way to two more bedrooms down a hallway on the west side of the home. The bedrooms were separated by a bathroom and linen closet at the end of the hall. The room to the south was in disarray similar to the tornado-stricken master bedroom, though on a smaller scale and without all the blood. A large pastel-hued reproduction of a flower painting had been unceremoniously dumped atop a pile of books, cake pans, family photos, and a dining room chair. The room's full-sized bed and two dressers were covered in wadded-up clothing and haphazardly bundled linens. On top of one dresser were a clear plastic tub of pet food, half a dozen containers of deodorant, and a professional photograph of Mary Jo and Blake. She stood behind him, her left hand placed gently on his shoulder, as they smiled into the camera. Beneath the picture were more images shot during the same portrait session. In one circular canvas print, Mary Jo and Blake stood with their two sons. Both boys had neatly combed blond hair, and Ryan, who appeared to be perhaps ten years old, looked dapper in a red tie with his striped shirt and jacket. Tyler stood beneath his older brother and flashed a toothy smile. Another frame housed three more happy photos beneath a mat that read THE HADLEY FAMILY.

The last bedroom actually had clear floor space, but it was still a mess. A giant painting lay facedown in the middle of the bed, beer bottles and cans littered the floor, looked behind and to the side, where his friends were nodding their heads. "Forever, if our demonstration goes as planned. But at least for two weeks if that's the most you'll give us." He sent her a stern look. "It is, after all, what you promised, and you've convinced us you're a woman of your word."

Suzie McCorkle stepped up and nudged him from behind. "Go on, Wesley, show her."

He cleared his throat. "There are some among us this morning who believe that the responsibility of getting you to stay falls squarely on my shoulders."

The crowd nodded again. Several individuals shouted words of agreement.

"With that in mind, I've come to offer you this." He brought his arm from around his back, and in his hand was a tall pink candle sitting in a delicate wreath of pink roses. Wes held it out to her in the palms of both hands, as if it were an offering from a knight to his lady love as she looked down upon him from a marble balcony instead of a weathered old porch.

"Tell her what it means," Suzie prompted.

Tears rolled onto Louise's cheeks. *I hope I know what it means,* she said to herself. And finding the promise shining in Wes's clear eyes, she knew she did.

He climbed halfway up the stairs, the candle outstretched. "It means romance, Louise. And love that lasts forever. And I offer it to you as my personal plea that you will stay, here, with me…" he glanced around at his attentive audience "…with *us,* in Bayberry Cove, as my wife."

The woman who'd only thought of candles as a

means to celebrate a birthday or combat a power out-
age suddenly became a true convert to their magic.
She swiped at her tears and blinked hard, not wanting
anything to blur her vision of Wes's fiercely determined expression. And because she'd always been a
woman who dealt in absolutes, she said, "Are you
fully and completely aware of what you've just
said?"

He dropped the candle to his side and gave her a
look so intense, so filled with longing, that she felt it
curl her toes. "Don't leave, Louise."

Her eyes remained locked with his for a wonderful,
magical moment of time. She was about to deliver
her answer when Mason hollered from the parking
lot, "Put the boy out of his misery, Louise. Say yes.
Let him give you that dang cottage you want so
much!"

Laughter sputtered from her lips. Real, honest,
heartfelt laughter. And the citizens of Bayberry Cove
seemed to utter a collective sigh of relief.

"And study for the North Carolina bar exam,"
Haywood shouted up to her. "This town needs a good
lawyer." He put his arm around Kate. "Looks like
I'm going to be in Ireland for a while going over the
cases of a couple of miscreant offspring of my future
wife's." He winked at Louise. "Don't know how
long that will take me, and I can't leave these folks
high and dry with no competent legal advisor."

"So what's your answer, girl?" Bobbi Lee said.
"I've known Wes Fletcher my whole life. He's a bit
stuffy, and he'll stand on his principles in the middle
of the town square until grass grows up around his

knees.'' She grinned at the object of her gentle chiding. ''But he's a good man and he'll make you happy. And he told me he'll do the cooking or bring you to the Kettle every night.''

Louise pulled her gaze from Wes and looked at Vicki, who had such a repentant grimace on her face that Louise knew her best friend had been a party to this little ambush. And then Vicki admitted it when she said, ''Hey, anybody can be a little sneaky if it's for a good cause.''

Louise laughed and focused on Wes again. She knew she would be here on the Fourth of July and beyond to witness the start of the candle store, the preservation of Currituck Sound and the continuing traditions of Bayberry Cove. And she would build her own future alongside this man in a little cottage that would once again be a gift of love.

''Bring that candle on up here, sailor,'' she said. ''I feel like lighting a fire.''

He gestured to his friends with his free hand. ''You can all go home now. Thanks for your help, but I've got a little private celebrating to do with my fiancée.''

And while the folks of Bayberry Cove dispersed to their jobs and their homes, Wes climbed the rest of the way, turned Louise toward the door and took her inside, where he proceeded to do just that.

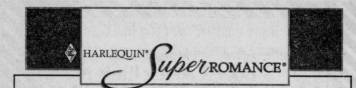

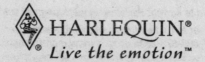

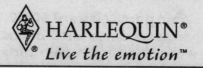

A Family Christmas
by Carrie Alexander

(Harlequin Superromance #1239)

All Rose Robbin ever wanted was a family
Christmas—just like the ones she'd seen on TV—but
being a Robbin (one of those Robbins) pretty much
guaranteed she'd never get one. Especially after
circumstances had her living "down" to
everyone else's expectations.

After a long absence, Rose is back in Alouette,
primarily to help out her impossible-to-please mother,
but also to keep tabs on the child she wasn't allowed
to keep. Working hard, helping her mother and trying
to steal glimpses of her child seem to be all that's in
Wild Rose's future—until the day single father
Evan Grant catches her in the act.

NORTH COUNTRY
Stories

Alouette, Michigan.
Located high on the Upper
Peninsula—home to strong
men, stalwart women and
lots and lots of trees.

Available in November 2004 *wherever Harlequin books are sold*

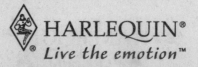

HARLEQUIN®
Live the emotion™

and a paper plate filled with either tobacco or, more likely, marijuana sat near the bed stand and in between a pair of Nike tennis shoes. It appeared this was Tyler's room. His unkempt bed bore blue sheets, a floral bedspread and unmatching floral pillowcase, and a Bugs Bunny comforter.

Meyer had to leave. Evidence technicians would be counting on her to help secure an affidavit and search warrant for the home. Until then, any evidence they gathered or photographs they took could potentially be tossed out in court. A mistake like that could jeopardize any case, and this one had more at stake than most. Two people were dead, and there was nothing natural about what happened to them.

Meyer stepped outside the home through the same front door she had entered and pulled the protective booties off her shoes. Sergeant Joseph Golino, who would ultimately conduct some of the interviews with partygoers in the investigation, stood with her for a quick briefing. Tyler was already in police custody, Golino said. The officers would need to get an affidavit and search warrant for him, too, to get a DNA sample and search for trace evidence on his clothes and body. Detective Chris Fulcher already was assigned to interview the 911 caller, leaving Tyler for Meyer to face. That didn't leave much time. If Tyler was to be charged in the death of his parents, he would have to appear for the first time before a judge within twenty-four hours.

CHAPTER 4

The television trucks and print reporters arrived swiftly. Those first words uttered into the police scanner—parents killed with the back of a hammer—were enough to get local media racing. Two deaths in one night was unheard of, after all. Maybe not in Orlando two hours to the north or Miami two hours south, but this was Port St. Lucie. Kids here smoked weed; they didn't kill people.

TCPalm.com, a news site dedicated to "Florida's Treasure Coast and Palm Beaches," was among the first to arrive. Photographer Deborah Silver captured images of the yellow crime scene tape and police gathering evidence in the shadowy windows of the once serene home. The double murder was bad enough, but as reporters learned about the party—a gathering of as many as sixty of Tyler's friends and acquaintances—the story began to explode. Reporters were learning the details almost as quickly as the police. Teens who'd been at the party the night before showed up to see if cops were really outside the house, as they'd heard, and they told some of the reporters about the shindig they'd left just hours earlier. Police, meanwhile, were getting phone calls from young adults and neighborhood parents telling them to check out Tyler's computer. *You need to confiscate it as soon as possible because Tyler posted on Facebook that he was going to murder his parents,* one tipster said. That part wasn't exactly true, but police quickly verified that the party invite had circulated on the social networking site, and that was enough to sink their stomachs.

"It was a merciless killing. It was brutal and the Facebook invitation—a party to have your friends and 40 to 60 people come over—I think speaks for itself," police captain Don Kryak told a reporter at the scene. Tyler had posted the invitation in the afternoon, Kryak confirmed, meaning that he'd invited people over before he inflicted the flurry of fatal blows. Kryak also verified the hammer rumor: "The blunt force trauma to the head and torso with a 22-inch framing hammer can effect a considerable amount of injury."

Some reporters swarmed the scene; others awaited Tyler's inevitable arrival at the county jail. As a sheriff's car pulled into the sally port, cameras zoomed in on deputies as they helped the tall teen from the backseat, where he'd been sitting with his hands cuffed behind his back. Save for the clanking of the jail door, the scene was quiet until a female reporter's voice broke the near silence.

"Tyler, Tyler," she called, prompting the teen to instinctively look over his shoulder for a split second before turning back around. "They say you murdered your parents. Is it true, Tyler?"

The deputies walked Tyler inside the jail and let the door clang behind him.

Reporters began approaching neighbors, some of whom had set up lawn chairs in their driveways to watch the police investigation unfold. Naturally, the media wanted to know more about who had been killed, and slowly, descriptions of Blake the "gentle giant" and Mary Jo the schoolteacher began to emerge. Blake worked for Florida Power & Light Company at the St. Lucie Nuclear Plant, a company spokesman said. "Our prayers are with the Hadley family at this time," Doug Andrews told reporters. Mary Jo had worked for twenty-four years as an elementary school teacher with the St. Lucie County School District. Like Blake's, her employer released a generic, if still genuine, statement: "The St. Lucie County School District family is deeply saddened at the tragic loss of one of our valued colleagues. Our thoughts and prayers are with the family."

Most neighbors agreed that they were shocked; they'd never seen much out of the ordinary from Tyler. He wasn't a model neighbor and he got in trouble from time to time, but what kid didn't? Soon, however, a former neighbor stepped forward to be interviewed by CNN's Jane Velez-Mitchell. Jason Maerki, who had moved from the neighborhood a few years prior, said Tyler was a disturbed youth who seemed to have dead eyes and was drawn to mischief.

"When I first moved in, I was warned by all the neighbors on the street that he was a troubled child, that he'd vandalized the house that I was moving into, and that I should keep an eye out for him," Maerki said.

He said his own son got in trouble once for setting a fire in a wooded area. Upon questioning the boy and his friends, he'd learned that Tyler had given his kid the lighter and instructions on what to burn. He'd scolded Tyler with little effect.

"Tyler was a very flat-lined person," he said. "He never showed emotion, whether it was happy or sad . . . He looked at me in my eyes and I could tell that he didn't care, that he enjoyed what had happened. Where it confused me is that he wasn't very aggressive to the other kids whatsoever. He was bigger than all of the kids that played in the neighborhood. He was the biggest one. I was more worried about him doing something to the children. Instead, I had to be more worried about him having them do things. He was more the type that wanted to sit back and watch things happen and really not have his hands in it."

Then there were Tyler's eyes, Maerki added. They were hollow, even in photographs playing with his children.

"At no time would you ever see any emotion out of him," Maerki said. "I don't think [I've] ever seen him smile. When he was in trouble, he wasn't like most kids who would put their heads down and feel bad. There was never any remorse or conscience when you looked into his eyes . . . I would hate to think it's only me that sees it."

Velez-Mitchell assured him it wasn't as images of Tyler's mug shots and photos lifted from his and his father's Facebook pages flashed across the screen. Maerki had met Blake Hadley after the fire incident, he said. He'd walked Tyler home after scolding him to face his parents, in part to ensure that Tyler didn't spin what had happened and make Maerki or his son out to be a bad guy. Blake met him at the door and, after hearing what had happened, apologized and sent Tyler to his room. He assured Maerki that he'd take care of it.

"I also told him at that time that there was a lot of people on the street that worried about him when he would walk around the neighborhood all the time,"

Maerki said. "His demeanor made you want to look out your window and see what he was doing."

The interview helped tell the story of the evil son, but it wasn't in line with the Tyler that most people interviewed by the media said they knew.

"I saw on the news people saying that they had an idea he was a troublemaker," Michael Mandell said. "I think some of them are just lying. I know there's one lady who lives toward the end of the street. He'd say hi and give her a hug all the time. I thought it was weird, but it turned out it was his old preschool teacher and he liked her. He was a nice kid."

HLN's Nancy Grace reported the news in her usual bluster, her voice at a near scream as she announced, "And tonight, a popular teen throws the party of a lifetime, inviting scores of friends by Facebook to a party at his place. Only two people don't show up: his mom and dad. They couldn't make it. They were locked in the bedroom—dead! Bludgeoned to death with a hammer!" She repeated the introduction at least twice as her show unfolded and broke for commercials, each time sounding slightly more outraged. *Nice kid* wasn't among her descriptions, though she did repeatedly call Tyler "popular," as evidenced by the sixty-some guests at his party. But Tyler truly knew only a fraction of the people who'd swarmed his house that night. Most were mere acquaintances, lured to the shindig by a game of Telephone and the promise of free booze and absent parents.

The Stuart News, based in Stuart, Florida, wrote a story within days of the killings that chronicled just how choked the area was with outside media. Journalists from NBC News and the *Today* show, the Associated Press, more than a dozen metropolitan newspapers, and several statewide television newscasts descended upon the small town. Robin Quivers of *The Howard Stern Show* mentioned the deaths during her news segment, which typically reached more than a million listeners on SiriusXM satellite radio. The story ranked second on NYDailyNews .com's most-read list and was the third-most-read piece on BBC Brasil. It also hit most-read lists on news sites in Canada and the United Kingdom, and outlets in Norway and Australia picked it up. *People* magazine featured it prominently on its website as well.

"This is an awful crime," Mark Potter, NBC correspondent, said as he waited for police to release copies of the official report to the many media members.

Port St. Lucie officials bristled at the attention.

"This could have happened to any city anywhere," Vice Mayor Jack Kelly said.

But police took the attention in stride. Officers were carefully combing the crime scene and balancing Florida's media-friendly Sunshine Laws with the need to protect evidence, the release of which they feared might jeopardize their case. And they were hard at work trying to make sense of the two Tylers they were hearing about: the dead-eyed sociopath capable of bludgeoning his parents, and the lovable kid who still had a soft spot for his preschool teacher. All investigators could really grasp at this stage was what they'd seen inside the home, and it was horrific.

"The crime scene was certainly a merciless killing," Kryak, a heavyset man with a shaved head and beard, told reporters. "It was brutal."

Kryak and Officer Tom Nichols were reporters' police liaisons on the killings. They were quoted in dozens of stories and in TV newscasts both stateside and internationally, including wire stories posted by the Associated Press and CNN. Nichols, wearing a burgundy tie and dark suit with sunglasses, said he couldn't yet speculate about any possible motive, but he told a group of reporters that it seemed Tyler wanted to hide what he'd done by tossing the household items atop his parents.

"It was a deliberate attempt to conceal the bodies inside the room," he said.

Both officers said police had a long investigation ahead of them. For detectives to truly grasp what had led up to the slaughter, they'd need to dig deep beneath the superficial headlines and figure out more than just what had happened. They had to learn why.

CHAPTER 5

Tyler Hadley sat quietly in the interrogation room. He wore black gym shorts, a black T-shirt, and black socks. He was not wearing shoes. This was how he'd been dressing in recent years, ever since he gave up his middle school skater-boy attire. Now black tees and gym shorts were practically his uniform. Sometimes he'd wear the T-shirts layered. Some shirts were plain; others had images or slogans. But they were almost always black and combined with black gym shorts. His friends figured he must have a pair of shorts for each day of the week.

Tyler had been in police custody for nearly three hours. No one had dared attempt to interview him. His inevitable defense lawyer would surely pounce to get dismissed any words he uttered before being properly told his rights. Even though Officer Greene had recited the Miranda rights when Tyler was first put in custody—right after another officer had wrenched open the bedroom door to discover Mary Jo and Blake inside—it still wasn't defense-proof. Department policy dictated that interviews and interrogations should be conducted, whenever possible, in front of audio- and video-recording equipment, and the police department's interview rooms were fully equipped with both. Though not all departments in the country follow those guidelines, the ones that do open themselves up to far fewer claims of coercion and misconduct.

Detective Meyer walked into the room at 7:57 a.m.— nearly three hours after police first entered the Hadley home. Meyer's demeanor was professional but casual. She had a job to do, and she was going to do it, she'd say, and if she was investigating a murder, she didn't care much about whether you were drinking booze on probation. Not her problem.

With the recording devices up and running, Meyer approached Tyler, who seemed largely unfazed.

"Hey, young man," Meyer said as she walked into the room. "Is it Tyler?"

Tyler mumbled a response.

"Tyler, you want something to drink?"

"Yeah."

It was standard cop routine: Break the ice, offer a beverage, get the subject comfortable. It was partly for psychological gain, and partly, too, to ensure that the kid couldn't later claim he was too sleep-deprived, too hungry, too thirsty to have made those incriminating statements. Tyler was still just seventeen, no matter how heinous the crime he was suspected of, and he no longer had any parents to help protect him from the big, bad police. Meyer played it cool.

"I got something cold," she said. "I got a Dr Pepper and I got a Vanilla Coke."

"Vanilla Coke."

"Vanilla Coke, you got it." Meyer left the room for a beat, then reentered. She'd found some water, too, she said.

"Can I have both?" Tyler asked.

Sure, Meyer said.

"Thank you." Tyler seemed awfully polite for a murder suspect.

Meyer settled into her chair and introduced herself. She began with the formalities—name and address.

"How long have you lived there?" she asked.

"My whole life," Tyler replied.

The teen's answers were clear and concise, Meyer would later write in her official report. He answered "without issue."

"You had a party last night, did you?" she asked.

Tyler nodded.

"Are you a senior this year?"

Yeah, he'd be a senior at Port St. Lucie High School, he explained.

"What time did your party start?" Meyer asked.

"Probably around, like, ten o'clock."

"A lot of people?"

"Yeah, a good amount."

The real questions Meyer wanted to ask were about Tyler's parents. But before she could, she'd have to read him his Miranda rights again, this time more formally. She handed him a sheet of paper listing the rights, and together they went through the list one by one.

"The first one is you have the right to remain silent. The second one is, anything you say can be used against you in court, okay? You've heard this before now, right?"

Tyler nodded. This was the spiel on every television cop drama ever created, after all.

Meyer went through the rest—the right to a lawyer, a lawyer would be appointed if he couldn't afford one, and if he wanted to talk without a lawyer, he could stop at any point to ask for one before answering more questions. She asked if he understood. He said he did. She asked him again. He said he did.

"Are you absolutely sure?" she belabored. She had to. She couldn't risk him saying later that he didn't understand his rights.

"I'm sure," Tyler said.

He marked on his sheet that he comprehended his rights, and then proved very quickly that he did indeed.

"Uh—I want a lawyer," he said.

Meyer didn't miss a beat. Those were the magic words to kill an interview. Anything said after that moment, even voluntarily by Tyler, could undercut the prosecution's entire case.

"Okay, all right," Meyer said.

She left the room without a good-bye. Two more officers entered.

"I need you to stand up for me," one said.

Tyler stood. As handcuffs were placed on his wrists, he asked for his water and Coke. The whole time, he was polite and cooperative, and he referred to the officers as "sir."

A few hours later, after a judge approved the search warrants, Tyler and Meyer met again. This time, she was to search him for possible trace and DNA evidence that might help her case. With Detective Fulcher at her side, Meyer slipped on some gloves and started to photograph Tyler. Then she used medical swabs to take both wet and dry samplings of his right hand, his fingernails, his right leg, some abrasions on his right collarbone. Then she moved to his left side, also swabbing some shoulder scratches and a cut on his lower left leg. She got swabs from the inside of his cheek as well.

Fulcher had Tyler strip and collected his black socks

and gym shorts. He took off one short-sleeved T-shirt to expose another. That one bore the words, GOT CRABS?—a play on the popular dairy campaign, "Got milk?" The clothes were bagged and labeled, and Tyler was given a white jumpsuit to wear instead.

Tyler had his wallet on him, and Meyer began sifting through its contents. She noted it had his Florida driver's license, a debit card in his father's name, and about $264 in cash. Shoved into the wallet was also a religious card bearing a quote attributed to Our Lady of Medjugorje. It read: IF YOU KNEW HOW MUCH I LOVE YOU, YOU'D CRY OF JOY.

CHAPTER 6

Back at the Hadley home, evidence technicians finally got the okay to start documenting. Officer Jeanine Marshall hit the scene at 6:07 a.m. Within ten minutes, she was wearing the protective gear she needed—booties and gloves, for example—to make sure she wouldn't contaminate evidence. She walked through the home, spotted the bodies in the master bedroom, saw the blood on the floor and furniture, and began taking overall photographs of the inside of the home. It was a long and labor-intensive process. First were the photographs documenting every blood spatter and drop she could find, mapping out the home's layout and party remnants. Technicians also numbered the floor tiles in the kitchen so the pieces would stay in clear order, and photographed in detail the red mop that had rested atop the mess in the bedroom. They shot images of the garage, where they found a bloody footprint and what appeared to be bloodstains in the utility sink. By the end, they would shoot well over one thousand frames.

Marshall didn't break for lunch until after 3 p.m. An hour later, when she got back to the scene, the search warrant had officially arrived. As it was being read, Marshall started to videotape the crime scene from the outside to the inside, still wearing booties and protective gear to prevent contamination. She documented the bloody shoe prints that led from the foyer all the way out to the sink in the garage. She also documented blood that had been cleaned from the tile and grout just outside the master bedroom, and beneath the mismatched china hutch and computer desk. Inside the master bedroom, she could see the blood spatter that covered the entertainment center, as well as the bloody drag marks that covered the floor. Marshall switched again from video footage to still images and focused in particular on the bloody shoe prints in the garage. She placed placards labeling each step and photographed close-ups of each at a ninety-degree angle for scale.

Outside, the onlookers had spread beyond neighbors. *The Hadleys are dead. Oh, but they were such a nice couple. Did you hear the boy threw a party last night?* The story had hit the morning news, so gawkers pulled up on the tiny street to stare as police bustled in and out of the house. It was a small town, and Mary Jo was especially well known because of her job as a teacher. By the time the rest of Port St. Lucie was waking up Sunday morning, text messages were flying among friends, and the rumor mill matched the reporting that was already on the television and Internet: Tyler Hadley had killed his parents and then thrown a party with their bodies still in the house.

Word reached Raymond McNamara, who quickly called his ex-wife. She in turn rushed to her daughter Meghan's bedroom. Did Meghan know Tyler? Did she know about this party? Yeah, Meghan said to both. She was actually *at* the party. Her mother recoiled and insisted that Meghan tell her everything.

About half an hour away in Stuart, Florida, Miles Petkaitis was starting to hear grumblings about a tragedy twenty-five miles to the south. As soon as he heard the Hadley name attached, he caught his breath. Maurice Hadley, Blake's father, lived just around the corner. He'd seen Blake, Mary Jo, and the kids gather there countless times over the years. Miles could look out his window and see into the elder Hadley's backyard. *The man's in his eighties,* he later said he'd thought. *How will he survive this?*

The news was spreading so quickly that police couldn't keep ahead of it to inform next of kin. Relatives started calling the police station. Some showed up at the crime scene. At both places, they were told only that a homicide investigation was under way. Kelly Reynolds, who was both Mary Jo's niece and one of her best friends, didn't believe the news at first. If police were outside the Hadley home, it was probably because Tyler had finally done what his mother feared most—suicide. But when Kelly reached out to police only to get stonewalled, her stomach sank.

About seven hundred miles away in Cullowhee, North Carolina, twenty-four-year-old Ryan Hadley's cell phone began blowing up with text messages and calls. *Something's going on at your house,* people told him. *Your brother snapped and killed your parents.* At first, it seemed absurd to Ryan. Why the hell would people tell him this? He'd just talked to his parents through text messages the night before. He called his father's cell phone, and then his mother's. Neither answered. He called his grandparents. Both sets lived within thirty minutes of his folks. Still nothing. Not a big deal, Ryan reasoned. Maybe they'd all gone to church together. It was a Sunday morning, after all, and his folks were active parishioners. Ryan tried to stay calm, but the calls and texts kept coming. He replied to more than one person not to believe anything they'd heard. It couldn't be true. How could it be? Wouldn't the police have reached out to him by now? No matter how calm and reasoned Ryan tried to remain, he couldn't keep still for long. The news was spreading like wildfire on the Internet, and it was starting to make headlines on major TV news networks. CNN began reporting about the allegations, relying on footage captured by affiliates. That likely would've happened with the murders anyway, but add in the party afterward, and the story elevated from sad-but-we've-heard-this-before to incomprehensible. Still without having heard from police, Ryan packed up and headed to Florida.

Inside Ryan's childhood home, Marshall worked alongside an investigator from the medical examiner's office to start removing the items that had been dumped atop Mary Jo's and Blake's bodies. In a detailed report she'd later file, she itemized everything: "bath and beach towels, pillows, mops, numerous papers, files, file cabinet, grocery items consisting of numerous loaves of bread, cherries, wet and dry dog food and dog bones, potatoes, gravy and condiments, coffee grounds, broken ceramics and glass, shoes, chairs, pictures with frames, candy and collectibles." The mops appeared to be stained with blood, she noted. The shoes nearest the entryway also had blood spatter on them, as well as blood on the tread.

Outside, officers secured the area around the house, both front and back. Patrol Officer J. L. Krause was situated along the backyard fence to ensure that no gawkers or media crossed into the crime scene. Officer Frankie Borges maintained the crime scene log to document the comings and goings of scene visitors—a potentially crucial component of proving in court that a scene wasn't compromised. Officer John Fazio kept watch on the back of the house until he was relieved that afternoon by Officer Anthony Romani. These "scene security" officers didn't go inside; their job was to make sure only authorized personnel got anywhere near the Hadley home.

Marshall and an investigator from the medical examiner's office slowly uncovered several towels draped over each victim. Then they saw the hammer—long, with a wooden handle, designed for framing houses. It was heavy-duty with a straight claw opposite its round head. The hammer lay between the couple, on top of Blake's arm and beneath Mary Jo's leg, with its head facing downward. Marshall saw bloodstains on its handle and head, so she snapped photographs and carefully placed it into an evidence bag for processing.

Next came the uncomfortable task of fully uncovering the bodies. As the towels came off Mary Jo's head, Marshall could see the skull fractures on the left side. The officer lifted the back of Mary Jo's shirt and photographed the wounds. Some were side by side and symmetrical. Others were round with a waffle-like print. She also had bruises on her right hand and left forearm.

Marshall moved on to Blake, photographing with a ruler for scale. Blake lay next to his wife, but stretched facedown in the opposite direction. His feet were closest to the bedroom door; his arms were outstretched toward the east wall. He was a large man who, now felled and prostrate, appeared helpless. As with Blake's wife, the towel that had been wrapped around his head was soaked in blood, and his burgundy T-shirt had been sliced straight through the back. Upon lifting Blake's shirt, Marshall saw deep, symmetrical wounds that seemed the same as those on Mary Jo's body. He'd been dressed casually this day, in blue shorts, white socks, and gray tennis shoes, and now everything was drenched in blood.

Detective Meyer returned to the Hadley home about 9:30 p.m. The couple's bodies were still there. Marshall and her cohorts had methodically removed the debris, taking the stuff out bit by bit and laying it on the sitting room floor, which Marshall had covered with a sterile paper to protect the items' evidentiary value. She didn't want the items to pick up fibers from other rooms; everything had to be just as it was inside the master bedroom to ensure it could stand up under the scrutiny of a shrewd defense lawyer. Meyer peered into the bedroom at the lifeless Mary Jo, the first time the detective had seen the mother of two cleared of all the debris. Despite the multiple wounds to the left side of Mary Jo's head, Meyer could clearly recognize her based on her driver's license photograph. The detective carefully removed the three rings Mary Jo still wore, bagged them, and labeled them as evidence. Next, she looked at Blake. He, too, had huge gouges to his head, but his face was unmistakable: This was definitely Tyler's father.

This was all Meyer needed for the next step in her investigation. She headed back to the police station and met again with Tyler Hadley. She'd just returned from his house, she told him. She'd seen the crime scene. He was to be charged with two counts of murder. Because he was a juvenile, he'd be taken to the Department of Juvenile Justice detention facility on Bell Avenue in Fort Pierce, not far from the power plant where his father had worked all those years.

Tyler nodded and said nothing.

CHAPTER 7

With Detective Meyer bouncing from crime scene to interviews all day Sunday, she enlisted the help of the police department's victim advocate to reach out to each set of Hadley's grandparents. Mary Jo's parents, Sam and Maggie DiVittorio, lived half a mile away in Port St. Lucie. Because of the proximity—and because Mary Jo was especially close with her mother—Ryan and Tyler grew up as much at their grandparents' home as their own. To get there by foot, it was a quick walk west on Northeast Granduer, a short jaunt on Larkspur, then around the corner to Horizon Lane. Or, if they were feeling particularly boyish, they could cut through some yards and trim a few minutes off the travel time.

Blake's parents, Maurice and Betty Hadley, didn't live within walking distance but were still very close. The city of Stuart was just up Florida's Treasure Coast in Martin County. Home to about sixteen thousand people, Stuart boasted a cute downtown with quaint stores and a historical museum, as well as waterfront restaurants and golf courses. Maurice, who went by Mo, and Betty perhaps weren't quite as close with their grandsons as Sam and Maggie, but the families were tight-knit nonetheless. It had always been important to Blake and Mary Jo that they raise their sons to value family. Living so close definitely helped, and their proximity was no accident.

Blake had grown up with his family in Fort Lauderdale, Florida, with two siblings—brother Michael and sister Linda. He was a towering man, about six foot four, and heavier set, and he always seemed acutely aware that his size could be intimidating. He didn't like that, so he worked to combat it. He was quick to smile and laugh, earning a reputation as a kindhearted giant with co-workers at the Florida Power & Light Company in St. Lucie County, where he was hired in 1981. As a young man, his size and slightly hooked nose gave him a goofy-but-lovable appearance. In photos, he seemed to hunch his shoulders just slightly, the way that tall people sometimes do, as if in an attempt to knock off two or three inches and fit in slightly better with the shorter folk around them.

"Something about him seemed like a giant teddy bear, it really did," recalled Miles Petkaitis, who grew up near Maurice Hadley's eventual home in Stuart, and whose father worked alongside Blake at the power plant. "He seemed like he couldn't hurt a fly. I know for a fact he did not have one bad bone in his body. I know he didn't."

Petkaitis had been to his father's work many times growing up. FPL, as the locals called it, was the largest electric utility in Florida, serving about four and a half million customers, and the state's leading employer with more than ten thousand workers. Under the NextEra

Energy Inc. umbrella, 2011 revenues topped $15.3 billion. On its company website, it boasted that it consistently outperformed national averages for service reliability, while customer bills were about 25 percent below the national average. FPL's power travels along seventy thousand miles of lines throughout half of Florida. The St. Lucie County plant was a clean environment, and a friendly one, despite the strict security and harsh fluorescent lights. Its severe industrial towers marred the otherwise serene view on South Hutchinson Island between Fort Pierce and Stuart in Jensen Beach, Florida. On one side was the Atlantic Ocean; the other, the Indian River. From an early age, Miles learned the importance of safety through his dad and Blake's work. Posters throughout the plant promoted STAR—an acronym for "stop, think, act, and review"—and being cautious became second nature to the men.

Miles's family knew Mo and Betty best of the Hadleys. Mo was a chatty guy. He'd regularly swing by to say hello and chitchat with the neighbors. He was elderly, past eighty, but in pretty good shape considering. Betty was just a sweet old lady whose life seemed dedicated to her children and family. Miles saw Blake with his folks a lot. They seemed to be a close and loving family, he would later recall.

"They're country folk. They're as American as you can get," he said. "Mo and Blake, they just had a very tight relationship, you could tell."

Blake was a true Floridian, having grown up without seasons, at ease with the sultry heat that made the state a haven for winter-hating snowbirds nationwide. His cousin Brenda Mayes recalled to reporters a time some forty years earlier when Blake and his family visited her in Indiana. It was wintertime, and the snow was wet and heavy.

"Blake had never seen snow, and he made snowballs," Mayes reminisced. "His dad bought dry ice so that Blake could take them back to Florida and throw them at his friends."

Blake loved his home state and stayed put for college, studying at Florida State University, where he was in the Chi Phi fraternity. The current incarnation of the frat is an amalgamation of three organizations that originally shared the Chi Phi name in the 1800s, the oldest being one founded in 1824 at Princeton. Blake graduated in 1980 and stayed in touch with many of his college buddies. "He was known by his brothers as a gentle giant, with a big heart and a ready smile," the Nu Delta Alumni Association posted on its website upon learning of Blake's death. He was quick to give encouragement or provide much-needed clowning around, they added. "He never had unkind words for anyone."

In photos from his college days, Blake looked awkward but fun. He wasn't the best looking, but there was something kind behind his dorky smile. He simply beamed. He'd make people laugh just by being goofy. Friends and family would tell Meyer that Blake's main goal in life was to make others happy. It was one of the reasons he wasn't great at disciplining his children, they would say. Even Tyler's friends—the few who'd met his parents—remembered Blake as a goofball, singing at random. One time, recalled Michael Mandell, Blake kept singing: *We are the Miami. Tuna. Dolphins.* "I just laughed," Michael said. Other times, while on the family computer, Blake would bellow, "Hedleeeeeeeey LA-MARR!" in an apparent reference to Harvey Korman's character in the cult Mel Brooks comedy *Blazing Saddles.* Michael didn't get the reference, but he laughed anyway. He couldn't help it. Blake was just silly.

That's what made it all the more difficult for Blake's

friends to grasp what had happened as the news spread that Sunday. Brian Nichols, a co-worker, reeled. He told reporters it was unbelievable; Blake was "so quiet and gentle." The two men had worked together for at least fifteen years. "I don't think I ever saw him get angry at anyone or anything, and we've been in some pretty tough working conditions together at times."

Parents Maurice and Betty said he'd always been that way: kind as a child, a good student, among the top ten of his class—top ten students, not percentile. More than two months after the deaths, the couple still struggled to even talk to Detective Meyer. The pain was so raw. Their happy-go-lucky son was gone.

Mary Jo was born in Braddock, Pennsylvania. Like Blake, she had one brother and one sister, Sam Jr. and Laurie. By the time Mary Jo hit high school, the family had moved to Fort Lauderdale. Mary Jo was a tall, pretty brunette with high cheekbones and dark eyes. She had a natural tan, a glow that didn't disappear in the winter months, and a button nose that turned up just slightly at the end. She was, in a word, cute. In high school, her reputation was as considerate and kind, schoolmate Cindy Montgomery recalled. Mary Jo wasn't the most popular kid in school, but she was well liked, and she stayed close with some of her childhood friends until the day she died.

It was in Fort Lauderdale that Blake and Mary Jo met. Though they physically looked nothing alike—Blake with his ruddy complexion and Mary Jo, more olive— they still seemed a natural couple. Both beamed when they smiled. Both were family-minded and outwardly affectionate. On their wedding day, Mary Jo wore a white gown with puffy sleeves and an ornate veil in her hair. Blake donned a powder-blue suit and white dress shirt with an upturned collar, a matching blue tie at his neck.

Many of his frat brothers attended the wedding, and the photos snapped are of a broad-smiled couple clearly in love, happy to have found each other.

Soon after they married, they decided to move ninety minutes north from Fort Lauderdale to Port St. Lucie to raise a family. Blake's father would tell a reporter that the couple built the white, ranch-style house and planned to call it home until their retirement—a milestone that for fifty-four-year-old Blake was looming ever nearer. About the same time that they moved to Port St. Lucie, Mary Jo gave birth to the couple's first child—a boy they named Ryan. They followed a tradition from Blake's side of the family by giving the boy his father's first name as his middle name. Just as Blake was Blake Maurice, Ryan was Ryan Blake. The family joined the St. Lucie Catholic Church in Port St. Lucie, where Blake and Mary Jo remained active members for twenty-five years. Six years after Ryan came Tyler. Mary Jo had trouble during the pregnancy, so doctors induced labor nearly a month before the due date. For three weeks, baby Tyler was in shaky shape, forced to stay in the hospital while his distraught mother went every day to stay with him. She doted on him and cooed over him, trying her best to compensate for the impersonal hospital room that served as his immediate home. Finally, his lungs developed well enough for Blake and Mary Jo to bring home their second child, and the Hadleys were whole again.

But it seemed Tyler would be prone to illness. At just three months old, he got chicken pox, again putting his life in jeopardy. And once again, Mary Jo and Blake doted on him and nursed him back to health. Then, as they readied to enroll Tyler in preschool, they discovered a hormone imbalance and took him to an endocrinologist, who prescribed a thyroid medication. Around that time, Tyler first started to worry outwardly about his weight.

Family members thought it odd that a little boy would seem concerned—no, obsessed, really—about becoming fat, and no matter how much reassurance Mary Jo and Blake provided, it never seemed to squash the fear. His grandmother Magdaline "Maggie" DiVittorio, a nurse, would later recall with some anger that Tyler's pediatrician made the grave mistake of telling Tyler he was "sturdy" around the time he was ten or eleven years old. To Tyler, *sturdy* meant "fat," and he became even more weight-conscious, Maggie later told a detective.

Like most teens, both Ryan and Tyler had acne for a time, and both took prescription Accutane. Though the controversial medication wouldn't be taken off the market until 2009 after being linked with inflammatory bowel disease, Maggie DiVittorio tried to talk her daughter out of giving it to the boys long before its dangers were well known. She called it poison, saying it gave the kids dry skin and dry mouth. Both boys took it for a long time, recalled Maggie. Mary Jo insisted on giving them everything they needed to bolster their self-esteem: braces, prescriptions, whatever it took. And when it was clear that her efforts weren't helping Tyler feel good about himself, she took it personally, wondering if she'd done enough or was somehow to blame. Friend Carmela "Mel" Jones said that Mary Jo worried that she hadn't bonded enough with him in his first few weeks and that he'd maybe end up small because of his early arrival, leading other kids to pick on him. She was fiercely protective of both sons, but more so of Tyler. Mel would later tell a detective that Mary Jo got defensive if anyone suggested she needed to be firmer with Tyler. People picked on him, she would say, and he was sensitive. To Mel, it sounded like the adoring mother was making excuses for her sometimes-spoiled boy.

That aside, there was one area in which Mary Jo

wouldn't budge: church. Each of her sons was an altar boy. Even as the kids became teens and started to rebel, their parents were adamant they attend every Sunday. Both went through phases of locking their doors in an attempt to ditch service, and while Mary Jo and Blake were considered pushovers by some family members, the kids didn't get away with skipping church.

From an early age, Tyler worried some family members because he seemed to inherently have an unhealthy fixation on the macabre. He made dark jokes, talked with strange fascination about killing himself, and generally seemed obsessed with death. Around age five, he joined the family for the funeral of a great-grandmother. Little Tyler kept asking to see his grandma, so Uncle Mike pointed out that Grandma was sitting in the crowd. *She's right over there,* Mike recalled to a detective.

"No," Tyler said. "I want to see the dead one."

As the boys grew, Tyler became unusually self-critical and negative. He'd accuse others of not loving him, of loving someone else more, or of thinking he was fat. He'd say this to Mary Jo, even, and the concerned mother would assure him that she adored him and that he was perfect. But Tyler didn't seem to hear her. His self-esteem likely wasn't helped by his parents' weight issues. Blake got even heavier as he aged and became medically obese. Mary Jo, meanwhile, gained a lot of weight in her pregnancies that she couldn't seem to shed. In the early 2000s, she underwent surgery to help her lose the pounds, and it worked—to a degree. One former student said she returned to school after the summer break looking as though she'd lost half a human. She was still on the heavier side, but considerably thinner than she had been for years, and she made walking the family's two dogs part of her regular exercise routine. The surgery and lifestyle change were in part to ensure she stayed healthy for her children. She wanted to live a long, healthy life so she'd be there for her boys as they became men and started families of their own.

Mary Jo was hired on to teach elementary school soon after she and Blake moved to Port St. Lucie. She taught in the St. Lucie County School District, eventually settling in at Village Green Environmental Studies School, a magnet school that concentrated on giving its kids tools to tackle environmental issues. The unique curriculum aimed to turn pupils into "world changers," and its motto was "Make a difference—the power of one." Each year focused on a concentrated area of study. For example, kindergartners learned generally about the environment, while third graders learned about energy. Mary Jo taught first grade, the emphasis of which was "recycle, reduce, reuse." On her home computer were reading assignments for her kids with titles such as "A Bed Full of Cats" and "A House for Hermit Crab." She carefully chronicled students' behaviors and progress and crafted calendars that she printed from her home computer. Her lesson plans were varied; one was called "hand washing," while others focused on vocabulary, grammar, and math.

Bernard Beaux Artabazon, known to friends simply as Beaux, recalled meeting Mary Jo in 2002, when he first began substitute teaching. Then thirty-five years old, Beaux had landed a long-term gig covering a multi-grade class thanks to a full-timer's maternity leave, and Tyler was a third grader in the class. Beaux began the job in the fall—the Halloween decorations still hanging in the hallways were dated—and was set to continue into the following year. It was a somewhat tumultuous time for Beaux personally, as he'd just moved to Florida to be close to his mother who lived there. He was going to school to become a teacher, and subbing was a way to get to know the area and make some money doing what he loved at the same time.

First, Beaux met Mary Jo through Tyler.

"He was lovely," Beaux later recalled of the boy. "He was a very well-behaved, polite, funny boy. He had a great sense of humor. But he was very shy, I would say."

Mary Jo was obviously active in Tyler's life. She checked in with Beaux often to make sure Tyler was staying on top of his studies—which Beaux found refreshing.

"I was a new sub and teaching another teacher's kid, so it was really nice that this parent was determined to make sure he was keeping up with what he needed to learn," Beaux recalled. "The way it is these days, a lot of parents don't get involved. They think that learning just magically happens at school."

And Tyler was engaged, astute. He was a good student and he followed the rules. After school, he often stayed and played in the hallways with other teachers' children, enjoying the school in a way that only those allowed to roam after hours can. They'd play games in the cavernous cafeteria as their parents wrapped up their workdays. Beaux considered those youngsters his surrogate nieces and nephews.

"When you work at a school, it's like a family," he said. "We were all very close."

He'd met Blake, too, through parties as some teachers retired or celebrated the holidays. He didn't know him well, but remembered him as upbeat and jovial, quick to smile. Mary Jo seemed more outwardly reserved; Blake, meanwhile, was just a fun-loving guy.

As Beaux got to know Mary Jo, he realized something about her that was at times lost on some of her colleagues: "She was frickin' hilarious," he said. "Mary Jo was so funny. I was a new teacher in a new place from a different state. It was so nice to meet someone like her."

Mary Jo was dry, sarcastic. A sly, knowing smile would sneak across her face as she subtly poked fun. She had a sharp wit, and sometimes, people had trouble getting the jokes. She'd deliver a line in such a deadpan manner that it went right over others' heads. Or the punch line would be in those impossibly expressive eyes of hers. She would point out a flawed idea by drily commenting on how "great" a plan it was. It perhaps sounded sincere, but the truth would flicker through her dark eyes, and Beaux would catch a glimpse and burst into laughter.

"I got her when I first met her," he said. "Some people would take her literally, but if you knew Mary Jo, you knew what she really meant. There was not this wall between her and me, like, 'Oh, I have to act this way around her.' She was hilarious to me. I got her humor."

But for all of her dry wit, she was always accessible to the children. One student, who planned after high school to become a teacher in part to honor Mary Jo, remembered her as being more like a second mother than a second-grade teacher.

"She had that mom instinct. She was a great mom. She was a great teacher," Chelsea Wells told a television reporter.

Mary Jo was a teachers' advocate, too, gathering her colleagues' concerns and presenting them to administrators, one union representative told reporters soon after the deaths. Vanessa Tillman, president of the St. Lucie County Classroom Teachers Association and Classified Unit, said Mary Jo was always calm when helping her peers. And she was an excellent educator.

"Besides the training and the scientific side, there's a true art to teaching, and [Mary Jo] was excellent when it came to both sides," Tillman told a reporter. "She was

interested in educating the whole child, not just the academic side, which is particularly important in early childhood education."

The parents of Village Green's students said she made
a lasting impression—even on children who weren't in
her class. Thirty-six-year-old Lauren Espitia said she
knew Mrs. Hadley's name even though her six-year-old
daughter Alyssa was just a kindergartner.

"She was the only teacher outside of Alyssa's main
teacher that she ever mentioned," Espitia told a reporter.
"I know she said she got to go to her room sometimes,
and [Mary Jo] was really nice and helped her with her
reading."

The day after the couple's bodies were found, a grieving Maurice Hadley told a reporter that Mary Jo was "the
best daughter-in-law you could have."

As a couple, Mary Jo and Blake didn't seem to fight.
They'd weathered some tough times, but they were still
fiercely in love. For nearly twenty years, in fact, Mary Jo
had kept the first email handle she'd ever created:
ilbh412—standing for "I Love Blake Hadley" and their
anniversary date. Still, Mary Jo occasionally got miffed
when she had to be the heavy when it came to the kids,
friends and family members said. Blake was just too good
to be a big disciplinarian, his brother Mike would tell a
detective. Blake wanted to make people laugh, make
them happy; being heavy-handed with his children wasn't
on the agenda. Not that Mary Jo always had to play the
bad guy. In fact, the role suited neither parent, so a lot of
times the kids just ran amok. And, some signs of spoiling
aside, that had seemed more or less fine until recently.
Sure, Ryan had gone through a rebellious phase, but he
was always smart about it and graduated to adulthood
relatively unscathed. As a youngster, Tyler was always

affectionate toward his parents, especially his mother. He would climb on her lap even when he'd grown too large for it. Some family members even called him a "mama's boy," and one relative said that as recently as a few weeks before the deaths, she'd spotted Tyler quietly leaning against his mother on the couch—a rare moment of affection for an increasingly out-of-touch teen.

The couple occasionally had run into some money problems—most recently fixed with a refinancing that had just come through on their house. Mary Jo's brother said she was especially relieved in the days leading up to her death because the mortgage restructuring had gone through, meaning they would be able to keep the home they'd had for a quarter century. They even started talking about renovating the kitchen to do away with the old appliances and apartment-quality cabinets. To keep things afloat, they'd asked to borrow a little money from Ryan, their oldest, and on Saturday, July 16, he mailed them a check and followed up with a text message to his mother, letting her know the money was in the mail. Ryan got text messages back from both parents separately, thanking him profusely and promising to pay him back very soon. Those messages reached Ryan within hours of his parents' deaths.

CHAPTER 8

Back at the crime scene, Officer Jeanine Marshall looked down at Mary Jo's lifeless body. The sight was beyond disturbing. So much trauma. Marshall got some cyanoacrylate hot shots—basically superglue—to fume Mary Jo's ankles for prints. She thought there might be latent fingerprints there left behind from when her body was dragged from the great room into the bedroom. Marshall put Mary Jo in a body bag, then closed it with the hot shots inside. After half an hour, she opened the bag to check for prints. No luck. Blake was also placed into a body bag, and at about midnight—nearly a day and a half after they'd been beaten to death—the couple was finally removed from the home.

There was still so much left to do. As the investigation continued, crime scene technicians would discover Mary

Jo's purse in Tyler's bedroom, as well as his father's wallet. In his room, too, was a prescription bottle of Endocet, a heavy-duty opioid painkiller in his mother's name. He'd taken framed baby clothes of his mother's—an outfit she wore when she was baptized—and tossed it in his room instead of hers.

Crime scene technicians gathered evidence to be sent to the Indian River State College crime lab for analysis and testing. The lab, located in Fort Pierce, boasted on its door the image of a seal that featured an outline of the state of Florida, the scales of justice and a microscope dangling from the jagged edge of the state's northwest corner. Scientists would huddle around such equipment for days to examine the evidence in what had quickly become one of the country's highest-profile slayings. The state-of-the-art facility worked in conjunction with the St. Lucie County Sheriff's Office. Forensic scientists could examine on-site a whole range of evidence, from ballistics to DNA samples, and the men and women wearing the lab coats underwent rigorous scrutiny: In 2006, after one chemist failed two proficiency tests, the lab's director ordered the retesting of 189 drug cases to ensure no one was behind bars—or on the streets—based on faulty analyses. For many in the law enforcement community, the self-correction served as proof of the lab's reliability.

"It may create a lot of work, but so be it, because somebody's due process may have been compromised," one public defender said at the time.

Another lawyer said he was amazed by the self-correction the lab initiated when it realized one of its scientists might have blundered.

"Maybe because they reported it themselves, that proves they are straight and narrow," lawyer Rusty Akins told a reporter. "I have to give them credit for that."

The evidence list from the Hadley home chronicled

page after page of seized items to be tested and inventoried: the hammer found between the victims, a pair of black men's socks, a black T-shirt, black shorts, a pair of size 14 Nike high-top shoes, a pair of size 10 women's sandals, fingernail scrapings, the red-handled sponge mop, a rope mop. Police seized electronics, too—a digital camera, a 16GB iPhone, two disposable cameras, a Toshiba laptop, a few external hard drives. And there was the biological matter seized—skull fragments from the master bedroom, possible brain matter, blood-soaked towels and sponges, and more than one hundred swabs of potentially biohazardous material.

Despite what seemed like a mountain of evidence in the Hadley case, including Tyler's statements to his friends both at the party and beforehand, the forensics team had to be just as diligent in its work as it would be in a case with an unknown suspect and no witnesses. Their job was to carefully chronicle what came into their office, determine whose blood was on what, examine the latent fingerprints lifted from technicians at the scene, and label everything for the likely trial that lay ahead. It would be exhausting work for days to come.

CHAPTER 9

Late Sunday, about the same time the Hadleys' bodies were transported to the medical examiner's office, Meyer got word from the victim advocate that Ryan had finally reached his grandparents' home. He was just blocks away from the house he'd moved out of only a month or so earlier. Some of his belongings were still in his old bedroom, buried beneath the household items that Tyler had tossed in there. Though his parents' bodies had been removed, the house was still a crime scene. Ryan couldn't go inside even if he'd wanted to.

Meyer knocked on the DiVittorios' door at 12:30 a.m., seventeen hours after her workday had begun. Sam Jr., Mary Jo's brother, answered the door with Ryan. Mary Jo's parents had finally fallen asleep, they said. Ryan knew from them only the basics: that Mary Jo and Blake were dead. All he knew about his brother was what he'd learned from newscasts and the rumor mill. He'd gotten nothing directly from police yet. Ryan had been crying all day.

"I apologize for the late hour," Meyer said after she, Sam Jr., Ryan, and the victim's advocate settled into a quiet spot to talk. "We've conducted quite a bit of an investigation today, and you were the first place that I came, okay."

She hesitated. "The investigation dictates that your parents are both gone, and they were killed by blunt force trauma."

"Like, do you know with what or—" Ryan stumbled.

"We have a good idea," Meyer said.

"Do you know who or, like, where?"

"We found them in their bedroom," Meyer replied.

Ryan nodded. "Uh-huh."

"And your brother's been arrested."

It was the first time the family had been officially told that Tyler was the suspect.

"Are you guys charging him with it or—"

"Yes," Meyer said, bluntly.

Sam Jr. interjected. "Is that definitive?"

"Yes," Meyer said again. "I'm really sorry."

Ryan looked devastated.

"I don't have tears anymore," he said.

Ryan Hadley had never been his brother's keeper. Not that he didn't want to be, or wouldn't have been if needed, but he had turned six years old the month before his baby brother was born, and six years is a decent span of time for siblings—when they're young, anyway. Those six years could prove to be nothing once they were both adults, but as children, the six years meant that Ryan was already in school before Tyler was born, he was out of middle school before Tyler entered it, and he graduated high school when Tyler was still in early adolescence.

But that divide had started to shrink in recent years. After Ryan graduated from high school, he stayed in the Granduer home with his parents, and he and Tyler started hanging out. Their favorite pastime was renting movies together—Ryan once said they must have rented every flick ever made—and they'd just chill and watch a film together. When Ryan moved to North Carolina in early June, Tyler tagged along for a day, helping his older brother unpack until Blake showed up with another truck full of belongings. Their parents had worried about how Tyler would handle the move, especially with he and Ryan having become so close. But Tyler seemed nonplussed about it. During the drive to Ryan's new home, he slept most of the way. After Blake showed up and the new pad was filled with Ryan's boxes, Tyler and his father headed back to Florida together.

Despite the brothers' bond, however, there was something off about their relationship, Ryan told Detective Meyer. Tyler was sort of untouchable, unreachable. Ryan would try to be the big brother, to coax Tyler into being comfortable with him, but Tyler had a way of keeping people at arm's length.

"He's kind of like a pathological liar," Ryan told Meyer in the early-morning hours after he learned of his parents' death and brother's arrest. "Like, it would be 11 o'clock at night and my parents would go to bed, and then they'd wake up at 1:30 or 2 o'clock in the morning, and Tyler wouldn't be in bed. And then he'd come home the next day at, like, 6, and they'd go, 'Where were you last night, we know you weren't there, we checked your bed,' and he would just act like he was there."

He wouldn't raise his hands and say, "Oh, you caught me," or 'fess up in any way, Ryan said. Tyler would hold on to the lie steadfastly, even to the point of getting angry at the accusation. It was as if Tyler had convinced himself of his own lies and replaced his reality with them. It was maddening for his parents. How do you argue with someone who's so out of touch?

"What—what was going on in that house?" Meyer asked Ryan.

"I know my brother's been getting into a lot of trouble lately, I can tell you that," Ryan answered. "Like . . . my parents have been trying to keep him home, trying to keep him from getting into the trouble that he's been getting into, trying to stop him . . . They've had him in counseling and all that kind of stuff . . ."

Ryan struggled and stumbled with his words. He'd seen his brother lose his temper a few times, but that meant maybe slamming a door, maybe even hitting a wall, but certainly never picking up a hammer. By now speculation was rampant that Tyler had maybe been pushed to do what he did, that he'd been abused or neglected. Ryan, who had just moved out of the home not six weeks prior, shook his head. No, that couldn't be it.

". . . There's nothing," he said. "My parents weren't doing nothing to, like—nothing bad to him, nothing. They were just being loving parents. They worried because . . . he was skipping school. . . . He dropped out of one school, went to college to get his GED, he got kicked out of that school, they got him back into high school, and then he kept skipping school. They were trying to track him on his phone to make sure he was going to school. That pissed him off, but there is no way that I would ever think that something like—like, seriously, like it's—it's like I don't even know how . . ."

Ryan grasped for more words.

"It's like . . . it doesn't even feel real right now."

"I know," said Meyer. She began to tell him what led police to the Hadleys' door—the anonymous phone call to the Orlando tipster line. But the pages of Ryan's mind were flipping rapidly, and he landed on another topic altogether.

"This is kind of off the wall, but do you know where my animals are?" Ryan blurted. The Hadleys had three pets: a black Lab, an old beagle, and a black-and-white cat. The black Lab had been locked in Blake and Mary Jo's bedroom. The cat wandered through the house as evidence technicians photographed blood spatter. Then there was the beagle.

"The beagle was on the back porch howling," Meyer said.

"Yeah, that's what she does," Ryan replied.

"She's a sweetheart . . . They're being taken care of, they're fed and they're together," Meyer said. "They won't be with strangers or anything else. They'll recognize each other, and they'll keep them together as close as they can . . . and we'll make sure you guys get all the numbers and everything so you can collect them."

"What's happening to Tyler?" It seemed a harder question to ask than one about pets.

"Right now, he's on his way to the jail," Meyer answered.

"Rock Road." Ryan knew the place. For longtime residents, St. Lucie County Jail went by the far less formal title—dubbed such for its address at 900 North Rock Road in Fort Pierce. The secure facility sat a couple of miles off I-95 at Rock Road's intersection with Colbourn. The area was hugged by tree-filled plots on three sides and a business complex to the east. A thick buffer of trees separated the jail from the closest subdivision—a smattering of homes with private pools to the southwest of the jail off Orange Avenue.

"Not everybody knows about Rock Road," Meyer told Ryan.

"I was born and raised here."

Though Ryan had lived in the Granduer home his whole life, including after high school, he'd started feeling antsy a couple of months prior. It was time to move out. He'd narrowed his choices to two: either move out with his long-distance girlfriend in North Carolina, or move to Pittsburgh with his cousin.

"I just figured if I was gonna move somewhere, I might as well move where she is instead of . . . keeping a long-distance thing," he said.

He lined up a job at Crossmart, but quit almost immediately. Things were computer-based and just not his bag. So he'd just landed a new job at a Pilot truck stop. He was set to begin work the next week. He hoped they would understand if his start date was delayed a bit now.

"How was everybody about you moving up to North Carolina?"

"My parents were very sad," Ryan recalled, adding that it was too tough to read Tyler to know if it upset him. "But my parents were upset . . . Of course they missed me, but they were happy. Like, my grandma told me every day how happy she said she was that I was actually doing what I wanted to do . . ."

"Okay, the typical parents sad," Meyer interjected.

"It wasn't like a huge dysfunctional family . . . They were really good people—like, I mean, really good people."

But things admittedly had grown tense in the house over the past year or so. Tyler's sneaking out, his off-the-wall lies, the teenage attitude on steroids—it was all getting to be a lot for Mary Jo and Blake to handle. Their boys-will-be-boys approach to parenting wasn't working on him. Ryan had gone through his bad-boy phase and come out the other side a mature man, responsible enough even to loan his parents money as they refinanced their house. It was slowly dawning on Mary Jo and Blake that they wouldn't be so lucky with Tyler.

"He was good his freshman year," Ryan recalled. "It was probably . . . just like last year, his sophomore year of high school, it really started to be, like . . . a problem. I always try to tell him that I'm there and . . . he doesn't have to hide something. Like, I know there might be some stuff you want to hide from mom and dad, but you can talk to me about it."

"Right, exactly, you're the brother," Meyer said.

"I'm your brother, and like he still—I'll ask him questions and he'll just deny this, or, 'Hey, dude, do you have a girlfriend,' 'No,' but then apparently he tells my parents that he's had a girlfriend for a year and a half, and then, like, all of a sudden he denies it."

Mostly, Tyler seemed like a typical teenager, but then these secrets would surface that caught everyone off guard.

"I don't know what he's doing when he goes out . . . I couldn't even get that out of him," Ryan said.

Plus, he'd started stealing. Ryan's parents were sure of it.

"They'd check the bank account. Forty dollars would be missing, and then the debit card would magically be not where they knew it was. They knew they put it somewhere, and then all of a sudden it would be over here or over there, and Tyler would say, 'I don't know what you're talking about, I don't know what you're talking about.' And it would always just be around, like, forty dollars, and next time they're missing twenty dollars out of a wallet, and they'd confront Tyler about it and Tyler would just deny it."

It had pushed Mary Jo and Blake to the breaking point. They knew something was wrong, Ryan said, but they didn't know how to help their youngest son. Their confrontations were met with lies, and their punishments weren't working, either. Mary Jo researched some counseling programs that she hoped would help. Ryan remembered his brother starting one, but then abruptly stopping. Ryan never knew why. About a month before Ryan moved out, his parents took Tyler to a facility called New Horizons, a treatment center for people with emotional and mental health disorders. Plenty of young adults struggling with mental health issues in St. Lucie County ended up at New Horizons. The name itself was the punch line in schoolyard bullying: *That girl should have a wing named after her at New Horizons*. Some treatment is outpatient, but more acute cases are recommended for inpatient care. Ryan said the center wanted to keep Tyler there, but he refused. The family thought Tyler might qualify for involuntary commitment, but no dice. The law that allows for that—commonly known as the Baker Act but formally the Florida Mental Health Act, passed in 1971—requires that a person either has a mental illness or clearly is harmful to himself or others. Had Tyler qualified, he could have been held for up to seventy-two hours even if he was medically stable.

"I don't remember what they said, why they couldn't keep him against his own will," Ryan said. Soon after, Mary Jo found a treatment center that offered intensive outpatient therapy, and Tyler started going. That, too, could have been forced on him under a 2005 change to the Baker Act, but that wasn't necessary. Tyler agreed to go, even if he told Ryan he wasn't thrilled about it.

Mary Jo had stumbled onto the various treatment options through a parent of one of Ryan's friends. The parent worked for the psychiatric ward at Lawnwood Pavilion Mental Health, a facility in Fort Pierce, and Mary Jo chatted her up to see what might be the best option for Tyler. To the few Mary Jo confided in, she said she felt Tyler was dealing with more than normal teenage stuff. She thought he might have a mental illness, and she worried that if it went unchecked, he could try to hurt himself. Just as Ryan was moving, his mom had reached out to yet another program. Ryan didn't know all of the specifics. His mother had been guarded when talking about it with others, family members included. Ryan gleaned that his brother was attending outpatient counseling several days a week.

"I think they were just trying to . . . figure out what was going on with him, and then this past time . . . he was actually in some kind of program," he said. "I know the lady would give him drug tests there. I mean, I guess maybe it was just to try to get him to change his ways or change his habits or whatever he was doing . . . or just, like, quit being so rebellious against my parents. It's not like my parents were asking for a lot."

It didn't take long for Tyler to fail a drug test, Mary Jo had confided in her older son. She worried that the treatment wasn't helping. Ryan wasn't sure if Tyler had been prescribed antidepressants or other medications in the program, but he and his uncle Sam did know that Tyler had been on thyroid medication for quite a while. In the home, officers found and photographed a bottle of Levoxyl, used to treat hypothyroidism. It was prescribed for people whose thyroid gland didn't produce enough thyroid hormone, without which patients might suffer from poor growth, slow speech, lack of energy, weight gain, or hair loss, among other things. Tyler for years had complained about his height—so much so that when he was barely a teenager, he was prescribed human growth hormone for a couple of years. His friend Michael Mandell remembered watching as Tyler jabbed himself in the thigh for the daily injection.

Michael wasn't sure why Tyler needed the treatment. Tyler was taller than most of his friends anyway, but he worried he wasn't going to reach his father's height. Tyler told Michael that with the HGH, he'd likely tack on another few inches. When HGH is prescribed legitimately, doctors have measured the patient's "bone age" and testes compared with his real age. If it seems his body isn't keeping up with his age, a doctor might prescribe the hormone. It's a risky proposition, though. Online, the hormone is talked up in chat rooms by young men desperate to add on a few inches of height or build more muscle mass. They routinely ignore the pleas from medical professionals who grace the boards, warning that taking HGH while still young can screw up their bodies. A few times, Tyler offered to let Michael inject him. Michael shrugged that off.

"I'm only interested in watching you stab yourself," he'd say with a laugh.

What Michael didn't know was just how expensive the treatment was. On average, and in injectable form, HGH can cost three thousand dollars per month. Mel, Mary Jo's friend, had tried to talk her out of giving Tyler the hormones. Mel had been debating the treatment for her own son but decided against it. It was too risky, and for what? A few extra inches in height? But Mary Jo was steadfast. She said Tyler was short and she worried he would be teased, so she was going ahead with the hormones. She wanted Tyler to be tall like his dad. Eventually, he was just shy of that—hitting six foot one to his father's six foot four.

When talking with Meyer, Ryan said he didn't know why his brother had been prescribed the hormone, but he remembered Tyler had taken it for a few years, and then switched over to the thyroid medication. Levoxyl—generic name levothyroxine—sometimes is used by people who just want to lose weight, regardless of their thyroid condition. It carries with it a warning through its listing with the U.S. National Library of Medicine, housed online at PubMed Health: "Thyroid hormone should not be used to treat obesity in patients with normal thyroid function. Levothyroxine is ineffective for weight reduction in normal thyroid patients and may cause serious or life-threatening toxicity, especially when taken with amphetamines." It also warns to be cautious when mixing with antidepressants or anti-anxiety medications. That was another drug discovered in the mess of the Hadley home: Citalopram, the generic form of Celexa, was found in a prescription bottle with Tyler's name on it. The drug was of the SSRI class—selective serotonin reuptake inhibitor—and generally was prescribed to treat major depression and anxiety disorders. In another bottle on the floor in a puddle of blood and tissue was a third medication in Tyler's name: hydroxyzine pamoate. The medication initially was released as an antihistamine in the 1950s, but eventually became recognized for its sedating effect and also was prescribed to treat mood and anxiety disorders.

Family members recalled Mary Jo asking her son if he'd remembered to take "his pill," and Mary Jo's mother, Maggie, had worried out loud the day of the deaths that Tyler would miss his dose. Truth is, though, Ryan didn't know which pills his brother was really taking.

"Why did mom and dad take him up to New Horizons?" Detective Meyer asked. "Can you remember if there was a specific incident or what happened?"

"I think he might have been talking about wanting to kill himself," Ryan answered. "And they were just worried that he might actually do it."

They didn't worry that he might hurt them, though. That never even crossed their minds.

CHAPTER 10

The next morning, Detective Meyer readied herself for another long day. She still had relatives to call and people to interview, autopsies to check up on and tips to chase down. Though she'd been up until past 2 a.m. early Monday, Meyer was back at the crime scene at 7:30 a.m. There she met Detective Sergeant Golino to review how the house had been processed. Several crime scene technicians and detectives gathered to update the duo. By now, with the bodies away from the scene and most of the debris that had been piled atop them gathered as evidence, much of the house was marked up with stickers, evidence labels, and pencil numberings. So much blood had pooled on the kitchen floor that investigators were confident Mary Jo, whose tennis shoes remained beneath the desk, had been bludgeoned there, then dragged to her bedroom.

Bloodstains on the floor beneath the bodies were in dried drag patterns, as well, bolstering the theory.

Because Blake Hadley's debit card had been discovered in the teen's wallet, Meyer had Detective Jim Jones contact Chase Bank, its issuer, to find out when the card had last been used. Jones was quick with an answer: Someone had used the card about 8:30 p.m. the night of the deaths. The bank agreed to send still images from the machine used to access the account.

Throughout the day Sunday, as officers kept the crime scene secure, teenagers had wandered by to ask what had happened. Some volunteered that they had been at the house the night before. The scene they described sounded pretty typical for a teenage "the folks aren't home" night of bingeing: beer pong on the dining room table, an occasional argument about missing weed or a stolen hat, items dropped and broken. Tyler seemed totally casual, at ease, throughout most of the gathering—with telling exceptions. One girl recalled Tyler yelling at guests to stay away from his parents' room. He seemed nervous and scared, but the friend dismissed it as him being protective of a part of the house he didn't want trashed. That wasn't unusual at these gatherings. It was obvious his parents didn't approve the party, so making the master bedroom off limits seemed reasonable. It was only in hindsight that the girl realized there was more to it.

Police grabbed short written statements from the inquisitive partiers who arrived at the scene and passed the information along to Meyer for her to pursue once she had time to breathe. Kimberly Thieben said she'd been at the party from about 10 p.m. to 1 a.m. Tyler was nice, she said, but mentioned that he was going to prison for sixty years. He'd rather die than go to prison, he added. Kimberly asked where his parents were, but Tyler never answered. Richard Wouters showed up at the party around

10 p.m., when the house was still locked up and about fifteen people waited outside as Tyler apparently did some last-minute cleaning inside. No one knew what was up; it was admittedly odd to be left on the lawn, but once people were inside, Tyler was a dream host. Bradley Dinger said Tyler was nice and told people they could eat whatever they wanted. Bradley had arrived about 11 p.m. and stayed until 3 a.m. Nothing seemed amiss. David Garcia had shown up about 11 p.m., stayed for two hours, then showed up again about 3 a.m. just as things were wrapping up. Tyler had told him he'd be going away for a while. David asked what he meant by that, but Tyler shook it off and said not to worry about it. David asked if he'd be coming back. Maybe, Tyler said, if he didn't kill himself first. Don't go then, David implored. Tyler said it wasn't that simple. Kenneth Mumma reported much the same: Tyler was in a good mood in general, even as he said he might be locked up for a while. Kenneth had no idea about the suicide comments until the next morning, when he heard from other shocked friends.

In all, nearly a dozen people at Tyler's party had heard him say he'd done something so bad that it would land him in prison for decades. And that didn't even account for the most shocking of admissions that he'd made to his best friend.

Michael Mandell first met Tyler in 2003, when the two were about eight years old. Michael and his family had just moved to the neighborhood, so the outgoing blond-headed little boy went for a walk to see the other houses and try to meet new friends.

"I didn't know anyone," Mandell later recalled. "I was going to give anyone a shot who wanted to be a friend."

He spotted Tyler playing in front of his Granduer home. Michael approached. Quickly they bonded over the things that little boys liked at the time—Pokémon trading cards, bike riding, skateboarding—and became fast friends.

"He slept over at my house that very first night," Michael recalled.

Tyler had light brown hair that he kept pretty shaggy when he was younger. His folks had him comb it for family photos, but Michael remembers it as always being a bit long, past his ears. They'd play basketball in Tyler's driveway with Tyler's older brother Ryan. Tyler was taller than Michael, an advantage on the makeshift court, but neither was a standout player.

"We had fun. He was always happy then, always happy," Michael said.

The two would talk Ryan into giving them a ride to the movies or the mall. Seems stupid in hindsight, Michael admitted, but like most American teenagers they wandered the mall with friends as a way to kill time and hang out away from home. They typically liked action flicks, but one movie, *Around the World in 80 Days* starring Jackie Chan, didn't fly. The two murmured to each other about twenty minutes into the film that it was boring, so they left before the first act was even over.

Then there was the mother of most teenage boy interests: girls. Both boys talked about girls at school that they liked, girls they wanted to ask out but couldn't, girls they'd love to date but would hate to bring home to their oh-so-embarrassing parents. For a brief stint in middle school, Tyler went steady with a girl named Jessica. She was the new girl at school, and her stay in Port St. Lucie was brief. The two were boyfriend and girlfriend for a couple of months before Jessica moved away. Tyler didn't seem too upset. It was the only time Michael ever saw his friend with an actual girl. Tyler would talk about girlfriends now and then, but it was always a John Hughes "you wouldn't know her" type of thing.

"I didn't assume he was lying, but sometimes he would tell me about a girl and he'd say her name, but I never saw her," Michael said. "I don't think he would really have a problem getting girls, but he was really nervous around them. And he wouldn't want to bring them home. He didn't know what his parents would think about it."

At first, Michael agreed. Bringing a girl home to meet the folks? Even the thought just sucked. But as Michael grew up, he realized he'd have to bring his girlfriends by, so he got over it. He told Tyler to suck it up, too.

"Once we got a little older, like got toward high school, I said, 'Man, come on, grow up, you gotta be an adult. It's not going to be the end of the world. It might be a little awkward, but it always will be. You'll get over that after the first few times.'"

But not everything about Tyler was typical for a boy. Michael once found him in the woods near his home with a bungee cord noosed around his neck.

"I'm gonna kill myself," Tyler said.

Michael protested. "No, you can't. If you try, I'll just pull you off."

"It seemed like it came out of nowhere," Michael recalled. "I don't know why he was saying that, but I'm pretty sure he was joking. He joked all the time."

Tyler was about ten then. He clearly had self-esteem issues, calling himself fat and ugly, saying he was stupid.

"He would say that quite often," Michael recalled. "It was always 'fat,' 'ugly,' 'stupid.' I'd say something like, 'Tyler, I'm not gay or anything and I'm not trying to judge you, but you're not ugly or stupid.'"

But Tyler didn't seem to believe that anyone could actually like him for who he was. Sometimes, out of the blue, he'd ask Michael, "Are you really my friend?" Michael would assure him that he was. He often wasn't sure what prompted the question.

Crime Stoppers was anonymous, but it didn't take long for Meyer to figure out who had placed the call. She started first with the 911 call that Jesse Duryea had made with his girlfriend. From Jesse, she learned that Michael had told him he'd called Crime Stoppers. Boom. It was as simple as that. Michael's was the voice on the tipster line that first notified police Tyler might have killed his parents. Michael seemed surprised when Meyer knocked on his front door. *I thought it was anonymous,* he said. Meyer assured him it was; she'd tracked him down on her own. He was immediately talkative, describing his decade-long friendship with Tyler and saying how shocked he was at everything unfolding. His parents were nice people, Michael insisted, and it seemed as though Tyler loved them. But in hindsight, Michael maybe should have listened to the "jokes" his friend had made for years about killing his parents.

Meyer stood on the front porch as they talked. She suggested the police station might be more appropriate. Michael agreed, as did his parents, so he and Meyer met back up at the station for a proper interview. Mike seemed dumbfounded that he could be caught up in such a mess. Tyler was his best friend; Tyler's family was like his family. He felt he knew Tyler better than he knew himself. Even after Mike had moved out of the Hadleys' neighborhood a few years earlier, the two stayed close. Sure, it was tough to hang out living five miles apart before they were old enough to drive, but once they got their drivers' licenses, they were tight again. Just days before the slayings, Tyler had come over to his house to play video games for an hour or two. Tyler never said a word about killing his parents or being mad at them. Everything was completely normal. Then Saturday, as he hung out at Tyler's with his girlfriend Morgan and Danny Roberts, Michael again sensed nothing wrong. Tyler was throwing a party because his parents were going out of town. Big deal. Kids in Port St. Lucie do it all the time.

Michael needed a ride to Tyler's, so Tyler picked him up about 10 p.m. and they drove straight back to the Granduer home. He hadn't been Tyler's first stop. Friends Jesse and Shannon already had loaded into Blake's truck for the trip across town. Tyler seemed totally normal, not hyper or nervous, Michael told Meyer. Never during that car ride did he suspect that his buddy had spent the past three hours scrubbing himself and his house of his parents' blood.

As people piled into the house for the party, Michael noticed that most of them weren't friends. At first, there were maybe fifteen people. Within an hour, another forty had arrived. It was tough even walking through the house. People were shoulder-to-shoulder, hollering and drinking. Some smoked dope; others wandered around the back- and front yards and played music from their cars. Tyler said he didn't care how many people were there; nor was he concerned that most were strangers. For a guy who so desperately wanted a party, he'd seemed awfully unimpressed with the grand turnout.

Meyer seemed genuinely concerned for Michael. He'd seen some awful stuff and lost his best friend in a horrific way. She asked how he was doing. Sad, Michael replied. Tyler's parents were really good people, and now they were dead. They were supposed to have a family reunion in six days in Pittsburgh. Everyone—Tyler excluded—seemed so excited for the trip. And Blake was one of the nicest people Michael had ever met. The two had bonded, and Michael looked up to him like a father. He and his own father didn't always get along, he said, and seeing

Blake dote on Tyler, well, he could tell he was just a really good man. Michael had heard Tyler complain about his folks, but he always thought he loved them still. He didn't know what had happened or when things went so far downhill.

The worst part, Michael said, was that Tyler didn't seem to regret a thing. He showed no remorse, and several times said proudly, "This is *my* house now." Michael, having been his friend's first confidant in the slayings, had suddenly been weighed down with horrific knowledge and a gut-wrenching feeling of guilt by association, all while Tyler had continued to party. Michael watched across the room as his friend laughed and drank and carried on as though nothing was wrong. This was what screwed with Michael's head the most, the reason he knew he'd have to call police. That became even more apparent when Tyler invited him back for another party Sunday night.

As forthcoming as Michael had been by calling Crime Stoppers and sharing details with Detective Meyer, he'd held back some crucial information. So many friends at the party were on probation; he didn't see a point in getting them in trouble by placing them at a home with underage drinking and drugs. What difference did it make, anyway, he figured. It's not like they could tell police any more than he already had. So he left out some details and names that would later make Meyer wonder if he was being completely honest with her after all.

Meyer had planned to follow up with Michael in a few days, but before she could set it up, he called her, clearly shaken. Could Tyler possibly be released from jail? he asked. If Tyler could kill his own parents, he could maybe turn on Michael, too, he worried. So Meyer headed to his home in the hope of calming his nerves. When she approached the Mandell family's ranch-style home, she didn't at first spot the teen with the nearly shaved head. Suddenly she saw him pop up in the door.

"You scared me," he blurted.

"Why?"

"I didn't know who it was."

"It's only me," she assured.

His demeanor matched up with his phone calls of late, especially the most recent, during which he pitched a bizarre conspiracy theory that maybe Tyler hadn't worked alone. Having seen the crime scene, Meyer was dubious, but she needed to hear Michael out. Besides, it was time for Meyer to more precisely map out the time frame with him. The detective started with Michael's phone. With his permission, she flipped through his call history back to the sixteenth, the Saturday when it all went down. Michael had been in some trouble for trespassing and was on probation. He'd been sentenced to perform community service, so on Saturday morning he'd awoken early to help work on a house with Habitat for Humanity. Based on his call records, he wrapped up a bit after noon and headed to pick up his girlfriend Morgan.

"I had to wait for her for a while," Michael recalled. "She was getting ready."

He and Danny started playing phone tag around 1 p.m. Finally, they connected, and Danny told him that Tyler invited them over to his house to hang out. Michael, still waiting in his car, nudged Morgan with a phone call at 1:06. She came out of her house and the two headed to pick up Danny. At 1:20 p.m., Tyler called from his dad's cell phone. By then, Michael was driving down St. James just shy of Airoso. He told Tyler he was on the way. But within minutes, his car sputtered. Dead battery. He, Morgan, and Danny left the car behind and kept walking to Tyler's house, which by then was only a few blocks away.

They were in the home stretch when Tyler drove by in his father's black truck, spotted them, and picked them up. Tyler wasn't alone. An older guy, rough looking, sat in the front seat. He seemed drugged out—high or drunk, it was tough to tell. Tyler drove them all to a Met Mart party store about two miles from Tyler's house, and the older guy got out, bought some booze, plopped it in the front passenger seat of the truck, and went on his way. Later, as Danny shared his version of the day with Meyer, he couldn't remember much about the guy aside from some sketchy details: He had a red bandanna in his back pocket, he was about five foot eight with shorn hair, he didn't wear glasses and didn't have facial hair of note. Danny had never seen him before.

"If I was actually thinking that [something] was going on, I would have remembered everything, but I don't. I don't remember," Danny apologized to Meyer.

As they all climbed out of the pickup, Michael noticed that Tyler's folks were gone. They went inside, sat down, and shot the shit. Later, Michael could barely remember what they talked about, it was so mundane. Just teenage stuff. But he did recall Tyler's plan for later that evening: After his parents came and packed for their trip to Orlando, he was throwing a party. By now it was almost 2 p.m., and Tyler had already posted about the party on Facebook. He'd messaged with several friends. The plan was in place.

At 2:30 p.m., Michael finally called his mom to tell her his car had broken down. He needed a ride. His dad showed up maybe ten minutes later, and Michael and Morgan left Tyler's house, leaving Danny behind to find his own ride home. It was easiest that way because Michael was on probation and his parents wouldn't have liked hearing that he'd gone out of his way to pick up Danny.

"That's, like, the only way it would have worked out

without his dad knowing," Danny explained. "He could have picked me up, but to his parents . . . His parents didn't really let him, you know, chill."

This was the part of Danny's story that most piqued Meyer's interest—the lead-up to the sudden "Run, run, run, go, go, go!" command that flushed Danny from Tyler's house as Mary Jo and Blake pulled into the driveway. Meyer, in an interview separate from Michael's, had Danny walk her through it.

"Okay, how are you planning on getting home?" she asked, taking the teen mentally back to the Hadley home.

"I was planning on Tyler driving me, you know."

"Okay."

"And, like, well at first . . . he said that his parents went to Fort Pierce and they were gonna come back, get packed and go to Orlando . . . Mike told me to just sit . . . because his parents weren't the way he made them come off, like [they were] not nice. But Mike said they were nice . . . Mike told me just to sit in there and when they come home, just be like that you walked all the way there and you just wanted to hang out with Tyler."

"Okay," Meyer said. "So why were you—I mean, why didn't Tyler just go ahead and take you home then?"

"I don't know . . . There's some other things he was telling me."

Danny sputtered as he explained. In addition to Tyler saying his folks weren't "nice," he'd also said that he'd asked for mental help but they refused. They didn't want the family to look bad, Danny said. Tyler had convinced him that his family cared more about their reputations than their son's mental well-being. He clarified that he'd heard this many times before, but with this new insight from Michael that the folks weren't all bad after all, maybe he could actually just hang out with Tyler while his parents got ready for Florida and stay until the party started.

As Danny waited, he tried the usual chitchat with Tyler, but it wasn't gelling. Tyler mostly sat quietly.

"He was always like that, you know," Danny said. "He was always quiet and never really let you know exactly what was going on."

Danny praised his house, the compliment quickly rebuffed.

"I guess he didn't really appreciate it, because he had . . . a lot of money, too, and he didn't appreciate that either."

"Okay," Meyer pushed.

"He had, like, $11,000. He had his own car."

"How do you know he had $11,000?"

"Because he told me he had $11,000."

"When did he tell you that?"

"Every single time we used to hang out, he would just open up his wallet and he would have, like, seven or eight hundred-dollar bills. Just like every single time I would hang out with him, he would have, like, a lot of money," Danny said.

And they hung out fairly often. Tyler was grounded a lot, but whenever he could get out of the house, he would hit up Michael and, in turn, Danny. They'd go to either Danny's or Michael's house and just chill. From other interviews, Meyer had gleaned that Tyler said something peculiar to Danny. She pushed him on it, assuring him that he wasn't in trouble but she needed every kernel of information he had. Danny began to spill.

"Sarcastically . . . he told me that—" Danny stuttered. "He told me that he bought, like, a pickaxe. But apparently that wasn't even used, but he told me that he had bought a pickaxe . . . He was like, 'The other day, I was about . . . to do it, I was that close, but'—like sarcastically, like you would never believe that he would do it because he was—he was always so sarcastic about it."

"Cover that conversation a little bit better for me, okay?"

"Yeah, he was like . . . joking around and saying, 'Yeah, I went to Wal-Mart and I had bought one of those wooden pickaxes with both sides and the other night, I was that close to doing it."

Danny couldn't be sure the comment came Saturday. It could've been during the week when he'd seen Tyler earlier.

"Okay, and then what else did he say?" Meyer prodded.

"He just was saying that he was so close to doing it, because he said his dad hit him, like punched him in the face, three times . . . He was really close to . . . killing them or something."

"So you kind of got the impression that he said that he was so close to doing it because his dad punched him in the face?"

"Yeah, but the impression he's always made was that he loved his mom, but he hated his dad. That's the impression I always got."

Danny remembered that Tyler said his dad had caught him doing something he really liked—smoking weed or drinking or something—and his dad just *wham!* hit Tyler in this face. Danny bought the story. Tyler had long said his dad knocked him around, and he'd have weird marks on his face that seemed to corroborate the claims.

"Tyler just apparently went in his room or something," Danny said. "He didn't really tell me everything."

This is why Danny wasn't keen on staying in the house, and why he was a bit surprised when Michael told him to chill, that they weren't so bad after all. But just as he settled in, the car pulled up in the driveway.

"So I just stand up, and I'm like, what do I do, what do I do, and [he] just like tapped me slightly and he's just like, 'Run, run, run, go, go, go!' And I couldn't—I don't know his house . . . I didn't know where to go. I tipped over, like, three things and then I opened the back two doors . . . and I just ran."

Tyler ran out alongside him and helped him jump the wooden fence.

"Why?" Meyer seemed incredulous. "Why?"

"I don't know," Danny said. "I just did whatever he told me to because I didn't know what was gonna go down, you know."

"But . . . why was it so imperative that you leave the house?"

Danny shrugged. He didn't know.

He never saw Mary Jo and Blake. Aside from Tyler, no one ever would again.

CHAPTER 11

As Meyer continued her interviews, Officer Marshall had more processing to do at the crime scene. She returned to the house about 7:40 a.m. Monday, chatted with Meyer, some other detectives, and a crime scene technician, and then continued tackling the mounds of debris that still remained in Mary Jo and Blake's bedroom. The goal, Marshall documented in a report, was to reveal any possible evidence that might be hidden in the mess. By now, all the blood in the house had dried, save for heavy areas where Blake's head had been. Joined at times by investigator Joel Smith, who also helped photograph the scene and debris, Marshall was careful to change her gloves every time she touched the blood for fear she'd contaminate evidence.

Each item she picked up, she paused and inspected in

the hope of spotting ridge detail from a fingerprint or tread from a shoe imprint. She stained the partial shoe prints she'd found in the master bedroom with aqueous leuco crystal violet, a presumptive test for the presence of blood. It would provide early confirmation that she indeed was looking at bloody prints, after which she'd swab each for DNA testing. She also photographed the prints by putting her camera on a tripod and illuminating the ridges with side lighting so that the patterns would show up in the images. The staining-and-photographing process took more than an hour.

She and a detective then began testing sink drains and the tub in the garage, as it appeared from the footprints that someone had walked between the bedroom and the garage several times. The front wall of the interior garage sink tested positive for blood, she'd later report. Marshall collected swabs for DNA testing and moved on to the master bath shower. That, too, tested positive. She gathered more swabs. Same thing at the spare bathroom sink and at the drain of the spare bathroom tub: Each tested positive for blood. Marshall tested a shoe print in Tyler's bedroom, but that one came up negative. She and a detective moved on to the kitchen sink, which tested a faint positive. Again, they grabbed more swabs.

Marshall next used a black powder kit and fiberglass dust brush to process the master bedroom and filing cabinet for latent prints. She saw several smudges and partial prints, but none was clear enough to be useful. Marshall contacted the utilities department to carefully drain the septic holding tank in the front yard; if Tyler had flushed anything down the toilets, it might still be in the tank, she reasoned. Utilities officials arrived and drained the tank, but it turned up nothing. Marshall moved on to the wooded lot to the west of the house—the same lot in which Tyler had played when he was a kid. She found some odd items—an airsoft gun, a sports trophy, shin guards, school yearbooks, and notes with Tyler's name on them—but they were covered with vines and faded, as though they'd been there a long while. Marshall photographed them and collected a few of the items for testing.

She eyed for latent prints, too, and then, after she finished with each item, she carefully laid it on the sterile blanket she'd set up near the sitting room. Because there'd been so much debris in the room, some pieces of paper were spotted with bloody shoe prints right on them. Marshall photographed those with a scale, and then placed the papers with the other evidence. Items that potentially had latent prints were carefully bagged for further processing.

Some of the items gathered yielded nothing, but dozens had prints that crime scene technicians hoped would prove useful at trial. The red mop handle collected not only had blood on it, but also held one fingerprint and possibly a palm print. An aluminum foil box had another palm print. The lower left leg of an armchair had two fingerprints; the top railing of the chair had three prints.

As Marshall sifted through the mess, she found a black T-shirt turned inside out. She eyed it and saw that it appeared to have blood spatter and bloodstains on it. She gave the shirt to a crime scene technician, who bagged it for DNA testing. Marshall carefully documented the items taken from the bedroom. They included bloody partial shoe prints on the floor by the porch door, at the foot of the master bed, on papers, on broken glass, and on a black plastic straining lid; and latent prints with blood on a black, spiral notepad, several pieces of whole or broken glass and ceramics, a glass candy jar, a ceramic coffee jar, and a wooden jewelry box. Once the room was cleared out, Marshall planned to focus on getting photographs of the blood spatter and drag marks on the floor.

She used a blow dryer on a low setting to gently clear away loose coffee grounds, animal hair, and crushed candy.

Inside the house, Marshall sealed each window with black plastic from the outside. She, Smith, Meyer, and Detective Kim Bailey began dousing the inside with luminol, a chemical that glows when it mixes with the iron present in blood. Even after Tyler's three-hour cleanup attempt, the dining room and bedroom gleamed a telltale blue. Marshall set up her camera on a tripod and opened the shutter for twenty-five seconds in each room, giving the camera enough light to capture both the darkened room and the highlighted, bloody areas. She documented blood on the spare bathroom countertop, inside the tub, on the shower curtain, and near the drain. A trail of bloody shoe prints glowed in the garage and in front of the sink, on the interior walls, by the drain, and on the faucet knobs.

CHAPTER 12

Ryan Stonesifer did not want to talk to police. Not even a little bit. Still, the seventeen-year-old walked in to the Port St. Lucie Police Department with his parents in tow. They all figured that he'd be asked to talk eventually. He might as well get it over with. Detective Meyer was still juggling other elements of the case, so Detective Lisa Carrasquillo took Ryan and his parents to an interrogation room and sat him down. The teen fidgeted in the sterile room, his legs bobbing nervously as he sat in a hard-backed chair next to a pair of handcuffs that connected to the wall. Carrasquillo quickly ducked out of the room, promising to return.

"Put your phone on vibrate," Ryan's mother told him.

"See all the little cameras?" his father said, pointing to

multiple electronic devices dotting the walls of the room.
"There, there, there."

"They're all around," Diana Stonesifer said.

"They're everywhere."

Ryan crossed his arms and kept rocking his knees.

"I've got bad breath," Michael Stonesifer blurted.

They all heard a beeping sound and assumed Carrasquillo had started the video recording. Ryan's mother got
nervous for him.

"He acts retarded in situations where he gets nervous,"
she said.

"It's ridiculous," his father agreed.

"Then why did you make me come?" Ryan asked.

"We can't leave you alone with them," his father replied.

"If it's ridiculous, why did you make me come?" Ryan
asked again.

"Because it's ridiculous that you have to do this," his
father said.

"So then I didn't have to."

"Yeah, it's the best thing," his mother said. His father
echoed her.

"Tell them about what he said," his mother said, "that
he wouldn't do that to his mom."

"Oh, yeah, I know that," Ryan said.

"That he loved his mom."

"I know. God, don't tell me."

Carrasquillo and Detective Jesse Inigo came back to
the room apologetically. Carrasquillo seemed harried and
a little disorganized, having searched for her cell phone,
only to find it back in the interrogation room where she'd
left it.

"We are so busy just interviewing so many people, as
you know," she apologized. The detective was pretty, with
long dark hair. She pulled the top up in a barrette to

keep it out of her face. Instead of a patrol uniform, she wore the casual clothes of a detective—in her case, a short-sleeved white blouse beneath a dark fitted vest.

She pulled a chair closer to Ryan and started easing him into questions.

"You're not in trouble or anything, all right?" she began.

This reassured his parents more than anyone. "Thank God," his mother sighed.

"Just to clarify," Inigo interjected, "you guys willingly came in. If at any point you want to get up, leave, just feel free to leave. We're not gonna stop you."

The Stonesifers nodded. The questions began: How did Ryan know Tyler? Through school. How long had they known each other? For about three years, since they both were freshmen at St. Lucie West Centennial High School.

"Tell me about Tyler," Carrasquillo prodded.

"I don't know, he's like . . . He's just a good friend," Ryan said. "He's always laughing and stuff, fun to hang out with. Just a normal kid."

They'd met the normal way kids at school meet—through classes and lunch—and started hanging out after school, too.

"Well, recently I've been hanging out with him, like, a lot. Like this last year, we hung out, like, every weekend, all of us. All of us was hanging out."

He elaborated "all of us" to mean his buddies Jesse, Michael, and a couple of other rotating friends.

"Since you were 15 years old and you've been hanging out with . . . Tyler, has he ever made any threats or said anything that was weird that . . . raised an eyebrow, as to why he would say something like that?" Carrasquillo asked.

"Never."

"Was he ever on any type of drugs that you know of?"

"I know he smoked . . . weed every once in a while, but nothing, like, serious."

"Okay, but what about pills? 'Cause I know he was taking some kind of pills. What pills was he on?"

"Uh, he did ecstasy."

"Is that his choice, just that one?"

"Well, he didn't do it a lot," Ryan clarified. "He did it, like, once or twice."

Carrasquillo glanced at Ryan's parents. She'd been a cop long enough to know Ryan likely wouldn't be as honest about drugs in front of his folks as he might if he were alone. She tried to calm him.

"Just relax, you're not in trouble. Okay?" she said.

"Yeah."

"And in addition to that, don't hold back anything because right now, even if your parents are here, it's cool . . . Trust me."

Ryan answered again: "When I was with him, he wasn't really doing a lot."

"But you know of him doing that stuff?"

"Yeah."

She asked where Tyler got his weed. Ryan said he had no idea. She asked, too, if Tyler had been punished recently or had a curfew. Ryan replied that he basically had to go home whenever his mom called, but that he otherwise wasn't restricted.

"How was his relationship with his parents?"

"I know he was really close with his mom," Ryan said.

"Okay, tell me about that."

"Well, if he'd get in, like, an argument or something with her, he'd have to apologize right away . . . He'd feel, like, really bad, like he couldn't do it, like, 'I can't believe I just said that to my mom,' and he'd walk back and talk."

One time in particular, Ryan remembered Tyler telling

his mom to shut up, then immediately feeling guilty. "He was like, 'I'm sorry for yelling at you,'" Ryan recalled. Another time, he said he felt bad he'd started a fight with his mom. Again, the guilt drove him to apologize.

"How long ago was that?" Carrasquillo asked.

"That was probably last month," Ryan replied.

"What about relationship with dad?"

"He never really talked about him."

"Never said anything, like, 'I can't stand my dad,' or 'My dad is a good buddy,' or 'Me and my dad and my mom are going away,' or anything like that?"

Ryan remembered that he'd gone to Georgia with his father on vacation. Tyler hadn't planned to go at first, but then changed his mind. That had been earlier in the month; Blake and Tyler returned home just three days before the killings.

"Do you know if Tyler was an abused kid?"

The question seemed to catch Ryan off guard. "No, I—" he stuttered.

"Do you think his parents beat him?"

"No."

Tyler got grounded for doing stuff he shouldn't have— like staying out too late or not telling his mom he was leaving, Ryan said. Mary Jo would react by grounding him for a day or so, taking his cell phone, those types of things. One night, in fact, Ryan got a text message from Tyler's phone—but it was really Tyler's mom looking for her son.

"She texted me one night and she was just like, 'Oh, it's Tyler's mom. If you see Tyler, just tell him to come home' or whatever, and I was like, 'Okay.'"

Tyler wasn't with Ryan that night, though. He didn't know where he was.

And then came the meat of the interview. Ryan and his parents had come to the police department not to talk about how often Tyler got grounded, but rather to talk about the party. The now-infamous party that Tyler threw with his parents' bodies locked in a trash-strewn bedroom. Carrasquillo told him she wanted to know everything about that day, and she slowed him down when he began speaking too quickly.

"Talk to me, in detail," she implored.

Ryan began talking. "He tells me on Facebook that he was having people come over, and that if I wanted to come, I could come. So I was like, 'Okay, what time?' He was like, 'Around, like 8:30–9 p.m.' . . . He gave me a phone number. I don't know whose phone number it was. He was like, 'Hit me up or I'll hit you up when it's gonna happen.' "

Ryan sat around and chilled most of Saturday before heading to Tyler's. The party was the only thing on his to-do list for the day. He got there, but the house was empty. He reached Tyler, who told him he wasn't home yet. That's when Ryan headed to McDonald's to kill time. When he came back, people were gathered on the lawn while Tyler moved about inside. Ryan was one of the handful invited into Tyler's room to hang out.

"We were all just sitting there," Ryan recalled. "I was like, 'You know there are people in your house, right?' and he was like, 'Oh, yeah, I don't care, it's whatever.' "

Ryan thought this was weird. People were doing stupid things in his house—smoking, doing drugs, all kinds of stuff—and for a guy who'd left his friends on his lawn as he seemingly safeguarded half the house, it seemed odd he'd suddenly not care at all what people were up to. Ryan took it upon himself to start playing the role of bouncer.

"I guess a different party got cancelled or whatever . . . So a bunch of people started showing up," Ryan recalled. "Tyler wasn't saying anything—like, people are breaking stuff and whatever—so I went outside and was telling everybody who was outside if they're not gonna stay, they need to leave."

If people were doing something he deemed stupid, he told them to bounce. Some were parked in the driveway with their lights and music on, a surefire way to attract police attention.

"I was just like, 'What are you guys doing?' Like, that's my friend's house, and I was just like, 'If you're doing stupid stuff, you gotta go' . . . So I was outside, like, the whole night, 'cause he wasn't saying anything to anybody, so I was doing it. I was outside just telling everybody to leave—for however many hours, I'm telling everybody to leave for a long time."

Finally, everybody did. It was about 3 a.m., and virtually everyone, all at once, walked out of the house, got in their cars, and just left. Tyler told Ryan they were off to another party. The timing was perfect: About then, police arrived to check on the noise, but the officers didn't investigate long as it was clear the party was wrapping up. Tyler seemed fine with that; he said he didn't want people there anymore anyway. Someone pulled up to the house and Tyler walked outside. That's when Michael Mandell approached Ryan.

Michael was panicked and weird. He grabbed Ryan and said they both needed to leave.

"I was like, 'Why? Whatever, I'm going to stay with Tyler and help clean up his house,'" Ryan recalled.

Michael insisted. "No, we need to go," he said. He tried pulling Ryan, who yanked away and told him to get off him.

Tyler came in and told them both to stay. That was fine by Ryan, but Michael was still visibly uncomfortable. As soon as Tyler turned around to go to his bedroom, Michael grabbed Ryan again and pulled him into the garage.

Again, he insisted they had to leave. Ryan relented this time. It was clear Michael wasn't going to stop insisting until he agreed to bail. Just then, they heard the doorbell ring. They thought it might be a cop, so both he and Michael left out the back and started walking home.

Ryan asked Michael what the rush had been.

"Tyler's parents are dead," Michael answered.

"Stop playing with me right now," Ryan shot back.

"No, I'm not playing."

Ryan blew it off. He figured Tyler hadn't wanted him to stay for some reason, so he and Michael made up an elaborate ruse to get him out of the house. He walked to a friend's house and crashed for the night, then got a ride home in the morning. That's when Michael called him and said he'd been telling the truth.

"And I went on the Internet and it was all over," Ryan said.

Meghan McNamara, jolted awake by her concerned mother asking questions about a boy named Tyler and a party the previous night, walked into the police station voluntarily and accompanied by her mother, much as Ryan had. Meyer was available for this visit, so she sat down with the obviously shaken teenager and asked her what she knew.

Meghan hadn't been at the party for very long, she said, maybe about an hour. She left with Jesse, Maggie, and a girl named Desiree—a friend who would later be the first to send a postcard to Tyler in jail. She'd seen nothing amiss at the party, so when Jesse began babbling about how he thought Tyler might have killed his parents, Meghan blew him off. She said she didn't believe him and headed home. It wasn't until Meghan's divorced parents started chatting about the party that Meghan realized Jesse might have been right.

Like most of the kids at the party, Meghan had learned about it through Facebook. She agreed to show Meyer the posts on her cell phone. Logged in as Meghan, Meyer flipped through the girl's newsfeed and spotted several messages from Tyler that he'd posted on his own page for friends to see. The first: "party at my crib tonight . . . maybe" came at 1:15 p.m. The next was a YouTube link to a video for the song "Feel Lucky" by rapper Lil Boosie. That was posted at 4:55 p.m. Then, at 8:15 p.m., came the more definitive: "Party at my house hmu" with a phone number. The last post was marked as having been left twelve hours earlier. It was about 4:45 p.m. Sunday as Meyer examined the phone, meaning Tyler had posted the message about 4 a.m.—just minutes before police got the first 911 call about his dead parents. The post read: "party at my house again hmu."

It appeared Tyler wasn't done celebrating.

CHAPTER 13

Kelly Reynolds was more than Mary Jo's niece. Even though the two were separated by nine years, they were very close friends. Kelly knew details of Mary Jo's life that Mary Jo's brother—Kelly's father, Sam Jr.—didn't even know. They were girlfriends more than typical aunt and niece. As Meyer approached Kelly's home in Port St. Lucie, she saw a grief-stricken woman leaning on her younger sister, Karrie DiVittorio, for support. Both were still shaking from the news.

"There are no words that can offer absolutely any comfort right now, because . . . if I could find them, they would be the first things out of my mouth," Meyer told them. "I'm so—sorry sounds so empty right now. I'm just at a loss with what to say to everyone."

"Yes," Kelly replied.

Meyer gently shifted gears to talk about the investigation. She was the lead detective, she explained, and she wanted to talk to Kelly because her father had mentioned how close Kelly was to Mary Jo. The investigation was still ongoing, so she wouldn't be able to answer some of Kelly and Karrie's questions, but she promised to do her best.

"The main thing is—is, has, you know, Tyler confessed to doing this?" Kelly asked.

"Tyler chose not to speak to me, which is his right."

"Does he have representation?"

"I'm sure that's being taken care of," Meyer replied. "I advised him through Miranda that he was entitled to it, so he understands that a court one can be appointed, and I spoke to Ryan last night. Ryan understands he is now his guardian and that he is going to be in charge of helping him with that."

She explained the process so the women would know what to expect from the upcoming few days. "It's not like we just kind of zoop-zing on through it," Meyer said. "They will tell him all his rights, they will walk him through the process . . . and that way he can make the decisions that he needs to."

"Does he show any remorse?" Karrie asked.

"Yeah," Kelly jumped in. "I mean, does he seem like he understands what's going on?"

"What do you know about what happened?" Meyer asked.

"We don't know much, other than what we've seen on the Internet," Kelly admitted.

Her sister added: "We've heard rumors that . . . it was a hammer. And that, uh, a few different scenarios, but that one of them was at the computer, one of them was possibly in the room."

"Is this on the Internet or are you actually hearing this from actual individuals?"

"Kind of both," Kelly said.

Meyer seemed perplexed and amazed at the rumor mill's overdrive setting. Details she hadn't expected to release were common knowledge to seemingly everyone. She asked if any of Tyler's friends—"kids"—had called either one of them. No, they said.

"Okay," Meyer said. "I know that someone else has received phone calls, and I was like, seriously? One, how did they get your number, and two, why would you make that phone call . . . I'm, like, wow, that's just callous, very callous people."

She spelled out for them what would be written in the forthcoming press release—the police department's official statement to provide the public with the info it was legally entitled to while holding back some of the details that might jeopardize the criminal case. In short, it'd say that police had established the victims died of blunt force trauma within the home well before midnight. Kelly and the family had been trying to piece a time line together, based on when Mary Jo had last talked to loved ones and when the media reports had said Tyler had planned the party. They knew there was no way Mary Jo and Blake would have given permission for a party.

"You're putting your time together correct," Meyer said.

"It's just very difficult," Karrie said.

The sisters laid out what they'd pieced together about the day of the deaths. They told Meyer that their grandmother, Mary Jo's mother, had talked with Mary Jo sometime around 7 or 7:30 p.m. Mary Jo had offered to come over to help her mom order some flowers for an anniversary party—a party that Mary Jo and Blake planned to attend while out of town the upcoming weekend—but Grandma DiVitorrio said no worries, just come over Sunday and we'll order the flowers then. (This information ended up being flawed; Meyer did more interviews and subpoenaed phone records and learned the conversation had actually taken place at 4:42 p.m.)

"Is Tyler showing remorse?" Kelly pressed again.

"There was a party Saturday night that started around 10 p.m. inside the home." That was Meyer's way of answering.

"Inside," Kelly confirmed.

"Until about two, three, four o'clock in the morning."

"When you arrived at the house, there were kids still at the house?"

"I don't believe so."

"But Tyler was there?"

"Yes. Inside the home."

"By himself?"

"Yes."

"So at this point, what is he actually being charged with?"

Meyer answered matter-of-factly. "He is being charged formally with two counts of murder, one for Mary Jo and one for Blake."

"And he knows that?"

"Yes, I told him myself."

It was too much to digest. The extended family had just gone out to dinner together that Friday night, Kelly said. They all went to LongHorn for steaks—the grandparents, Kelly, her husband and two daughters, her mother and stepfather-to-be, Mary Jo, Blake, and Tyler. It was to celebrate the birthday of one of Kelly's girls. Everything had been fine, Kelly said. People were talking, having a good time. Everything seemed normal. Still, Kelly had known there were troubles in the Granduer home. Mary Jo had confided in her that Tyler was becoming a handful.

"Tyler has been really giving them a run for their money for a while," she told Meyer.

Mary Jo had always been reticent to talk about family problems. She seemed uncomfortable burdening others and perhaps a bit worried that they'd judge her family too harshly. She never seemed to have problems with Blake, but in the past few months she'd slowly opened up more about Tyler—his drug use, his sneaking around, his issues at school. Mary Jo said he was sad a lot and stealing money, too, so she'd told Kelly that he'd been put into counseling. After a lot of research, she'd discovered REGA Mental Health Center, a facility designed for adolescents and adults "who require an intensive treatment program under a structured and safe environment, but that do not require an inpatient or residential treatment," its website touted. It was meant to treat a host of disorders—depression, bipolar, substance abuse, and eating disorders. All of those conditions seemed plausible to Mary Jo. REGA has two programs, one called Partial Hospitalization Program, in which patients spent six hours a day, six days per week, at the center undergoing a variety of therapies. The other, Intensive Outpatient Program, was slightly less structured for patients who didn't need quite as much supervision. Patients typically attended three hours a day, three days per week. (Family members weren't sure in which program Tyler was enrolled, but based on descriptions provided to Meyer, it seemed more likely he was involved in the Intensive Outpatient Program.)

The sessions were covered by Blake's insurance, and Mary Jo was so committed to the counseling idea that when Blake planned an annual trip to Georgia that Tyler normally would have attended, she paused. Leaving meant he'd miss some of his counseling sessions, which his doctors advised against, and Mary Jo told some friends that she was starting to think the sessions were helping. She told her friend Mel within two weeks of her death that the improvement was subtle but there; Tyler perhaps was over the hurdle. And Mary Jo was so happy about it, Mel later said. When she would check up on him, Tyler actually was where he'd said he'd be, and he was coming home at night. He started pitching in around the house more, and Mary Jo was starting to see a glimpse of the son she used to know.

"She said he seems to be doing a lot better," Kelly recalled. "Anytime we were together, he seemed to be more talkative . . . I mean you could never say anything to him, but when he started the counseling, he would talk to you. If we saw him, he would give you a hug . . . He didn't do that before."

Mary Jo wrestled with the trip, though. On the one hand, maybe the counseling was doing its job and interrupting it would be a mistake. On the other, Tyler might benefit from hanging out at his uncle Mike's cabin. Tyler himself wasn't much help in making the call. He didn't seem interested in going; nor did he seem to care about missing therapy. So Blake and Mary Jo struggled with the trip decision on their own. Ryan was supposed to visit there from North Carolina, so the brothers would be together for a bit with their dad. Surely that would help Tyler's mood. In the end, she and Blake decided he should go. Maurice Hadley, Blake's father, said Blake was sure the trip would be good for him. Blake had slowly started to confide in his dad about Tyler's attitude and drug use, and Maurice admitted that he thought Blake could've been stricter with the boys. Around the time of the Georgia trip, he and Mary Jo seemed to be stepping up and making tougher calls. Tyler didn't want to go to Georgia, Blake said, but—in typical "it's my way or the highway" dad talk—he was going anyway. Tyler would take some time away from therapy and then start his counseling sessions back up Monday—the same day that Meyer approached Kelly's home for an interview.

The hugs that Tyler had started to give were a throwback to the Tyler his family knew years earlier. He'd always hug both sets of grandparents at each visit and tell them he loved them. But in the previous year or so, all that affection had stopped, and some family members assumed they'd never see that side of him again. When he started hugging again, well, that was a breakthrough in Kelly's eyes. She assumed the counseling had been working. Before, he'd blow people off, sulking quietly. Or they'd say something he didn't like and he'd get mad.

"Or he'd just be, like, whatever, I'm stupid, or . . . you'd know that he just didn't like himself . . . He thought he was fat."

"Yeah, he would say that a lot," Karrie agreed.

At family gatherings, both Ryan and Tyler struck others as being a bit spoiled, not only by Mary Jo and Blake, but by the DiVittorio grandparents. They spoke with condescension enough to grate on Kelly, who saw them as straight-up disrespectful. Mary Jo would reel them in occasionally, but her and Blake's parenting style didn't involve much more than a "knock it off" here and there. They never got to the point of yelling at the kids in public, Kelly recalled.

"If he was being rude at the table, then of course she would say something," Karrie said. Usually he'd stop after that—or get one more word in, and then stop. Typical teenager.

To an extent, anyway.

"When Ryan was Tyler's age, you know, Ryan was giving them a hard time, too, but never to the extent of this," Kelly said. "When Ryan got to be in the 18 range and he was graduating high school . . . he just matured in a different way . . . I had kept saying to Mary Jo, I don't know, I know Ryan gave you a hard time, but not like Tyler is doing to you."

Mary Jo tried to understand what was behind Tyler's attitude, but she couldn't seem to pinpoint it. She didn't understand why he was so angry, why he felt the need to sneak out. Even when he got his own car, he would steal theirs in the middle of the night rather than go joyriding in his own. And the lies were so unnecessary. Sure, sometimes they were clearly meant to keep himself out of trouble, like when he lied about sneaking out, but other times the fibs were just inexplicable. It's not as though his parents cared if he had a girlfriend, so why did it seem he'd sometimes invent one, only to deny that he'd ever mentioned her later?

Several times, Kelly had suggested that Mary Jo take a harder stance. "Maybe when he sneaks out you need to call the police, or maybe when he does things you need to call the police, and she said, 'I don't want to get the police involved, I don't want to get the police involved.'"

Kelly didn't even think they tended to yell back at him when he was a jerk.

"The impression that I'm getting is just . . . they're trying to control and he's like, whatever, I'm out of here."

"They were never yellers," added Karrie.

Especially Blake, the sisters agreed. He rarely raised his voice to either of the boys.

"He was their friend, you know," Karrie said.

That was how it looked to outsiders at least, but Kelly acknowledged that the family didn't necessarily see the real Tyler.

"My grandmother just said yesterday that Mary Jo had said to her . . . 'You only see him when he's good, you don't see him when he's bad,'" Kelly said. "I think she was trying to hide a lot of the stuff from us."

CHAPTER 14

Blake and Mary Jo raised both children Catholic, and they were heavily involved in the St. Lucie Catholic Church. Mary Jo was so proud of her faith that when her mother had her baptism outfit framed for Mary Jo's fortieth birthday, Mary Jo hung it on the living room wall by the front windows next to the fireplace. When Tyler was younger, he took his first Holy Communion with one of Kelly's daughters. He wasn't as enthusiastic as his parents, but he played along, mostly because his parents didn't give him a choice.

"I don't think he believed," Kelly told Detective Meyer. Tyler largely went to church because Mary Jo made him, she said. Mary Jo figured it was typical kid resistance and didn't stand for it, Kelly added: "That's something that she said: 'This is our religion, and this is what we do, and you're doing it.'" It was the one tough stance the parents consistently took.

Blake and Mary Jo tried to give Tyler academic advantages with the goal of preparing him for college and a successful career. Instead of attending the same public elementary school as his friend Michael, Tyler went to Lincoln Park Academy, a magnet school that dubs itself a "premier college preparatory secondary school." The academy was a bit farther away in Fort Pierce, about a twenty-minute drive from his Port St. Lucie home, and it boasted a well-defined discipline policy, progress reports sent to parents every two weeks, and regular homework. Another emphasis: "character and citizenship education."

Tyler wasn't a standout student, but neither was he a bad one. He tended to average between a 2.0 and 3.0, getting mostly B's and C's, and he scored well on Florida's Comprehensive Assessment Test. The basketball and football he played at home largely stayed at home. When family members encouraged him to play, he'd say he wasn't good enough.

"I think he used that as an excuse a lot of times," Karrie said.

But he did start showing interest in music. He picked up the drums pretty quickly, getting private lessons from a tutor so he could play an electronic set at home and percussion in the school band. He also played trumpet. Michael Mandell remembered going to see him play once in middle school. Tyler seemed to love it, he recalled, and Mary Jo and Blake were very supportive. That night, his grandparents went, too, and everyone went out for dinner afterward to cap off the night.

Tyler wished aloud sometimes that he and Michael could go to the same school. Sometimes he'd say that he wished Michael's mom was both of their mothers and Tyler's dad was both of their fathers. That way, he would say, they could be brothers. But they didn't go to the same school until high school, and by then Tyler's path seemed to have already started veering off course. He started selling marijuana, according to several friends, including one girl who told detectives she used to buy regularly from him. Another friend said Tyler started using ecstasy, which had an odd effect on him. Tyler seemed especially serious. "Why do you look crazy?" one friend asked him when he was high on the drug once. Tyler told him not to worry, he was just fucked up.

Tyler didn't drink much around Michael, largely because Michael hated alcohol. A relative was an alcoholic, Michael said, so he despised the stuff and was quick to let people know it. He got especially mad when people were drunk around him and started arguing as though they were making any sense. More than once, Michael had been known to go to the fridge during someone's drunken rant, grab whatever beer was left, and empty the cans down the drain. Michael guessed he saw Tyler drunk maybe a handful of times at most. But Tyler did other things around him, and even in jail, after his parents were dead and his future bleak, Tyler reminisced in letters about the good old days, when he'd smoke twenty marijuana blunts in a row, get drunk off beer, and take an ecstasy pill or two. A friend of his named David rattled off to police all the pills he'd known Tyler to pop: zannies, bars, French fries, monkeys, and half a dozen other slang terms. The terms described everything from alprazolam—brand name Xanax, an anti-anxiety medication—to cigarettes made from tobacco and cocaine paste. French fries were crack, while bars were heroin mixed with alprazolam.

At school, Tyler was known as a strange mix of quiet guy and big talker. He didn't say a lot around people he didn't know well, but with his friends he joked and pulled pranks. Michael remembered hearing about Tyler messing around with a group of friends at school a couple of years back. The kids had managed to get into the school's auditorium with no one else nearby. They climbed atop the walkway that overlooked the seats below, where the senior class was meant to gather for a meeting the next day, and peed all over them.

"He told me one of his friends took a shit off one of the seats," Michael recalled. Looking back, though, he no longer knew if the tale was true. It had turned out that Tyler said a lot of things that weren't quite true.

"I guess it could've happened," he said.

When he was allowed out, Tyler would still manage to get in trouble. In June 2010, he was accused of hitting someone while driving his father's truck. The family of the injured child was suing the Hadley family for fifteen thousand dollars, according to a newspaper report, and court documents showed that Tyler had been scheduled to give a deposition in late August in the case. The letter summonsing him was postmarked July 8.

Tyler talked a big game about killing people or himself, but he didn't seem to have the chutzpah to follow through on any of his rants. Friend Danny remembered that he kept a Baggie of pills in the door of his car just in case he wanted to off himself at some point. Danny didn't know if he was serious or not—Tyler did seem miserable at home, after all—but it seemed like the Baggie was more for show than anything else. He rarely seemed to get angry, which made it stand out even more the one time his friend Dennis saw him pissed. Dennis told detectives that Tyler and another friend had tried to rob someone over drugs, and the would-be target smashed the back window out of Tyler's car. Tyler came back furious and tried to recruit friends to go with him to get back at the guy, Dennis said, but no one would join him. That was the only time Dennis had ever seen Tyler angry. (Friends of Tyler's parents remembered the car window being smashed, too, and recalled that Mary Jo said it was the result of Tyler being bullied and picked on at school.)

After high school started, Tyler seemed to skip school all the time, often inviting Michael with him to play hooky. Michael did a few times, but he didn't want to get caught, and besides, he had plans to graduate and get a job—maybe become a cop, even—so he usually turned down Tyler's invitations. But Tyler kept skipping. Michael told him to knock it off. He was grounded so often that Michael had to find new people to hang out with, and Tyler was even getting a little jealous.

"Are you still my friend, Mike?" he asked once when Michael was hanging out with a new friend more often.

"Yeah, you're my best friend forever," Michael replied. But Tyler would skip school and end up grounded for a week at a time, and Michael got bored. He had to hang out with someone.

"I'd get frustrated," Michael recalled. "I'd say, 'Do you really like staying in your room with nothing to do so much?'"

Mary Jo was confused. Tyler had never hated school so much before. She didn't know what was prompting his revolt. She and Blake tried to get tough by taking away the things that Tyler loved—his phone or his laptop—and grounding him as punishment, but nothing seemed to stick. Mary Jo even began driving Tyler to school and dropping him off right at the door. It didn't matter, Kelly Reynolds later told Detective Meyer. Tyler would walk in the door and, once she was gone, walk right back out. The problems peaked around Christmastime 2010, Kelly said.

"He wouldn't go to school for a full week, or he'd go to one class and he'd leave," she recalled. "Right around Christmastime, he basically had failed the semester and begged Mary Jo and Blake to let him" go to Indian River State College, the adult education school.

IRSC hosted what was called the Drop Back In Academy, designed for people wanting to get their degrees after dropping out of high school. It boasted more than fifty sites in six locations around the county with twelve Florida-certified teachers. The courses conformed to state standards, and the program was under the umbrella of Alternatives Unlimited, which was headquartered in Baltimore. The parent company launched in 1997 and programs quickly expanded to multiple states nationwide, according to its website. In 2012, AU had schools in Alabama, Arizona, California, Florida, Illinois, Kansas, Maryland, Mississippi, Missouri, Nevada, New Jersey, New York, North Carolina, Ohio, Tennessee, Texas, and Washington. The program touted the idea that all students could learn, but some might not learn in traditional ways. Plus, the alternative education path has long been considered a viable option for kids who have been bullied in regular school, or for students who've ended up parents a lot sooner than their own folks would have preferred. The program, open to students age sixteen through twenty-one, was free, and for some it was a godsend.

"These kids need this school. It is doing something for them that no other school did. My stepdaughter goes there and she's doing great," Port St. Lucie resident Julie Lambert said in a May 2011 article published by TCPalm .com.

But Mary Jo was adamantly against Tyler dropping out of regular school to attend the alternative education program.

"She did the whole truancy thing," Kelly recalled. "You know, 'They're gonna come after me because you're not going to school.'" Tyler's response? "I don't care."

"It got to the point where she was either taking him to

the bus stop every morning or they were physically taking him to school, but she said it didn't matter if we took him to school or took him to the bus, because he would leave anyway," Kelly said.

Tyler kept pressing for IRSC. He said he hated school, couldn't stand it, and finally Mary Jo and Blake caved. But it didn't last long. Tyler got caught smelling of marijuana and he was booted from the program, Michael recalled. Mary Jo and Blake were at their wit's end. They pushed him back into public school—Port St. Lucie High School— while encouraging Tyler to get a job and be more responsible. Tyler claimed to have applied for jobs everywhere, but Kelly didn't know if that was true or just a line he fed his folks. When Kelly's own daughter landed a job, Tyler seemed genuinely annoyed. Tyler would say that employers didn't want him, that they weren't interested in hiring him because of some shortcoming that Tyler never could articulate when pressed.

"So . . . he took it personally," Meyer said.

"Right," Karrie replied.

Mary Jo and Blake tried to appease him. When he continually snuck out and stole their cars in the middle of the night, he complained it was because he felt cooped up without a car of his own. His parents thought maybe he was just restless.

"He really wanted a car desperately, and, you know, they were not in the position to get him a car when he turned sixteen," Kelly said. Eventually, though, they worked out the finances and got Tyler the gold Lincoln his friends would quickly covet. (He'd tell them that he paid for the car himself; his family disputed that in interviews with detectives.) After Tyler got the car, he seemed happier—but not for long, Kelly recalled.

"Once he got the car, it gave him more freedom to just take off and do what he wanted to do," she said.

Mel Jones, Mary Jo's friend, said that by the time 2011 rolled around, Mary Jo was downright miserable over Tyler's antics. Mel had known Mary Jo for twenty years. Their families attended the same church, and Mary Jo taught both Mel's niece and nephew in elementary school. In the mid-2000s, Mel was hired to teach first grade at Village Green, and for the last five years the women had taught in adjacent classrooms. Mary Jo confided in Mel as they grabbed lunch or went shopping. Mel knew that Tyler was finally going to counseling for his depression, drug use, and to work on an eating disorder. Mary Jo was alarmed at his weight loss, estimating that he'd shed some fifty pounds in recent months. Mel agreed that Tyler looked thinner. She'd run into the mother and son at JCPenney the first weekend in July, where the two were shopping for clothes for Tyler. Mel told Tyler he looked good. *What are you wearing now, a 32 waist?* she asked. Tyler's doctor had actually said he'd gained a few pounds, Mary Jo replied, thinking she was highlighting good news. Tyler countered that he had to lose weight.

Mel's son and Tyler had been friends for years, but as much as Mel loved Mary Jo, she eventually had to forbid the kids from hanging out together. The families would be having a good time when Tyler would suddenly say things to his mother that made Mel uneasy, asking if she hated him and wanted him dead. Mary Jo would reassure him that was nonsense, but it never stopped the bizarre questions and comments, and Mel didn't want her own son exposed to it anymore. When the boys were in the eighth grade, she put a kibosh on the friendship, and the year that followed marked Tyler's most dramatic decline. Not only did his grades drop and his truancy skyrocket, but he became downright nasty to his parents. Mel told police that she'd come over near Christmastime to visit with her friend, and as they talked, Tyler told his mother he needed something. Mary Jo replied that she and Mel were in the middle of a conversation. Tyler barked that he needed it *now*. When Mary Jo later remarked that the kids emptied the fridge of soda without putting new cans back in, Tyler replied, "Oh, my God, that's what you are going to do, complain? You just hate everyone, mom." Mel tried to steer clear of the confrontation and suggested they have a glass of wine. "You going to get drunk?" Tyler shot at his mother. "You going to be an alcoholic?" Mary Jo told Mel she hoped it was just a phase.

But recently, Mary Jo admitted to Mel, things were getting worse, not better. Tyler's anger seemed to have gone from a simmer to a boil, and she didn't know how to help him. Mel suggested she Baker Act him; Mary Jo shook off the notion. She didn't want to make Tyler even angrier. But the suicide comments—those crushed Mary Jo the most. Once, Mel asked a question that would later haunt her: Do you think Tyler would ever hurt you? Mary Jo replied adamantly that he couldn't, he wouldn't. No, that wasn't her Tyler.

As Tyler supposedly looked for work, more money started disappearing from his parents' accounts and wallets. It would never be a huge amount—forty dollars here, another twenty there—but it got so bad that Mary Jo warned relatives not to leave purses around him when they were gathered for get-togethers. Even that wasn't foolproof.

"Anytime we would go over there, I would always leave my purse in the car, lock the car up, you know, keep the keys with me," Kelly told Meyer. "I wouldn't bring stuff like that into the house, and I had told my daughter that as well . . . One time she forgot, brought her wallet in and it was right on the table. She left and, you know, a couple of hours later, the money was gone."

Again, it wasn't a huge sum, just fifteen dollars, but it was beyond aggravating. Kelly told Mary Jo about it, and Mary Jo confronted Tyler, but he denied it. Kelly didn't believe him, reinforcing her stance that Mary Jo should call the cops if he kept up his shenanigans. He simply didn't have the hard life he seemed to want to present— nor did he have the world's worst parents, despite what he told his friends.

"I think he felt that they were intruding on his life . . . You know, 'Why do you have to know everything?' " Kelly said. "I mean, my daughter says that to me . . . My response is, 'Because I'm your mother, and that's it.' "

Despite Tyler's bitching, Kelly and Karrie still figured he'd live at home for a long time after high school, the same way his brother Ryan had.

"Ryan lived there until he was twenty-four. I assumed Tyler would probably do the same, because Blake and Mary Jo always took care of everything that they needed," Karrie said.

"I never felt that Tyler . . . couldn't wait until he turned 18 to leave, because where would he go, what would he do?" Kelly added.

As Kelly and Karrie talked to Meyer, they couldn't help but return to the same questions that the detective simply couldn't answer: Did Tyler show remorse? Was he on drugs when he did it? Why would he have done such a thing? As Meyer readied to leave Kelly's home, Karrie blurted, "Does it seem like it was violent?" She immediately ridiculed herself. "I mean, I know it was violent, I mean, that's a ridiculous question."

"No, it's not, young lady. No, it's not," Meyer assured.

"Was he, like, in a rage or . . . I don't know, it's just weird for us to understand."

"I know, I know."

"Like, did he snap?"

"Right, uhm," Meyer hesitated. "But [then he] had a party afterward."

Her words intentionally vague, Meyer explained that first there was the act—the beating deaths—and then there was the decision to have a party. And after the party, there was talk that Tyler might throw another party the next night. In other words, the "I just snapped" defense didn't seem plausible.

"We knew there were issues," Karrie said, "but never anything to—"

Meyer interrupted her. There was no point in looking back for red flags, she assured. No one ever says, "I knew this person was fully capable of murder." There's a reason the post-tragedy refrain is, "I never saw this coming."

Kelly couldn't hide her disgust.

"To have a party, to know that your parents are in the goddamn house, you know?"

Did any of the kids know beforehand what had happened, Kelly wanted to know.

"Everything we're learning is not indicating that any of the kids were aware of what was in the master bedroom, and the door was locked."

Kelly's daughter Taylor didn't quite buy that.

"How do a lot of other people know what happened?"

"They think, they think," Meyer replied.

"A lot of people have come to me as my friends, and then they were like, 'Oh, well, he told me he did this.' And I was like, 'You don't know anything; if I don't know anything and my family doesn't know anything—"

"They're saying that Tyler told them?" Meyer interrupted.

"Yeah, a lot of people are writing on Facebook, 'Oh, you have no heart, why would you kill your parents with a hammer?'"

Meyer explained that from the very beginning, the rumor mill had picked up that Tyler had killed his folks with a hammer. That's because the phone calls alerting police told them as much. So one person at least had to know something, she said. And then it was a domino effect.

"I guess my last question is, was Blake sleeping?" Karrie asked. It'd been a question on many family members' minds. Blake was so big, so huge, he could have taken Tyler down. "How did he not stop it or do something, you know?"

"Nobody knows that but Blake, and he took that with him," Meyer said. "Based on my experience—I've been doing this eleven years—based on my experience and the things that I've seen, my image of what I saw, I would say [he was] just frozen."

"With shock," Karrie said.

"He was shocked," Kelly repeated.

"Shock, fear," Meyer offered. "Again, he's the only one that knows, but it's just . . . a person can only take a certain amount of shock, and this well exceeded that . . . 'Frozen' probably would be the best word that I can think of."

CHAPTER 15

On Tuesday morning, Tyler Hadley stood before a judge for the first time. The teen wore a sleeveless, V-neck uniform issued by the St. Lucie County Jail, and had his hands shackled in front of his waist. Though he'd initially been arrested as a juvenile, the gravity of the crime meant he faced as an adult two charges of second-degree murder. As the judge communicated with him via videoconference, Tyler was unfailingly polite. Asked if he was Tyler Hadley, he replied, "Yes, sir." Asked if he had a lawyer, he answered, "No, sir." He looked neither ashamed nor proud, but rather as though he were answering questions posed by a DMV employee renewing his driver's license. Tyler didn't have a lawyer at first, but he soon was assigned public defender Mark V. Harllee of Indian River County, who filed for his client a plea of not guilty.

"There is a very long, significant, documented history of mental illness in young Mr. Hadley, and this is going to be a major issue in the young man's case," Harllee told reporters. It was the only comment the lawyer would make publicly about the case.

Harllee worked as chief assistant public defender beneath Diamond Litty, who had held the elected position of public defender for nearly twenty years. Not all states have such offices. In Michigan, for example, defense lawyers are usually in private practice in addition to being in the pool for available court-appointed attorneys. Some are cleared to handle misdemeanor and less serious infractions; others are approved for the heavier task of handling murder and manslaughter cases. When the court appoints them, lawyers are paid by the county. When hired individually, they're paid by their clients.

As an employee in Litty's office, Harllee worked fulltime as a public defender assigned to people who couldn't afford a lawyer on their own; he drew a state salary. Harllee earned more than $146,000, far less than someone in private practice likely would with a little hustle. Litty was generally a popular figure—a smart, attractive lawyer with short, blond hair and a fit frame who usually ran unopposed in her reelection bids. That changed in 2008 when challenger Don Chinquina launched a campaign to dethrone the longtime defender, criticizing Litty's ongoing refusal to provide a public defender at a suspect's first appearance. Those appearances—such as the one at which Tyler stood alone for on the Tuesday after his parents' deaths—are considered crucial by some, in that proper representation could mean that low-risk offenders are allowed out on bond, freeing up cramped jail space. Litty insisted that her office not step in until the suspect was deemed indigent. Her critics declared that put her clients at an immediate disadvantage, and they complained

that taxpayers had to foot the bill for a new jail to allevi-
ate overcrowding when initial representation might have
had the same effect.

"Failure by the office to promptly become involved in
cases can mean indigent clients may not get bond they
can afford and stay in jail longer than necessary, potentially losing their jobs," the TCPalm.com wrote in an editorial that declined to endorse either Litty or Chinquina
for the post. "Keeping those clients in jail also increases
costs for taxpayers."

Litty opened herself up to further criticism in early
2008 when it was uncovered that an unlicensed intern
had been allowed to handle cases in St. Lucie and Indian
River counties for several weeks. The intern was supposed to be certified by the Florida Supreme Court; Litty
said the certification process got backed up around the
holidays without anyone noticing. Chinquina pounced on
the oversight and filed a complaint with the Florida Bar.

But the anti-Litty campaign failed, and the Republican
kept her post in 2008.

Harllee, too, wasn't without his critics. A balding,
ruddy-faced man, he served as Litty's top lawyer, assigned
to the most complicated and highest-profile cases that filtered through the understaffed office. Despite a reputation as a solid public defender, anti-Litty campaigners
accused him of forcing clients into plea deals they didn't
want for the sake of maintaining a good relationship with
prosecutors and judges.

His reputation took a hit in November 2008, when he
was stopped outside his home south of Fort Pierce for
driving drunk in his state-owned car. Police reports at the
time said he'd driven on the wrong side of the road and
nearly struck a Fort Pierce police car. Harllee refused to
take a breath test on-site to determine his blood alcohol
content. A dash-cam video installed in the police cruiser

showed Harllee losing his balance while trying to hold up one foot.

"I'm not intoxicated, okay?" Harllee insisted. When the officer placed handcuffs on him, Harllee pleaded, "Please don't do this."

The incident put lawyers and judges throughout the Nineteenth Judicial Circuit in a bad spot. Because Harllee oversaw cases throughout Indian River, Martin, Okeechobee, and St. Lucie counties, then-governor Charlie Crist had to issue an executive order allowing the counties' judges and prosecutors to recuse themselves from handling the case. More than a year after his arrest, Harllee pleaded no contest to misdemeanor driving under the influence and was ordered to pay fines and court costs, have his driver's license suspended, attend DUI school, and have his car outfitted with an interlocking device to ensure the engine wouldn't start when the driver was impaired. The prosecutor had asked for a six-month jail sentence, from which Harllee was spared.

"I deeply regret putting myself in this position. I have embarrassed myself, my office . . . and I'm grateful for whatever the court wants to do," he told the judge upon his sentencing.

The judge decided against jail time in part because Harllee hadn't been in trouble for drunken driving for twenty years. (His previous arrest was in Gulf Breeze.) He faced no further punishment from Litty, his boss, according to a TCPalm.com editorial that sarcastically declared Harllee "fortunate to have such a compassionate employer."

"I feel strongly in light of all the circumstances that the judge acted both fairly and appropriately," Litty told a reporter at the time.

All controversy aside, Tyler would later praise his lawyers and Harllee in particular, calling them a fantastic team with his best interests in mind. He regularly updated his grandparents about meetings he'd had with Harllee and the forensics experts and psychiatrists his lawyers lined up for him. Aside from his first statement alleging that Tyler had mental health issues, Harllee rarely spoke to the media at all.

By now, much of the world knew Tyler Hadley's name. Newspapers across the country ran a wire story headlined, "Tyler Hadley, 17, Throws a Party After Murdering His Parents." It began, "A Florida teenager is accused of stashing his parents' dead bodies in a bedroom before welcoming dozens of Facebook friends to a party at his family's home on Saturday night." The story described Tyler as a high school dropout who had "previously injured a child in an accident" while he drove his father's car. Another story, written by Associated Press reporter Matt Sedensky, presented a fuller picture of the teen: "Neighbors knew Tyler Hadley as a polite and respectful teen who played basketball with his father in the driveway and built forts of junked wood as a kid—not as someone who could kill his parents and throw a party while their bodies lay tucked beneath towels and other items in a locked bedroom."

Media scrambled for photographs of Blake and Mary Jo and quickly released their driver's license images. In Blake's, his smile was broad and slightly goofy, his graying brown hair cut short and parted on the left. Mary Jo's curly hair hit just past the nape of her neck. Her eyes were kind and her smile serene. This was the world's introduction to the two lives lost: a smiling, seemingly all-American couple who were conscientious enough about others that they both made a point to be organ donors.

Raeann Wallace, who lived next door to the Hadleys, said she used to ask Tyler to watch her house when she was out of town. She'd see him in his yard as she packed up her car for a trip and she'd call out, "I'm leaving for a few days. You make sure no one messes with my home," she recalled in an interview. He was always polite and seemed eager to help. She often saw him playing hoops with Blake and his brother Ryan.

"How do you go from shooting hoops with your dad in the driveway to beating him with a hammer?" she wondered out loud to more than one reporter.

Blake and Mary Jo largely kept to themselves, she added, though they'd run into each other occasionally at grocery stores or restaurants. Mary Jo was especially nice, Raeann said. She shuddered when imagining the brutality the couple had faced. Someday, she said, Tyler would realize what he'd done and he'd buckle to his knees in remorse.

The more shocking headlines were based on a purportedly anonymous friend, but the details could have only come from Michael Mandell, or at least someone with whom Michael spoke. As far away as Australia, a story ran under the headline, "Dying Mum Asks Killer Son: Why?"

It was more media attention than the generally safe city knew how to handle. Not two weeks earlier, Orlando had seen a similar crush of reporters as the trial wrapped up against young mother Casey Anthony. Anthony had been charged with killing her two-year-old daughter Caylee in a case that made headlines worldwide. The mother had been photographed partying in the days after her daughter's disappearance, bolstering prosecutors' theory that she killed her daughter to allow herself to again live a carefree lifestyle. Public opinion was against Anthony, so when the jury came back July 5 with a verdict of not guilty, outrage followed, and many in the area—even as far away as Port St. Lucie—were sick and tired of reporters.

The detectives in the Hadley case, starting with Meyer, made it known that their opinions of reporters were less than flattering. Meyer warned Ryan Hadley the first day she talked with him that members of the media were going to grab onto the story like pit bulls. If he declined comment and reporters continued to badger him, he was to call the police immediately.

"We're here for you guys," she told him. "We're not gonna tolerate that. I know there's a freedom, and I know they have whatever they want to squeal at me. I don't care."

She promised to send a marked unit to wherever Ryan was staying to make things uncomfortable for reporters.

"We're not gonna let them just abuse and just be in your face because there's just no reason for it. So just don't hesitate, if it gets overwhelming, to call us. We can send a road unit up, and we will very politely and eloquently say, 'Back off.' "

Seeing the throngs of reporters at the funeral reinforced the distaste, but there was no denying that the Hadleys' story had resonated with millions of people worldwide, far beyond the Sunshine State. Tyler's Facebook page was blowing up with messages that he of course couldn't see. Tyler's cousin told police that his friends were writing messages calling him a monster and asking how he could do such a horrific thing. Some of his friends posted in response to defend him, saying he'd clearly been pushed to do what he'd done by parents who refused to leave him alone. A public Facebook page was created in memoriam of Blake and Mary Jo, and it quickly had about eight hundred "likes." Some self-described family members wrote heartrending messages there, saying how much the couple would be missed and how loved they were. Meanwhile, other Facebook pages popped up, too—these glorifying Tyler. They drew hundreds of followers, but many of the comments were angry messages left toward the pages' creators, accusing them of being heartless and callous. It seemed sadly inevitable that Tyler, whatever his reason for bludgeoning his parents, would be celebrated in some circles as a hero. One made a crude reference to a popular Beastie Boys song: "You have to fight for your right to party—sometimes til death."

One page had as its profile image the photo Michael Mandell shot just after he spied the bodies in the Hadleys' bedroom—the image of Michael with Tyler holding a Solo cup. Registered as a "public figure," the page declared, "This page is NOT Tyler Hadley but is a close friend of his." Immediately, the page had about five hundred "likes," but the number plummeted to eight after the page kept getting reported as bogus to Facebook authorities. "I am not Tyler Hadley, stop reporting my page," the creator implored at one point. Most of the posts were short and crass: "Tyler Hadley be gettin them hoes" (sic), "supporters of Tyler Hadley unite," and YouTube videos of rapper Lil Boosie, whose music Tyler allegedly listened to as he amped himself up for the attack. One buddy wrote, "never going to forget the weeks leading up to the incident. never gonna fucking forget the shit we did" (sic). Others weren't so willing to fondly reminisce. Wrote one poster, "Fuck tyler hadley and fuck your bitch ass for supporting this type of madness" (sic). Wrote another, "hope your buddy gets the death penalty . . ." Another page, called Tyler Hadley 1, was equally crass and controversial. One series of posts was simply the lyrics to Peter, Paul and Mary's "If I Had a Hammer." Another read, "I guess his parents got hammered before the party even started."

The purpose of Tyler's initial court appearance was to get the charges on the record and get a defense lawyer assigned to the case, but Chief Assistant State Attorney

Tom Bakkedahl, who represented the prosecution, told reporters he planned to seek first-degree murder charges from a St. Lucie County grand jury. That carried a maximum penalty of life in prison. Had Hadley committed the crime not a decade prior, he would have been eligible for the death penalty, but in 2005, in the case *Roper v. Simmons,* the U.S. Supreme Court eliminated the death penalty as being cruel and unusual punishment for juveniles. Five years later, the court ruled that sentencing juveniles to life without parole was also unconstitutional—unless the crime involved killings.

The death penalty is "simply off the table; it's not a viable option," Bakkedahl told reporters. "Despite the fact that the case may otherwise in all respects warrant the death penalty, we are prohibited from seeking it as a result of him being approximately six months short of his 18th birthday."

Bakkedahl—a tall man with a slightly crooked nose and thin-lipped smile—wasn't shy about his pro-death-penalty stance. The lawyer had started working as an assistant state attorney in Martin County in July 1996. Nearly four years later, he headed to a similar position in St. Lucie County, and five years after that he moved up the ladder to chief assistant state attorney in the Nineteenth Judicial Circuit. He was a true Floridian, having earned his bachelor's in political science from Florida State University, followed by his law degree at the FSU College of Law. Like Harllee, he was middle-aged and white, his face a bit red, and his daily attire usually a simple suit with a white dress shirt and patterned tie. He wore his hair in a short crew cut, not unlike Tyler's, and when his forehead knitted as he made a serious point, a deep line cut between the brows above his pale eyes.

Bakkedahl had been an outspoken proponent of the

death penalty, writing in 2009 a piece for TCPalm.com in which he slammed capital punishment opponents for claiming that the punishment cost taxpayers too much money. At that point, he'd handled ten cases in which he'd sought the death penalty. In his early comments to reporters after Tyler's arrest, he seemed frustrated with the U.S. Supreme Court ruling that prohibited him from seeking death in the case because of Tyler's age. Bakkedahl seemed to take the "our hands are tied" position on the matter. In his earlier writing, he'd criticized defense lawyers who claimed that capital punishment was cruel and unusual because of the delay between conviction and execution, countering that those same lawyers were the ones who caused the massive delays by retaining experts "in an effort to persuade the jury to spare the defendant's life" and by exhausting convicts' appeals options. "Assuming, arguendo, that the valuation of an innocent human life is the appropriate subject matter for a cost-benefit analysis, I would suggest the expense is well worth the effort," he argued.

Looking at the other death penalty cases Bakkedahl had recommended, it seemed likely that Tyler's case would have been among them had the law allowed. In 2009, after Dale Middleton killed a neighbor with a knife to steal a large-screen television—which he later sold for a lousy two hundred dollars—Bakkedahl argued for death. Middleton had seen forty-nine-year-old Roberta Christensen with a stack of cash she'd received as tips from her job as a waitress, so he went to her home hoping for money. When he couldn't find any, he stabbed Christensen in the neck so hard that the vertebrae in her spine were cut.

"The life ebbed out of her in her own bedroom, where he had no right to be," Bakkedahl had told the jury in his impassioned closing argument. "He is a murderer! . . . What we have here is a killing done in a cruel and unusual manner!"

His plea was heeded: In August 2012, an Okeechobee County jury voted unanimously that Middleton should face the death penalty.

Bakkedahl wouldn't get to make such a plea on behalf of Mary Jo and Blake Hadley, and it seemed to frustrate him. Life in prison without parole was the "only viable option," he said. "While it may not be satisfying to me, that's all we've got."

At around 3 p.m. after Tyler's first court appearance, Assistant State Attorney Bernard Romero signed the arrest affidavit that would lock up Tyler for the foreseeable future. In the stilted language of the law, it spelled out each of the second-degree murder charges the teen was facing so far: "July 16, 2011 Tyler Joseph Hadley did unlawfully, by an act imminently dangerous to another and evincing a depraved mind regardless of human life, although without any premeditated design to effect the death of any particular individual, kill and murder . . . a human being, and during the commission of said offense the defendant carried, displayed, used, threatened to use, or attempted to use any weapon, to wit: a hammer, in violation of Florida Statutes 775.087(1)(a) and 782.04(s)."

Prosecutors didn't believe the part about the crime being "without any premeditated design," but until they could get a grand jury to indict Tyler on first-degree murder charges—a must, per Florida law—second degree would have to suffice. The arresting paperwork contained sad tells, such as the area reserved to jot down which parent or guardian officials interviewed to preserve the juvenile's rights. "Unable to contact," read the form. Elsewhere, it listed his parents' names under "critical alerts": "Hadley,

Blake. Father—Deceased. Maryjo Hadley [sic]. Mother—Deceased."

Under "risk assessment," Tyler scored zeros nearly across the board. He had no prior history, he wasn't on probation, he had no outstanding cases pending. He ranked "low" when weighing his likely risk of reoffending, which factors in social history and behavior indicators. But that mattered little, because he rang in the highest risk possible by being charged with a crime that carried a potential life sentence. On a scale that determined he had to be jailed with a score of 12 or more, Tyler hit a 15.

But while Tyler was being charged as an adult and being housed in the county jail rather than the juvenile detention facility, he wasn't going to be mingling with adult inmates anytime soon. First, because of his erratic behavior when he was arrested and his comment to Michael that he planned to kill himself, he was housed in the medical ward on suicide watch. After that, he was headed to isolation until he officially turned eighteen.

Instead of a cake, Tyler's birthday present would simply be a transfer to the big-boy side of the jail.

CHAPTER 16

As their younger son appeared before a judge and their older son tried to make sense of an unfathomable ordeal, Blake and Mary Jo Hadley lay inside the medical examiner's office in Fort Pierce awaiting examination. As much as everyone wanted the answers to come quickly, investigators had to be methodical and precise, or else they risked jeopardizing one of the most important and highest-profile cases Port St. Lucie had ever seen. So after the bodies were removed from the home, they were transported to the District 19 medical examiner, where they were kept cooled in a room until 9 a.m. Tuesday. That's when Chief Medical Examiner Roger Mittleman and Dr. Linda Rush-O'Neil began the hours-long task of examining both bodies inside and out—Blake and Mary Jo, respectively—to ensure nothing was overlooked or taken for granted. Others with a stake in the case, including Chief Assistant State Attorney Thomas Bakkedahl, Detective Meyer, and Officer Marshall, attended.

Marshall began alongside O'Neil. Again donning protective gear, she started photographing Mary Jo overall, then taking close-up shots of the forty-seven-year-old's injuries with scale. She documented what O'Neil described as defense wounds on Mary Jo's arms, wrists, and hands—evidence of blows that were likely inflicted as she tried to shield herself from the hammer—and she took pictures of the clothing that had been laid out on a sterile blanket, paying special attention to the tears on the back of Mary Jo's blood-soaked shirt. O'Neil and an assistant moved across Mary Jo's body slowly, allowing Marshall to take pictures of the injuries before and after they shaved away any hair in the way.

Many of Mary Jo's injuries were to her upper torso and head. Her spine had been fractured—possibly from her back hyperextending during the attack—and seven ribs broken. Three of the rib breaks punctured her left lung. After O'Neil opened Mary Jo's skull, Marshall documented the extensive injuries visible to the brain. The claw portion of the hammer matched many of the injuries, Meyer later reported. O'Neil counted about fourteen wounds across Mary Jo's back, and, while talking with Meyer during the exam, she described the left side of the woman's skull as being "pulverized." From the crown of her head toward her left ear was a gaping cut. Just below that, another laceration ran toward the front of her face. The skull had been smashed like an egg, O'Neil told Meyer.

"There were fragments of skull and brain tissue exiting this head injury," Meyer reported. "On the top of her head was a circular laceration with tissue missing and the skull visible."

In a separate room, Mittleman documented his findings during Blake's examination in detached fashion:

*The body is that of a well developed, obese white
male weighing 302 pounds and measure 6 feet 1
inches [sic]. The appearance of the deceased is
consistent with the stated age 54 years. The scalp
hair is brown, straight and approximately one inch
in length. The irides are gray and the conjunctivae
are unremarkable. Native dentition is evident.
Along the mucosa of the upper lip there are a few
small dark contusions with one of the bruises having a small laceration. Along the lower lip mucosa
in the midline there is a small contusion/laceration
of similar appearance as above. There is no evidence of genital or perianal trauma.*

In layman's terms: Blake was obese, had his own teeth,
brown hair (though in reality, the brown was being over-
taken by silver), gray eyes, and cuts on the inside of his
mouth. Mittleman then moved on to Blake's clothes. He
noted Blake was wearing a T-shirt and jean shorts, both
of which were stained with blood. The back of the T-shirt
was cut open in five places; the front was cut in another.
The examiner noted, too, bits of material he'd found on
Blake's body: a green shred of cellophane on his right
arm, thin threadlike material at the tip of the right thumb,
a tiny fleck of white material on the left pinkie, and a
strand of brown hair on the right hand.

The examination of the injuries was far lengthier.
Blake had been savagely beaten, and Mittleman's job was
to clearly document every bruise and every cut with precise measurements in painstaking detail. And there was
much to document. The injuries were so extensive that

the examiner broke them down into body parts, beginning with Blake's head. "Examination of the head reveals multiple blunt trauma injuries," the section began.

Among the findings: Blake's nose had been broken at the base. A small, linear abrasion ran across the center of his forehead, measuring just shy of a centimeter. Near his left temple was another abrasion, this one nearly two centimeters long. Directly anterior to that abrasion was a cluster of small red contusions—injuries that reddened, but didn't break, the skin. The cluster was about 7.5 by 5.3 centimeters. Inside the left ear was a vertical slice, about 3.5 centimeters long by 1 centimeter wide. Near that, at the rim of the ear, was another abrasion. Turning Blake's head to the right revealed even more gruesome damage. A cut along the right ear extended upward to the right side of the head, measuring thirteen centimeters long—about the length of a ballpoint pen—and four centimeters wide. Beneath this, the skull had been smashed in several spots. The fractures were visible through the skin, causing parts of the skull that are normally jointed to tear apart. The right temporal lobe—the front part of the brain containing the sensory center of hearing—had multiple lacerations, as did the right cerebellar hemisphere—the part that controls balance and muscle movement. The brain itself was encased in blood from the beating.

At the base of Blake's skull, in what's called the occipital region, were five lacerations, the largest of which was nine centimeters long and gaped open another centimeter. The shape of the cut seemed to match up with the other lacerations, a sign that the same weapon had been used in all. Several of the cuts made inverted V shapes in the skin. In all, there were twelve skin injuries of the head, and extensive damage to the brain encased inside.

Mittleman next moved down to Blake's neck, where he noted a long but superficial cut on the right side a few centimeters beneath the right earlobe. Just below that were two parallel red abrasions, and a similar pair of abrasions lay on the left side of the neck just behind the left ear. Moving down to Blake's shoulders, Mittleman documented three oblong patches of closely spaced abrasions and two lesions along the right shoulder, and four-sided abrasions atop the left shoulder. Blake's chest had even more bruising—again, most of the abrasions were in parallel lines—as well as a pair of lacerations, one deeper than the other.

Beneath Blake's sliced T-shirt was a cluster of five wounds and a long abrasion measuring more than eleven centimeters, or about four and a half inches. Though the weapon tore through the T-shirt and occasionally pierced the skin, the wounds weren't deep enough to reach into the chest cavity or damage the rib or spine. Moving on to Blake's right arm, Mittleman noted eleven injuries, as though Tyler had been blindly swinging in a frenzy at his father's upper body, perhaps in an effort to bring the large man down. Some of the injuries were more abrasions, but others were actual cuts. The right humerus, or the long bone extending from the shoulder to the elbow, was broken, and the elbow was marked by cuts and bruises. The back of Blake's hand had been bruised—had he raised it to block a blow at some point?—rounding out the injuries. His left humerus was broken as well, and two abrasions lay atop the wound. "After a spared area of skin," Mittleman noted, "there is another such abrasion measuring 2.0×1.2 cm in dimension. Incision into the latter site reveals blood extravasation in the underlying subcutaneous tissue." In other wounds, blood had pooled beneath the wound. On the back of the arm were more abrasions and bruising, as well as a shallow cut connected with a long bruise—this time, nearly fourteen centimeters in length—and more cuts to the elbow. In all, there were twelve injuries to his left arm.

Blake's legs hadn't been spared, either. Each had bruises and cuts, and the fibula of his left leg had been shattered. Along the left ankle were two cuts, one measuring four centimeters, the other more than seven. On the lower half of the left calf was a gaping cut measuring eight centimeters long and about an inch deep. Red dot-like abrasions, about one millimeter in diameter, speckled his right leg. In all, Mittleman documented ten injuries to Blake's legs.

Though Blake was obese, he'd been generally healthy before the beating. His heart had a normal size and shape without the scarring that indicates disease. He had some mild plaque in his coronary arteries, as much a sign of age as anything. Mittleman noted there were no laryngeal petechiae or neck bruising—meaning that it didn't appear Blake had been choked. His lungs were healthy, the liver showed no signs of cirrhosis, and his spleen and kidneys were normal. He'd already had his gallbladder removed, and as Mittleman examined Blake's stomach, he found that he'd eaten that day, clearly oblivious to the fate that awaited him. His toxicology results were clean for all tested drugs—barbiturates, cocaine, opiates, and the like—though testing showed he'd likely had a drink or two at some point, as his blood alcohol content was 0.02 percent (far below the 0.08 percent that is the legal limit for driving under the influence).

Mittleman's ultimate findings in Blake's autopsy were brutal: "Multiple blunt trauma injuries of skin (65), soft tissue bruising, massive skull fractures, lacerations of right cerebral hemisphere and cerebellum, subdural ecchymoses, humeral fractures, left radius fracture and left tibial fracture." Cause of death: blunt trauma injuries. Manner of death: homicide.

Though Blake and Mary Jo had been attacked differently, resulting in a variety of injuries, the conclusion of Mary Jo's exam was ultimately the same as her husband's: homicide caused by blunt trauma. After the autopsies, Mittleman examined the previously processed hammer that police believed was the murder weapon. The hammer weighed 880 grams, or about thirty-one ounces, and had a round, flat surface at one end that measured just shy of four centimeters. The other end had two sharp claws measuring about 1.2 centimeters in length along each sharpened edge, with a 0.9-centimeter gap between the edges. Mittleman found that the weapon was consistent with dozens of the injuries, including four on the back of Blake's head, three on the right side of his neck, and several on his shoulders and chest.

"It was, for lack of better term, horrific," prosecutor Bakkedahl told reporters after watching the autopsies. "The injuries were just massive."

He was baffled at how polite Tyler appeared when addressing the judge for his initial court appearance when juxtaposed with the brutality the teen had unleashed on the people who'd brought him into this world.

CHAPTER 17

Ryan Hadley was suddenly both next of kin in a homicide case and the legal guardian of the killer in custody. He wasn't sure how to process it all. After spending much of Sunday—the day he learned of his parents' death and his brother's arrest—in tears, he'd finally hit a wall. He couldn't cry anymore. He'd sat with his uncle Sam in shock as Meyer described the next steps in the case to him: He'd be assigned a victim advocate; he'd get financial help paying for his parents' funeral because they were homicide victims; he'd be the go-to person for police as the trial date neared. It could take up to three years for the case to hit a courtroom, he was told. He couldn't fathom it.

"This is where we're supposed to have those amazing words and we just don't," Meyer apologetically told him.

"There are no amazing words for this," Sam said.

"I mean, your immediate family is gone in one day," said Ryan.

Meyer hadn't been able to tell him everything about the investigation. Some elements were still unclear, and others were too sensitive to release publicly—even to family members. Asked if Tyler was on drugs when he swung the hammer, Meyer replied, "We'll go with 'unknown.'"

"You, under your investigation, think he was the sole person involved?" Sam asked.

"He's been the only arrest."

"That's all you can tell me?"

Meyer relented slightly. "There is no reason—"

"No reason to think otherwise," Sam finished for her.

Meyer told him they'd likely be able to visit Tyler soon, but it wasn't like on TV shows where people arrested get a phone call immediately, she said. The family would soon learn that nothing was like the TV shows.

"Ryan, I wish I had amazing words of wisdom," she said.

Ryan sat across from Tyler behind the glass dividers inside the visitor area of the St. Lucie County Jail. He'd visited briefly before, the only relative who could stomach it, but he hated being there. The two were separated by a line of partitions meant to give a semblance of privacy. Each brother picked up a telephone. The conversation started slowly—a "what's up?" from each of them, followed by complaints about the phone reception—but soon Ryan was talking about his plans to go back to North Carolina in a few days. He was drained, he had a job to start, and he needed something to focus on aside from upcoming funerals and court dates.

"Oh, really?" Tyler asked.

"Yeah."

"And then what—like, are you going to a grievance counselor?"

"Yeah, I've already been doing it."

Tyler said his first meeting with a counselor was coming up the following week.

"What's everybody been up to?" he asked.

"I don't know, not much," Ryan said. "I've been doing nothing but running around and shit 'cause I have a ton of shit to deal with now, every day, nonstop."

"You can come to jail and have gravy and biscuits," Tyler joked.

"Shut up."

"It's really good."

"I'd rather not."

Tyler, who'd been dressed first in a white jumpsuit after his arrest, and then in blue for his arraignment, was now in orange. He explained he was still on that "medical thing"—suicide watch—as doctors tweaked the medications he was being prescribed behind bars.

"Yeah, that sucks," Ryan said.

"Yeah."

"You don't know what shit I have to do now, Tyler." Ryan seemed overwhelmed.

"What do you have to do?"

"Oh, my God, Tyler, there's so much shit."

"Like what?"

"I have to find health insurance 'cause I don't have health insurance. I got to deal with all this stuff, the house, with the cars, I have to get all this shit . . . All these problems that are now on my ass."

Tyler seemed oblivious. "I'd rather have your problems now."

"Huh?" It was almost as if Ryan had misheard. His brother, who'd gotten them both into this mess, who'd picked up a hammer and bludgeoned the life out of their parents, seemed incapable of stepping outside himself long enough to empathize with the slew of responsibilities now weighing down on Ryan.

Tyler changed tacks. "What are they gonna do with everything? . . . Did they take the cars yet?"

No, Ryan said. Everything was his decision now, and he'd had no time to decide.

"What about the house? I mean, is it going to go into foreclosure?"

"I'm just gonna let it go," Ryan said.

The family's pets had been divvied up. Ryan took Sophie, the protective black Lab, one set of grandparents took Molly, the fourteen-year-old beagle, and cousin Kelly took the black-and-white cat, Tinkerbell.

"How's Sophie doing?" Tyler asked.

"She's good."

"Are you staying at the house or grandma's house?"

"I can't stay in that house," he said. "I can't even go into the house."

This, too, seemed to roll off Tyler. He mumbled, then asked, "Are you guys, like, well?"

"Yeah, everything's completely different now, but I guess everybody's doing as good as they can."

Tyler hoped his grandmother—his mom's mom— would visit him soon. The two had always been close.

"They said they can't do it yet," Ryan told him.

"What do you mean, 'They can't do it yet'?" Tyler asked.

"They don't feel up to it."

"Right, right . . . Tell 'em I understand."

"The only reason I've really been coming is 'cause I knew I was gonna leave soon."

"You didn't have to come." Tyler sounded borderline defensive.

"Well, I wanted to come . . . and I knew if I didn't come now, I didn't know when I would ever see you again, so . . . Hard for me to come, to be honest with you. Every time I'm here I feel like I'm gonna have a heart attack."

Tyler said he understood. He was surprised anyone had come to see him, he admitted. Surprised that the family was showing him so much support.

"Nobody supports what you did whatsoever, though," Ryan corrected. "That shit's never gonna change. No idea how you could even do that . . . Just fucked up."

"Just—just tell everybody I love 'em and that I said hi," Tyler said.

"I will."

Tyler talked again about his medication. He was in a process, he said, in which doctors would give him one drug, then another, to see what was working. It was a long-ass process, he said, and it really sucked.

"I'm sure life for you is gonna pretty much suck for the rest of your life now," Ryan said. "Not gonna be great for me, either."

The two tried to change the pace of the conversation. Ryan had gone to Busch Gardens in Tampa Bay the day before with a few friends to try to blow off some steam and get away from the heartache. He told Tyler, who perked right up.

"Any new rides there?"

"They have a new roller coaster . . . It was called 'The Cheetah Hunt.' It's really good."

It seemed so silly for one brother to be talking about a sixty-mile-an-hour roller coaster ride through glass to the brother who'd just killed their parents. Ryan started to say his good-bye. He said he'd mail Tyler letters on postcards—the only form of mail that prisoners at the county jail were allowed to receive. And he told Tyler not

to expect to see him for a while because he was going
back home.

"Tell everyone else I said hi," Tyler implored again.

Ryan agreed before saying good-bye.

"I love you," Tyler said.

"Love you," his brother responded.

They hung up the phone, and Ryan left Rock Road.

CHAPTER 18

Tyler Hadley remained in his jail cell as nearly a thousand mourners gathered July 23, 2011, to pay respects to his parents. Somehow, in the midst of the chaos and grief, Ryan and his grandparents had managed to forge ahead and make arrangements for Blake and Mary Jo at the St. Lucie Catholic Church, where they'd been members for a quarter century. The church was beautiful, its entrance tall and grand and its walls a cream stucco, with red Spanish tile on the roof. Palm trees dotted the surrounding landscape.

The service, held one week to the day after the couple's death, drew not only people from throughout the region, but family members from all over the country who had rushed to be by Ryan's side. Within the hours after they learned of the death, family members started trickling in, Ryan had told Detective Meyer, especially from Blake's side of the family. Now they gathered for the final farewell.

Outside, it was a beautiful, albeit hot, day. The sun shone from a steel-blue sky. Mourners carrying bouquets of flowers filled the parking lot and filed past sheriff's deputies stationed to keep watch. Inside the sanctuary stood three large posters with a collage of photographs of the couple and their two sons—including the one accused of killing them.

Beaux Artabazon, who'd become a full-time special education teacher the year after he started subbing at Mary Jo's school, was leading a different life altogether by the time he arrived for her funeral. He'd moved to Florida from Virginia to be close with his mother and was forever grateful he had: Within five years, at age sixty-seven, she was diagnosed with lung cancer and died three weeks later. The death gutted Beaux. He'd been the type of teacher to routinely go in on Saturdays, and it was over one hardworking weekend that his mother had begun experiencing chest pains and feeling as though she couldn't breathe. Beaux didn't have a cell phone, and no one else was at the school to answer calls, so his mother sat there, enduring the pain, until he finally came home.

"That kind of is indirectly related to why I quit teaching after my mom died," Beaux later recalled. "I couldn't get over that—that I wasn't there at home when she needed me. It haunted me that she sat there having a hard time breathing, thinking I would be home any minute."

The year was 2006. Beaux rushed his mother to the hospital, and, after a long wait followed by an impersonal exam, the doctor announced bluntly that she was dying of lung cancer.

"It's from the smoking," he said unsympathetically.

Three weeks later, his mother was dead, and Beaux

reexamined his life. He quit teaching, moved in with his sister, and tried to find the "great lessons in love" that are hidden in every horrible situation.

It was a fluke that Beaux learned of Mary Jo's death as quickly as he did. He didn't have a television set—wasn't a fan of cable—but he'd happened to swing by a friend's house the morning after the fateful party. That friend had the news on in the background, and the urgency of the "two dead" report caught everyone's attention. When Mary Jo and Blake's names were mentioned, Beaux muttered that he knew them and inched closer to the television set. He immediately regretted having announced his connection to the victims. His friend let out an incredulous, *"Really?"* and began asking far more questions than Beaux was comfortable answering.

"A sick feeling washed over my whole body as it dawned on me what I was paying attention to—because I'd just heard their names," he recalled.

Eventually, Beaux went home and started getting emails and messages through Facebook from people wanting to let him know what had happened, hoping they'd catch him before he learned it from the news. It was too late.

The next week, Beaux was dressed for their funeral. So many tear-streaked faces. He spotted a former student of his and said hello. The kid hadn't really known the Hadleys, but he'd seen the news coverage and was drawn to the service.

"Even if you know the person just kind of marginally, this kind of thing touches you," Beaux said later. "You feel like, my god, I knew them and I liked them and I wish I'd kept in better touch with them."

Beaux couldn't help but compare this turnout with his own mother's funeral, which was dwarfed in comparison. People who learned peripherally of his mother's fall to cancer weren't nearly as likely to come to her funeral as those who heard of the Hadleys' deaths at the hands of their own son. Both deaths were gruesome, Beaux thought, but people have a bizarre fixation on the macabre, a determination to burden themselves with the circumstances of others' untimely demises.

"For some reason, we can sort of put our attention on how they died and just think about how sad and tragic and horrible it is. What must it have been like? Were they aware, were they awake, were they pleading? Were they thinking, 'My god, my baby, what is he doing?!' "

Beaux tried to shake such thoughts off. They weren't productive. They were the types of questions that could leave a man glued to his couch, unable to see the point in everyday living. But this day, the day of the funeral, he had come to the church to bid farewell and pay his respects. He hugged former colleagues he hadn't seen since the last party, and they shared their disbelief and recalled happier times.

"We always say we should get together more, and it was a horrible way to be brought together. It was really heavy; *Big Chill* ain't got nothing on this," he said.

TV crews, while respectful, were still there. They camped out in a back parking lot and interviewed whoever was willing. It seemed so crass, insensitive. Beaux felt sick about it.

"The whole situation was so personal, so private, and it was being broadcast all over the country," he said.

Beaux spotted one of Tyler's longtime friends—he couldn't recall the boy's name—but his voice cracked as he described him.

"Oh, bless his heart, the tears hadn't stopped," Beaux recalled. "He was just broken up. That was so sad to see."

Inside the church, the priests never directly talked of the gruesome end to the couple's lives but rather focused on celebrating their accomplishments, their joys, and their legacies. They also talked about love and forgiveness, asking those who'd gathered to pray for Tyler—and forgive him. One mourner read the thirteenth chapter of First Corinthians—the oft-cited passage about love being patient and kind that's read at nearly every chapel wedding ever performed—because that was the passage Mary Jo was supposed to read at service the Sunday her body was discovered in her home.

Ryan, wearing a black suit with a red rose pinned to his lapel, seemed stoic but dazed, unable to do much more than politely nod at the hundreds of strangers who descended on the church, according to one family friend. The tears that had dried up the night he spoke with Detective Meyer returned as pallbearers ushered out two matching wooden caskets to load into a waiting hearse. Media members were asked to stay outside, and so they did, filling the public sidewalks as mourners entered the church for the service and left afterward. Most seemed gripped with shock.

"This is a kid that most of us here have known our whole lives," Cameron Adams, one of Mary Jo's former students who also knew Tyler, told a reporter. Adams had known Tyler since the first grade, and Mary Jo had taught him when he was a student at Bayshore Elementary School. She'd taught his brother, too, and Adams had met Blake several times. He felt like he could tell Mrs. Hadley anything. She was so nice and open. He remembered that she'd had a weight problem until the year after he had her. When he saw her after the summer, it was like she'd "lost a whole other person," Adams told Meyer. (He didn't know the reason was weight-loss surgery.) Nothing seemed amiss from either Mary Jo or Tyler. The boy was quiet but nice and never said anything negative about his parents. As they grew older, Tyler got skinnier and tall, and he was a tad more hyper than he'd been in his younger years. He was the type of kid who was louder around you if he knew you, Cameron explained. In other words, he was pretty damn normal.

Adams said he'd run into Tyler at a Circle K gas station the day before the murders, an account he'd shared with investigators. It was Adams's birthday, and he and his girlfriend had stopped to get cigarettes and a couple of drinks before hitting Benihana for hibachi with Cameron's parents. He and Tyler chatted for about five minutes, he recalled. Tyler told him things were good; Cameron mentioned it was his birthday.

"Happy birthday," Tyler responded. "How old are you?"

"Nineteen," replied Adams, sensing that maybe Tyler was feeling out his age to know if he could ask him to buy him some booze or not. Then Tyler mentioned the party he planned to throw the next evening. He invited Adams to come hang out. Adams had considered it, but ended up catching a movie with his girlfriend instead. One different decision, and he would have unwittingly been at a party with the body of a former teacher in the next room. The next day, July 17, he read something from a Facebook friend about "this parent-killing thing," he later told Meyer. He went to TCPalm.com and was floored that he'd talked to Tyler not twenty-four hours before the kid apparently slaughtered his parents. And now, a week later, he was at a funeral for a teacher who'd helped shape his formative years.

The tragedy seemed to strike every age range. Some tearful children, apparently students at Mary Jo's school, clutched their parents' waists. Teenagers—those who knew Mary Jo, Tyler, or both—stepped somberly from the church. Raeann Wallace, the next-door neighbor who'd asked Tyler to watch her house several times while she vacationed, emerged from the church in tears, her eyes red as she clutched two gold crosses she wore around her neck, according to the *Palm Beach Post*. One news photographer snapped a picture of Ryan hugging his grandparents, and another of a sobbing grandmother carrying a red carnation as she was helped into a car. After the service, the Hadleys' family members and closest friends had another private service. And after that, the couple's bodies were to be cremated and their ashes buried.

Beaux, who'd gathered with other teaching colleagues, remembered the priest's words on forgiveness and repeated them to the group.

"He pointed out that now is the time for us to engage in forgiveness. When we have something terrible like this, it's time to remember that forgiveness is a virtue," Beaux recalled. "I repeated that, and I said that I was really glad that he said that."

Several in the group stiffened. Some were not quite ready to consider forgiveness. One woman, who'd been among Mary Jo's closest friends, said simply: "I'm not sure everyone is to that point right now." She motioned to her husband, who had been very close with Blake. It was clear that he wasn't ready to provide Tyler with any absolution. Not yet, anyway.

"There seemed to be a general feeling of resistance," Beaux said. "The wounds were so fresh. That may be why I haven't heard from the others a whole lot since then. Everyone's in their own place about it."

But Beaux set about immediately to forgive. It's how he handles crises. To others, he knows it can make him sound callous, as though he's okay with the heartache caused, like he's taking a "c'est la vie" approach to a friend's horrific death. But he figures he has a choice: He can either wallow in the inexplicable, playing the horrific scenes over and over in his mind until he's paralyzed with grief, or he can choose not to focus on the things over which he has no control.

"I kind of realize that I'm an observer here. I'm watching what's going on, and I don't have to react to everything in my experience. I can observe it and learn from it," he said.

For him, forgiveness was the only path.

"Really, the easiest thing to do is allow forgiveness to happen," he said. "That's a lesson that Tyler has to learn because he needs to forgive himself, but it's the most important one. We're the only ones who feel the pain of non-forgiveness."

CHAPTER 19

Mike,
I prayed every day that you would write me. I just
got your postcard and my prayers are answered.
Thank you for writing me. I thought everyone for-
got about me. I don't give a fuck about anyone else
writing me just as long as you write me. Actually, I
wouldn't mind getting a card from Jesse. Tell him I
said what's up. I have dreams almost every other
day that I'm on the outside . . .

At first, Tyler seemed certain no one would talk to
him again after they learned what he had done. Offered
the chance to make phone calls twice by jail guards, he
declined, saying he had no one to call. Before long,

however, he slowly started getting word from the more forgiving of his family members. And so, from his jail cell on Rock Road, Tyler began writing letters. He wrote to his friends, to his mother's parents, to the family members who cared to hear from him. He could only receive letters that were written on standard-sized postcards— one of the rules of the jailhouse, so there was no chance anyone could sneak anything to him in an envelope or package, and prison guards had easy access to read whatever was being written to the prisoners.

He wrote to Michael Mandell often, reminiscing about getting fucked up and hanging out. He wrote about his defense lawyers and their strategy. Dozens of letters were photocopied and saved by prosecutors as part of Tyler's case file. In one rambling note, he wrote Michael that if he went to trial, he'd be fucked, save for "something in the defense that could keep me out of prison." He was hoping for the best, he said. It was lonely in jail. He missed Michael and his friends. He missed sneaking out late and joyriding and doing dumb stuff and "getting fucked up." He wanted nothing more than to throw back some beers and smoke a strawberry white owl. Despite that, he admitted that it felt kind of good to be sober. His head was nice and clear for a change. He was working with two private investigators, two researchers and two main attorneys, and in December, he would get a forensic toxicologist to evaluate him. If all went well, he'd be able to cut a deal, he suggested—maybe he'd even see the outside of prison in 20 or 30 years.

"I swear to you, Michael, the devil had a hold on me," he wrote. "I talked to him and he talked to me. That's why I seemed so crazy toward the end."

He implored Michael to hop on his Facebook profile and tell his friends that he missed them and was sorry for the grief he caused. He asked that Michael drink himself stupid "like I used to do."

He prattled on for pages, saying how grateful he was that most of his family was forgiving and helping him get through the tough times. He said he thanked God every day for them. His DiVittorio grandparents and brother regularly put money in his account so he could buy food and items from the jailhouse canteen. He worried that he'd "be talking like I'm black soon . . . It's contagious." He encouraged Michael to study hard and make something of himself. Tyler said if he got out, he'd want to become a priest. "I can't wait," he wrote. He'd been reading "like a bitch"—Harry Potter ("their [sic] good as fuck") and James Patterson were favorites. He complained about having to be locked up so long—"It sucks knowing that on my birthday the only thing I get is an orange uniform"—but he didn't talk about his parents, about whether he missed them or what they likely would have done for that upcoming eighteenth birthday.

And he thanked Michael again for writing. In huge capital letters that took up the bottom quarter of the lined page, he wrote: "I LOVE YOU."

His grandma DiVittorio wrote to Tyler the most often, sometimes sending two and three postcards in a day, their two-inch-by-three-inch boundaries simply insufficient to hold the many things she wanted to say to him.

In one postcard, she wrote that she and Tyler's grandfather had just come back from their jail visit. Please, she begged him, don't read the newspaper or pay attention to the news. She implored that he trust in his defense team and stay strong. Don't even worry about getting a GED, she suggested. Like most of her notes, she closed it with, "We love you. God bless you.—Grandma and Grandpap."

Another card shared with him a version of the Apostles'

Creed, the basic expression of Christian faith recited in thousands of churches in every country worldwide. One version is this:

I believe in God, the Father almighty,
*   creator of heaven and earth.*
I believe in Jesus Christ, his only Son, our Lord,
*   who was conceived by the Holy Spirit*
*   and born of the virgin Mary.*
*   He suffered under Pontius Pilate,*
*   was crucified, died, and was buried;*
*   he descended to hell.*
*   The third day he rose again from the dead.*
*   He ascended to heaven*
*   and is seated at the right hand of God the Father*
almighty.
*   From there he will come to judge the living and*
the dead.
I believe in the Holy Spirit,
*   the holy catholic church,*
*   the communion of saints,*
*   the forgiveness of sins,*
*   the resurrection of the body,*
*   and the life everlasting. Amen.*

This time, Grandma DiVittorio signed off with an addendum to her usual "God bless you." "Remember: What would Jesus do?" she wrote.

Tyler received other types of mail, too. Mike Hadley, Blake's brother, typed a note to Tyler on a homemade postcard. One side bore the pertinent addresses. From the other beamed a smiling photograph of Mary Jo. "It is October 4, 2011, do you know what today would have been?" the card asked, then answered its own question in

The Hadley family lived near the picturesque waterfront along Florida's Treasure Coast. *(Courtesy: Amber Hunt)*

Blake Hadley worked for Florida Power & Light Co. at the St. Lucie Nuclear Power Plant, a short drive from the quaint home he shared with Mary Jo, his wife, and Tyler and Ryan, the couple's two sons. *(Courtesy: Amber Hunt)*

The family's simple, white house on Northeast Grandeur was built in 1988 and had about 1,500 square feet of living space and a pool in the backyard, according to the St. Lucie County Office of the Property Appraiser. *(Courtesy: Amber Hunt)*

Tyler Hadley, in the black T-shirt, is pictured at a Christmas event with his best friend, Michael Mandell (in white), and two people depicting Joseph and Mary. *(Courtesy: Michael Mandell)*

Michael shot this cell phone photo of Tyler while the two hung out a few months before Tyler's arrest. *(Courtesy: Michael Mandell)*

Police descended on the Hadley home after receiving 911 calls from Tyler's friends claiming that he said he'd killed his parents. In this photo taken Sunday, July 17, 2011, Port St. Lucie Police Department crime scene technician Joel Smith works late into the night inside the home. *(Courtesy: AP Photo/*The Stuart News, *Deborah Silver)*

A photo of Blake and Mary Jo Hadley in happier times was among the items police discovered tossed haphazardly throughout the home. Later photos of Mary Jo show her thinner thanks to weight-loss surgery. *(Courtesy: Port St. Lucie Police Department)*

To reach Mary Jo and Blake's bodies, investigators first had to dig through piles of blood-soaked household items and debris that police say Tyler tossed on top of his parents before locking them in their bedroom. *(Courtesy: Port St. Lucie Police Department)*

Blood spatters are visible on an entertainment center in Mary Jo and Blake's bedroom, as well as a mop investigators believe Tyler used to clean up elsewhere in the home. *(Courtesy: Port St. Lucie Police Department)*

Beer bottles and Solo cups litter the home after Tyler hosts approximately 60 friends for a party while his parents' lifeless bodies remain locked in their bedroom. *(Courtesy: Port St. Lucie Police Department)*

Evidence cards mark possible blood evidence inside the Hadleys' garage. *(Courtesy: Port St. Lucie Police Department)*

Tyler's friends told police that the teen spent much of the night here, in his bedroom, with a select group of teenagers, drinking beer and smoking. *(Courtesy: Port St. Lucie Police Department)*

Police talk to the media outside the Hadleys' home on Monday, July 18, 2011. *(Courtesy: AP Photo/*The Stuart News, *Deborah Silver)*

Port St. Lucie Police crime scene investigator Jeanine Hickox talks with a police officer at the Hadley home as investigators continue gathering evidence inside. *(Courtesy: AP Photo/*The Stuart News, *Deborah Silver)*

Nearly a year after the deaths, the Hadley home remained abandoned, with signs posted warning against vandalism. *(Courtesy: Amber Hunt)*

Police released these photos of Blake and Mary Jo to media in the days after the couple's slaying. The images are from their Florida driver's licenses. *(Courtesy: Port St. Lucie Police Department)*

Tyler Hadley was arrested and booked in the St. Lucie County Jail on charges of first-degree murder. *(Courtesy: Port St. Lucie Police Department)*

Michael Mandell, left, poses with Tyler, holding a Solo cup, in Tyler's garage. Michael told police he snapped the photo after Tyler confessed the slayings to him. *(Courtesy: Port St. Lucie Police Department)*

Tyler spent time in solitary confinement in the St. Lucie County Jail. He was moved to the jail's general population on his 18th birthday, where he awaited his impending trial. *(Courtesy: Amber Hunt)*

a run-on sentence: "Your Mom's 48th birthday, it is a very sad day for us we will never be able to wish her a happy birthday again only through our thoughts and prayers."

Across the bottom, written in all caps, was the message: IF YOU'RE GOING THROUGH HELL . . . KEEP GOING.

CHAPTER 20

Detective Meyer started monitoring Tyler's correspondence barely a week after his arrest. She wanted to know everyone he called and wrote, and she collected copies of all of his correspondence that didn't relate to his communications with his attorney. The prosecution's hope to level first-degree murder charges hinged in part on proving that Tyler had planned his crime, that it wasn't a so-called crime of passion that usually resulted in a second-degree murder charge—and the difference was huge: If Tyler was convicted of first-degree, he'd automatically be sentenced to life behind bars without any chance of parole. He'd forever be locked up. The judge would have no wiggle room on the mandatory sentence. But if Tyler got second-degree, he could be out in a few decades. With Tyler being so young to begin with, that could mean he'd be able to pick up his life on the outside at about the same age he'd ended his parents' lives.

It was during such a checkup with the jail that a deputy told Meyer about George Brown, an inmate who'd been housed next to Tyler in the medical ward immediately after the arrest. Brown was housed in Medical Pod H for nearly three weeks. For about nine overlapping days— beginning the Monday after the slayings—Tyler was next door in Pod G. Brown hadn't been comfortable with some of the things Tyler had said to him, so he came forward and asked to speak to a detective.

Such a development wasn't unexpected. Tyler was by far Rock Road's most infamous inmate, and with that notoriety came the likelihood that other inmates might want to cash in, swapping (possibly bogus) information for time shaved off sentences. But Brown didn't seem interested in that. The twenty-two-year-old, with an anarchy sign tattooed on his right shoulder, had a lengthy rap sheet dotted with charges of burglary, selling stolen property, grand theft, and commercial fraud. For his most recent offenses, he faced a decade or more behind bars. Still, he turned down Meyer's offer to fetch his lawyer and didn't ask for a sentence reduction. Rather, he said Tyler had made some comments that bothered him, and he had to tell someone. The two were in adjacent cells on suicide watch, he said. Tyler introduced himself, but Brown, who hadn't seen TV or read any newspapers of late, didn't know who he was. The two first started talking by yelling over the wall, but then discovered they could talk quietly through the metal plates on the lower portion of the wall that separated their cells.

At first, Tyler wouldn't tell Brown what he had done to land in jail. Eventually, he said he beat "them" with a hammer.

"Holy shit," Brown responded. Tyler just laughed.

Tyler slowly told him more, revealing that the "them" he'd beaten was his parents. "They deserved it," he supposedly told Brown. One tried to get away, he added, but Tyler gave chase and won.

Brown asked more questions. Tyler laughed in response. After a few days, Brown finally was allowed some of his belongings and he saw news coverage of the murders. He told Tyler through the wall what the stories said about him, what it described him doing, and Tyler replied, "Nice, ain't it?"

"George told me that Tyler isn't worried at all about being in jail and that he believes he is only going to go into a State Hospital instead of prison," Meyer reported. "He said he doesn't seem scared at all."

Tyler's laughter was the worst, Brown told Meyer. It bothered Brown immensely that Tyler could seem so happy after what he had done. Brown missed his own parents while in jail; how could Tyler take his for granted? Didn't he miss them? He asked Tyler once if he regretted anything. No, Tyler said.

Some of the details Brown passed on to Meyer matched other tidbits that had trickled in from friends—mostly Michael Mandell, who seemed to remember more from the party every time Meyer talked to him. Tyler had needed to pop three "beans"—or ecstasy pills—before killing his folks, Mandell said. Brown, too, said that Tyler told him he'd had to get high before swinging the hammer, though he didn't tell Brown what he'd taken. He allegedly told Brown that after the killings, he smoked some weed and made party plans.

"I asked [Brown] if Tyler was worried that his friends would find the bodies or see them during the party," Meyer wrote. "He said Tyler was planning on showing his friends what he had done."

By this point, Brown had heard about Tyler's friends,

too. Tyler talked about Michael Mandell a lot, saying that Michael was his best friend and would never rat him out. He knew someone called police, but surely it wasn't Michael.

That delusion wouldn't last for long.

CHAPTER 21

Police normally like to keep quiet sensitive information key to an investigation—for example, details about how many times Mary Jo and Blake had been wounded in the attack and what Tyler did immediately after the deaths. For Meyer, it was crucial information, and early on she was under the impression that only Michael Mandell had actually seen Blake's and Mary Jo's bodies, making him the star witness for the prosecution. Soon, however, Meyer realized that Michael hadn't been able to keep quiet at the party—or afterward, for that matter. Still visibly shaken, he appeared on one TV newscast describing what he had seen. Standing on his front porch wearing a T-shirt bearing the Busch beer logo, Michael fielded questions from an off-camera reporter.

Michael: "He told me if I looked at it enough, I could

see signs. I looked at the floor, I could see signs of blood. That's when I went around back and looked in his parents' bedroom."

Reporter: "After you saw this scene, what did you do?"

"I was in shock. I was sitting down, I didn't know what to do."

"Was he worried about what to do with the bodies or anything like that?"

"No."

"Did he act like he was concerned about getting in trouble?"

"He was going to commit suicide once he got caught, but that failed."

"Was he on any sort of drugs or anything?"

"He was on ecstasy," Michael said. "I think he just threw a party because he knew he was going away and he wanted to see his friends one last time. I feel like, this kid that I've known all my life, I don't know him."

The minute-long footage of him went viral online and was shared with other newscasts, and suddenly Michael became a small celebrity—the friend of a killer. Police initially tried to shield the identity of their tipster, calling him "MM" in public documents, but the effort was pointless. Within days, everyone following the case knew who MM was and what he had seen.

Meyer seemed perturbed at the free fall of information. When she interviewed partygoers, she didn't know if they were describing things they actually saw and heard or things they'd gleaned from the news. She tried to pin Michael down precisely to learn whom he'd talked to and what he'd said.

"The reason I'm asking, it's not because I think you were lying to me or anything like that," she told him. "And I get that this screwed with you bad, all right, and I totally get that. But what I need to know is, I need to know exactly everybody that I need to talk to . . . You were just overwhelmed, you were totally overcome by all of this, you don't know what the hell to do and you felt the need to just—you had to get some support."

"Yeah," Michael agreed.

"Okay, and that's cool . . . That doesn't mean you did anything wrong or anything bad or anything like that, okay. But I just need to know."

Michael began to map out those he'd spoken with: Jesse Duryea, Dustin Turner, and Ryan Stonesifer. But Justin came with his friend Desiree, and he apparently told her, Michael acknowledged. Ryan was the last person he told, he insisted, and Ryan didn't seem to believe him.

"He kept saying, 'If you're gonna kill me, Mike, just do it.' I don't know, maybe he was all freaked out about everything," Michael recalled.

Dustin was the only one who looked into the room, Michael said. This was after Jesse left. Michael said when Jesse left, he felt alone, weighed down by the knowledge, so he showed Dustin. That's when Dustin bailed, too.

"As soon as he saw it, he said, 'I was never here, I'm getting out of here.' . . . And he just left," Michael said.

After that, Michael stayed at the party, "just talking and bullshitting," for a few hours yet.

"You didn't tell anybody else?" Meyer pressed.

"That's literally it. I didn't tell anybody else."

Until Ryan Stonesifer, just as the two were leaving.

Meyer drove home her need to know everyone and everything Michael had told.

"The last thing that I want to do is be surprised by something you know that somebody else tells me, okay?" she said. "If you're being completely straight with me and you're being completely honest with me and these are the people that you told, okay. If there's anybody else, then I need to know and I need to know now . . . I don't want any surprises. I need to know what you did."

Michael nodded and then backtracked on a couple of details. He hadn't walked home from the party, like he'd first said he had. He'd been trying to avoid giving police Ryan Stonesifer's name—not knowing that Ryan himself had already planned to go to the police station with his parents in tow. Rather, Michael got a ride with Ryan's brother and friend. And while at Ryan's brother's house, Ryan told them what had happened.

"He just said that, you know, that party you were at, there was dead bodies there . . . I don't think they believed him at first, but then he kept freaking out about it," said Michael, before apologizing for not coming clean sooner. "A lot of people are just simply scared of the police."

"Why? I'm a nice person," Meyer quipped.

With as many people playing round-robin with the gory details of the case, it was getting easier to understand how so many people Meyer encountered knew more than they should have—and to grasp why Ryan Hadley had received so many callous text messages with details he should have learned only from police.

CHAPTER 22

The round-robin routine hit the headlines as well. As he sat in jail, Tyler's mood seemed to fluctuate with every news story about his case, prompting him to write agitated letters to his friends. In one, to Michael Mandell, he said that most of the stories were filled with lies. He wished his friends wouldn't talk to police and reporters, he said. Sometimes he even wished they'd just backed off the night of the party and let him down the pills as he'd planned. All his friends were snitches. He felt like everyone turned their backs on him. "I wish everything could go back to normal," he wrote.

CHAPTER 23

Detective Meyer had to track down as many of the partygoers as she could—especially those who'd heard
anything about the deaths while at the house. Desiree
Gerhard was toward the top of her list. Desiree, called
D-Ray by her friends, was a thin, pretty blond with a
Twitter account that on the one hand showed her holding
an adorable white-and-black cat, while on the other featured a profile picture of her making duck lips with two
girlfriends, one of whom was flicking off the camera. That
sort of contradiction appeared elsewhere in Desiree's
life—summed up pretty succinctly with one ironic tweet:
"I hate school bt i love english clasz" (sic). Desiree had
known Tyler for about two years, having met him through
Jesse, their mutual friend.

Desiree recalled for Meyer as much as she could about

the party. She remembered arriving sometime between 10 and 11 p.m. after a friend named Mike dropped her, her sister, and Jesse off. The same friend came back for the trio at 1 or 2 a.m. Unlike the first people to arrive, Desiree didn't have to wait outside; about ten or fifteen people were milling around inside Tyler's home already. She'd sat at the computer—the same one Mary Jo had sat at less than eight hours earlier—and tried to pull some music up on YouTube, but she never got it to work right. Tyler was flitting around most of the night. She saw him for about ten minutes before he left for nearly half an hour, apparently to get more booze. After he got back, a wave of new people hit the house, ready to party. That was likely around midnight.

By then, Michael Mandell had grabbed Jesse and told him what Tyler had said. Jesse had started looking around, suddenly noticing the droplets on the walls and wondering if they were, in fact, blood. Jesse pulled Desiree to the front yard and said that Tyler had killed his parents and they needed to call her friend Mike for that ride home. Desiree did, though she didn't really believe Jesse. Tyler was acting completely normal. When she walked back into the house, she aimed to find Tyler and ask him straight up. She looked in Tyler's bedroom, but he wasn't there. She walked from that corner of the house into the living room and spotted him. She got close to him and nearly blurted out the question, but there were so many people around, she lost her nerve.

She'd been among the handful of friends to get invited into Tyler's bedroom, where he and his closest friends sat around, smoked pot, and drank. They stayed there even with the rumor floating that Tyler's parents were dead somewhere inside the house. It was too unfathomable to think it was anything more than a prank. Desiree said there was marijuana on Tyler's dresser that everyone was smoking, but she never saw any cocaine or pills. She'd been drinking from the half bottle of gin she'd brought to the party, but almost everyone else was drinking beer. When asked where his parents were, Tyler repeated the line that they'd gone to Orlando for the weekend, which seemed plausible. She'd never known Tyler to have a party before, and she knew his parents wouldn't have been okay with one if they were in town. It was a far more likely explanation than him having killed them. In the time Desiree had known Tyler, she did hear him say violent things about killing something or other, but it was usually while playing video games. She did know that he likely had a drug problem, though. One night, she ran into him at O'Malley's Sports Bar & Grill on Southeast Morningside Boulevard. Tyler seemed fine and ended up joining Desiree and her friends. They ended up in a car together, and suddenly Tyler started vomiting everywhere. Desiree took him back to her house and took his shirt off because he had puked down the front of it. He was out of it, completely unaware of his surroundings. He didn't seem to know she'd taken his shirt off. He fell asleep on her bed and urinated all over himself. When he finally woke up, he flipped out about being shirtless—some family members reported they'd never seen him without a shirt, not even while swimming—and kept asking where the shirt was. The next week, Desiree learned that Tyler had gotten in trouble with his parents and was going to counseling for drug use. She didn't know much about his parents, but Tyler's mom did call her once looking for him. Desiree said Mary Jo was very nice about it, simply asking if Tyler was with her, and when Desiree said he wasn't, she asked that Desiree please tell him to come home if she ran into him. It especially struck Desiree that his mother had apologized for bothering her, Meyer noted in a police report.

Back at the party, when Desiree's ride finally showed up, she ducked out with her sister and Jesse, with Jesse saying his mom was mad at him and he had to get home. After they left, they went back to Desiree's house, and Jesse couldn't stop talking about what Mandell had told him. He couldn't believe that Tyler would do such a thing, but it ate at him too much for him to fall asleep. Desiree, meanwhile, was beat. She nodded off. When she awoke, she learned that Jesse had called 911 and reported what Michael had told him.

Friend David hadn't heard anything that pointed. He'd arrived at the party about 10 p.m., and then left for another party at 1 a.m. He swung back by Tyler's at 3 a.m., just as the last group of partiers headed out. As Tyler turned back to head into the house, David called after him and thanked him for the good time.

"The party was fun," Tyler agreed. "I might have another one tomorrow night."

David told him to hit him up, because he'd definitely come back for another party. Tyler agreed and asked David if he wanted to hang out now for a while. David declined.

"Well, I might be going away for a while," Tyler said. David asked if he was going on vacation, to which Tyler simply replied he was "just going away."

"Are you coming back?" David asked.

"I don't know because I am thinking about killing myself before I go away."

"Why are you going to kill yourself?"

"'Cause I don't want to go away," Tyler replied.

David didn't know what he meant. Tyler stayed vague. The conversation ended with him telling David again that he might have another party. The next morning, he got a phone call from a friend who said police were at Tyler's house. He was sure it meant that Tyler had killed himself, and the very first rumors that flew were just that. Friend Kaitlin, who'd known Tyler for about three years and was at the party briefly, stopped by the house to pay respects to Tyler's parents. She was heartbroken to hear he'd killed himself, and completely shocked when she learned at the scene that he hadn't. His house had smelled like party, not like death, she'd told an investigator later.

Most people who attended the party hadn't heard anything abnormal. Sure, there were drunken and drugged-up rumors about Tyler saying weird things, but this was a house filled with young adults messed up on all sorts of illegal substances. Bizarre behavior was to be expected. At one point, someone walked into the house with a mailbox. Tyler freaked out, his friend Stephanie said, because he thought bringing a mailbox into the house was a felony and that police were surely on their way. Soon after, Stephanie, who'd had a little crush on Tyler, left the party for a stint and came back a few hours later. Sure enough, as Tyler predicted, police were at his doorstep. Stephanie decided to go home for good. The next morning she got a text message from a friend named Amber about how "creepy" it was to think about what Tyler had done to his parents, that it "just sucks how his mom was trying to get him help, and now he took their lives."

The interviews with the dozens of young adults who attended the party were divvied up among detectives. Some were useless and incoherent. One nineteen-year-old named Dennis scrawled on a witness statement form: "I kame to his house and talked 2 him 4 a littlebet and I left Tyler" (sic). But many of the kids seemed to have distinct but overlapping versions of what they'd seen that night. A seventeen-year-old named Josh showed up just after 1 a.m. Josh had met Tyler when the two were both freshmen at Centennial High School, and though the two weren't tight, he knew Tyler as a jokester. A mutual friend texted him about Tyler's party, so he left a previous party and showed up late. When he arrived, one of Tyler's friends—likely Ryan Stonesifer, who was the self-appointed bouncer for the night—warned him, "This is my friend's house, don't mess anything up." Josh noticed that people were spread all over the house. He spotted Tyler with some beer, and heard someone yelling about stolen marijuana.

It was the first time Josh had been in Tyler's home, and he had noticed it was dirty. He assumed that was from the party, though, in hindsight, he remembered that when he was playing water pong (during a spell when the beer had run out) the ball rolled beneath the dining room table and into a nasty brownish liquid. He wiped the ball off on the tablecloth and kept playing. That was within feet of where Mary Jo had been slain.

Another partygoer, Courtney, told Meyer she'd known Tyler for about a year, having met through mutual friends on Facebook. They went to different schools and had maybe met in person just a few times. Still, they'd struck up a friendship by sending private messages back and forth, in which Tyler would listen to Courtney's problems—her parents getting divorced, the death of a friend of hers, how stressed she was at her job. Tyler told her he was there for her. In turn, Tyler complained about his falling grades and his parents getting on his case. They wanted to stop him from going out so much, he'd said. Courtney said they were just trying to do their job as parents, and then she'd try to change the subject so he'd focus on something else. To her, he was acting like a normal teenager.

The night of the party, she drove the half hour to his house and partook with the other minors. She showed up alone and sat on the living room couch. She heard some commotion from the dining room area, near the door to the master bedroom. Someone had apparently tried to open the door. Tyler was yelling not to go in there. Courtney figured Tyler was trying to keep partiers out of his own room and thought nothing of it. All in all, it was a regular party. Until it was on the news the next day.

CHAPTER 24

In an October 2011 letter to his friend Desiree—nicknamed "D-Ray"—Tyler insisted he wasn't the psychopath that some people seemed to think he was. He certainly hoped Desiree didn't think of him that way. "I just made a life-threatening mistake," he wrote. Why weren't his friends writing him much? He'd heard from his family, but he rarely got notes from friends, he said. He felt neglected, forgotten. And he was bored, stuck in protective custody, though he wasn't sure why.

He killed time mostly by playing cards, reading and watching TV. He worried about going to trial. At this point, a guilty verdict meant an automatic sentence of life imprisonment. "That's the thing that haunts me every day and makes me wake up in cold sweats most nights," he wrote. He'd fucked up, sure, but it'd suck to not get a chance to live his life just because of a mistake.

He suggested that Desiree go to church. Behind bars, he was seeing his priest from the outside every week, and it was helping him trust that God had a plan for him. If only it hadn't taken a stint in jail for him to find God, he said. If only.

CHAPTER 25

As Meyer tried to track down the rumors that originated with Michael Mandell, another friend showed up at the police department and proved that Mandell wasn't the only one with a propensity to share too much. Tyler himself had offered some unsolicited details, though he was cagey when it came to specifics. Mark Andrews had known both Ryan and Tyler Hadley for about nine years. He lived on Northeast Emerson and knew Tyler and Michael as being best buddies. They were a little weird, he recalled, playing with bottle rockets and pulling cruel pranks.

"They basically, like, took bottle rockets, they'd light them, they'd throw them out in the street. If a car went by, it'd scare the people that are driving—that kind of thing," Andrews said.

Back then, Michael was more of the troublemaker, and Tyler seemed more a follower. He still had a dark sense of humor, though. He was the guy who'd call a friend a faggot, then laugh it off. But he'd take it another step, Mark said: " 'I'm going to kill my parents,' laughing about it."

Carrasquillo seemed surprised. "Even then?"

"Yeah."

"When he was young?"

"Yeah, but everybody kinda does that. Their parents piss them off, so they're, like, 'Man, I'm gonna kill my parents, yeah, yeah, ha ha ha, never mind, I'm just joking.' "

"So he has said this in the past?"

"Yeah."

"When was the first time you believe he said something like that? . . . Why would he say that?"

Mark dug back in time.

"I think he was like ten, but his parents . . . had pissed him off somehow and he comes over to my house . . . He's, like, 'Dude, I'm gonna kill my parents.' I'm like, 'Dude, man, don't do that, man. Don't sweat it. It's not worth it. Everybody's parents piss them off. Everybody's parents do these sorts of things.' "

This seemed to reach Tyler.

"He's, like, 'Yeah, man, you're right,' starts laughing about it. We start joking around."

"That was when he was ten," Carrasquillo repeated.

"Yeah. I never thought he'd do that," Mark said. "His parents—like, sure, they were assholes sometimes, but they were nice people."

Though they'd been friends for years, Mark fell out with both Tyler and Michael because he'd started using drugs and, at the time, Tyler and Michael weren't using. The three grew apart, aided by Mark's move from the neighborhood, and by the time they hooked back up about a year before the fateful party, Mark had largely moved past his drug phase, while Tyler was waist-deep in his own.

"I've done a lot of things, but he started getting into it a little bit too heavy," Mark told Detective Carrasquillo.

No longer did Michael seem the leader in the friendship, either. Mandell had evened out, and Hadley had taken over as troublemaker.

"You ever gone to a high school and there's just that one kid that everyone thinks is going to bring a gun to school and just shoot people?" Mark asked.

"Uh-huh," the detective replied.

"Yeah, he kind of reminded me of that—but at the same time, he didn't. He didn't like to fight. He would talk out his mouth a lot, but he would never do it . . . I just didn't really think he'd be able to do something like this."

Mark ended up at the party because a friend saw Tyler's post on Facebook and wanted to go. Mark was reluctant, but the friend sweetened the deal by offering gas money if he drove. They first arrived during the on-the-lawn blackout, then came back around 11 p.m. when the party was bumping.

"There was, like, cars lined up [and] down the road. And I'm like, 'Dude, this doesn't look like the kind of party I need to be at right now.' He's like, 'Why?' I'm, like, 'Dude, I'm on probation. This doesn't look like the kind of party I need to be at' . . . But when we pulled up, I saw a couple of people I knew. So I was, like, okay, I'm gonna go inside real quick, say hi to them. So I park my car. I get out, he gets out, and I go inside. And I look around and I see a bunch of people."

Inside, a fight was under way. Someone hollered about someone stealing his weed. The kid was flipping out, arguing with some others, reinforcing Mark's gut feeling that this was not where he wanted to be. Mark made his

way around the party mostly to say hi and bye: "Nice seeing you, but look, I can't be here. I gotta go." At first, he
didn't see Tyler. But as Mark was about to leave, Tyler
spotted him and approached.

"Dude, can I talk to you?" Tyler asked, Mark told the
detective.

"Yeah."

First, Tyler asked for help getting people from the front
lawn into the house. People were spread out, hanging
everywhere, which would put a target on the place for police. Mark, no stranger to partying, knew the drill: The
kids would draw cops, the cops would make some arrests
and break things up, and a lot of people who were already
on probation would suddenly be in far deeper shit. But
once everyone was inside, Tyler still wasn't done with Mark.
The two walked toward Mark's van and then climbed inside. Tyler pulled out a wad of twenty-dollar bills; Mark
estimated he had a good three hundred dollars on him.
He counted out about sixty and asked Mark to go to the
store and buy him some beer. Mark declined.

"Dude, I need to talk to you," Tyler said again.

"What?" Mark asked.

"I did some things."

"What do you mean?"

"Dude, I might go to prison, I might go away for life.
I—I don't know, dude, I'm freaking out right now."

"What are you talking about?"

"I know you're not going to believe me. No one will
believe me. I freaking killed somebody."

"What are you talking about?"

"Dude, as in I—I—I killed somebody."

Mark's reaction was a lot like Dustin's: "You killing
somebody is your own business. Don't be telling me that
sort of thing."

Mark didn't exactly buy it. People say a lot of weird

things when they're drunk and stoned, and Tyler especially had a history of making up stories. Tyler, too calmly, said that people would learn soon what had happened.

"He said, 'you guys will find out in a week what happened,' because he was telling us he's either gonna kill himself or he was gonna go to prison or something. He's like, 'You guys will find out in a week. I don't have to tell you guys anything else; you'll find out in a week.'"

Mark remained dubious. "All right, dude," he said. "Well, look, just be easy, okay? And I'm just going to forget about this. I didn't hear anything about this."

The detective took notes as Mark relayed the conversation. Mark said he'd had no clue it'd be *that* type of party. Tyler had mostly been sedate when he knew him, low-key.

"When I heard he was throwing it, I thought it was going to be, like, okay, ten people come over, smoke cigarettes, watch a movie, chill and hang out," he said. ". . . Then when I get there and see all that, I'm like, 'What the hell?'"

Even as Tyler confided that he'd killed someone, he wasn't coming completely clean. Mark asked where his parents were, and he said they'd taken a trip. But that didn't jibe with what Mark knew about the family. They rarely took trips, he said, and when they did, they always took the family's SUV—the same vehicle that was now still parked out front. Tyler insisted they were in Georgia, and when Mark asked about the car, he said he'd driven them to the airport. That seemed reasonable. A lot more reasonable than the idea that Tyler had actually killed anyone.

"I thought he was just talking out his ass like he usually does because that was the kind of person he was back in the day," Mark said.

Tyler got out of the van and headed back inside. Mark pulled away and began heading home. Before he got very far, his cell phone rang. It was his friend Dustin.

"I'm down the street, man. Come get me. We gotta go now," Dustin said.

"What's going on?" Mark asked.

"Dude, just come get me."

As police learned, it turned out that while Tyler was laying things out for Mark, Dustin had approached Michael, who seemed uneasy. Michael said he didn't want to go back inside Tyler's house.

"Why? What's going on? What are you on? Are you okay?" Dustin asked.

"No, I'm not anything. I'm completely sober right now, but I'm not going in the house."

Dustin pressed. "I've known you so long, dude, just tell me what's going on."

Michael still hesitated. "I'm afraid to tell you because I'm afraid Tyler is going to kill me."

Dustin insisted again; Michael finally relented. He took Dustin to the back of the house. According to Mark, who relayed the story to Detective Carrasquillo, Dustin started to sense something was seriously wrong. He started to sense he might see a dead body. Michael opened the door to the tornadic bedroom. Dustin took a step back.

"It looks like you guys just trashed the room."

"No, wait, look," Michael insisted. "Do you see that?"

He used his cell phone as a flashlight. Dustin looked again and saw blood splattered everywhere. He took another step back. Was this a practical joke? Had these people gone so far as to make fake blood and wreck the room? Michael insisted he look again, this time pointing out the leg. Dustin didn't want to know more. He immediately walked away and down the street, calling Mark to come pick him up. The two went to a store, bought some cigarettes, and then went to Mark's house. Dustin pulled Mark outside on the front stoop for a smoke and told him what he'd seen. The next day, they talked to Mark's parents. Beyond that, they kept quiet. They weren't sure if they should come forward. Both were on probation, so neither was even supposed to be at such a party. Mark had fought so hard to get his life straightened out. He was off drugs and only drank anymore. It had taken a year and a half for him to land a job, but now he worked for a doctor at Lawnwood. Dustin had just been released from the Brevard Correctional Institution in April on a child abuse conviction and was trying to find work to step up as a father to his young daughter. If they came forward, they risked violating their probation, which meant risking everything else. But as Carrasquillo told Mark, if they hadn't come forward voluntarily, it would have made police suspicious when their names inevitably cropped up in the investigation—especially knowing that one of them had spent time alone with Tyler talking in a van.

Mark was still guarded, however. He at first refused to give his name, and he clammed up when asked for others' names—even Dustin's. While Mark was talking with Carrasquillo, Detective Inigo was interviewing Dustin in a separate interrogation room. Like Mark, he refused to give his name.

The detectives decided to combine the interviews in the hope of getting some more information. It turned out Inigo had been hitting a wall with Dustin for completely different reasons. Carrasquillo walked Mark into the room and apologized for interrupting.

"These are boys, and there's a lot of stuff that he may not want to say because he's here and vice versa, so if we get them both together, then maybe they both can talk to us and it's easier."

"I agree," Inigo said. He continued: "We know that what happened was messed up, we've established that. We're not afraid of him in that sense. But the one fear that [Dustin] has is that he's going to be labeled a snitch. And I'm telling you that No. 1, you guys aren't snitches because everybody who looks at this story, the first thing that they think is, 'That's fucked up, this dude killed his parents.' And what we want to make sure of is that there was nobody else in the house, there was nobody else that helped him out, because our fear is that there might be somebody out there that might do somebody else—to your kid, to your family. That's all we want."

Snitching. So many criminal cases have gone unsolved or been hampered because of the absurd notion that protecting someone who's broken the law is more important than providing peace and resolution to victims. In hoods across America, graffiti artists have tagged bridges and buildings countless times: SNITCHES END UP IN DITCHES and STOP SNITCHIN'. And those neighborhoods know no racial or socioeconomic boundaries. The sentiment is as prevalent in Detroit and New York City as it is in Sioux Falls, South Dakota, and Port St. Lucie, Florida. It's maddening for police officers trying to tease out the truth from reluctant witnesses. In the Hadley case, the fear of snitching and self-incrimination—mostly on the part of people with "papers," or who were already on probation—meant that detectives had to work much harder to get information that should have been flowing in freely from outraged and heartsick friends. Instead, the best they were getting was sketchy details from reluctant witnesses who, like Mark and Dustin, didn't even want to give officers their names.

"We're gonna waste an hour and change just trying to find the identity of you, right?" Inigo tried to reason. "And when we talk to somebody else, we have to spend another hour and a half trying to find out who this person is, who may have nothing to do with anything, just say, 'I was at the party and I saw nothing.' That's an hour and a half, you know what I'm saying? If you tell us what direction to go, we can save time in trying to find out who it was and who was where so in case there was somebody else, we can find out who it was, man."

"I—I just got out of prison," Dustin said.

"And you have a kid," Carrasquillo acknowledged.

"You did nothing wrong. Did you assist in the murder?" Inigo asked.

"No," Dustin said.

"You did nothing wrong," Inigo repeated.

But Dustin said reassuring cops had burned him before.

"I heard that when I got arrested, 'Just tell me and you'll be okay,'" he said.

The detectives assured him again. This wasn't some burglary; this was murder. They needed information. They didn't care about drugs or violating probation by going to a party. Finally, the guys gave up their names. Dustin still wasn't comfortable, though. He said he worried for Michael Mandell.

"Mike would have been arrested if he had something to do with it," Carrasquillo dismissed.

"I'm not talking about Mike being arrested . . . I'm talking about the whole reason I didn't call [police immediately] . . . Mike said, 'Man, please don't tell nobody, I'm scared Tyler will kill me.' So that's why I didn't call."

"Okay," Carrasquillo nodded. "And Tyler is in jail and Tyler is not going to see the sun again."

"I know," Dustin said.

"So what are you worried about? You know what I mean? He's gone."

Because Carrasquillo had been with Mark, and Inigo with Dustin, she hadn't had a chance to question Dustin about what he saw in the bedroom. She seemed flabbergasted he didn't push Mandell for details.

"Weren't you like, 'What the fuck? What happened? Who did this, how did it happen?'"

Not at all, Dustin said.

"You didn't get frickin' details?"

"No, I didn't want to know," Dustin said. "I didn't want to know anything. The only reason I talked to him is because I've known him for a while and he's shaking, he's freaking out. He looked like he was on something, but then he didn't—he looked shocked. He looked really, really shocked. You know, so I'm like, 'Dude, what's wrong with you?' 'Man, I can't tell you, man, you know, I can't tell you.' I said, 'Bro, come on, I've known you for a long time, you can tell me anything.'"

After Dustin saw the room, saw the blood, saw the leg, Michael begged him: "Please don't say nothing."

"I wanted to," Dustin acknowledged, "and he knew that I did. He could tell that I did."

They considered telling police the day after the party, but in a misguided attempt to reach cops, they showed up at the crime scene. Reporters were swarming, and some approached to ask questions.

"Oh, God, no. You don't want to talk to the reporters," Carrasquillo said. "Wrong place. Should have went to the police department."

Seeing a dead body in real life wasn't anything like seeing one on TV, and Dustin admitted he was having trouble sleeping at night. While hanging out with friends, he didn't like being left alone in a room, so he'd sometimes follow people from room to room, quietly hoping to keep their company.

"I know I look like a pussy," he said.

Inigo shook his head. The whole machismo thing is bullshit, he said. Being upset at the loss of life didn't make someone less cool or manly.

"You're human beings," Inigo said.

Mark said he felt sorry for the other kids who were at the party, so many of them far younger than he was. "That kinda screws with somebody's head," he told the detective. "Hey, I just got drunk, high or whatever at somebody's house, and there was dead people in it."

As the days dragged on, it became clear that the case was screwing with a lot of people's heads.

CHAPTER 26

Michael Mandell still wasn't sleeping well. He was trying desperately to balance the loyalty he felt for his longtime friend with the grief that genuinely consumed him at losing the Hadleys. They had, after all, taken him in as Tyler's best friend, inviting him on family trips and taking him to dinner too many times for him to count. Tyler had been his best friend, and they were his best friend's parents, and he felt the sting of their loss. His entire world was upside down, and even though he did the things you're supposed to do—sending flowers to Tyler's grandparents, for example—he couldn't get his head on straight.

Maybe that's why he was briefly taken in by a coked-up friend's conspiracy theory.

Michael had called Detective Meyer rambling something about another friend having maybe helped Tyler pull off the crime. *Remember Danny, the boy I left at Tyler's house just a couple of hours before the slayings? Well, a mutual friend thought Danny knew too much about the crime—the type of stuff only the killer would know—and he'd seen Danny with a pocketknife. Maybe Danny was in on this thing, too. Tyler had said before he couldn't kill his mom, right? So maybe Danny took that job on for him.*

Dubious, Meyer agreed to meet with Michael to hear him out, which led her to Paul Robertson (name has been changed). Paul was eighteen years old and lived less than three miles from the Hadley home. He wasn't friends with Tyler, but he was friends with a lot of Tyler's friends, and he wasn't even at the infamous party. Rather, Paul had a gathering of his own that night because his mom was at work, and he always threw little parties when she was away.

Paul knew Danny well enough—they smoked together and occasionally hung out—but they weren't really tight. Because Danny lived just up the street, they were more friends of convenience than anything else. Danny had been by earlier Saturday, after bolting from Tyler's place and before both Paul and Tyler's parties, to hang out and smoke with Paul and another guy not-so-creatively called McLovin. (The name got popular with the 2007 coming-of-age comedy *Superbad,* in which a nerdy kid names himself McLovin when getting a fake ID so he can buy booze.) While those three hung out and smoked, Danny mentioned Tyler's party and said that Tyler had used his dad's phone number when he put it on Facebook. Paul shrugged this off.

Danny left, and returned very early Sunday, around 5 a.m., Paul said. Paul noticed he was wearing different clothes, and he and McLovin were acting strangely. Danny told him to put on the TV news.

"I didn't ask him why, I was just, like, yeah, and I just put it on," a panicky Paul told Meyer.

"Okay, but by this time it's all on the TV," Meyer tried to assure him.

"No, not yet—not yet," Paul insisted.

"Yeah, it is."

Meyer tried to cut through the bullshit. Paul was all over the place. Was he worried just because Danny had changed clothes? She told him to slow down.

"All right, this is my first time talking to a detective," he blathered. Finally, he got it all out: When Danny and McLovin came over at 5 a.m., they seemed skittish. McLovin appeared to be soaked in sweat. They told him to flip on the news, and as they were watching the breaking story and images of police over on Northeast Granduer, Paul felt like the duo knew too much before it was reported. They didn't seem upset about it, either, but rather, he said, more as though they might have been proud of Tyler for finally doing it. And after the guys left, Paul found a pocketknife in his bathroom with what looked like blood on the blade. It was a small, silver knife with an image of the Confederate flag and a cannon on the handle. In a panic, Paul grabbed the knife, walked up the street, and threw it into a canal near Preston.

"So instead of turning it over to law enforcement, knowing that . . . all this stuff is going on, you got rid of it?" Meyer asked.

"I was afraid. I'm not even gonna lie. I was scared out of my mind that Danny had actually did it [sic] and was at my house and I was trying to get my facts straight before I was going to report anything," Paul said.

Paul confronted Danny about the knife. It was his, Danny acknowledged, but he'd carried it with him because someone had tried to rob him recently. Paul pushed harder.

"Bro, you need to tell me now if you have anything to do with this," he pleaded. "If you do, you need to go and tell them what you know, because I know you know more than me, because you're the last person to see this man before he did this."

Danny seemed offended, Paul said. "He told me that he didn't have anything to do with it, and he was like, 'Do you really think I would honestly kill somebody and then come hang out with you?'"

That could have been the end of the story. After all, as an admirably patient Meyer pointed out, Paul's story actually gave Danny an alibi. His phone showed that Danny had left Tyler's house around 3:30 p.m. because that's when Danny called to hang out, and Danny stayed with him until 9:30 p.m., nearly the time that people started showing up at Tyler's house for the party. And Danny's ability to supposedly know "too much" could be excused because by the early morning hours, text messages were flying all across town with details—some true, some mistaken—about the crime. But Paul wasn't satisfied, and Danny decided to screw with him. He and some friends went back and forth with Paul, alternately assuring him Danny had nothing to do with it, and then subtly planting it back in his brain that he was involved all along. Mostly they were screwing with him because they knew they could, and because they thought it was ludicrous he'd even be suspicious in the first place. He fell victim and stayed up all night, playing Columbo and interviewing his friends. He couldn't sleep off his suspicions. Even Danny told him to take a shower and get some sleep because he was working himself into a frenzied state of paranoia.

"Is that all you smoked is weed?" Meyer seemed ready to pinpoint the cause of the paranoia. She'd been a cop a long time. These theories didn't sound like the type that came without the assistance of some illegal substance.

Paul stumbled in his reply. "That's it, that's it, I—"

"No, tell me the drugs," Meyer insisted. "I'm not here to jam you up over it. Tell me the drugs that you did Saturday night."

"I did some blow."

"Okay, so you had blow, weed and alcohol?"

"That's it."

After a pause, she told him to relax. Danny left Tyler's well before the Hadleys died. He wasn't at the house when they were killed. Although she didn't spell out the specifics for Paul, Meyer had uncovered a McDonald's receipt that placed Mary Jo and Blake in a McDonald's drive-through in Fort Pierce at 2:57 p.m. The couple had bought a large Coke and a medium chocolate shake.

Paul exhaled. "Thank God, holy shit."

"You gotta quit with the conspiracy theories, okay?" Meyer implored. "Do not screw with this. Don't go running your mouth, okay? You just let this go, all right, because I understand your concern and it's absolutely phenomenal that you were willing to go out on a limb like this and contact police. Dude, my hat is off to you, I commend you, it had to be very scary to make that phone call . . . I can tell you without divulging my entire investigation, and I am the lead detective in this, that at 4 o'clock when Danny arrived here, everything was still okay over there."

This finally seemed to appease Paul, who said he maybe needed to lay off the blow.

Even after Detective Meyer debunked the theory that Tyler's friend Danny had a hand in the slayings, she still had to search for the knife Paul said he'd tossed, just in case. Officers combed the creekbed where he said he'd tossed it but came up empty. And that wasn't the only false lead. Officers had to sift through countless tips from people claiming to have information that Tyler hadn't worked alone. It seemed every couple of weeks, someone had a new "maybe so-and-so was involved" hypothesis that Meyer dutifully investigated. On August 11, nearly a month after the slayings, she got her most pointed tip since Paul's. The caller asked to remain anonymous but wanted Meyer to know that the neighborhood was abuzz. A teenage girl had been talking to one of the Hadleys' neighbors and said there was no way Tyler could have managed the deed solo because his father was simply too large. Surely, he had to have had help. The neighbor was also suspicious about Michael Mandell's phone call to the Orlando tip line. Why would he drive all the way to Orlando unless perhaps he needed to distance himself further from the crime?

Meyer had answers to both of these riddles: Blake Hadley likely was killed in his own bedroom, negating the need for an accomplice to help move his body through the house. And Michael Mandell had first tried to call the Treasure Coast Crime Stoppers but got no answer. The next number he called was for Orlando, and he didn't leave Port St. Lucie to dial. His phone records backed up his claim, and multiple witnesses placed him in Port St. Lucie around the time he called the Orlando number.

Still, Meyer followed up with the teenage neighbor, and in the detective's subsequent report it was clear she wasn't thrilled about it: "Due to the 'teenage female' discussing what she had 'heard,' I attempted to and was able to identify her for follow-up." The girl, Shelby, lived right behind Tyler's home. She and her mother agreed to chat with Meyer, and both seemed surprised that the little bit of neighborly chitchat Shelby had engaged in had been reported back to police. Yes, she'd talked with neighbors, she acknowledged, but she never pretended to have inside information. She said she'd had trouble envisioning Tyler committing the murders, but law enforcement and the news both reported that he did, and she assumed they knew better than she. "She had nothing else to contribute to the investigation, had not heard anything from anyone, and did not attend his party," Meyer wrote in her report.

But Shelby's short-lived involvement was symptomatic of a bigger issue: People would not shut up about this case. The rumor mill was in overdrive.

CHAPTER 27

Meyer let a few days pass before following up with Ryan Hadley and the rest of the family. She wanted to know more about what was going on immediately before the attack, but the first time she had talked to Ryan—in the early-morning hours of Monday, July 18, just after his parents' bodies were removed from the home—he was in too much shock. The same was true for Salvatore "Sam" DiVittorio Jr., Ryan's uncle and Mary Jo's brother. Because Ryan didn't want to be interviewed alone, and because Meyer wanted their answers to stand independent of each other, she interviewed Sam first.

As the days had passed, Sam had flipped through his mental memory book of Tyler growing up and a few things started to push to the forefront. He remembered that Tyler had started saying negative things about himself—"I suck" stood out—when he was as young as three or four years old. Then, as Tyler hit his early teens, he started calling himself fat, dumb, and ugly. Tyler had the typical teenage acne, and he was particularly hard on himself because of it. The family would ask him why he said such hurtful things about himself, and Tyler would reply that he didn't know why. Sam said the whole family constantly reassured him, telling him that he was indeed popular or that he could be an athlete if he wanted to be, but Tyler wasn't swayed. In Tyler's mind, the negative stuff he told himself was the truth, and there was no convincing him otherwise.

Tyler's standoffishness was difficult for Blake especially. He and Tyler had gotten along well when Tyler was young—even Michael Mandell remembered that his buddy had seemed to get along best with his dad when they were kids—and Blake adopted an open-door policy for his family. If anyone had a problem, they would talk about it and work things out together. But Tyler wouldn't bite. He was quiet, Sam said, and never talked about things that were troubling him. Instead, he'd hold it in.

Sam told Meyer that he and other family members would try to get him to open up, and Tyler would say, "Everything is fine." They shrugged it off as typical teen stuff. In hindsight, they wished they hadn't.

Tyler wasn't particularly looking forward to the upcoming trip to Pennsylvania his parents were planning. It was a family reunion that had been planned long in advance. Because he couldn't be left home alone, he was being dragged along, and about two weeks before that fateful Saturday, Mary Jo and her mother had taken Tyler to go clothes shopping. Sam knew Tyler wasn't excited about the trip, but he thought maybe the new clothes would have brightened his mood, at least. (Police found some of those clothes, tags still attached, in a partially packed suitcase in Tyler's bedroom after his arrest.)

Sam struggled to pinpoint a trigger, but the best he could come up with was that Mary Jo and Blake were finally getting tough on him and punishing him for his wild behavior. They didn't like Tyler's friends, they took his phone to curb his socializing, they grounded him on occasion, and they wouldn't leave him behind when they went out of town. It was normal parent stuff in reality, but maybe to Tyler, who'd been allowed to pretty much do as he pleased for much of his life, it felt too much like a noose. Mary Jo and Blake had never yelled at the kids, had never hit them, and only recently had even scolded regularly. They'd even had to make sure Tyler couldn't find his car keys, and they hid Mary Jo's purse from him, Sam told Meyer. They were flabbergasted and frustrated, and their "tough love" approach was pretty wimpy by a lot of parents' standards. Mary Jo wanted to believe she could love away all of Tyler's troubles, but she had started to realize he needed more than love. He needed professional help.

And that tore at the woman who prided herself on having a tight bond with her students. She never felt like she had that connection with Tyler, Sam said.

"Mary Jo had come to [our] mom and told her she wanted to see about getting Tyler some psychiatric help because she believed he had the symptoms of a mental health issue," Sam told Meyer, according to a police report.

Sam was clearly still reeling. He was so confused; how could Tyler have been raised in a home with zero violence and then commit the most violent act anyone could imagine? Aside from the stuff the family had written off as teenage angst, Tyler had been so normal. He was close with his grandpa, Sam Sr., the junior said.

"They were buddies," he recalled. Until recently, Grandpa would pick Tyler up at the bus stop to hang out after school. Tyler sometimes borrowed money from his grandparents, too, but Grandpa would ask for a chore in return to make him earn the money—maybe mow the lawn, for example—and Tyler would do it, no problem. Tyler often went on errands with his grandfather just so the two could ride around together. Never was there any hint of what was to come.

"Not at all, ever," he said in disbelief.

Ryan Hadley was equally flummoxed. Meyer asked how often his folks yelled, but Ryan said the only time he'd ever heard his father yell was when his parents were trying to refinance the house some ten years prior—and even then, the yell was directed to someone at the bank on the phone, never at his family. And Mary Jo just didn't yell, period. She had what Ryan called a "teacher voice"—stern but not loud. Growing up, the kids didn't have many rules. If they went out, they were given an 11 p.m. curfew. They were supposed to tell their parents where they were going and whom they were going with. The rules were pretty loose, prompting some family members—Blake's parents and Kelly, Mary Jo's niece and good friend—to say they were too lax. The Hadleys weren't doormats, but they didn't like confrontation and particularly had a hard time if Tyler got angry. They felt awful after arguments and often cut punishments short because the tension was too heavy in the house.

Ryan remembered his own period of rebelliousness, but it was nothing like what Tyler was doing. The money stealing and out-all-night business was pushing the boundaries in ways Ryan never dared. It got so bad that Mary Jo bought both boys iPhones over the winter specifically so she could use the tracking device on Tyler's phone. The device infuriated Tyler (Ryan admitted it "kinda sucked," too, but understood his mom's reasoning), but it ultimately came in handy. One night, Tyler didn't come home, so Mary Jo used the tracker to locate him. He'd said he was going to the movies, but instead he'd gone to a friend's house and gotten drunk. Mary Jo told Ryan about the ordeal the next day. Some thirty kids were hanging outside the house they'd found their son in, she'd said, and one of the kids even thanked them for getting Tyler because he was so drunk.

That incident infuriated Tyler. He yelled that he needed his privacy. But it didn't change his habits. He'd still stay out late, claiming to have been one place when he was obviously somewhere else. Sometimes Blake would walk onto the front porch at nine or ten in the morning to find Tyler there, having never come inside from the night before. They took his car keys away and hid their own, but Tyler would then just steal Blake's bicycle in the middle of the night. Mary Jo started using Tyler's phone to track him during the school day, too, revealing that he often wasn't there. He was skipping school nearly every day, but when she confronted him about it, he would either lie and say he'd been there, or just say he hated school. Once she called him during the school day when the tracker showed he clearly wasn't there. He answered in a hush and claimed he couldn't talk because he was in class. He held fast to his lies.

Ryan, remembering his own comparatively tame days of sneaking out, tried to tell Tyler not to do anything stupid while he was wandering solo. He suggested Tyler reel it in a little, too, to give their mom a break. Tyler didn't listen. Even though they seemed to be getting closer as they grew older, Ryan never really reached his younger brother as he would have hoped, he acknowledged to Meyer. The two went to Applebee's a lot to grab food, rented movies, ate frozen pizza, and watched recorded

TV shows on the family's DVR. Ryan told Tyler he should focus on schoolwork more and consider college, but Tyler said maybe he should just go to boot camp because no one liked him anyway.

And the self-esteem issues went deeper than the comments. Over the winter, Ryan started noticing that his brother spent a lot of time in the bathroom. Once, he saw Tyler puke all over himself. Several times, Tyler would eat an entire pizza, and then go take a shower. Ryan could hear the puking noises coming from the bathroom, and then, when Tyler came out, he'd say he was hungry and ask to go to McDonald's. Mary Jo had found vomit in the backyard, too, Ryan said. This apparent bulimia seemed to last for a couple of months before the family stopped seeing outward signs.

The whole family knew that Tyler was using drugs and drinking, though no one was quite sure to what extent. Ryan never saw him drunk, he said, but he suspected his brother was either drunk or high because he'd sleep until well past noon. Plus, when Tyler borrowed Ryan's car, Ryan would find pieces of marijuana in it afterward. The smoking worried the parents more than it did Ryan. Mary Jo wanted to switch Tyler's psychiatrists in part to address the pot use. (On the Hadleys' dresser, scrawled on a yellow legal pad among a handful of "to-do" notes, police discovered the name and phone number of an area doctor. Next to the name was a note from Mary Jo: "Psychiatry," it read. A different psychiatrist's name was on the bottle of antidepressants police found at the scene.) Ryan drove his brother to his psychiatry appointments from time to time. Tyler didn't seem to mind counseling. He said it was no big deal. Still, he quit after a few months, and the tiny bit of progress that he had made vanished. The night before Blake and Mary Jo were to head to Orlando for a weekend anniversary trip in April 2011, Tyler didn't come home. When they finally found him, he was a drunken mess. They obviously couldn't trust him to stay home alone with his brother, so they forced him to go on the trip, leaving Ryan behind. Even at Ryan's most rebellious point, he'd never pulled a stunt like this one. Tyler protested that he didn't want to go. He said he'd rather kill himself. His parents didn't back down, and Mary Jo told a friend that Tyler threw up everywhere all the way to Orlando. But when he got back, Tyler was happy and smiling, saying he'd had a great time. His parents had bought him a Joe's Crab Shack T-shirt, and Tyler was wearing it.

Even with all of this going on, the fights never got out of control, according to Ryan. Tyler was quick with the quintessential teenage comeback—"whatever"—and he occasionally yelled and slammed doors, but he never got in their faces or seemed at all like he wanted to fight. Ryan never heard him say he hated their parents, never heard him threaten anyone, never even considered that Tyler might be the slightest bit violent. And the Hadleys, for all their attempts to get Tyler on the right track, never seemed at all concerned that he would turn on them. Their only fear was that he'd hurt himself.

For Mary Jo, the pros of sending Tyler on the trip to Georgia seemed to outweigh the cons. Maybe time with the guys in the family was what he needed—a chance to recharge and relax. He'd ditched one therapist already, and Mary Jo worried that if pushed too hard, he'd walk away from another—one that finally seemed to be getting through to him. Though at least one family friend told police that the new counselors suggested he not take the break, Mary Jo envisioned him with his brother and father and couldn't help but think that he'd enjoy their time together more than he would being cooped up at home.

Mike Hadley, Blake's brother, hosted the mini reunion

at his cabin with his wife, Cindy. Blake and Tyler arrived July 9 with plans to leave July 12, but they ended up staying an extra day. Blake was all for pulling Tyler out of counseling for the trip, Mike later told Detective Meyer. His brother thought it'd be good for Tyler to get away, be a kid, spend some time with his family. Tyler by now was enrolled in some online classes to try to bring him up to speed after dropping out of one school, then getting booted from the alternative education program at the local college. Blake would instruct him to tackle his homework while in Georgia, and Tyler obliged. From home, Mary Jo would call and check online to make sure Tyler was keeping up.

Five days after investigators turned the Hadley home into a cordoned-off crime scene, Detective Meyer called Sam DiVittorio, Mary Jo's brother, and told him the house was ready to be released. The logistics involved hadn't been pleasant. Police aren't tasked with, or equipped for, the grisly duty of cleaning up blood and tissue, so the department gave the family a list of biohazard cleaning companies that could handle the job. Most accepted homeowner's insurance, Meyer had told a stunned Ryan the day he learned of the deaths.

The family met Meyer outside the home on the afternoon of July 22, 2011. Sam had asked for the keys to Mary Jo's and Blake's vehicles, which Meyer handed over after he signed a form acknowledging receipt. Everything had to be carefully documented, keeping in line with the meticulous chain-of-custody protocols meant to ensure that nothing was lost, overlooked, or stolen. As the family walked inside, they were greeted with a home still in disarray. The naked walls, the piles of broken household items—all of it was still the cluttered mess it'd been when police arrived on the scene, and nothing like the warm and familiar home Ryan had left behind not two months prior.

Sam was confused. Did the police department take everything off the walls? he asked Meyer. Had they left this mess behind? No, the detective explained. Officers had simply processed the house, photographed the wreckage in detail, and collected items they believed would prove useful in trial as evidence. There were still elements of the crime itself that hadn't been publicized. Sam asked, not for the first time, how many times Mary Jo and Blake were hit.

"Multiple times," replied Meyer, declining to elaborate.

Sam asked where it happened. Meyer delicately told him that based on the evidence and statements investigators had collected, it appeared some of the attack was at the computer desk. The rest was in the master bedroom. Meyer, predicting that the bedroom would be tough for loved ones to face, had pulled the door closed after the search was completed. No one had to go in there who didn't want to face it.

Not two hours after meeting the Hadleys at the house, Meyer returned to Tyler to meet with him and his public defender so that she could take photographs of the injuries she'd noticed on the teen that she'd earlier documented in writing. Harllee met her in an interview room at the jail, and as the two waited for officers to bring Tyler down, he asked if the parents had a will. Meyer didn't know. He requested she pass along his condolences to the rest of the Hadley family, and said he'd heard that they'd hired a family attorney. Meyer responded again that she didn't know.

Tyler walked into the room, his hands cuffed, wearing a navy-blue smock issued by the jail. He and Harllee met in private first, out of Meyer's earshot, and afterward

Meyer tried to locate the marks she'd seen before. The goal was to photograph them with a scale held next to them, allowing investigators—and, just as important, jurors—to grasp their size and scope. Meyer found and photographed the scratch she'd seen before on Tyler's left leg, as well as some scratches under his left arm, but the rest of the marks had already faded. The wounds he endured in the attack barely lasted a week; the ones he inflicted ended two lives.

CHAPTER 28

In June, not a month before the deaths, Blake and Tyler made the trip to Georgia to stay with Mike and Cindy. It was the trip over which Mary Jo had agonized, not knowing if it was going to help or hurt Tyler to go. Mary Jo told Ryan she'd taken Tyler to the New Horizons treatment center and that they'd gotten him some counseling, too. Even she and Blake were planning on going to counseling as a couple in the hope of figuring out how to best help their troubled son.

Ray Ankrom had also joined that get-together. Ray was married to Linda, Blake's sister. After the crime scene had been processed, he approached Meyer. Tyler had said some things not only in Georgia, but in the past in general, that in hindsight seemed worth exploring. Tyler was what Ray called a "blurter," blurting sometimes-inappropriate, random comments in front of family and friends. It had the effect of being particularly jolting because the boy was otherwise on the quiet side; suddenly he'd then open his mouth and say something completely off the wall. Ray remembered asking Tyler, then age seven or eight, what he wanted to be when he grew up. Tyler blurted out that he wanted to be a cop so he could arrest people like Tyler that said "stupid" things. Ray was shocked.

Ray had moved to Georgia, just about ten minutes from Mike's cabin, more than three years prior and would still go visit his family members down in Florida, usually making the trip about three or four times each year. Blake was a quiet man, Ray said, but he and Linda had learned through Mary Jo the troubles they'd been having with Tyler. At first, Ray told her not to worry, that Tyler was just being a teenager. Mary Jo said no, it was more than that. During one of Ray's trips to Florida, Tyler plopped down next to him and said he'd heard that Ray had once gone to jail. Ray hadn't, actually; he'd simply taken a tour of a jail once. He'd never want to go to jail, Ray added. Tyler just looked at him and said nothing more about it, Ray told Meyer.

Now, Ray told Meyer, he knew that Mary Jo was right all along. Her son was no typical teenager. The signs were so heartbreakingly clear—maybe not that Tyler was homicidal, but the boy had at times tossed out red flags that someone should have heeded. First, there were the odd trips to the bathroom. The teen would eat a meal, then head to the restroom and stay there for an abnormally long time. It was so frequent that Ray finally asked Blake what was up. Blake replied that he and Mary Jo thought Tyler had been purging, that he was bulimic, because he thought he was fat. Ray was shocked. Even though he'd heard Tyler call himself fat since childhood, *bulimia*? It was so extreme. Ray had never viewed Tyler as being overweight. Mary Jo and Blake had weight issues, but Tyler was just a normal kid, he recalled. He remembered the couple putting Tyler on human growth hormone, and he knew of no medical reason for it. Tyler was simply shorter than he wanted to be, and his parents forked out the money to help him get taller.

The visit to Georgia was pleasant overall, and Tyler and Blake even stayed a day longer than they'd planned. Blake wanted to take his son on a hike. Tyler had rebuffed a hike the day before, but Blake had spotted a bridge that he was sure his son would like to see, so the next day he convinced Tyler to meander out into the woods with him, his aunt, and his uncle. Ray gave Tyler a walking stick to use on the trek, but before they even hit the trail Tyler had started hitting everything with the stick. Ray told him to stop it, but Tyler said he had arachnophobia and was whacking at spiders. He wouldn't stop. Ray had to tell the seventeen-year-old that the stick was for walking, not for hitting, and then he was forced to take the stick away. It was behavior expected in a toddler, perhaps, but not a near man. Tyler just laughed, Ray told Meyer.

When they reached the bridge that Blake had wanted to share with his son, Tyler said it was awesome. And afterward, as father and son got ready to drive back to Florida, the teen smiled and effused about what a great time he'd had. But looking back, Ray didn't know how genuine any of it was—and he remembered another odd "blurt" that Tyler made while they were all hiking.

As they were walking, Tyler blurted "Menendez brothers" seemingly out of nowhere.

Ray acknowledged knowing who the infamous parent-slaying brothers were. Tyler responded that they were heroes. They're not heroes in my book, Ray replied.

Nothing more was said about it.

Then there were the drawings. One night, as the group of family members sat at the dining table, Tyler asked for some paper. Cindy handed him some plain white sheets, and Tyler began to draw. He told Mike it was therapy, meant to relieve his stress. He sketched away, and when he finished, the image was haunting: He'd drawn a two-story house, similar to the cabin in which they were staying, and it was engulfed in flames. Mike was taken aback. That's pretty dark, he told Tyler. What are you trying to imply?

"Oh, nothing," Tyler answered.

On the backside of the paper, Tyler drew a volcano, a knife, and a nuclear plant—like the one where Blake worked. Mike had never seen Tyler draw at all before. These drawings gave him the creeps.

The weirdness continued throughout the visit: Every night at 2 a.m., Tyler would wake up and wander. He and his father were sleeping in the loft of the cabin, and Mike could hear him moving around. The first night, Tyler came downstairs and walked outside. Mike said he and Cindy were in their bedroom. He looked up and saw Tyler standing ominously outside their window, his hands pressed against it as he peered into the bedroom. Mike was unnerved and told Blake about it the next day. Blake said Tyler sometimes roamed at night. They decided not to confront him about the Peeping Tom business.

One morning, Mike walked onto the porch of his cabin and had to double-take at the sight. Spit and slobber covered the porch, all over the handrail and down the steps. Again, Mike turned to Blake. I don't understand why kids these days are always spitting, Blake replied. Mike asked his brother to reel in his son: Tell him to respect my property, he implored. Later, it was suggested that the goop all over the porch wasn't spit and slobber after all, but remnants of Tyler purging his meals.

The family debated a movie to rent to watch together. Tyler offered a suggestion: *The Texas Chainsaw Massacre.* No, no, Cindy said. She didn't like those types of movies. But it's hardly violent at all, Tyler protested. Cindy reiterated: Not in my house. Tyler suggested another one: *Full Metal Jacket.* This had played into a conversation Mike and Blake had about the potential of Tyler joining the military. Blake had warned Tyler that the military would be mighty tough on him. Tyler said he'd just kill them. Would you kill the sergeant? someone asked. Sure thing, Tyler replied, just like they do in *Full Metal Jacket.* Mike and Cindy assumed he was joking. That kid was always joking around. Like the time he told a cousin he had a black woman in his head who talked to him. It was just a crazy, off-the-cuff remark for the sake of shock value. Wasn't it?

And then there was a moment of prophecy: As the family gathered around a creek, Tyler began heaving large rocks into it, watching them bust open. You're being a little rough, Mike told him. Blake chortled: Yeah, Tyler is getting ready for his new career when he'll be surrounded by barbed-wire fence. Everyone laughed, having no idea how close to the truth Blake's comment had come.

But there were genuinely jovial moments on the trip, too, like when Ryan came down and joined his brother for a golf cart ride. The two had a blast zipping around the property. And Mike and Cindy got to have a heart-to-heart talk with Tyler about his friends. They weren't real friends, Mike told him. They were just using him as company while they all got high. *Trust me, they're not your friends,* he insisted. Mike opened the door for Tyler to call him, anytime, with the hope that he'd confide in his uncle perhaps a little more than he would his parents. Tyler seemed receptive, but he never called.

As Blake and Tyler drove away, Blake called his

brother from his cell phone to thank him for the trip. It'd been good for Tyler, he said. Mike could tell that Blake was elated. Tyler seemed happy, so he was happy.

As Mike and Cindy reflected on the trip for Meyer, they couldn't help but wonder: Could the devastation have happened then? Was the image of the burning cabin a sign of what Tyler was contemplating, or was it truly a way to blow off steam? And what of that nuclear power plant drawing? Was that foreshadowing of a bull's-eye on Blake's back? Ryan, too, struggled. He'd moved out so recently. Michael Mandell once said he thought Tyler was waiting for Ryan to move before he killed his parents. Mike and Cindy weren't so sure. If Ryan had been there, would he have been another victim? Or would he, as Ryan feared while mired in survivor's guilt, have been able to stop his younger brother before the bloodshed?

CHAPTER 29

Finally, after months of speculating, Tyler figured out why he wasn't getting much mail in jail. He met with Harllee, his lawyer, and learned that a jail official was holding back the postcards addressed to Tyler and handing them over to Tyler's lawyer instead. Tyler didn't know why, but in early October 2011, he finally saw a backlog of letters that had been sent to him. He wrote to his Di-Vittorio grandparents how elated he was to "know I have people thinking and caring for me." As always, he wrote of his worry about reaching a plea deal. He was petrified at the prospect of life behind bars. "I can only hope everything goes well so I don't get a life sentence," he wrote. In signing off, he asked his grandparents to send his love to his brother Ryan.

CHAPTER 30

"Menendez brothers," Tyler had blurted. What an odd thing to reference while hiking with the family. Uncle Ray hadn't found it as funny as Tyler's friends surely would have. But that's how Tyler seemed to joke, even around his family. He maybe cleaned up his language and left behind the mutilated-cat jokes that his friends so enjoyed, but he seemed to thrive off making others squirm, no matter the audience. Menendez brothers struck Ray as undeniably unfunny, but also as just another off-the-wall, Tyler-being-Tyler attempt at shock comedy—until it was far too late. Then it became gut-sinking prophecy.

It's difficult to determine if Tyler knew the intricate details of Lyle and Erik Menendez's case—undoubtedly the most famous case of parricide in modern history. Uncle Ray didn't press him on the issue, and, in more than eighteen hundred pages of police reports and interview transcripts, his friends and family members haven't talked of the 1989 murder case in any detail. But there are parallels that can't be denied, and differences too distinct to allow the cases to be clumped together.

For starters, there were two of them. Lyle, age twenty-six, was born first to Jose and Mary "Kitty" Menendez; Erik followed two years later. The attractive, dark-haired brothers grew up lavishly by most American standards, first in Princeton, New Jersey, where Jose worked as a corporate executive and Kitty was a stay-at-home mom. When Jose got a job as an entertainment industry executive during the boys' teen years, the family migrated to Beverly Hills, California. Jose's salary jumped to more than a million dollars a year, give or take—basically upper middle class by California's impossible standards— and the boys were groomed for success. They took private tennis lessons and got expensive cars as birthday presents. After high school, Lyle enrolled at prestigious Princeton University. Their father reportedly envisioned a Kennedyesque dynasty for his family. But that dream was dogged by the boys' apparent apathy and troubled behavior. They were pinned with burgling neighbors' homes to the tune of more than a hundred thousand dollars, caught only when a friend ratted them out. Lyle's Princeton endeavor was marred when he was placed on academic probation for poor grades and discipline problems, followed by allegations of plagiarism.

Jose's Kennedy dreams abruptly ended August 20, 1989, as he and his wife settled in to watch a James Bond flick in the den of their home on North Elm Drive in Beverly Hills. Lyle and Erik walked in with shotguns they'd bought three hours away in San Diego. Lyle leveled his gun at the back of his father's head and pulled the trigger, spattering Jose's brains across the room. Kitty tried to run but was shot in the leg. The blood from the wound gushed to the floor; she slipped in it and fell. Two more shots were fired. The boys realized they needed to reload, so one ran out to Lyle's car for more ammunition, then came back and pressed a shotgun to Kitty's face. The blast left her unrecognizable. The boys rushed to a movie theater to buy a film ticket to establish an alibi, and then claimed to have made the gruesome discovery afterward. "Somebody killed my parents!" Lyle screamed tearfully to a 911 dispatcher. The scene was horrific; the tears, convincing. It wasn't until six months later, after the orphaned boys had spent nearly a million dollars on trips, restaurants, Rolexes, and other luxuries, that police had pieced together enough evidence to arrest them. Crucial evidence came from their own mouths: Erik had confessed to a psychologist, prompting Lyle to threaten the doctor's life. (It was the threat, not the confession itself, that voided the rule of patient–doctor confidentiality.) In light of that, the defense immediately shifted from "we didn't do it" to "we were abused," and the eventual six-month trial—aired on then-nascent Court TV—centered on accusations that Jose had systematically assaulted the boys, both physically and sexually, for years, while Kitty sat by and did nothing. Problem was, neither Erik nor Lyle had told anyone of the years of abuse, nor was there any physical evidence. And prosecutors presented a compelling motive of their own: greed. The brothers stood to inherit some fourteen million dollars in their parents' deaths.

As with Tyler, some family members immediately sided with the boys. Even without having seen or heard of any abuse, they deemed it possible. They attacked the victims' characters in the media, calling Jose demanding and impossible to please, and Kitty unloving and withdrawn. One non-family witness even implied that Kitty perhaps had been trying to poison her family. And the boys testified in great detail about the alleged sex abuse, describing bizarre rituals in which their father would put tacks in the skin of their buttocks and force them to perform oral sex. Lyle said on the stand that he'd abused Erik himself when they were both very young, and he offered a tearful apology for acting out on the behavior he'd learned from their father.

It made for fantastic television and difficult deliberations. Though the brothers were tried simultaneously, they were assigned separate juries. Each ended with a mistrial, the jurors unable to decide if they'd truly been driven to kill or if they were simply greedy, cold-blooded murderers. A second untelevised trial ended with guilty verdicts, and each brother was sentenced to spend the rest of his life behind bars.

Tyler had alleged abuse several times to a few friends in a matter-of-fact manner, directing it at his father. It was a claim that his friends either didn't believe—*he was always joking like that,* they'd later say—or didn't question—*who would make up that kind of story?* And when word of the slayings spread, many who hadn't thought much about the claims beforehand quickly embraced them as true. That was the only way the deaths made any sense. Surely, Tyler had to have been acting out against his parents for a reason. But, as with the Menendez brothers, there was no documentation, no claims with specific dates or corroborating details, that backed up the attention-getting stories. Instead, there was the opposite: a slew of family and close friends who said that there was no way, no how, the Hadleys had ever hurt their children. Even relatives who very quickly seemed to forgive Tyler shared no concerns of abuse or neglect with Meyer. Tyler needed help and needed God, they told him in letters, but he also needed forgiveness.

Though stories of parricide can be found in ancient literature and modern-day thriller flicks, killing one's parents is actually incredibly rare. One of the most famous cases of alleged parricide in American history is that of Lizzie Borden, a thirty-two-year-old New England spinster whose father and stepmother were brutally hacked to death on August 4, 1892, in Fall River, Massachusetts. Prosecutors painted Lizzie as an ungrateful daughter frustrated with her father's miserly ways. Andrew Borden was a wealthy bank president, but he was so tight-fisted that he refused to splurge on the indoor plumbing that Lizzie's friends enjoyed. On a hot August morning, Lizzie's stepmother Abby was found in a guest bedroom of the family's home, dead from some eighteen axe blows to her head. An autopsy indicated she'd died at least an hour before her husband. Andrew Borden was discovered with eleven whacks to his head on the family's couch, where he'd apparently been attacked after falling asleep. Lizzie's trial was a media circus. Her face was plastered in photographs and courtroom etchings across front pages nationwide. But while the media seemed to have convicted her from the start, the jury couldn't do it. In June 1893, after barely ninety minutes of deliberation, they acquitted Lizzie Borden of both slayings. She went on to live a wealthy life in ostracism, until her death of pneumonia at age sixty-six in 1927. Still, her case continues to fascinate, and, deservedly or not, her name remains synonymous with parricide even 120 years after the deaths.

Statistics cited by Kathleen Heide, a professor of criminology at the University of South Florida and author of *Why Kids Kill Parents: Child Abuse and Adolescent Parricide,* indicate that on average, about five parents are killed by their biological children in the United States every week. Slayings of mothers and fathers each make up about 2 percent of the approximately fourteen thousand homicides each year in which the victim–offender relationship is known and reported to the FBI. The killing of both parents at once is rarer still. Heide's study of statistics between 1976 and 2007 showed that most people who killed their parents were adults, and that long-term abuse often played a role in the household before the deaths. Parricide was often characterized by overkill—the killer might fire a gun fifteen times instead of once, or continue stabbing long after the victim was dead. And it's impossible to predict, Heide determined, partly because it's so statistically unusual. She determined some factors that increase the likelihood that a juvenile might kill his parents: The youth is raised in a chemically dependent or dysfunctional family; an ongoing pattern of family violence exists in the home; conditions inside the home worsen, and violence escalates; the juvenile becomes increasingly vulnerable to home stressors; and a firearm is readily available in the home environment. (Heide spelled out these factors in an interview with *48 Hours* in July 2012.) In her studies, Heide determined that most parricide cases are committed by offenders who fall within three categories: severely abused children, dangerously antisocial children, and severely mentally ill children. Each category presents different motives. Abused children kill to stop the abuse, while antisocial children kill to further their own goals. In those cases, the youth sees her parents as an obstacle to overcome, a speed bump on the road to getting what she wants. Those children are often out to inherit money or gain more freedom with the parents' demise.

Antisocial kids who start acting out for personal gain need to be reeled in, according to Heide. Otherwise, "the youth often will engage in criminal activities that may include violence toward people or animals, destruction of property, deceitfulness or theft, and/or serious violations of rules by parents, such as staying out all night or being truant from school," Heide said in a question-and-answer with *48 Hours*. "At this point, the youth will likely be diagnosed as having a Conduct Disorder. If this pattern of violating the rights of others continues past age 18, it is likely that this individual may be diagnosed as having an Antisocial Personality Disorder. This type of parricide offender is far more dangerous to society than the first in terms of re-offending and hurting other people in the future."

Diagnoses with mentally ill children usually include long-standing battles with psychosis and severe depression. The juveniles often are on psychotropic medication. "They may report hearing God's voice commanding them [a hallucination—false sensory experience] to kill the parent," Heide said.

"In parricide cases, I have seen good parents overindulge their children with fatal results," Heide continued. "These parents often love their children very much and do not want to fight with them over 'little things.' These parents reason that these challenges—staying up late, getting another toy at the store—are not really important. The problem is that over time, the 'little things' become bigger and bigger issues. At 15, 16 or 17 years of age, the son or daughter is now saying, 'I am going out, I am taking the car, I am dating who I want.' The parent appropriately steps in and says 'no.' However, the adolescent has not learned to respect the parent and to accept the parent's authority. The youth has not learned that you do not always get your way. The youth has no frustration tolerance, meaning that he does not know how to deal with disappointment, and gets angry. Sometimes the anger is so intense that it erupts into deadly rage."

Jurors would eventually decide that the Menendez brothers would fall within the second category—antisocial behavior—though the defense their lawyers mounted characterized them as belonging to the first. They were victims, not merciless killers, Leslie Abramson, one of the lead defense lawyers, argued again and again to an audience of millions. It's the most common narrative arc available in a crime that is so incredibly uncommon. Paul Mones, famous for being the first American lawyer whose specialty was defending kids who kill, has written books and papers about abused children driven to do the unthinkable. His book *When a Child Kills: Abused Children Who Kill Their Parents* not only became must-read material for people working with abused children, but it's been cited in research and opinions handed down by state appellate courts. In the days after Tyler's arrest, people searched for that narrative arc. Questions of abuse inevitably surfaced. *What else could drive a teenager to kill his own parents?*

Maurice Hadley was still grappling with that question months later, when Detective Meyer returned to interview him and his wife, Betty. The emotions were still too raw for Betty, who had trouble talking about the deaths or her grandson. She wasn't ready to forgive Tyler, and she certainly couldn't visit him in jail.

"I told her that was completely up to her and Maurice," Meyer would write in her case report. "While they were fine speaking to me, it is still a very emotional subject and Betty had difficulty speaking. Maurice and I spoke during the majority of the interview."

The couple had struggled for two months trying to figure out what went wrong and when. Sure, Blake and Mary Jo could have been stricter, but plenty of people make missteps in parenting without paying the price with their lives. Tyler was well behaved in their home, and he hugged them and told them he loved them, just like you'd expect any child would. Blake had told his father about some of the troubles of late—the drug use and sneaking out particularly—and while everyone was concerned about him getting his life straightened out, they certainly never worried about him becoming violent. That didn't seem to be in Tyler's nature. Still, Maurice acknowledged that Tyler at times behaved bizarrely. During Blake and the family's last visit to Maurice and Betty's home, they had been reminiscing about Ryan and Tyler's childhoods. As they sat around, each shared memories of the boys growing up, mostly fond memories of boys being boys. But Tyler's memory wasn't as sweet. He recalled standing in front of the open refrigerator when his grandfather snapped, "Shut that damn door!" Maurice was shocked; of all the thousands of little moments over all the years, this was the memory that popped to mind? Of being yelled at for leaving the refrigerator door open? Maurice didn't remember the specific incident, but he didn't doubt it, either. He told Meyer that Ryan and Tyler were typical boys who did typical boy things—like roughhousing and wrestling and standing in front of the fridge the way kids sometimes do. And the grandparents, while doting and adoring, sometimes told them to knock it off. It all seemed so normal.

As Meyer's investigation unfolded, she began to uncover a side of Tyler that no one—not his parents, his grandparents, his brother, or even his best friend—had fully grasped. They'd seen hints here and there, but if they'd known the full truth, they might have been more concerned.

Among Meyer's findings:

He told some friends that his father sexually molested him, though no one stepped forward saying they witnessed any behavior that would remotely support the contention—including Ryan, who lived in the home for more than two decades. Tyler never raised the allegation after his arrest, either, which would have made for a potentially compelling defense. And he didn't make the allegation to his close friends, like Michael Mandell, who actually knew and interacted with his family. Rather, he told people on the periphery who were less likely to call bullshit on the claim.

He'd also told some of his friends that his father was dead, and that Blake was his stepfather. He'd randomly say that his dad died when he was young, and he never corrected himself. Mandell heard him say it once to other friends in his presence, but, because Michael had been friends with the family for so long, he knew it wasn't true.

"I remember thinking, 'Why would he even say that?' " Michael later recalled. "I can't even begin to think why he'd say something like that."

Michael didn't call Tyler out in front of their friends, though, and eventually he forgot about it. Tyler had most recently had made the claim when it was actually true. The night of the party, a female friend named Ashley had gotten in a van with Tyler and another friend for a beer run. When the older friend went inside to make the buy, Ashley chatted with him and mentioned her mother having passed away. Tyler said his father, too, had died. The way he said it, she assumed he meant that his dad had been dead a long while, not that he'd been bludgeoned just hours earlier and was inside the house where she and others had played beer pong. But as Meyer was learning, some of his friends never knew the truth, and in fact still believed that Blake wasn't Tyler's biological father long after the news of the slayings had spread.

The tale about Blake not being his real father apparently helped perpetuate another story: that his parents beat him. Tyler told tales of abuse to some friends, but never to his closest buddies. It seemed more as though it was a lie designed to elicit sympathy from strangers.

"I heard that he got hit," Dustin Turner told detectives as Mark Andrews agreed beside him.

Michael said none of it was true. Blake wasn't remotely threatening, and he certainly was no child molester. The parents perhaps had started punishing their son for getting in trouble, but they weren't violent people. No one—not Tyler's brother, not his grandparents, not Michael—told Meyer of a single instance of abuse, and many said there was no way that either parent ever hit the boys. If anything, they should have turned to corporal punishment, some relatives would say.

"They never, ever got physical as far as I know," Mandell said. "They'd take away his phone or his laptop, it all seemed pretty minor to me. When I was little, probably until I was maybe 5 or 10, I'd get a little spanking if I did something. He'd just get grounded."

A friend named Angelica trekked to the police department after she'd learned of the deaths. She'd known Tyler for six months and had seen him a few weeks earlier at a different party. Tyler had been grounded, but he'd sneaked out and stolen his parents' car. He was on all sorts of drugs, Angelica told an officer, so he wasn't coherent when he parked the car and forgot where it was. He and Angelica stumbled around in the darkness until they found it at the other end of the street, after which they sat inside it. About an hour or two later, Blake and Mary Jo showed up and screamed at him, dragging him home. Based on this, Angelica told detectives that Tyler was pushed to it by his parents' behavior.

Tyler was "under a lot of pressure," Angelica insisted. "Like, his parents would never let him be himself and, honestly, I think that they caused everything that just happened because, like, he was probably mentally abused. He was not allowed to be himself. His parents always expected him to be someone else that he wasn't and that's not right. Anything Tyler would do, he'd be wrong for it. No matter what he did, he would be wrong . . . Honestly, he got crazy 'cause of it and if you have that much hate for somebody, then you actually would do something like that."

Angelica had attended the notorious party but hadn't noticed anything amiss other than the old beagle hanging out in the only available bathroom. Officer Carrasquillo, who interviewed Angelica, asked her if she knew that Tyler's parents had placed him in a counseling program and had been trying to help him. "Angelica became defensive," Carrasquillo reported, "and stated that maybe Tyler didn't want to be help [sic], his parents kept pushing him and he was probably sick of being pushed. She then said, 'If his parents cared a little more then he probably wouldn't have been popping pills.'"

Betty, Blake's mother, had babysat the boys from the time they were babies until they hit about six or seven years old. The kids were sweet and got along well, despite—or maybe because of—their age difference. There were no red flags, they insisted, not even in recent weeks. Meyer asked if Tyler ever seemed angry or said he was mad at his parents. Maurice said no, but that he knew Tyler wasn't happy about his parents clamping down, trying to regain control. Blake had told his parents that he'd even taken Tyler's bedroom door off its hinges and confiscated his cell phone. They'd gone through the phone to try to figure out with whom Tyler was running around. They were waging a parental war in the hope of winning back their son. At times, it seemed they'd won small battles. Betty remembered seeing Tyler lean up against his mom while the two sat together on the couch. And Blake's description of Tyler on the Georgia trip was of the Tyler they'd known for years—a cutup who joked and played and went for walks with his family.

Meyer had to ask uncomfortable questions: What about the molestation rumors Tyler had spread to friends? And the allegations that Blake sometimes punched him? Maurice and Betty were adamant: Neither had heard any such allegation of any kind from the boys toward their parents, neither in jest nor in anger. Nor had they seen either parent hit or even threaten to hit the boys.

But while the family didn't see any signs, Tyler's friends should have. Had anyone truly been listening to what Tyler Hadley had spouted in the weeks before his parents' deaths, they would have realized he was spelling out in detail what he was about to do and how he would do it. In the days after the slayings, Meyer learned about one particularly disturbing omen. Sitting in one friend's room while a group of five friends smoked pot and drank beer, just two weeks before the murders, Tyler said in his usual "I'm sure he's just joking" way that his parents were going to get it. Everyone laughed, as usual. Friend Matt Nobile said they "were talking twisted and have a sick sense of humor," Meyer later reported.

Tyler said it again. "I'm going to kill my parents." This time, he appeared serious. Still, everyone laughed.

Tyler continued to ponder the act. He'd have to catch them off guard, his dad especially. He'd steal their money and throw a big party. After some thought, he clarified that he didn't want to kill his mom, so if someone wanted his car, the gold Lincoln, they'd have to do that job. Danny Roberts said, sure, he'd like Tyler's car, so he'd take on Mom. They all laughed the whole time they talked, everyone assuming that Tyler was joking. They even talked about how to do it. Tyler thought an axe would be most efficient. In hindsight, it was a gut-wrenching conversation, but Nobile told police that such twisted talk wasn't un-usual for the friends. That was their modus operandi: to say obscene and offensive things for shock value. They'd joke about lighting churches on fire, killing babies, and mutilating cats. It was biting humor mixed with a bit of teenage one-upmanship. *Who can be the most shocking today?* But on this day, about two weeks before the deaths, the only real topic of conversation was Tyler's plans to kill his parents. And even though the others were laugh-ing, Tyler looked as though he was playing the straight man in a comedy routine. He was the Dean Martin to the group's collective Jerry Lewis.

After learning of this gathering, police began ques-tioning the friends who'd heard Tyler spell out his plans. One initially denied it, saying Tyler had never really said anything about his parents, good or bad. When the officer pressed him, the friend cracked.

"I didn't think he was serious," he said. "Like he was just saying, like—" He took a deep breath. "Shit! He was saying how he wanted to kill his parents and have a big party after. I didn't think he was serious!"

Later, Tyler supposedly told a friend that he'd almost bought an axe but got stopped by police. Nobile didn't think Tyler made it to the store, though Tyler apparently told someone he'd indeed bought a pickaxe at a Walmart in the days leading up to the slaying. Why he'd settled on a hammer was anyone's guess.

The dead-parents jokes became so commonplace that when Nobile and Tyler chatted about the impending party on the fateful Saturday, even then they talked of Tyler killing his parents. Matt thought they were still joking, he'd tell Meyer in an interview, during which he shared the last written exchange he'd had with his friend prior to the party. In the Facebook messages (apparently written

with disdain for intelligible, properly spelled and punctuated English), Nobile started by asking, "did u do it" (sic).

"no but imgonna bet."

"u really should now they called the 5-o on you," Nobile
replied. The term *5-o* is derived from the once-popular TV
series *Hawaii Five-O,* which aired from 1968 to 1980. It's
doubtful the teens knew the slang's origin, but even thirty
years after the show's end, *5-o* remains synonymous with
police.

"when? now" Tyler replied.

"do it"

"don't worry I am then imhavin a party"

"yea party time nigga"

That was Matt's final comment. He told Meyer he had
no idea he was egging on a kid who was genuinely contemplating killing his parents. It was only a joke, he insisted.

All of the harbingers and the macabre joking made the
case of Tyler Hadley even stranger. As far as Meyer could
determine, there was no abuse or trauma that led to Tyler's fury. There was only his intense desire to have a
party he knew his parents wouldn't allow.

CHAPTER 31

In September 2011, Ryan Hadley found himself filing paperwork that no son should ever have to file: He asked a state court to block his younger brother from any chance of inheriting their parents' money. It wasn't that Ryan was being greedy and wanted his parents' life insurance policy and retirement investments all to himself—he routinely was slipping money into his brother's jail canteen fund, after all—but the state of Florida or overriding federal laws could automatically aim to split the parents' legacy between the two surviving sons, even though one of them was suspected of causing their deaths.

Through Port St. Lucie attorney Stephen Navaretta, Ryan Hadley filed the civil complaint in St. Lucie County Court citing Florida Statute Section 732-802. The complaint read in part: "A person who intentionally and unlawfully kills another person is not entitled to reap the benefits of the unlawful and intentional deaths and by virtue of that statute is deemed to have been disqualified from receiving life insurance policy benefit payments, pension plan benefit payments, or any other entitlement that otherwise would vest by virtues of the deaths of Blake M. Hadley and Mary Jo Hadley."

Nothing in the complaint indicated that Tyler had been eyeing an inheritance. Rather, it seemed more a preemptive move on Ryan's part to keep the payout from getting muddled by bureaucracy.

CHAPTER 32

Inside St. Lucie County Jail, Tyler was an unparalleled celebrity. After all, jail was for two types of inmates: people who'd been sentenced to less than a year behind bars, usually for something far less serious than murder, or people awaiting trial. Tyler fell into the latter category, and with so few homicides in the area each year, his was by far the highest profile. The cold-blooded crime caught the attention and imagination of the other inmates. Especially Justin Toney.

Toney met Tyler on Tyler's eighteenth birthday. That's the day that the teen was able to move into the general population of the jail. Tyler didn't need any introduction. He was a tall boy, a big guy, Toney recalled—much bigger than he'd seemed in the newspapers—and Toney, who'd spent no time in the Florida Department of Corrections, was amazed that the two were in the same dorm of the jail.

"The first couple days he didn't say nothing," Toney later recalled to a detective. "He came in on his birthday and everyone was like, 'Dude, happy birthday,' you know, 'cause we were trying to make him, like, not uncomfortable."

But Tyler slowly came around. He wasn't an especially talkative guy, but when people asked him questions, he answered—often with a directness that made them sorry they'd asked in the first place. Toney became something of a friend. Tyler would approach with a bowl of ramen noodle soup and start with a "What's up, man?" The two would talk about Toney's recent court appearances and his upcoming release.

"He's like, 'I don't even want to talk to you short timer,' " Toney said. "And we like, we just laugh about silly, stupid little short stuff."

By the time Meyer caught up with Toney, he wasn't sure he wanted to be interviewed. Though he'd been the one to reach out to officials first, the twenty-three-year-old had just reached a plea deal in his case and could have walked away from the whole experience rather than risk being thrust into a highly publicized case that was destined to be CNN fodder if it ever went to trial. Plus, Tyler had trusted him. Toney was torn.

"I just feel wrong for listening to him and then going and tell everything he told me," Toney told Meyer. "I would be pissed if someone did that to me, too, you know."

Meyer played it cool as she tried to encourage him to clear his conscience.

"I'm here to listen," she told him. "I could sit here for three hours and listen to everything that you want to tell me, but if you don't, you don't . . . This is something that,

that people are coming to me with just because of their
conscience and their morals, the fact that they want to do
the right thing. And you know you're not the first person
that's come forward."

After a few minutes, Toney relented. "I can't believe
I'm fucking doing this. So what do you want to know?"

"Everything," Meyer replied.

So Toney started talking.

He'd been fascinated, in a way, by Tyler. It wasn't every
day you met someone accused of killing their parents,
right? So Toney sidled up and started asking Tyler what
had happened. He wanted to know every detail, every
thought process along the way. Plenty of people think
about murder, but there aren't many who actually go
through with it. Toney couldn't shake his morbid fascination.

"At first he was telling me it was the medication he
was on," Toney said. "I was like, 'Dude, I'm not fucking
buying it.' I kept picking his brain . . . I kept switching
from subject so subject about, you know, 'What made you
choose a hammer?' And he said that he had some loppers
he was gonna use, like the things that you cut bushes
with. He was like, 'I had those. I had, like, a choice of a
few different things.' "

"What made you want to do it?" Toney asked.

Tyler said he'd wanted to have a party and he knew
they wouldn't allow it. He'd been thinking about it for a
few weeks before it happened.

"He was like, 'We were at LongHorn, me and my
grandparents and my mom and my dad . . . I was even
thinking about it then.' "

Meyer had heard about this LongHorn visit before. It
was the night before the deaths, when the family had
gathered for a dinner to celebrate Kelly's daughter's birthday. But, according to Toney, Tyler had been thinking

about it a lot longer than that—maybe three or four weeks. The plan had brewed slowly, and his intent all along was to kill himself rather than go to jail.

And even jail didn't stop his suicide plans. At one point, he told Toney he'd looked for ways to do it in jail. He got down on all fours and mimed banging his head against the concrete floor.

"He was like, 'I was even gonna do this,'" Toney said, mimicking the bashing motion. "I was like, 'Oh, my God.' So I mean, he definitely had a thought to kill himself . . . It was definitely premeditated for sure, 100 percent."

"All this just to have a party?" Meyer asked.

"That's what he said."

"Okay."

"I guess . . . right after he killed them, he went to their bank and got money out of their bank or something."

"Okay."

"I'm not sure if he said $5,000 or what, but I know he spent, like, two grand on the party. He said it took him forever to clean up, clean up the blood. I asked him who he hit first and he was like, he just said he hit his mom. I guess she was on the computer or something. And then he said his dad seen him and just ran away. And I said, 'Did they try to stop you?' And he was like, 'No, that's how I knew that they really loved me.'"

Toney stopped cold. That line struck him.

"I was just, like, dumbfounded, you know. If you found out right then that they really loved you, why would you continue?"

As the days passed, he asked more questions, over the objections of some cell mates who found the line of inquiry far more upsetting than intriguing. He asked Tyler if he'd seen their brains. No, Tyler said, but he saw brain matter.

"I just kept going and asking him just little stuff, and

he kept answering," Toney said. "I said, 'Did the dog try to stop you?' He's like, 'No, that little fucker knew what was up.' I'm like, wow. Yeah, it was pretty intense, the conversations.

"Then one day he looked at me—and, dude, he looks like the devil, like when he looks in your eyes . . . that's Satan right there—and he's like, 'You really want to know what it was?' He's like, 'I don't think it was the medication.' He's like, 'It was the devil, because the devil is drugs and money.' That was his exact words: 'The devil is drugs and money.' "

The revelations Tyler shared were bit by bit over a span of weeks. Each time they talked, Toney would press for more details. He couldn't help himself, he later told Meyer. He just found Tyler fascinating. Disturbed and fascinating.

"He would just utter little shit," Toney recalled. Like when Tyler said his dad had endured sixty-something double stab wounds from the hammer. Toney asked why Tyler didn't stop hitting them.

"He's like, 'I hit 'em and I just figured I had to finish the job.' "

"Does he mention his mom and dad? Does he call 'em 'mom and dad'?" Meyer asked.

"Yeah, he calls 'em mom and dad . . . Every now and then he'll be like, 'Yeah, man, I regret it. I wish I had a mom and dad.' Everyone in the dorm will, like, look at me, like, 'Dude, leave him alone,' you know. But . . . like I say, that's just one of the most horrific crimes . . . I want to pick his brain. I, you know, want to find out . . . what would possess someone to do that to their mom and dad."

"Does he talk about them? Does he talk about being angry with them or mad at them?"

"He said that they were arguing for a couple of weeks," but he never alluded to any violence, Toney added. He said they were fine, they weren't molesting him or anything. He killed them simply because he knew they wouldn't let him have the party.

And in Tyler's mind, the party was apparently worth it. He repeatedly told his jail mates that they should've been there. Turns out, Toney could have been there. He happened to be two streets away the night of the slayings. He told this to Tyler.

"He was like, 'Yeah, man, you should have come to the party. It was awesome. We had so much fun at the party. I was . . . really, really drunk. We were smoking blunt after blunt.' He spent, like, two grand on drugs, weed, beans and alcohol, liquor and other stuff."

His account to Toney matched what he'd told Michael Mandell: He'd taken three pills of ecstasy. Also, his drink of choice at the party was gin, and he smoked a lot of weed in his bedroom with his friends.

The paranoia Tyler had about his parents' affection—"you don't love me," "you think I'm fat"—hadn't disappeared in prison. But Tyler cared less about how Toney felt than who he was. Each time the two talked, Tyler would quiz him: "You're not a cop, are you?" Toney would laugh and say he wasn't. "Are you sure?" Tyler would press. Toney insisted.

Just as Tyler was in his letters to family and friends, he seemed with his jail mates to be obsessed with getting a plea deal. At first he'd hoped for an insanity defense that would land him behind bars for maybe ten to fifteen years. Soon that crept up to twenty or thirty years. And then even that seemed a long shot to Tyler.

"He's like, 'I'll gladly sign forty right now. I'll sign forty. Even fifty, I'll sign fifty,' " Toney relayed.

Though Toney started out the conversation with Meyer nervous about being a so-called snitch, he eventually offered to get more information for her. "I can fucking pick

his brain and he will tell me. He confides in me," Toney
said. "I don't know why, but he definitely confides in me
for sure." Meyer turned him down, saying she'd never put
him in a spot to collect information but was happy to hear
what he'd learned about Tyler so far.

The reason for Toney's willingness to come forward
was simple: Tyler freaked him out. He seemed unrepen-
tant and heartless. Despite how prisoners are portrayed in
movies and on television, the inmate serving time for the
craziest crime doesn't necessarily get respect. There's a
code behind bars, and Tyler, by describing in remorseless
detail how he'd murdered his own parents, was breaking
the code. Most prisoners would love to see their families
again. Most would give anything to spend even a single
night on the outside eating Mom's cooking one more
time. Tyler didn't seem tough and hard-core by recount-
ing the deaths in gory detail. He seemed sick.

When newcomers would enter the jail and get around
to know the inmates, Tyler was especially crass, Toney
described.

"Every time someone new comes in, he'll be like,
'What's up, man? You know who I am? I'm the hammer
boy.'"

Toney found it disgusting. It was one thing for the
other inmates to christen him with a tasteless nickname—
they'd started with Ham, and then, after Tyler protested,
settled on Hambo and Bamm-Bamm—but christening
himself was another story.

"To introduce yourself like that after the horrific crime
that you just fucking committed, you're definitely sick
for sure. You are definitely sick. I mean . . . he's definitely
not insane. He knew what he was doing."

"How do you know that?" Meyer asked.

"I can tell by the way he talks and the way he expresses

himself, and it wasn't because he's crazy . . . He's trying to get an insanity plea . . . Hell, no, he's not insane. Not even close."

There's a fine line between disturbed and insane in the layman's world, sure. But in legal terms, the boiled-down definition of *insane* is actually pretty simple: Did the suspect know the difference between right and wrong when he committed the crime? Without that right–wrong distinction, insanity pleas would be far more commonplace. The insanity defense is used in fewer than 1 percent of felony cases and is successful in maybe one-quarter of those, according to an oft-cited eight-state study of criminal cases in the early 1990s. The fact that Tyler was unquestionably disturbed and without apparent remorse—at least when talking to his jail mates—might mean he was crazy by everyday standards, but not necessarily in clinical or legal terms.

Toney felt Tyler was trying to seem insane simply for a plea, but he wasn't buying it. One day, as Tyler was still on twenty-three-hour lockdown in his cell, Toney positioned himself in Cell H so that everyone else in the dorm could see him. He nearly taunted Tyler: "Dude, you're not getting an insanity plea . . . Dude, you're getting life."

"No, man . . . Ask Cell H," Tyler implored.

Toney went down the line: "So-and-so, do you think Hambo is getting life?"

One by one came the responses: "Yeah, he's getting life."

"No, man," Tyler said. "I'm gonna get an insanity plea. I'm gonna get an insanity plea."

"He's stuck on that's what he thinks he's gonna get," Toney said. "There's definitely something wrong with him, but he's not crazy. He might be a little lost—of course he's gotta be lost—but . . . but I don't know."

In a lot of ways, though, Tyler was normal, too, Toney said. He'd laugh and be chatty. His visits with his grandparents always gave him a morale boost.

"He was so happy when he talked to one of his friends one day. He was like, 'Yeah, man, my homeboy just picked up.' "

Toney had been listening. He'd heard Tyler say his name twice—"It's Tyler . . . Tyler Hadley"—so Toney realized the kid must have asked "Tyler who?" But when the conversation started, Tyler was in a much better mood. Tyler said he had a girlfriend who'd write him, though Toney wasn't sure if that was true. In fact, Toney was pretty convinced Tyler was gay—an assertion Tyler's best friends couldn't deny or substantiate in hindsight. Still, hearing from his "homeboys" and "homegirls" clearly perked the kid up. And Tyler regularly had money put in his canteen from either his maternal grandparents or his brother Ryan—who had inherited a decent chunk after the deaths—so Tyler didn't want for much.

"Hell, no, he's not happy to be here, but he damn sure laughs," Toney said. "He laughs and jokes with us."

Though sometimes, Tyler was the only one laughing. That sense of humor that his friends shook off as being a little dark, a little twisted, would pop out in ways that bugged not only Toney but other cell mates as well. Tyler started offering to sign newspaper stories with his picture in them or images of hammers. He signed several for Toney, who thought maybe he could sell them online. But the clippings contained more than just autographs, and the messages they bore were the final straw for Toney, who struggled for days before mentioning to a guard that he might have information prosecutors would want to hear. On the one hand, Tyler had been open with him and had pressed so hard to ensure Toney wouldn't talk. But on the other, he seemed far too proud of his crime, and he clearly had to pay for what he'd done. So, after some soul searching and a "do the right thing" talk from Meyer, he agreed to eventually turn over several autographed sheets of paper from Tyler. The one that bothered Toney the most read:

"I don't know if you're a fan, but you should be. It's hammer time. —Tyler Hadley."

CHAPTER 33

In late November 2011, depression began to take hold of Tyler behind bars. At least, that's what he told his maternal grandparents in a letter. He worried that his medication wasn't working, so he was making plans to talk to the jail's mental health officials. He thought about the upcoming holidays, and the realization that he'd be behind bars for Christmas caused him to crumble in tears. He kept praying and asking for God's help, he said, but sometimes he felt like God wasn't there.

"I hate when thoughts like that come into my mind," he wrote.

He felt remorse, he added. He worried for Ryan, that his brother might hurt himself from the stress. He knew his brother missed their parents. "I really miss them, too," Tyler wrote. He wasn't a psycho. He'd keep praying, keep looking for the reason this all happened. (Everything does happen for a reason, right? So the saying goes.) And he'd reach out to St. Rita and St. Jude, whom he understood to be the saints of impossible cases. Because, really, that's what his was.

CHAPTER 34

Michael Mandell wasn't doing well. He was haunted by what he'd seen in his friend's house, haunted by having turned Tyler in to police. When he closed his eyes, he saw blood spatter and Blake Hadley's lifeless leg. He wasn't sleeping much, and when he did, he had nightmares. He was growing paranoid of people around him, and he couldn't stomach the thought of starting his senior year of high school after having become a local celebrity for all the wrong reasons.

"I think about it every day and I don't stop thinking about it," he told one journalist. "It's terrible. I hate it."

Instead of attending Port St. Lucie High School, Michael opted to be homeschooled. He took Meyer's advice and started counseling, but coming to grips with what had happened was slow. He'd known Tyler for ten years.

Ten years of playing football and basketball, going to movies, talking about girls, experimenting with drugs, hanging out, and playing video games. Ten years of having each other's backs and spending the night at each other's homes. Ten years of being brothers in every way but blood.

"That was my closest person I ever had to me, and I'm kind of lost without that person," he said.

Michael flipped through photographs of himself as a child almost wistfully. He sent one image of himself on a swing, a huge smile cutting across his young face beneath a mess of blond hair, to a writer who'd asked for pictures of him and Tyler together as children. Michael was alone in this photo, and his title he'd given the image was heartbreaking: "Carefree days." In another image, he stood beside a gawky Tyler amid nativity scene reenactors. The two boys smiled awkwardly, clearly posing for a parent more enthusiastic about the Christmas scene than they were.

At first, Michael didn't write Tyler behind bars. His parents didn't want him to, and lawyers advised against it. And, frankly, he was a little mad at the guy. He knew Tyler wanted to reach him, though, because a mutual friend told him that Tyler had asked for his street address. She didn't pass it along, uncertain that Michael wanted to rekindle the friendship. And he didn't—for a while. But in truth, he missed his buddy, so he fired off a "what's up?" postcard that eventually made its way to Tyler, who replied in elation. After that, Michael wrote a few more letters, but it became clear through Tyler's replies that he wasn't receiving them.

"I don't know why," Michael later said. "Maybe his lawyer wasn't giving them to him, but I'd get letters back that said, 'Why won't you write me?' when I had been writing."

Michael started hating the idea that he was the prosecution's star witness in its case against Tyler, too. He withdrew from police. He'd answered their questions so many times, he said, and he was just tired of repeating himself, so he quit returning phone calls. That seemed to be a mistake. In March 2012, police showed up at Michael's door about a loitering charge. Michael argued that the charge was bogus, but police pushed inside the home and arrested him. Michael ultimately was accused of resisting arrest and battery, which he denied—"I would never hit a cop. I called *them*"—and finally ended the case by agreeing to write an apology letter.

The kid who'd grown up thinking he might want to become a cop had a different goal in mind: Now, if he could just get his shit together—which even he admitted was becoming more of a long shot—he wanted to go to school and eventually become a prosecutor.

CHAPTER 35

As Michael pulled away from his childhood friend, Tyler seemed determined to keep in touch. In one letter, he said he knew he shouldn't write anymore, that Michael's mom didn't want the two to stay in contact, but said that he couldn't help it. He missed him.

The sentiment didn't keep him from bitching at Michael, too, though. He'd been in the newspaper four times that week, he wrote, and he begged Michael not to go to the media with this latest later. "PLEASE!!!!" he emphasized in all caps. "Please man, sorry to say this but you've kinda fucked me over enough," he wrote, before quickly backtracking that he wasn't mad, though. He'd landed himself in jail, he added, but then returned to the "why did you snitch on me" theme soon after.

Tyler didn't seem to realize that Michael wasn't turning

over his personal letters. Rather, reporters who submitted Freedom of Information requests to the prosecutor were given most of the letters without redaction. Dozens of pages of notes both to and from Tyler were handed over, highlighting the teen's innermost thoughts and fears—not to mention underscoring how his tone and demeanor seemed to change when writing his grandparents versus, say, his friends. To his grandparents, he wrote of depression and God. To his friends, he swore and reminisced about smoking pot and ordered them to drink beer on his behalf, even though most of them were underage.

But in this October 2011 letter to Michael, Tyler did express a sentiment he'd also shared with his family: remorse. He'd heard that Michael was having trouble sleeping at night, and that made him sorry. "I know you've been going to counseling and shit and I feel terrible for that," he wrote. Tyler, too, was in counseling, he said, trying to deal with flashbacks. They kept him up at night and made him sick. A doctor was coming up from Tampa to evaluate him, he wrote. If all went well, maybe he'd only get 10 to 15 years in a state hospital.

"I hope we can still be friends and chill when I get out," he wrote.

CHAPTER 36

Though most of Tyler's friends were more than willing to let Detective Meyer flip through their cell phones and jot down time stamps of text messages and phone calls that would help police map out a chronology for the day, Meyer still needed to secure search warrants for Tyler's Facebook page, his parents' bank records, the family's computers, and all three of their cell phones. It was crucial to establishing a time line that supported prosecutors' theory that Tyler alone killed his parents. Beginning August 30—more than a month after the deaths—Meyer finally got the legal authority.

First, there was the pertinent Facebook information. Meyer had requested access to all stored communications and files associated with Tyler's account. The warrant requested Neoprints, which are an expanded view of a

user profile providing profile information and wall post-
ings, as well as messages to and from the user that haven't
been deleted. It also requested a compilation of all the
photos uploaded to the account and photos in which Tyler
had been tagged. Of greatest immediate interest to Meyer
were the status updates about the party. In order, they
were:

"party at my crib tonight . . . maybe"—posted at 1:15
p.m. July 16.

"party at my house hmu" with Blake's cell phone
number—posted at 8:15 p.m. July 16.

"party at my house again hmu" with the same phone
number—posted at 4:40 a.m.

Three minutes after the last post, police arrived outside Tyler's home and peered at him through a crack in
the blinds as he paced erratically.

Meyer matched this information with Mary Jo's cell
phone records. At 12:41 p.m., she exchanged text messages with friend Jennifer Archer, who asked Mary Jo
some banal questions about newspapers and a shopping
trip. At 4:42 p.m. July 16, Grandma DiVittorio called and
chatted with her daughter for fifty-seven seconds. That
meant Mary Jo was alive three and a half hours after
Tyler first posted about his tentative party plans—and
nearly two hours after Tyler chased Danny from the
house and shoved him over the backyard fence.

A few hours later, at 7:48 p.m., one of Mary Jo's friends
and fellow teachers, Peggy Hoffman, sent her a text message. Peggy never got a response, which was uncharacteristic of Mary Jo, who always responded to texts. Jen
Archer also sent a message that night, at 8:54 p.m., and
didn't get a reply. Detective Meyer was able to confirm
through cell phone records that Mary Jo never read those
messages. By then she was dead, Meyer concluded.

Included in the long list of "if onlys" was the discovery

that Mary Jo's friend Mel had tried desperately to get her away from the house Saturday. They'd talked the day before: Mel wanted Mary Jo to come with her to the green market. No, Mary Jo had said. She didn't want to leave Tyler alone. Mel tried to plead and insisted they'd only be gone an hour, but Mary Jo still refused. She planned to stay at home with her son in the morning, after which she needed to go grocery shopping. She'd hoped to get Tyler to tag along on that, but as it turned out, he refused, and while Blake and Mary Jo headed out for some errands, Tyler apparently plotted their deaths and planned a party to celebrate.

CHAPTER 37

When Jen Archer saw the police tape hugging the Granduer home, she thought for sure that Tyler had finally followed through on his threat to kill himself. Poor Mary Jo, she thought. Jen sent a message to Mel, and then learned that there apparently had been a party at the Hadley house. Jen's stomach sank. She knew Mary Jo would never have permitted a party, she later told Meyer. It was far more likely that whatever horrible thing prompted police to string up their yellow-and-black tape had nothing to do with suicide.

Jen and Mary Jo had been friends for more than a decade, meeting after Jen was hired as a first-grade teacher at Bayshore Elementary. They became even closer when Jen and her family moved into the Hadleys' neighborhood soon after. The Hadleys and the Archers regularly went out together. Michael Mandell remembered joining them on weekly trips out for dinner, when he recalled that Mary Jo often grabbed the bill for her friend's entire family. Mary Jo looked after Jen's clan as though it was an extension of her own, and the day before she died, she had even given some of her boys' less worn shoes to Jen's family so they could make use of them. Jen's husband wore a pair that very night to work. Just like Mel, Jen had a son who for a while had been one of Tyler's friends. But Tyler had been kind of a jerk, taunting the boy that he didn't play sports well or that he didn't have the latest electronics like Tyler did. They quit hanging out. In an attempt to gain insight into whether Tyler was at all normal, Mary Jo had once asked Jen if her son said the same things Tyler did—that he hated himself and was fat and ugly. No, Jen said. Not at all.

As Tyler seemed to unravel in high school, Mary Jo could always turn to Jen. Not only was she kind and a good listener, but she had a close family member who suffered from bipolar disorder. The mental illness is marked by a pendulum of mood extremes: depression one week, elation or irritation the next. Jen and her mother attended a mental health support group to help them cope, similar to how Al-Anon helps family members and friends deal with having alcoholic loved ones. Jen had tried to convince Mary Jo to attend a meeting because of Tyler's behavior. Maybe he had a mental health issue, she suggested. At first, Mary Jo resisted, saying Tyler was just being a teenager. Finally, on Monday, July 11, Mary Jo agreed and tagged along to a meeting. When called upon, Mary Jo told the group she was there because her son was suffering from depression and an eating disorder. After the meeting, Mary Jo told Jen she was happy she'd gone, and that she planned to go more often.

CHAPTER 38

Leveling second-degree murder charges against Tyler had been no problem. All authorities needed for that charge to move forward was enough evidence for a reasonable person to determine that the teen was likely responsible for his parents' deaths. To make the charge stick, prosecutors would have to prove three elements: that the victims were dead, that Tyler was the one who killed them, and that the killing was unlawful—not, say, in self-defense—and resulted from "an act imminently dangerous to another and demonstrated a depraved mind without regard for human life." The archetypal second-degree murder scenario is the one at the heart of more than one prison classic: A man walks in on his wife in the midst of an affair and, in the heat of passion, pulls a gun.

But to up the ante to first-degree murder in Florida, a

grand jury had to convene to weigh things further. First degree required intent and premeditation, a pairing that several of Tyler's friends told investigators he most certainly had. All those supposed jokes spanning several years about killing his parents would surely help the state's cause, as would some of his friends' statements that Tyler had even claimed to have bought a pickaxe and hovered over Mary Jo and Blake's bed "so close" to doing it. If the grand jury panel believed that Blake had indeed hit Tyler, as the teen had at first told Michael, that could endanger the first-degree charge. And the stakes were naturally high: Second-degree murder meant that if Tyler was convicted, he could be sentenced to any amount of time behind bars, up to life. The death penalty was never an option then. But when a jury trial returned with a guilty verdict in a first-degree murder case, there wasn't a chance at parole. Sure, Tyler had narrowly missed the death penalty window, but as he made clear in his dozens of jailhouse letters to friends and family, he was mortified of facing an automatic life sentence.

In September 2011, a grand jury convened behind locked doors before Circuit Judge Dwight Geiger. The twenty-member panel heard evidence for four hours as it was presented by Chief Assistant State Attorney Tom Bakkedahl and Assistant State Attorney Bernard Romero. (The process at this stage doesn't allow for the defense to put up its own evidence, but rather gives the prosecution a chance to show it has enough to warrant the charges.) One of Hadley's uncles testified, as did Detective Meyer, the medical examiner, and a crime scene investigator, among others, Bakkedahl told reporters.

"We felt there was sufficient evidence to support the first-degree murder charges, and we planned all along to submit the case to the grand jury," Bakkedahl said. "It's the first step in a long journey."

The panel reached its decision in just fifteen minutes, TCPalm.com reported. For the indictment to pass, at least twelve members had to vote for it, but officials didn't release the exact numbers of the vote. Judge Geiger accepted the indictments and ordered that Tyler be re-arrested on the new charges and remain in custody without bond. It was a milestone, but the "long journey" Bakkedahl described had months and months yet to go. He estimated that the case wouldn't get to trial for at least another year and a half.

From inside the county jail, Tyler was clearly uncomfortable with the new charges. The thought of a life sentence kept him awake at night. "If I get found guilty, I get an automatic life sentence without parole," he wrote to friends. "That would fuckin suck mad dick."

CHAPTER 39

Tyler was part celebrity, part freak show at Rock Road. Inmates such as Justin Toney wanted to get inside his head, hoping to find out the inner workings of a madman. It's the same insight sought after by fans of forensics shows on television or readers of true crime books. But not everyone was a fan. In December 2011, two jail mates he managed to piss off over a birthday cake beat him viciously. Woodson Fluerine, booked in November 2010 on charges of being a minor in possession of a firearm and ammunition, was readying to celebrate his eighteenth birthday just two weeks prior to Hadley's. In what seemed like a gesture of goodwill, Hadley offered to make him a "jailhouse cake." In inmate parlance, that meant taking cookies (usually with creamy centers that can be made into a frosting) as well as other sweets—honey buns and candy bars usually do the trick—crushing it all up, and then mixing it with a bit of water, wrapping it in plastic, and letting it set for about half an hour. It was by no means a recipe you'd find in a Julia Child cookbook, but for inmates, it was a highly anticipated birthday treat.

Fluerine accepted Tyler's gracious offer and planned his jailhouse coming-of-age around the birthday cake to come. But when the cookies arrived for the cake, Tyler changed his mind about making the cake and gobbled them up himself. Fluerine was not a happy birthday boy.

"Fluerine became irate at [Tyler] and told him he had ruined his birthday plans," according to court records.

To even the score, Fluerine asked Tyler to come to his cell for a chat. Other inmates were instructed to distract deputies and block the view into Fluerine's cell during the confrontation. Once Tyler arrived, Fluerine began pummeling him. He threw one punch after another, stopping at points to talk to Tyler before the flurry continued, according to security video of the attack. Tyler never defended himself. Another inmate, Michael Garofolo, joined in, punching Tyler three times in the face. The beating lasted six agonizingly long minutes, and the two inmates were eventually charged with felony battery by a person detained in prison or a jail facility. But the assault went unreported for nearly two weeks. When officials finally realized what had happened, they asked Tyler why he hadn't told anyone.

"I don't know," he replied.

Tyler told a friend in a letter that the beating topped off an already bad week for him.

"I'm just depressed as fuck cuz I'm gonna be in here for Christmas and my birthday. I'm already havin a shitty week cuz I got jumped by 2 people over fuckin cookies," he wrote. "Now I'm sittin in a dorm by myself."

Investigators tried to speak with Fluerine and Garofolo, but both requested legal representation, shutting down the interviews.

Beyond taking a beating for six minutes, and the bizarre autograph signing, Tyler was earning a reputation for other weird behavior behind bars. Former inmate Justin Toney had a tough time explaining it to Meyer, but Tyler seemed to be confused about his sexuality, talking one minute about girls, and then the next, well, acting like this:

"He'll sit in front of the dorm and just, like, act like he's sucking a dick—straight up, no joke," Toney told Meyer. "He'll be like—" Toney made a sexual noise. "He'll go to everyone's window and tilt his head and try to kiss 'em through the glass. The dude is real weird."

Toney felt Tyler was trying to seem insane, but Meyer knew from her previous interviews with family members that the sexuality question had come up before. Not only had Tyler never had a girlfriend, save the short-lived flame in middle school, but he at times told his family he wasn't sure he was all male. It had come up in odd ways for years, but most recently family members heard Tyler talk about it during the trip to Georgia with his dad. As the group walked back to the cabin after an outing, he said suddenly that he thought he was part girl because he was so emotional.

"No, you're all boy," replied his uncle Mike, dismissing the comment as a joke.

Tyler kept on. He said, no, he thought he was half boy and half girl—transgendered, maybe. Mike continued to argue it, and Tyler continued to insist. But his tone of voice was such that they couldn't tell if he was serious or not, so once again they assumed he was being shocking for shocking's sake.

This was a side of Tyler that Michael Mandell never

saw. He never once heard his friend question his sexuality or imply he was either transgendered or gay. Several other friends agreed: Tyler might've made odd jokes, but he didn't seem conflicted about his sexuality.

CHAPTER 40

Behind bars, Tyler was taking up a pastime that he'd avoided as a teenager. He was reading voraciously. It didn't seem to help his language skills much, based on the letters he sent from jail, but he said he was learning to enjoy the written word more than he'd expected. He was in the midst of *Jurassic Park* when he wrote a letter to the whole Reynolds family on October 27, 2011. He also loved the Harry Potter series.

And when he wasn't reading, he told his loved ones that he spent a lot of time crying. He'd curl up in a ball and cry for "a long while" on most days. He hated doing it, but it helped make him feel better. Sometimes, too, he wrote letters to God. The unsent writings helped him blow off stress and feel less guilty. "Working out helps, too," he wrote, though lately he'd been too lethargic to do much of anything. He was confined to his cell 23 hours a day still, though his 18th birthday was looming. That's when he would have more freedom with the older inmates. He hoped it'd break the monotony, but he admitted he wasn't sure if he was ready to graduate.

"I'm not scared, just a little nervous," he wrote, then quickly admitted that he maybe was "a little afraid, but I guess that's normal."

CHAPTER 41

If Tyler had thought his parents were strict, settling in to the St. Lucie County Jail must have been quite a jolt. Even after he was taken off twenty-three-hour lockdown, he had very little freedom inside the jail. The car his parents had bought him, the iPhone they'd occasionally taken away as punishment, the parties he so desperately wanted so throw—they were all luxuries he'd abruptly flushed away in a few minutes of fury. In letters to family, he described even his recreation period as being far from recreational. Guards would lead him outside into a gated area, where he'd remain in shackles as they stood watch. Aside from getting fresh air, "you don't actually do anything," he complained in a letter to an aunt and uncle. Most of the time, he stayed in his cell, reading books from the jail library and writing. The latter pastime relieved stress, he said. His grandmother DiVittorio urged him to avoid books that were "too gruesome."

While most of his letters complained of his incarceration and fretted over the possibility of a life sentence behind bars, he occasionally expressed remorse without ever referring directly to his parents.

"I want to say I'm really sorry for all the stress I've stirred up," he wrote on October 6, 2011. "I know everyone probably thinks I'm a psychopath and all. But I really am sorry for everything. I've been praying every day for forgiveness and for a decent plea offer."

Tyler wasn't a dumb guy, and at times, his broken-record reference to plea deals seemed designed more for the prosecution to read than for his letters' recipients. Surely he knew that his letters were being read—at least within a couple of months, after the first batch was released by prosecutors to inquiring media members, prompting a slew of new stories about the case. "Teen Accused of Killing Parents Wants to Become Priest," multiple headlines read. Michael Mandell again appeared on television newscasts to share the letters.

"I want to get out and become a priest. I can't wait to do good in school and don't mess up," Mandell read from one letter. "I'm not mad at you for what you did that night. I'm actually really grateful that you did that, because if you didn't, then I wouldn't be here. Thank you."

In most of his letters, Tyler spelled out his hopes for a plea: He wanted to spend somewhere between fifteen and forty years in prison (depending on the day and the letter recipient), he wrote, so he could someday get out and reunite with his friends. In his first letters, he wrote that he surely would be convicted if his case went to trial. But in later letters, after some had been released to some media, the tone changed. Tyler no longer said he was terrified of trial; rather, he wrote that there was "something in the defense" that would get him off entirely. Was it possible that was planted to shake up prosecutors?

That "something" likely was based in Tyler's long-standing mental health issues. He indeed had a documented history with depression, as well as recent bouts of behavior that had convinced his mother he might suffer from bipolar disorder. If his lawyer Harllee's comments to reporters were true, mental illness would play a crucial role in trial—if trial ever came. It was clear that Tyler hoped it never would.

"I should get [a plea offer] since it's my first offense," he wrote to his aunt and uncle. "I have a great defense team and their [sic] doing anything and everything to help me. I have a whole bunch of people who want to help me. My grandma tells me every time that everyone is praying for me. I'm grateful that I have such a loving and caring family looking out for me."

No one loved and cared for Tyler as openly as Mary Jo's parents. They were quick to forgive the grandson who'd torn their family apart. Perhaps they sensed that's what their daughter would have wanted. Mary Jo had said to friends so many times how much she worried for Tyler and how much help she knew he needed. Tyler, in turn, relied on Grandma and Grandpap DiVittorio for nearly everything, from money in his canteen to a steady stream of supportive letters that never failed to tell him how much he was loved.

Their visits were sometimes strained because Maggie's hearing wasn't the best, for which she apologized profusely. She even got new hearing aids in the hope of curbing the "whats?" and "could you repeat thats?" that she found herself saying each visit. At first, Tyler's visitations fell on Sundays, and each week Maggie and Sam went through the rigmarole of a jailhouse visit. Sometimes, Kelly—Mary Jo's niece and good friend—would come as well, taking with her a few family members. Tyler could only put a handful of people on his list of approved visitors, so not everyone who wanted to see him could visit. But he placed calls often, sometimes to friends. After one chat with a "homeboy," he came back to his cell beaming, reinvigorated, according to jail mate Justin Toney. When the phone lines were down or no one was home to take the call, Tyler seemed despondent. He'd write his grandparents letters that he knew would reach them after their next visit, but it was a way to reach out and relieve stress. Maggie wrote constantly, too.

Across the top of one postcard that was made out to "my dearest Tyler," she had scrawled "God bless you" before writing about how her heart was breaking. Tyler had called the house that morning, but Grandpa had tried to answer the couple's new magnified voice phone and messed it up. "Sorry, honey," she wrote, adding that she knew she likely would see him in person before he even got the postcard, but the incident bothered her so much that she had to write immediately to tell him what had happened.

One day in early October 2011, Maggie and Sam made the trek to the jail only to be turned away. Jail officials told them there was an electrical problem inside the facility and visitations were canceled across the board. "I'm sorry we have to wait another week," she told him in a letter she wrote as soon as the couple returned home. "We just want you to know we love you and are here to help you any way we can."

Tyler wrote an impassioned letter to his grandparents, saying how upset he was that the jail canceled visitation. He'd been looking forward to it so much that he had to fight back tears. "It's like the only thing I have to look forward to," he said. He prayed that they'd be able to visit next week, and he talked of the guilt that was "swallowing" him whole. He blamed the "darn pill" he took for making him do what he did.

On its own, it might have seemed a heart-rending letter. But within days, he'd written another letter—this one profanity-laced and complaining about being bored and weighing whether he should eventually become "a priest or some shit"—to a girl who lived on his street that took an entirely different tone. He signed that letter with "FTP"—an abbreviation commonly used for "fuck the police."

His letters to his grandparents were quite different from letters written in the same time period to friends. Just as Mary Jo had once told her parents that they only saw the good Tyler, it seemed that even behind bars, Tyler was careful to craft the image his grandparents saw. Within the same week of the letter in which he blamed "that darn pill" for his actions, he wrote a profanity-laced note to a girl who lived down the street from his Granduer home and who was friends with a jailmate of his.

"How's life on the outside? It's boring as fuck in here cuz I'm in protective custody," he wrote. *"It's bullshit that he was only allowed out of his cell for an hour a day, he complained, and he worried that if his lawyer was right, he'd likely be in jail for at least a year and a half before he even got to trial. He'd rather take a plea than risk getting life in prison. "Fuck that. I wanna get out and become a priest or some shit" he wrote. He'd been reading the Bible and it spoke to him, he added. Then he signed the letter "FTP."*

*   *   *

In June 2012, a U.S. Supreme Court ruling came down that could help ensure Tyler's worst fear of life imprisonment wasn't realized after all. The court ruled that sentencing minors to life in prison with no chance of parole violates the Eighth Amendment's ban on cruel and unusual punishment. The opinion, announced by Justice Elena Kagan in *Miller v. Alabama* and *Jackson v. Hobbs,* came down to a five-to-four vote, and continued the trend that *Roper v. Simmons* began in 2005 by prohibiting juveniles from getting the death penalty, determining that children can't be automatically punished the same way as criminal adults. The opinion was a split between liberals and conservatives, with swing vote Justice Anthony Kennedy making the final decision.

The Supreme Court opinion was based on two separate capital murder cases in which the convicted killers were fourteen years old. In both cases, the children were charged as adults and, when found guilty, given mandatory life imprisonment sentences because their respective states (Alabama and Arkansas) didn't give judges any wiggle room when sentencing in murder convictions. Lawyers for the defendants argued that juveniles have long been viewed as less culpable than adults because of the "immaturity, impetuosity and failure to appreciate risks and consequences" that goes hand-in-hand with childhood. And they argued that life without parole is similar enough to the death penalty to warrant that defendants "should get individualized consideration when facing such a severe sanction," according to a SCOTUSblog explanation. (This is why states with the death penalty have two phases when doling out the ultimate punishment—one phase for determining guilt, and another for deciding if the death penalty will be applied.)

By making youth "irrelevant to imposition of that

harshest prison sentence, such a scheme poses too great a risk of disproportionate punishment," Kagan wrote.

"Even a 17½-year-old who sets off a bomb in [a] crowded mall or guns down a dozen students and teachers is a 'child' and must be given a chance to persuade a judge to permit his release into society. Nothing in the Constitution supports this arrogation of legislative authority."

The ruling meant that if Tyler were to face trial, a guilty plea wouldn't automatically mean a life sentence anymore. Instead, the judge would have the ability to weigh the circumstances and decide if Tyler should stay behind bars for life—or if he'd get his wish and be released long before he reached his parents' age.

CHAPTER 42

Life crept forward at an agonizing rate. Maggie DiVittorio returned to work but had trouble focusing. She'd gone from having her daughter and her daughter's whole family living just blocks from her home, to having the family torn apart, her daughter slain, her youngest grandson imprisoned. The North Granduer home that had once been a happy gathering place for holidays and family affairs now sat as an overgrown, abandoned reminder of what once was. Even Ryan was gone now, trying to get his mind and life straight in North Carolina. "I am trying to work, but I am not having much luck," Maggie wrote Tyler around Thanksgiving. "I don't like this time of the year. It gets dark too early and I can't stop thinking of you." For the DiVittorios, there were no more phone calls from Mary Jo, no more family trips to church, no more steak house dinners together. The family reunions, like the one Mary Jo and Blake had planned to attend in Pittsburgh and the annual trip to Uncle Mike's cabin in Georgia, would forever be incomplete.

Ryan turned twenty-four in November 2011, his first birthday without his parents or his brother. Tyler sent him a card in North Carolina, where he'd then been living for five months: "I know this is probably the worst birthday ever for you and I'm sorry for everything. I know I say that every time I write you, but your [sic] going to hear that from me for the rest of our life. I miss you alot [sic]. I'm very thankful for having a caring/loving brother. HAPPY B-DAY."

The holidays were particularly difficult, highlighting just how changed life was for everyone. Tyler got a few cards in jail, but none of the adoration and gifts that he'd received from his parents each of the eighteen years prior. And he no longer received letters from some of his friends. It wasn't clear if the friends' letters had been confiscated, as Michael Mandell suspected, or if they chose not to write anymore, but four days after Thanksgiving, he sent a letter to Desiree's home and addressed it to "whoever the fuck's over there and shit."

The letter probably was a waste of paper because no one would likely write him back, he said. Maybe it was because they were on the witness list, but that wasn't a good enough excuse for him. "It seems like all my friends fuckin forgot about me," he wrote. "That's a really shitty feeling." Life in jail was rough and left him depressed a lot. He got shit from other inmates for what he was accused of doing. His only hope was that things would be more "bumpin" on the adult side of the facility.

Behind bars, even while he preached a newfound respect for sobriety, Tyler professed that he was learning new and innovative ways of getting high. "Coffee and cough drops," which he'd mentioned in a few letters to friends, was a potentially dangerous combination of the dextromethorphan in some cough drops mixed with caffeine. The mix could cause what's called serotonin syndrome in some people—especially those who also were on serotonin-boosting antidepressants—producing such high levels of serotonin that it basically mimicked the high of cocaine. In letters to his grandparents, Tyler denounced all of his previous drug use; in letters to his friends, he suggested they try tripping jail-style.

Desiree did write back, apologizing that it took so long. She and another friend had attended one of his court dates in the hope of seeing him, she said, but without luck. Both girls encouraged him to keep his spirits high and gave him their phone numbers so he could call anytime. "Keep ur head up, Boo," Desiree wrote. "And do you think we would ever see each other again?"

But more and more, the friends that authorities said Tyler had killed to impress were drifting away, graduating from high school and moving on with their lives. The Facebook fan pages were losing their followings. Tyler's name would pop up in the news with each new court date or quarter turn in his case, but the headlines were getting smaller.

At the anniversary of the Hadleys' deaths, TCPalm. com wrote about the still-empty house on Granduer that looked "like the many abandoned buildings in a city hit hard by the scourge of foreclosures." The house's white siding was shadowed with mildew, and even in just a year's time, a section of the privacy fence surrounding the backyard pool was collapsing, reporter Tyler Treadway wrote.

Michael Mandell was especially ready to move on, though he wouldn't entirely be able to until Tyler either pleaded guilty or faced trial. Michael remained the prosecution's star witness, providing much of the calculated detail that would likely come into play if a jury had to decide between second-degree and first-degree murder—the rev-up to the crime while listening to Lil Boosie in the garage, the five minutes' contemplation behind his mother's head, the moment he locked eyes with his father and chased him down. Michael's testimony was key if the prosecution wanted to prove that Tyler deserved a sentence of life in prison.

Though he'd written his friend a few letters early after his arrest, Michael was grateful that it appeared only his first letter reached Tyler behind bars. It took him a while to come to grips with the demons his friend had unleashed upon him, but slowly, Michael decided that Tyler wasn't an influence he wanted in his life anymore. They'd been like brothers for a decade, but so much had been based on half-truths and lies, and the burden Tyler had placed on him by sharing that horrific secret one hot night in July was more than Michael could bear. He lamented the day he ever walked around the block and introduced himself to Tyler Hadley. If only he hadn't been so outgoing. If only Tyler hadn't been out in the yard at that moment.

"I really was the happiest kid ever," Michael said. "I could write a tragedy just at what has happened to me since I moved to Port St. Lucie, I swear."

CHAPTER 43

February 1, 2012
This is to all the people who followed my case. I
want you all to know I regret what I did but I have
found God. I realize I shocked the world and I'm
sorry. —Tyler Hadley

CHAPTER 44

As the second anniversary of his parents' deaths neared, with a trial date tentatively scheduled in a few months' time, Ryan Hadley made his own headlines—this time, for something positive. The now-twenty-five-year-old had tried to donate the Granduer home to needy people, but red tape kept him from pulling it off. So instead, he donated part of the inheritance he had received from his parents to help Habitat for Humanity refurbish a foreclosed home that they dedicated in Mary Jo and Blake's honor. On July 9, 2013, John and Sharon Kerr were moving into the home in the 2900 block of Southeast Pruitt Road, about nine miles from the house in which Ryan and Tyler had been raised.

"I am grateful in spite of my loss," Ryan wrote in a letter

that was read at the home's unveiling by St. Lucie Habitat for Humanity executive director Garret Grabowski.

Grabowski continued: "It's important to him to let everybody know that he didn't run away from this. He's really going above and beyond to make things right. By giving back to the family that received the house, that's just a tremendous gift."

It was telling that Ryan somehow felt it was his duty to "make things right"—atoning for his brother's sins as though they were his own.

Detective Meyer's initial guess that the trial could take years to arrive proved right. It had always appeared on track to be a slow-developing case, but some had hoped a spring 2013 trial was realistic. Instead, it was about that time—in late April 2013—that Tyler's lawyers filed a notice declaring he would rely on an insanity plea in his trial. In her announcement, public defender Diamond Litty said that, at the time of the slayings, Tyler was "laboring under a mental disease, infirmity or defect, to wit: depression." The filing also declared that Hadley was "involuntarily intoxicated" when his parents were killed. In the filing, directed to Judge Robert R. Makemson, Litty spelled out the defense witnesses she intended to tap: Dr. Wade Meyers, director of forensic psychiatry at Hasbro Children's Hospital in Rhode Island; and Dr. Kathleen Heide, the author of *Why Kids Kill Parents* and the researcher whose statistics on parricide were the most often cited in courtrooms across the nation. Tyler had long hinted at aces up his lawyers' sleeves. Perhaps it was these high-profile experts to which he was alluding. He just wanted fifteen years. Hell, he'd even sign away forty years if it meant avoiding trial. At least, that's what he said when life imprisonment was to be automatic with a guilty verdict. Now maybe he was feeling a bit bolder.

Tom Bakkedahl, the prosecutor on the case, wasn't surprised by the notice. He told a reporter that his office had long been prepared to receive it.

"We're going to have a doctor who will examine [Tyler Hadley], complete discovery of their experts," he told a television reporter. "We will move toward trial. That's really where we're at right now."

To another reporter, Bakkedahl said: "I retained an expert some time ago in anticipation of this defense . . . So my expert has been reviewing all of the materials in the case."

He didn't buy insanity as a defense, Bakkedahl added.

"If I believed he was insane, or if I believed he acted in self-defense, or if I otherwise believed he had a viable, absolute defense to the crime, I wouldn't be prosecuting him. That would be unethical and illegal, so you can draw whatever conclusions you want from that."

Friends and neighbors weren't surprised, nor did anyone seem to be really bothered by the delay. Tyler was, after all, behind bars. His brother Ryan was rarely seen around town anymore. It was mostly Mary Jo's and Blake's parents who served as the heartbreaking reminders of justice still unserved, and they didn't seem to be in a hurry to have Tyler convicted, either.

Donna Montero, who lived directly behind the Granduer home, told a reporter that she considered the insanity defense filing to be inevitable.

"That's a pretty basic public defense strategy," she said. "I mean, what else are they going to say? There's not a whole lot you can do, except [claim] insanity. It wasn't, as far as my knowledge, that he was abused at all, so it wasn't that he just snapped because he was tired of getting beaten . . . So what are you going to say? There's not much left to say except 'temporary insanity,' in my opinion."

The "involuntary intoxication" portion was a little harder to reconcile. Hadn't Tyler told his friends that he needed to get stoned to be able to muster the stomach to kill his parents? How could there be anything involuntary about getting high on purpose? To pull off proving Tyler was involuntarily intoxicated, his defense lawyers would need to prove first that he was intoxicated, that the intoxication was involuntarily created, and that his mental state at the time met the jurisdiction's test for insanity, according to a 1992 rundown by psychiatrist Robert Goldstein. Though their court notices didn't spell out specifics, onlookers surmised that they would likely try to convince the jury that he'd been suffering from pathological intoxication, and that his prescribed medications interacted with his recreational ones in a way that he as a layman couldn't have predicted, causing him to do things he wouldn't normally do. It would no doubt be a difficult defense to mount, especially in the face of countless letters to friends in which he reminisced fondly about his drugged-out days far more often than he expressed regret over what those drugs supposedly made him capable of doing.

For Michael Mandell, the heartbreak didn't stop. In 2012, just two days before Christmas, Michael's mother, Michele, died of cervical cancer in their Port St. Lucie home. It had been nearly a year and a half since the Hadleys had been slain, and Michael still hadn't shaken the demons from that night. Now his mother was dead, too, at just fifty-four years old—the same age Blake had been. Michael had helped nurse her through those final days. It was a slow and agonizing death. Though Tyler's trial date was still pending, and though Michael had aimed to stick around Florida until the case was over, he couldn't sit still anymore, waiting for the trial to finally come and his life to hopefully get recharged. He packed his bags and headed to Michigan to get a job, figuring he'd head back down to Florida for the trial. Things were going well for a while. He worked fifty-hour weeks at a car plant and made a decent wage. Then he got caught in one of Michigan's infamous wintry downpours of snow and sleet and rain and slammed into a highway sign on Interstate 94 going some seventy-five miles an hour. He walked away uninjured, but the car was totaled. He flew back to Florida and started crashing with friends, hoping he could scrounge up enough grant money to go back to college.

"All I know is that God would not have given me all of these obstacles if He did not know I could deal and learn from them," he told a reporter.

He wondered sometimes if Tyler truly had any grasp of the damage he'd done when he swung that hammer in that goddamn frenzy. Sure, two people were dead, but it was even more than that. Two years later, Michael still wasn't sleeping right, wasn't eating right. He had trouble trusting people, even friends he'd known for years. And Michael wasn't even the most directly affected. Tyler's grandparents, his brother . . . If Michael couldn't sleep at night, surely they couldn't, either. So how the hell was Tyler managing, having been the one to cause all of this?

The scene plays out in Michael's mind sometimes: Tyler standing there, in the kitchen, that twenty-two-inch hammer in his hand. Mary Jo at the computer, oblivious to the six-foot-one mass of fury eyeing her head. Sometimes Michael prays for an alternative ending. Maybe Tyler squeezes his eyes shut, quietly shakes his head, and rests the hammer on the kitchen table, walking away and posting to Facebook: "Party's off." He continues counseling that Monday, and he slowly sorts his demons. Or maybe Blake steps into the kitchen just a little sooner— soon enough to not be paralyzed by the sight of his bludgeoned wife. Maybe Blake shrugs off that need to be liked, that desire to be the loving, buddy father, and overpowers his son while his wife dives for the phone and calls police. Maybe these things happen, instead of the hammer swings and the cleanup afterward, and the kids are bummed that the party's called off, but they forget about it soon enough because there are so many other parties anyway.

Michael prays for an alternate ending pretty often, but he knows there will never be one. Tyler swung the hammer. There's no rewind button, no ability to undo or delete. No matter what a jury decides, Michael will see his surrogate father's lifeless leg when he closes his eyes and wonder what his path would have been if his best friend had simply stayed his best friend and not become a killer.

EPILOGUE

Inside the courtroom sat several of Tyler Hadley's relatives. His maternal grandmother, the one to whom he'd been writing letters since the week of his parents' deaths, looked somber, worried, her forehead knitted as she sat by her husband, Tyler's grandfather and Mary Jo's dad. Reporters had filtered into the room and jockeyed for the best position to watch the day unfold. It was Wednesday, February 19, 2014. Word had spread that the long-stagnant case was about to be injected with new vigor.

Some reporters were skeptical. It seemed that each time the case inched toward resolution, something happened to throw it off track. Back in early 2012, Assistant State Attorney Bernard Romero had said he expected the trial would start within months. That never happened. Then came 2013, and defense lawyer Mark Harllee said he anticipated the case would get underway early that year. Instead, the first half of the year went by, and then Harllee suddenly left his job—whether by choice or not, his boss wouldn't say—which delayed the case further. Public Defender Diamond Litty took over as Hadley's defense lawyer and tried again to get the first-degree murder charges tossed in favor of less severe charges. That didn't happen, either.

Now, as reporters, family members and court gadflies gathered together in Judge Robert Makemson's courtroom, word was that something major was about to finally happen.

Tyler was led into the room by guards. He wore the orange jumpsuit of an adult prisoner, and he was barely recognizable. Two and a half years prior, when he was arrested and his mug shot first splashed across TV screens and in newspapers nationwide, he'd stood before a judge as a skinny teenager with an almost gaunt face. Now he was heavy, his face round and his frame lumbering. He appeared to have packed on at least 20 pounds, maybe more, and not of the hardcore pumping-iron variety. After years of battling what his parents thought might be an eating disorder, it seemed Tyler had finally gained the weight he'd been so dreading. He was doughy.

Makemson, flanked by the American and Florida state flags, took the bench and plowed ahead. Earlier that week, a court spokesman alerted reporters that Hadley was readying to change his plea. Though the teen had long maintained that there "was something in the defense" that could clear him of murder, his hopes of leniency had been dashed repeatedly. Litty had again tried to get the judge to toss out the first-degree murder charges as the trial date approached, but Makemson refused. Word was that Tyler didn't want to take the risk of allowing a Florida jury to convict him of the charge.

Instead, he'd change his plea to no contest.

A plea of no contest wasn't a traditional guilty plea. It meant that while Tyler wasn't admitting that he killed his parents, he acknowledged that there was enough evidence to convict him. The plea technically is called "nolo contendere," a legal term that comes from the Latin phrase for "I do not want to contend." No contest pleas are treated as guilty pleas when it comes to sentencing, and Tyler would stand convicted of the crime if the judge accepted the plea. But if anyone sued him civilly, his plea couldn't be used as proof of guilt in a trial.

Makemson, charged by law to make sure such pleas are given freely and voluntarily, pressed Tyler. "I want to make sure you understand exactly what you're giving up," he said: the presumption of innocence, the ability to mount a defense against the allegations. All of it would be gone if Makemson accepted the plea. The judge asked if Tyler wanted to change his mind.

"No, sir," Tyler said.

And with that, it was done. Hadley was convicted. Not guilty, but convicted. Next came the mitigation hearing, during which witnesses and experts and law enforcement officers were tapped one last time for testimony so that Makemson could decide how many of Tyler's adult years would be spent behind bars. The prosecution asked for two consecutive life sentences; the defense argued for parole within his lifetime—possibly after as little as 20 years behind bars. Makemson sided with the prosecution. Over the pleas of Tyler's maternal grandmother, the judge decided that Tyler should never be part of the outside world again. The crime had been "brutal, horrific," he said; the punishment must be severe.

"These attacks on his parents were very painful, both physically and emotionally," Makemson told the courtroom. "I say emotionally because they realized their own son was killing them."

It was time for the community to move on and for the Hadley family to at least try to heal.

Michael Hadley, Blake's brother, said after the plea hearing that he felt dreadful.

"The family has grieved for so long, and we're hoping to find some closure for this horrific situation that's happened to our family," he said. "It has just literally turned us upside down. But we're doing good. Everybody is getting it together."

He said it was Ryan—Blake and Mary Jo's oldest son and Tyler's brother—the family worried about the most. In a flurry of hammer swings, he lost his mother, his father and his brother. The family he'd lived with for twenty-three years was gone, wiped out in a single night.

"We pray for Ryan every night," Michael said. "Bless his heart. He's the one that's hurt the most out of all this."

ACKNOWLEDGMENTS

As always, I owe huge gratitude to my husband, Elijah Van Benschoten, without whom I wouldn't be able to tell these tales, largely because he makes sure I eat while I'm writing—something I've never been that great at remembering. I'd also like to send love to my son, Hunt, who was born during the writing of this book. I love you, kid.

Thank you goes to my agent, Jane Dystel, who's a fantastic cheerleader and advocate. Gratitude as well goes to St. Martin's Paperbacks and, most directly, my editor April Osborn. I miss my Knight-Wallace Fellows and am forever grateful for their continued support, encouragement and feedback.

For this particular project, many thanks goes to Matt Sedensky of the Associated Press, who did a fantastic job covering the case and staying on top of Freedom of Information requests.

Also, I send a special salute to Michael Mandell. Without his candor and assistance, I feel this book would be missing its heart. Keep your head up, Mike. You're going to be okay.